I0669398

About the Editor

LIZ GRZYB was born in the middle of a thunderstorm in Perth, Western Australia. She is the editor of acclaimed paranormal romance anthologies *Scary Kisses* and *More Scary Kisses*, paranormal-noir anthology *Damnation and Dames*, and the website ticon4.com. Liz is also the fantasy editor for *The Year's Best Australian Fantasy and Horror* anthologies from Ticonderoga Publications.

Dreaming of Djinn

Also edited by LIZ GRZYB

Scary Kisses
More Scary Kisses
Damnation and Dames (with Amanda Pillar)
The Year's Best Australian Fantasy & Horror 2010 (with Talie Helene)
The Year's Best Australian Fantasy & Horror 2011 (with Talie Helene)
The Year's Best Australian Fantasy & Horror 2012* (with Talie Helene)

*forthcoming from Ticonderoga Publications

Dreaming of Djinn

edited by

Liz Grzyb

Ticonderoga publications

*To the fabulous Mystique Dancers,
who take me
on a magical carpet ride every time
I dance with them.*

Dreaming of Djinn edited by Liz Grzyb

Published by Ticonderoga Publications

Copyright © 2013 Liz Grzyb

Introduction copyright © 2013 Liz Grzyb

Typeset in Sabon and Penhurst

A Cataloging-in-Publications entry for this title is available from The National Library of Australia.

ISBN   978-1-921857-35-5 (trade paperback)
            978-1-921857-36-2 (ebook)

Ticonderoga Publications
PO Box 29 Greenwood
Western Australia 6924

www.ticonderogapublications.com

10 9 8 7 6 5 4 3 2 1

ACKNOWLEDGEMENTS

Liz would like to thank Marilag Angway, Charlotte Nash-Stewart, Joshua Gage, Angela Rega, Alan Baxter, Thoraiya Dyer, Barb Siples, Pia Van Ravestein, Havva Murat, Cherith Baldry, Anthony Panegyres, DC White, Richard Harland, Jetse de Vries, Dan Rabarts, Jenny Schwartz, Jenny Blackford, Faith Mudge, Russell B Farr, Kate Dunbar-Smith, Kate Williams, Andrew Williams, Debbie Wilson, Jacinta Rosielle, Angela Challis, Shane Cummings, Ambre Hillier, Michael Hillier, Tasmar Dixon, Mel Donald, Phil Ward, Helen Grzyb, Amanda Pillar, the English Department, Lina Piscitelli, Ruza Foster, Nikki Irwin, Andrea Orlowsky, Hilary Donraadt, Frankie Bertolini and all the girls at Mystique.

Contents

Introduction

The idea of *Dreaming of Djinn* has been floating around in my head for a few years. When I edited my first anthology, *Scary Kisses*, I joked that the next one I did would have to combine two of my biggest loves, belly dancing and speculative fiction. While it's taken a few detours, *Dreaming of Djinn* grew out of that vision, fusing the magic and exoticism of Scheherazade's *Alf Leila wa Leila* (*Thousand and One Nights*) with the questioning, exploratory nature of the speculative fiction genre.

The Thousand and One Nights seems to me to call out for speculative reworking. The whole idea of a young woman, seemingly in the lap of luxury in a gilded cage surrounded by silks and satins and with slaves to do her every bidding, but only being in that position in order to stop the king from murdering another innocent with every daybreak in revenge for the adultery of his sister-in-law, his wife and his concubines (let's not open the can of worms about equal opportunity here!) is the ultimate questioning of right and wrong. Telling stories, using the power of words to stop these atrocities is the ultimate in the writer's craft, surely! The subject matter of Scheherazade's stories themselves are intensely speculative—"The Voyages of Sinbad" tell of exploring new lands, "Aladdin and the Lamp" of magic and betrayal, "The City of Brass" involves robots and automata.

There are so many references to Scheherazade and *The Thousand and One Nights* in Western culture which focus only on the orientalist view of the Middle East and even now still show a one-sided view of women. The Disney movie *Aladdin* showcases sensual women dressed in diaphanous silks as political and sexual pawns. Even *I Dream of Jeannie* is merely wish fulfilment from another blonde djinni dressed in pink chiffon! With *Dreaming of Djinn* I wanted to reinvent elements of this orientalist idea but also question it through exploring different threads of the same cloth. In addition to portraying sensitive yet strong male characters who have vulnerabilities and flaws, the stories in this book also show powerful female characters who, like Scheherazade who worked within the avenues open to her to fight against oppression, are able to forge their own way in the world, all while still paying tribute to the original mood of *The Thousand and One Nights.*

I really need to thank Angela Rega at this point. We had spoken together of our mutual love of dance and speculative fiction, and when I was editing another anthology she sent us a version of her story which has been included in this book, "The Bellydancing Crimes of Ms Sahara Desserts". This was the story that tipped me over the precipice and made me realise that this combination of seemingly disparate ideas could really work together: crafty and caring djinn, a bellydancer named Sahara Desserts, and sweet yummy desserts—how fabulous!

Once I started reading submissions, the vast array of ideas in the stories sent really amazed me. Speculative fiction writers and the way they look at the world surprise me constantly, but I couldn't help but be blown away with the ways these authors had approached the theme. The tales within these covers link to the original idea in very different ways. Some recreate the horror provoked by the idea of King Shahryar killing hundreds of young girls in revenge for his wife's adultery. Other stories evoke the sly humour of "Ali Baba and the Forty Thieves", the intricate politics of royal marriages, intrigues woven by jealous courtiers, or the rules and dangers surrounding dealing with various supernatural or magical creatures which makes up such a huge volume of the original stories.

The landscape is incredibly important in many of these tales and help to give a firm connection to the original *Thousand and One Nights.* Some are set in arid deserts populated by ifrits, some in the claustrophobic, jasmine-scented drawing rooms and gardens of royal palaces, in bustling streets redolent of incense and magic, or dim, smoke-filled tents. Whether a historical Middle Eastern setting or a more modern or futuristic situation, the sense of place is firmly in dreamland.

Take a piece of sweet *lokum*, a glass of mint tea and dive into the djinni's bottle. There on the magic carpet, I hope you will be horrified, delighted, but ultimately entertained by what you find.

LIZ GRZYB
GREENWOOD, MARCH 2013

Shadow Dancer

Marilag Angway

"She is a girl."

A frown marred Desha's beautiful face.

The man before her grunted. "So were you when you started."

"She is a *little* girl." Her eyes narrowed after further examining what was supposed to be her charge. "And her colouring is off. She stands out like a camel in a pen of horses."

The girl couldn't have been more than nine or ten in age, her pale skin dirty but no sign of physical scarring. The skin was the least of Desha's problems, however. Pale skin could be painted over and tanned after some seasons under the scorching desert heat. It was the girl's overall appearance that disturbed her.

Hair as yellow as the desert sands and eyes as bright and clear as water. Infidel hair and infidel eyes.

"I am a dancer, not a djinni," Desha snapped. "I cannot work miracles."

"And you dancers have your own essence of witchery." The man's eyes narrowed. "Do I have to tell you that this is what the padishah wants?"

Desha shrugged. Many would gasp and shiver at the mention of the king. Desha was not one of them. "He can order all he wants, but even the padishah cannot force me to do the impossible."

"There is no impossibility," the man replied on reflex.

The dancer rolled her eyes and completed the saying. "There is only success."

Desha sighed. She examined the girl again. There would be a lot of work to be done. The girl returned her gaze, blue eyes determined, blazing. Desha bit her lip. She crushed her pity and looked away. After all these years, she still hadn't learned detachment.

"I suppose I can have dyes regularly administered on those locks of hers. Wigs, too. And there is paste for her skin. But short of a djinni, her eyes I can do nothing about."

"No djinn. You just make sure nobody gets close enough to see them."

Desha frowned again. "The padishah cannot spare one wish on this child?"

He shifted uncomfortably. The king had many djinn to his calling, but everyone knew he would not use magic on himself. Or his family.

The hesitation was enough for Desha to guess the girl's parentage. The dark visitor saw the shift in her gaze and he shrugged. "Out of the question, Desha."

Desha made the proper sign of respect. Then she knelt down and peered up at the girl. "You said the padishah wants this?"

"Heard it directly from him."

She looked at him. "Why me?"

He grinned. "You are the best."

"It will be a difficult path."

"That is so."

"And the girl is aware of this?"

"Yes." The answer had come from the eager charge. "I shall endeavour to make the padishah happy."

Desha slapped her cheek. This surprised the girl, though she did not cry out. The dancer glared. "Leave your desires behind you. You have no need for it where you will walk, where you will dance. At the end of your training, it will not be said that you *desire* to be what you are. You will only *know* that it is what you are, and nothing else. Do you understand?"

Harsh words needed to start early. Desha would not have it said that her dancers grew weak with love for their king. The king did not deserve their love. Not for what he expected of them.

The girl hesitated, but she nodded in the end.

"Leave her, Zemir."

He nodded. "I assured the padishah that you *are* the best option for this. Do not make me regret my decision."

"What do you take me for, *dozd*?" It was said that Desha's glares could induce the stopping of hearts. She gave one such glare then.

Zemir smirked. "Save the anger and insults, Desha. I say it out of formality. And did anyone tell you that you look beastly when you frown?"

Before she could respond, the man leapt from the window and rolled gracefully onto the awning that always broke his fall. Desha contemplated having the awning removed, just to give the nightly visitors a more trying ordeal. But the thought was fleeting, like her love for the King of the Thieves.

The girl was silent. Desha realised she didn't even know her name.

"What did the padishah call you, child?"

The spark returned to the girl's spring-blue eyes, one of pride and honour. "Morgiana."

"Morgiana." It was a fitting name for one of the King's brood. The name of a queen. Desha shook her head. "Do not be so flattered. You will not be known by that name any longer."

She saw the girl's eyes fall. Desha schooled her expression to remain stony. She motioned for the girl to come and step to the centre of the room, in front of the standing mirrors that were arranged on three sides. Morgiana obeyed.

Desha looked at her from all angles. There was no telling how the girl would grow up to look, only that she would be fair-haired, blue-eyed, pale-skinned. Whether her curves would grow in or not was something only a magus could predict.

She forced Morgiana to look at herself in the mirrors. "All of you will change, child. From the hair on your head to the paleness of your skin. You are too *visible* now. What you want to be is *uniform*. You want to blend in with the dancers, yet gain skills to attract the *right kind* of attention. What you are now is a weakling pawn that can be kidnapped because of your ties to the padishah. There will be very few girls who look like you, and you are easily recognised."

"You said you can change my hair and my skin," Morgiana said.

Desha slapped her again. "No impertinence."

Morgiana bit her lip.

Desha walked to her changing table. Her hands hovered over powder and dyes. Once she decided on the proper tools and shades, she turned her attention back to Morgiana. She smiled, though she knew by the girl's saddened expression that her own eyes gave no warmth. That was how it was meant to be. Seduction is an art; emotion a hindrance. And love?

Love is a toy to play with and discard.

"Today and the rest of your life as a dancer, you will be Gia," she said. "And your first lesson is concealment."

• • •

They fussed like she expected them to. By the morning light, everyone had already heard that the king's Right Hand came to visit. The dancers knew of the informer's aversion to the Realm of the Dancers, so if he came at night, it was only for one reason alone.

To deliver a new student.

One by one, the dancers trickled down those cobbled steps and into the common hall. Each face was shrouded behind a thin, sheer veil that rippled as she moved. The hall held at least a dozen dancers when Desha arrived, her charge shadowing her footsteps.

One dancer squealed. Another, Desha noted, blew a jealous snort and stomped off. But the majority of the dancers had chosen to stay, not to poke or prod the girl, but to stare and take in the view. Whose child was she? Why was she there? Was she a replacement for a dancer who'd lost favour with the King? Dancers were as expendable as the clothes they arrived in.

Desha had proven adept at learning concealment skills. What the other dancers saw was not an infidel's child. Instead, they saw a miniature version of themselves. Desha allowed herself a touch of pride in her transformation of the girl. She had not slept, choosing instead to cover Gia's arms with ointment that darkened her skin and powder to keep the ointment from melting in the heat. She had had no time to dye the girl's locks; instead she cut them and found a dark wig, painting only the girl's eyebrows to match it.

The effect was satisfactory, and had Gia been older, she might have risked the dancers' envy. But for a girl her age, she was nothing but adorable in the eyes of the older dancers.

"Oh, Desha, she looks like you," one giggled.

"She looks like all of us," another pursed her lips.

"So my statement was not wrong, Reeshi!"

Desha caught the second speaker's eyes. Reeshi watched her with a suspicious, dark brown look. Desha winked. She mouthed *later* and left it at that.

One of the dancers gasped. Desha's attention snapped back to Gia, who had looked up.

"But, Desha, her eyes are *blue*."

"Have you not seen blue eyes before, Nemesh?" Desha would have to be careful with their fussing. Dancers talked, and unlike the king's informers, their mouths sometimes danced faster than their hands and feet.

"Well, of course I have, but she is a *dancer*. Dancers look like us."

"No man will be watching her eyes."

Reeshi brushed past Nemesh and examined Gia as well, then led the girl toward the table with the few students they had. Beside her, Desha followed.

"Infidel eyes," Reeshi said flatly, though quietly enough that only Desha heard.

Desha shrugged. "A custom order from the padishah."

"So it is," the other dancer looked over her shoulder. "Does she know what is expected of her?"

"As much as I could say without completely frightening her." Desha had chosen instead to show the girl some of the skills involved. The rest could wait for her next assignment.

"Your name?" Reeshi asked the girl.

"Gia," Desha answered quickly, noticing her mouth purse to form an 'M'. She watched Gia scratch her cheek. "Gia of Jimoor."

Reeshi laughed. "Appropriate." Desha had expected Reeshi to find amusement in giving the city's name to an infidel.

The two dancers sought seats nearby. Desha murmured a brief command to Gia, who nodded and went to mingle with the girls her age.

Once the women had finished whispering about the arrival, they dispersed, most back to their rooms to prepare for the night's performances. Others had already covered themselves, prepared to go out for early assignments. Reeshi and Desha were two of the few who stayed with the other dancing instructors, their skills valued at a higher price.

"If I recall correctly, it was not your turn for a student," Reeshi finally commented after they had broken their bread. She ripped a piece off her loaf and dipped it into the bowl of olive oil. "Some have waited their turn for over a season. It was Nemesh's due, and once she is stopped being curious, she will begin to ask more questions."

"I do not claim to know the thoughts of the padishah, any more than you do, Reeshi." Desha watched Reeshi chew her bread thoughtfully, and followed to do the same. "I do not claim to be above his commands, either."

"Rightly so," Reeshi replied. "Still, blue eyes could have fetched a better price elsewhere."

Desha knew where Reeshi's thoughts lay. Why had the Guild of Shadows brought a girl into the Realm of the Dancers when they could have further profited by sending Gia to the more affluent High Court? The ladies there would grow up without having to hide themselves, for the men who sought them were looking for the exotic.

Desha shook her head. "I do not claim—"

"—to know the thoughts of the padishah," Reeshi quipped, amused. "Yes. So you have said. You wonder still."

"As much as you."

Desha and Reeshi ate their breakfast silently, both stealing glances toward Gia. The girl did not have a hard time making friends, though perhaps this was due to her oddly coloured eyes. Most of the young girls sat close, striking conversation with the new student, their faces expressing the same curiosity as Nemesh and the others.

A runner interrupted Desha's thoughts, and she nodded him permission to approach. He handed her a parchment with the king's seal, a black scorpion with a red stinger. Desha waited until the runner had left before unsealing the parchment. She unrolled it slowly and read the summons.

Reeshi tilted her head. "Working tonight?"

"Looks like." Which meant scouting had to be done beforehand. Desha rose from her seat. "We shall talk another time."

Desha tapped Gia silently on the shoulder, and the girl made her excuses. She followed her teacher to the door.

"We have work to do, Gia, so I suggest you take note and watch. Under no circumstances are you allowed to do anything else. Do you understand?"

"Yes, teacher."

Desha nodded, though she knew that the girl would not understand. Likely, she would be a hindrance to the assignment. Desha should know, she'd blundered her first shadow mission, after all. Every starting dancer blundered her first mission.

Desha was one of the best. She'd not blundered a mission since.

• • •

The target was a high-end client at the High Court, a Siesh nobleman with too much money and very little to do with it. After some discreet whispers—and a brief visit to one of the Unnamed—Desha discovered that the nobleman stuck to a particular schedule. He would walk to the High Court in the morning, speak briefly with the ladies and gentlemen of the Court, and then extract his favourite lady to accompany him for the rest of the day. Because he always chose the same lady, Desha knew that taking the guise of a High Court female was not a possible solution.

But she also heard that the man loved social gatherings, and that he would host one that very night.

And what was a social gathering without entertainment?

"The padishah certainly knows when to pick his opportune moments," Desha commented aloud, with only Gia to hear. She turned to her little shadow and grimaced, remembering that she would have to explain and set forth certain rules. "One thing you need to know, Gia, is when a *dozd* gives you an assignment, he wants it done as soon as possible. Some of them, like the padishah and his informers, even go so far as provide you a manageable time to accomplish the mission."

She saw Gia struggling to ask questions, so Desha nodded, allowing her to speak. "But, teacher, what *do* you do for the *dozd*?"

Desha raised an eyebrow. Then she silently cursed Zemir for not telling her of the depth of Morgiana's ignorance. "We are the silent harbingers of the *dozd*."

"I do not understand."

There was so much the child needed to learn. Desha was beginning to feel that she was the wrong person for the job. Why hadn't Zemir gone to Reeshi? Or, better yet, one of the *actual* instructors? She did not have the patience for this.

Desha took a moment's breath and exhaled. "In short, Gia, we investigate the target, assess his character, find his treasure stash, and open the way for the *dozd* to plunder as they so choose."

Gia's eyes widened. "So we are helping the padishah betray and steal?"

"Girl, what do you think the *dozd* do?" Desha asked incredulously. Could the little Morgiana have been so sheltered? Thieves are thieves! "What else do you expect of them?"

"I . . . " Gia's head drooped.

Desha looked around the street, watching the cloaked faces of men and women pass by. They barely glanced Desha's way, but some did look at Gia. She was so small, people *would* be tempted to ask questions. She pulled Gia away from the open path and dragged her quickly to a narrow alley.

The stone in the narrow alley was cool, a welcome reprieve from the hot air blowing across the open streets.

"What did I tell you the first time you came to me?" Desha asked.

Gia paused in contemplation. "To erase all desires."

"You erase more than that, little shadow. When you agreed to work for the padishah and do as he wishes, you have signed a bond that would make you his loyal servant. It is a bond with words, but it is a bond still. You are his eyes and his secret voice. You do not think about the consequences, but you should know what they are. You do not act against your conscience because you are not to have one. Not where our missions are concerned. Your targets are many, they are not always villains, and they may be merciful and kind. But that does not matter."

Desha nodded out at the street. "Now, if you have no more of your questions, we can go on with this assignment. I have some observing to do."

Gia scratched her cheek. She had been doing that since Desha slapped her. Desha wondered if Gia was remembering the sharp sting. The girl nodded.

They stepped back out.

· · ·

Sula Sab Jibnn was an infidel. That had escaped the whispers, though why, Desha did not know. He had the infidel's hair of red clay, and the marble white skin of the northern barbarians who had once tried to stake claim on the desert kingdom of Salaithra. But that had been centuries before, when the sand djinn had not built their wall of storms around the twin cities of Jimoor and Siesh. It was difficult enough to travel past the desert that surrounded Salaithra, but any would-be conquerors also had the highly difficult task of passing the perpetual sandstorm that raged around Salar borders.

A legacy from a desperate sultan. Or was he a wise one, for wishing those barriers up?

Whatever the case, the old sand djinn continued to churn their magic, and no infidel had been able to enter since.

What infidels did remain, however, had been the ones left over from when the borders were still open. Salaithra had once dealt trade with outsiders, and many had come from all manner of direction. The northerners offered gems mined from their mountains, the southerners wood and skilled soldiers. The west had remained a bit more aloof, but for the occasional wind magus who traipsed in and studied the djinn in return for bottled magic. The east brought with them metal and horses. Yet no matter which direction, it was the magi that the Salar community coveted most.

The magi were blessed with skills no pure-bred Salar possessed. Most of them had come from the east. These magi, these soothsayers, were respected, for they held powers of insight and prediction that were coveted across the desert kingdom. Sometimes, with a substantial amount of money, soothsayers could even be bought.

Sula Sab Jibnn had one such magus in his employ. The man had a similar colouring in his skin to his master, but the magus was ebony-haired and chocolate-eyed. He had high cheekbones, long, bony fingers, a lizard's grace, and a scorpion's speed. It would be a mistake to underestimate him.

Desha smiled thinly. The magus would be difficult, but not impossible to sidestep. For, unlike the djinn, with powers from the sheer force of smoke, vapour and sand, the magus is limited to his reserves. The magus is human, the djinn are not. For that, Desha would face a magus any day.

There is no impossibility, there is only success.

The dancer had wheedled herself into the entertainment that would perform at Sula Sab Jibnn's gathering. Every entertainer usually went under the scrutiny of the nobleman's soothsayer, who examined them for possible wrongdoing. Desha had experienced a soothsayer's gaze, and no doubt he would see a future where she was involved. But she also knew that the foretelling of the future was limited. Futures hinged upon a branching of limitless possibilities, and what the magus did was choose the most viable future. For that, the magus depended on his knowledge of personality. He would delve into Desha's inner being and pick the future she would likely enter.

And so, as the magus stared at the beautiful dancer, Desha opened up. She allowed him to see her as she had been, before the King of the Thieves called upon her services to his order. Light, strength, passion, trust, humour.

The magus let her through.

Gia, on the other hand, was more difficult. The magus had reeled back, as though startled at what he saw. Desha frowned. What *did* the magus see?

In the end, it might not have been as disturbing as she feared, because the magus recovered himself quickly and produced a thin smile. He let Gia through.

The infiltration was a success. Desha turned to Gia and nodded. Now it was onto more pressing matters.

• • •

Every night she danced, Desha fell in love.

She knew she was discarding the rules she'd placed upon her students. She knew, if the dancers watched her face carefully, that they would recognise emotions that Desha should have crushed when she received her golden sash. She fell in love anyway.

The dance was why she lived and breathed. When the music gave its cue, Desha would step onto the stage with the others, the bangles on her wrist sparkling gold, the bells around her ankles polished, tinkling silver.

That night, her dark hair was pinned up with jewellery loaned to her by the house, and Gia had helped her put on the tiered skirts and the top, which ended playfully just above Desha's midriff. Purples and blues wound their way around the orange and yellows.

Gia's eyes shone with envy. Desha grinned, the excitement of the dance overtaking her usual no-nonsense attitude. "You will be able to wear these when you come of age, when the dance mistresses find that you are ready. But tonight, you shall watch. Come, hand me my dagger."

It was this statement that made Gia blink a few times over.

This time, Desha smiled, though the mirth did not climb to her eyes. "Before pleasure, there is business. A woman is allowed to protect herself, no?"

But it wasn't just a simple knife that Desha wanted. She'd already equipped herself with smaller daggers around her waist, hidden beneath folds of purple-blue skirts and a golden belt. No, it was the khanjar that she wanted.

Before entering Sula Sab Jibnn's territory, Desha had given Gia her khanjar, a curved dagger sheathed within camel hide. Warriors and assassins could easily discern typical blades, but the khanjar was not a typical blade. It was Desha's favourite tool, dancing or otherwise.

Desha tried to remember the last time she had to use it for her defence. Only once, a lifetime ago, she mused.

What she *did* use the khanjar for, well, that was part of her appeal as a dancer. It was her speciality.

Desha unsheathed the khanjar. The dagger's hilt formed a loop so a hand could easily clench it. Desha pulled a sheer, magenta sash from her waist and tied a triple knot around the loop. To test the sturdiness of her knot, Desha bade her charge to move away as she threw the dagger ahead of her. Before it could hit anything, she used the same hand to reel the sash back, and the dagger stopped its journey. Desha gave her sash a hurried twist and the dagger fluttered back to her hand as the end of the sash did.

The dancers who stood nearby clapped with awe. Desha knew none of the dancers in that room belonged to her order. It was a relief: two dancers with the same assignment usually spelled trouble.

Shortly after her small demonstration, she and the rest were ushered out of the changing rooms. The other dancers squealed and giggled. Desha remained silent, but she knew her face beamed as the music began to play and the host climbed to his feet to make his introductory speeches. Desha glanced only once to make sure Gia was near the stage. The girl, while ignorant of the dancer's trade, at least knew how to look scarce when she had to. Gia sat on an abandoned cushion to the side, servants bustling around her. None had reprimanded her, for she'd pinned the apprentice insignia upon the cloth near her breast. Only teachers were allowed to chastise their apprentices.

Desha nodded once to acknowledge her student, and her attention turned back to the task at hand. Entertain the man first, lull him to false security. By the end of the night, he would be sleepy and drunk and distracted. He would not care when a dancer slipped out of the celebration hall to pad toward his private chambers.

The music blared, a light, festive tune. The dancers tapped their feet in unison, clapping along as they moved toward the large, circular stage, the crowd surrounding them. Bells jingled, jewellery sparkled, and the frenzied, feverish movement energised the dancers and the crowd.

The dance was animalistic, sensual, joyful, free. Desha loved it to the core of her lithe frame and her light feet. She swayed her hips and moved her hands, she spun and spun, her skirts waving around her like the flutter of wings. Each dancer was given space to show her unique tricks, and Desha watched as one dancer after the next bent and twisted, somersaulted and hovered in the air. Then it was her turn, and she pulled out her sash.

There was a collective gasp, and the music stopped. Sula Sab Jibnn roared with anger. Desha hesitated, her face showing some surprise, though she had half-expected the reaction.

"What's the meaning of this?" Sula Sab Jibnn turned to his magus, who also paled. He repeated the question again. "What's the meaning of this?"

Desha deferred to the lord of the house, and she placed the khanjar down on the floor. She knelt low, her head bowed. "It is but a dancer's gimmick, my *agha*," she murmured, trying to soothe the lord's fury. Infidel descendants were always so hot-tempered! "If you will let me show you . . . "

"It is so, Sula," the magus replied, his voice showing none of his pale anxiety. "I have Seen that she will conduct no harm upon your most noble person."

Desha stiffened. If the magus changed his mind, one word would silence Desha for all eternity. The king had no patience for failures, she knew that. But the magus said no more, and he retreated back to where he stood, behind his employer.

Sula Sab Jibnn hesitated, weighing his magus's words. Grudgingly, he nodded. "This had better be a good trick." He waved his hand, and the music began to play again, the room returning to its festive mood.

This paved the way for Desha's dagger tricks, and she smiled, dark eyes shining in the candlelight. She released her sash and spun it in the air, using the khanjar as the necessary weight to manipulate the sash. Desha wove her arms around, her feet and her hips in time to the movement of the sash, which crinkled the air in streaks of magenta lightning. She could hear the gasps and screams as she lunged, and then the cries of delight and whoosh of relief when she pulled back. The lord of the house roared with laughter when he saw the skill displayed before him.

A few more ladies danced after her, and Desha blended back into the fray. When the performance was finally over, the crowd clapped and whistled, and coins flew at their feet. The dancers stooped to pick what coins skidded nearby, but Desha only pushed them further away from her.

"You have done well," Sula Sab Jibnn said, approaching Desha. Beside him was his mistress, a plump redheaded beauty with smoky gray eyes and audacious curves that would make anyone jealous. "Stay and enjoy the rest of the feast. You entertainers more than deserve it."

Desha bowed low. "I thank you, my *agha*."

"But next time, you should be careful where you point your daggers. There are too many people in the twin cities wanting me dead," he said sombrely, passing her by without waiting for a reply.

She glanced at Gia, who had approached her with a mixture of admiration and fear.

"Do not look so stunned," Desha frowned, the love for the dance slowly dissipating. "And stop shifting your eyes."

Without another word, Desha retreated from the party, a dancer blending to the shadows. While the guests laughed and talked, one dancer and her apprentice moved unseen, their small frames disappearing back into the dancers' changing rooms and emerging out as servant girls on their way toward the lord's private chambers.

• • •

The magus waited for them in Sula Sab Jibnn's private rooms.

"I must admit, I had almost doubted myself when you pulled your dagger out on the open floor," he said, respect in his voice. The room was barely lit by torchlight, and darkness fought with flame. It was difficult to see the magus's face. "I thought then that you might have been an assassin, and that would have been my end."

"As well as your master's," Desha replied dryly. She sighed. "Would it be better if I went and stabbed him?"

"For you, maybe. For me, well, that depends, doesn't it?" The magus approached them.

Behind her, Gia held her breath. Desha shook her head. She was not to interfere. At first, the dancer had contemplated telling her charge to run, to escape and return to their troupe house. But that would mean conceding to the magus. Telling her student to retreat was as much an admission of cowardice and hopelessness as any.

There is no impossibility, there is only success.

Desha recited the words bitterly in her head. No matter how many times Zemir insisted that the dancers had a different type of magic, Desha could find none upon her person. She relied only on her wits, her nerve, and her skill. She was not like the King of Thieves with his djinn, nor was she the sultan with his army of magi. She was just a dancer who worked for the shadows.

She would play their game.

"You have not alerted the guards yet," Desha noted.

"No," the magus admitted. "But you forget I have Seen your future."

"Futures," Desha corrected. "They are undetermined events until the very moment one decides her course."

The light flickered briefly onto the magus's face, and she saw a look of surprise there. "You are well-versed in our soothsaying magic."

"A girl has to make do."

He chuckled.

The magus had ample opportunity to strike. Why didn't he? She was becoming irritated; Desha hated being toyed with. "Well? Let us not dance around this impasse. What will you do, magus?"

There was no answer. Instead, the magus leaned over to look at the girl behind Desha. Gia stiffened and he said, "Nothing that would render harm upon either of you."

He saw the puzzle in the dancer's eyes, and he shrugged. "Unlike most of my greedy colleagues serving under the Shahanshah, I have some code of honour. It is not the soothsayer's way to harm. What you do here is your choice, and I will not stop you."

The explanation only further confused Desha. She had never heard of a magus who didn't harm. Many a thief had been lost after being subjected to the will of the magi. "Then why are you here, if not to stop me from opening the doors?"

"I . . . " the man hesitated. He looked over at Gia again. "You have a strange student. I was overly curious. I Saw . . . "

He didn't continue the statement, partly due to his reluctance, and partly because he heard a noise from beyond the private quarters. Desha also heard it, and her hackles rose to a momentary panic. They were here, and it was time. But there was a watcher within Sula Sab Jibnn's private quarters. The thieves tolerated no watchers, and it would be on Desha's shoulders to fix this predicament.

With a quickness that put even the magus off-balance, Desha pulled at her sash and released her dagger toward the watcher's head. Even if he had Seen the movement, he was not fast enough to block or avoid it. At the last minute, Desha twisted the dagger, the khanjar's hilt making impact. He crumpled to unconscious surrender before Desha could re-sheathe her khanjar.

Gia whimpered beside her, but Desha glared her back into silence. She bent over and gave the magus an extra push. The man slid to the side of the bed, hidden from anyone who stepped in from the window. Then Desha moved with dancer's grace and hurried to the now-open balcony.

"Desha," Zemir grinned. The stars could not find Zemir if he so chose to blink out of existence. Desha had to squint to find him. He nodded acknowledgment at the girl before him. "I see your witchery is working."

She rolled her eyes, choosing to ignore his banter. "The padishah has his humours, I suppose."

"On the contrary, I personally requested for the mission," he replied. "Your report?"

"All is clear." Years of experience had given her confidence. She would not give a sidelong glance at the magus unconscious and hidden further inside the room. She also knew that the thieves would not approach the proximity of the bed, for the treasury was nowhere near there.

Desha felt the tension in the air, and she sensed Zemir's muscles stiffen beneath the folds of dark clothing. For a brief moment, she tensed as well. Had he sensed something wrong? "I heard voices in here. Was there a watcher?"

"No." She hoped Gia was a fast learner. "Gia and her incessant questions. You know how the younger girls are."

"I see," Zemir said. "Well, you know what to do with watchers if it comes to it."

Desha nodded. Thieves are not seen. The watchers are routinely silenced or led away. Those aware of a robbery were always silenced. Desha felt a shiver running down her spine. She knew what category the magus fell under. And yet . . .

Zemir had two other thieves with him. Quickly, the men climbed the coarse walls and reached the balcony where Zemir stood to bark his orders. All three crept to the treasure room, a location one of the informers—Zemir, probably—had previously sought out. Desha was to stand watch as they pilfered. And for her services, she would be paid a percentage. The thieves took care of their own.

The money was never something Desha cared for. Taking it made her feel just as sordid as the High Court ladies. But the ties that bound between the king and his dancers were strong, and Desha was not someone willing to break away from ancient magic.

The thieves carried Sula Sab Jibnn's wealth upon their backs. The treasury must have been vast, for it was the king's way to take only a fraction of the nobleman's worth. It would do no good if they robbed the man dry; they would lose a future target. If Sula Sab Jibnn can regain his losses, then there's a chance to steal from him again. Of course, the thieves would have to deal with added security, but they relied on the dancers to see that through.

Zemir gave one last nod before he and his thieves disappeared into the night once more. All that time, Gia and Desha remained demure, silent. Unsaid between them, was the thought of the watcher, the magus on the floor of Sula Sab Jibnn's bedroom.

The magus lay still as stone. Desha watched his chest rise up and down, and knew that he was still alive.

Her hand pulled at the khanjar around her waist. Her throat became desert dry. She did not want to kill this man.

Gia protested as well, and Desha looked at her. She needed to teach the girl the dangers of sympathy. Emotion is a hindrance and love is a toy to discard. To fail in learning these matters would only lead to further failures in the future. The magus could prove to be a threat to Desha's well-being, and Gia's as well. It would be better to send him the scorpion's sting now, while he was still asleep.

The choice before her was clear. She repeated the dancer's rule over and over. Her khanjar gleamed with the need for blood.

Gia stood between Desha and the magus. Desha narrowed her eyes and moved to strike her. But even with the threat of physical harm, Gia stood her ground. The girl flinched only once. Teacher and student stood frozen as if time had slowed and stopped for them.

Wordlessly, Desha sighed and sheathed the khanjar. She beckoned to Gia, whose face lit up with utter relief. Desha did not bother to scold her on the expression of emotions. For the dancer, the giving of life was a failure on her part, and she would have to live with it. They climbed down the stairs to rejoin the guests below.

"He will make our living as dancers difficult in the future, Gia," Desha told her charge. "You will soon know how it is to fail in your role."

Gia nodded, her face thoughtful. "But, teacher, you and Zemir said so yourself. There is no impossibility, there is only success."

"No impertinence." But Desha felt a smile creep toward the corners of her down-turned mouth. She shrugged. "Perhaps. Only the future can tell what the magus will do."

And only the magus can choose what fate awaits him.

For now, Desha could wait. Gia would be her constant worry, but even so, she could tell that the girl learned quickly. She looked past the dark ointment and the black wig. Beneath, she saw the yellow hair and the pale skin, the vibrant blue eyes singing with determination. Yet for those physical differences, Desha knew that Gia was a dancer, for Gia was a girl with the same drive as Desha. The same strength and the same passion. The same sympathy.

The magus was right. There was something unusual about Gia. She was an infidel's daughter, with the heart and the soul of Salaithra. A melding of both worlds, Desha thought wryly. The future was looking more and more like a whirlwind dance.

Perhaps Zemir chose truly after all.

Afterword

The tale of Ali Baba is probably one of the more popular folktales stemming from Arabia. We have a poor merchant's son who becomes gravely involved in a feud with the forty thieves (something about Ali finding a cave and taking the money conveniently hidden inside). But nowhere in the tale does it say he emerges victorious alone. In fact, the story of Ali Baba does not end the minute he obtains his riches. It does not even start with Ali Baba's stumbling into the thieves' cave. No, I believe the true beginning is when slave-girl Morgiana enters the scene in order to save him from the vengeful King of Thieves and his menacing Forty.

This, to me, is where the inspiration for "Shadow Dancer" emerged. Ali Baba, as good as he is portrayed to be, is still a thief. A lucky thief, for he manages to escape the King of Thieves' clutches more than once. Yet behind this lucky thief stands a beautiful, clever, dangerous slave girl, whose name is often forgotten amongst the pages of the folktale. In my world of Salaithra, this slave girl exists in the form of a young apprentice, whose story begins the day she promises her servitude to the King of Thieves, the Padishah of Jimoor. A shadow dancer's path is not an easy one to follow, as Desha will illustrate to the young Gia. But then again, what path was ever easy for a woman with talent in ancient Arabia?

Parvaz

Charlotte Nash

Some days, when the alley streamers snap in the breeze, and I smell the upper atmosphere come down to mingle in the detritus of these shops and stones, I sit in this chair and fester an evil longing for what can never be again. My shoulder aches where the bone healed amiss, the wasted muscles clamped and remembering my body stuffed into this human form; my treasures broken down and sold. And the one who both saved me and chained me.

The bells ring from the shop door. A woman is there, framed in the doorway. A shock of ebony hair, a silhouette of arms and hips. And desire stirs, low down in my brain. She approaches tentatively, as if she smells something that makes her nervous, as if it is too dark for her to see. She moves like a hunted thing, making my spine tingle and my leg muscles burn. I rise, silent, and watch her from this doorway. Her fingers moving to the glass case nearest, her eyes flickering to the side, lingering on the jewels. She has the sway of a princess. She wears loose culottes like a veiled dancer. An exotic thing that lived in the palace, perhaps, when I lived in the mountains long ago. My desire unfolds until my mouth is dry, my neck sore from the clench of hunting muscles, but I won't allow more. Above her shimmering pants is just a T-shirt, her features too light for a sultana. Besides, there would be questions, and I need her to pay.

I show myself, and she jumps a fraction, which sets my heart racing, pupils expanding, the shop with its cases and old wood and silken drapes suddenly blooming in spectrum shift. The detail floods my consciousness: a mouse lurks in the far corner, thinking himself unseen; beetle bodies on the door lintel, their rainbow shells dull; dust and wood polish and earthly things. Cloying. And my plodding, human brain tries to give it all meaning.

I'm overcome and stagger, strike my knee. Pain sends the human brain away and brings me clear. The woman rushes over. I smell her relief, and her perfume; she sees an old man, a weak man. She has dismissed what scared her only moments ago. But I am neither old, nor weak, nor a man, and she smells familiar . . . of blood and feathers.

She helps me aloft the floor. "Goodness, are you alright?" she asks. "Do you want me to—"

Just a small stumble, a slip! I protest, allowing my hand to linger on her proffered arm. My own skin feels strange, but her form underneath it familiar. Bones in meat.

"You have beautiful things," she says, allowing the moment to pass. She moves to the cabinets. I slip into the counter and shadow her interest.

She stops by the middle case. "These here." She traces the outlines. My gaze is steady even as my heart is twisting in my human chest, seeing what she is seeing. These are brooches, all wings. Wings half-furled, wings in glide . . . and below them, feathers in silver and gold and platinum. All my treasures remade.

She sighs. "Birds," she says, as if this conveys something. I say nothing. So many customers begin this way.

"I love birds," she continues. "Such freedom. I'm sure I'd love to be able to fly. To be so carefree. Is that why you make these?"

Her gesture indicates the shop. She already knew of this place, perhaps. From a friend, or by reputation. The odd jeweller down the little side alley in this big, ugly city, where every piece is a wing or feather, or a beak. But she is mistaken—of my reasons, and what she sees. *No*, I say, but softly, and she pays me no attention.

I hope that she will pick quickly, but she dithers as they always do. I rub my shoulder, and look out the window. She moves across the shop, but I still smell the feathers on her skin.

"I have a bird," she says softly, when the silence becomes uncomfortable for her.

Ah, I say, though I mean it explains how she smells and not because I am interested. She is waiting now for me to ask what sort of bird it is, but I do not care. Instead, I ask what she is looking for.

"Something," she says vaguely, browsing distractedly, until she looks in the cases opposite. Her turned back brings me a memory, though it should not. A cave; and that smell of blood and feathers. I have been too long in this body, and yet can never leave.

When I look up again, she is gone. The door is closing with its cheerful chime. I turn the latch and flip over the sign. *Parvaz* is closed for now.

I numb the human in me with spirits and perch on an old chair to go over my books. My saviour . . . and my gaoler is due his fee. There is enough for this time, but not yet for the next. I glower at the closed shop with its cases, its propensity to attract customers. Its position beneath the perfect and unattainable sky.

• • •

Two weeks pass and I sell only a little. The customers like the jewels; they come to the shop from the tent markets outside, happy and pleasant; but they do not like me. My mood matters, and I work on improving it, like the helpless living thing I am. That desire to live is what got me here. I spend half a day mulling on this, then I improve.

Therefore, I am surprised and annoyed when she comes back. The girl with the ebony hair and the preyish ways. I rub my shoulder, wondering if she could know my thoughts. She hovers in the doorway. I stare. She looks different, though I know it is her. She has changed her hair, perhaps.

"Hello again," she says. Advances two tentative steps.

You were here before, I manage. I stand behind the counter, feeling my human self all thin and fragile. As if I could crack my skin like an eggshell and emerge again. I fix on her, then realise I am not blinking. I have to remember to do that. I do it twice. Slowly. She seems to settle.

"Do you do custom pieces?" she asks quickly. She blinks. Her eyes are very green. The flesh around them is soft. My hands clench against the wood. It takes a long moment to recover. I apologise and lie: ask her to repeat herself; I am not sure what she has said.

She does, but as I form the word *no*, two thoughts clash together. The first is that this is a sale. The second is how little money I have for the djinni.

And what he will do to me if I cannot pay.

So I nod. She smiles, a tiny movement at the edge of her lips. She is nervous again; she feels exposed. I see the pulse at her neck and wrists. I wish she would leave.

Do you know what you want? I ask. I rub my jaw with the back of my arm, and it feels odd. Smooth where there should be feathers.

She is already turning to go. "I will do a sketch and come back?"

Relieved at the distance, I nod. She is gone again. The smell does not linger long, but my shoulder is itching now.

I go to the back room and pace about my chair, scratching. My eyes fall absently on the ledger. I strain my good shoulder, searching my back with my paltry nails. I find a lump.

I seek the tiny relief room with its mirror. I undo the buttons and pull my shirt away. The scar wraps my arm like a strangling snake. I pull the wasted arm forward. Something is there, its tip protruding through my skin. I think of burrs, or parasites.

I snatch the fine pliers from my workbench and close them about this thing. I tug. It comes loose with a sting I've known before, and I thrust the offending object up to the light. A white feather, a bloody quill. I lose my grip and the pliers fall. The feather floats to the pale porcelain sink, where it sticks, fanned and wetted. I hold myself, shivering, as the blood creeps pinkly into the barbs.

• • •

She comes back in two days with a white sheet folded in her hands. She looks different again, hair piled high on her head, her neck exposed. I try not to look further, but retreat into my human brain, the one that thinks of how to handle tools and work metals, and not about how to hunt; or how to rip out a slender throat.

She unfolds the sheet and pushes it across. I look down and the picture shudders in my vision. *No, no! I cannot make this!*

She sees my expression. "I'm sorry, the drawing isn't very good," she stumbles. "It's a necklace, you see?"

I do. I see the curve of the band intended to grace her neck, and erupting from the side of it, the motif she would have me create. The rendering is so good, it could fly off her page.

I cannot make this, I say, pushing the paper back towards her. I hope to convey that I have not the skill for such a design, though I do. But this thing is too large, and renders an image the djinni forbade me to make.

Her big eyes are sad. "Oh please!" she begs. "You're perfect for it. No one else can make it!" She gestures around the shop, as if to remind me that I make wings and beaks and talons already. But never a form complete. Never that. The djinni would have me.

"How much do you need?" she says quickly. And this is the critical moment. I have not sold enough this month. And the djinni can have me anyway if I cannot pay. I stand there, in dithering silence, my fingers moving like inch-worms against the glass. I tell myself I can stop before the size is too large, that I can tell her I cannot do it later. I will sell other things, and destroy this piece without finishing it.

She raises her eyebrows, hopeful. I look away. I name a hideous price; more than enough to pay the djinni for a half-year.

She nods slowly. "I will pay you half now?" she asks. Her hand darts to her bag. So swift. So unexpected. I catch her before I realise what I have done. She stares at me, frightened green eyes, my hand closed about her wrist.

No, no, I say, dropping her. In my head, my tongue is tasting her blood. *Pay when I finish*. For then there is no transgression until the end.

She almost protests, but I have scared her. She leaves me with the drawing and the rising panic in my ill-fitting body prison. I go to walk into the back, but a fit comes and I throw the paper down. My head is full of her design: a bird, wings outstretched, a hunting form, talons out, eyes focussed. I felt that, once. I shrug off the human brain, and the smell of prey sharpens. I leap onto the cabinets and scan the revealed shadows. The mouse is still there; I sense him. I wait, watching him along his usual track. I pounce.

The cabinet crashes to the side. I'm aware of the mouse steps, accelerating. But this body is ungainly. My good shoulder crashes into the wall. A silk drape comes down. I chase the small grey haunches and lose the ability to recall.

When I wake later, it is dark and I am under a cabinet. The shop is a mess. There is fur on my lips and blood in my mouth. Even after I have cleaned, I am not sure if it is mine or mouse.

• • •

I work on the piece in a feverish state. For the first two days, my hand shakes whenever I think of it, and I cannot begin any part of the bird. I raid my treasures and make the circlet from a platinum sword pommel. I select diamonds for inlay, from a sultana's bracelet, and gold and silver from other jewels that once sparkled in the mountain sun.

She comes back in two days. I show her the circlet, and she leaves quickly. I stare after her again, trying to place how she looks different each time. Maybe just because I have been dreaming of her blood and flesh.

I make the parts for the bird over the next three days, but I do not meld them. Each is small enough not to exceed the djinni's conditions, but even still, I begin to dream of the night I hunted, and woke up in the djinni's palace, a slave for eternity.

The next time the woman returns, I refuse to show her my work. *I am not happy with it*, I say. *Besides, my tooth is hurting and it gives me a headache.* She purses her lips. She tries to persuade me. She is excited to see her piece, she reassures me she will love it. I refuse more sternly. I tell her to come back later, that I am not feeling well.

After she leaves I stare at the pieces on my bench, holding the tooth through my pallid cheek. Sales are still not enough to meet my payment. But I am scared of this piece, of making a whole picture. My human mind is strong on craft and finances, but it has limits in regulating my real self. If I make this thing, will my mind break? Will I hunt this woman and kill her? Will I be found, imprisoned and unable to pay the djinni?

My fingers slip inside my lips to test the tooth. I grunt, surprised, as it comes away in my hand. My focus shifts to the twisted roots, pinkly stained. Am I hallucinating?

I lie on my cot and push the tooth back into place. It fits with a dull pain, and later when I wake, it sits solid in my gum.

My hand sweeps the work pieces into a box and shoves them beneath the cot. Then I dream of the mountain air, of wings so large they spanned the peaks, a cave of treasures, and a dozen other things gone forever. And I wake with my shoulder aching and tears on my cheeks.

. . .

She returns again in two days, in a suit this time, her hair braided tightly behind her head. She smiles again. "How long to go now?" she asks. "Can I pay you?"

I don't respond, but this time I take her to the workbench. I have taken the fragments from the box, unchanged. I have prepared this moment. I tell her I cannot complete the design, but that she can take the pieces to someone else to assemble. I have not been well, I say. I show her my hand. It shakes with the restless nights and the fear of being imprisoned. But if she will buy the pieces separate, I can pay the djinni; another month will go on.

She purses her lips, but she puts a kind hand to my shoulder. "But I want you to finish it; you have to."

I stare at the platinum wing, at the exquisite detail on the feathers. No wonder she does not believe I cannot complete it. But I wish she would not touch me, those blood-smelling fingers on my wasted flesh. I step away.

"Do you know what this is?" she says softly, tapping her finger on the now-smudged drawing. "I looked up the name of your shop," she continues, as if this will explain it. "*Parvaz.* Persian. And so"—she taps the drawing—"is this *rukh.* So, you have to finish it. Please. No one else can. I have your money all ready."

I stand a long moment, my true name tripping ugly memories, knowing I have no time to make other sales. My shoulder aches. I dare not look at her.

Friday, I say. *Come back Friday.*

. . .

When she is gone, I open the shop windows, and the door. Outside, the market tents crowd together under the building walls and sky. The breeze snaps pennants at the tent crowns, the air cool. I look for ebony hair. There is none, but I am bothered the same.

I make a wheeling turn back into the shop. The breeze is lofting the silk drapes, like it did in a sultan's palace, long ago. I stop in the entrance to the back room, see the pieces lying on their table.

She said *Persian* . . . unusual. And she said *rukh,* not roc. Perhaps she is a scholar? But her keenness to pay . . . I rub at my shoulder. The ache is dull now, as usual. I stand there and ponder, as the sun goes down and evening comes.

Then, I go to my workbench, take up the pieces; both those in gold and the ones in my head. And I smell jasmine coming in from the street.

• • •

I am dreaming again, though this is a place I have been before. Another cave in my mountains, but one lower down, reachable for a great bird with a broken wing. I am frantic in the way living things are when they are going to die and can't accept it. I know who lives here and should not go in; this djinni is clever; he knows how to trap things, even one as great as I.

I should not go, but I want to live. I need the djinni's magic. For how can a rukh hunt with this useless wing? A piece of feather drifts to the djinni's feet. He seems a saviour. He can make me a human body, where a wing is not essential. But I must pay him each moon, in human money, not with my treasures. And those I cannot sell as they are; they must be transformed, but never as a bird-form complete, or weighing more than my broken feather. He twirls the white shape in his hand. I will starve slowly, or take this chance.

• • •

I work through the remaining days and Friday comes with the piece finished on my bench. It violates the terms of my salvation. Too large; showing a bird-form complete. In those last hours, its emerging splendour sent me mad with memory. Snow-melt I could taste, clear skies I could see. But now it is done.

My shoulder aches. It should. She is nearly here. I have put this puzzle together. My heart bounds for what could happen now.

The bells chime on the door, and she enters. Again, different. Sharper, less feminine. I show myself.

She smiles, again, a quick movement. My reflexes scream, but I control them now. I am focussed.

I am hunting.

"You are finished?" she asks.

I nod and beckon her towards the workroom. She comes closer. I shift my shoulders against the prickle there, like feathers pushing against a cloth. She pauses in the door as she sees the finished piece.

Her *rukh* streams in gold, platinum and jewels, immaculate. She grasps it in her hands, testing the weight.

"I should pay you," she says.

This, here, is the moment. I look her in the eye as she hands across the cash. The contract closes. As soon as I take the notes, her smile twists. For a second, I see the flames dance in her pupils, confirmation of who she is.

"You are mine, *rukh*," she says. She does not bother to disguise her voice now. It is the rumble of the djinni. My mind gives me pictures of dungeons in his mountain palace. The djinni bounces the piece in her hand. "Too heavy for our contract," she says. "And a form complete, besides."

I am not blinking now. I am fixed, waiting for what she will do. My back itches, my shoulder burns.

"You will be my slave now," she says, slipping the piece about her neck. My blood thrums as I see her pulse there, just against the circlet. She shakes her head. "I have waited a long time, *rukh*, to have you like this."

You tricked me, I say. *You asked me to do this!*

She laughs, not unkindly. "There is no rule against that. Now come."

My vision focuses on that one square inch of flesh. *But you have broken a rule too*, I say. *You were too confident. You forgot something.*

She laughs, amused. Her pulse rises and falls. "And what is that?"

I can hurt you.

She laughs again. "You are trapped in that form, *rukh*, and I am immortal. You cannot hurt me."

My smile, if I could, would be slow. *But your magic does not work in human form.*

I feel the feathers rip through my skin, the talons burst my shoes. But my beak is what kills her. It plunges into that soft neck and spills blood and flesh across the floor. I feast on her lifeless form, hunted and destroyed. And it tastes like winging over imaginary mountains, like freedom I once had.

❀

Afterword

"Parvaz" was one of those stories that crystallised from mental images I'd been filing since childhood. When I was quite small, my Dad took me each week to our local newsagent to buy a new edition of Story Time magazine. Each illustrated issue came with tapes and contained both stand-alone, and serialised or episodic stories. All the classic fairy tales were in there, but I was particularly taken with Aladdin, who always had perilous adventures in exotic places and escaped with fantastic riches. In one of the tales, Aladdin meets a roc, whose egg is so large it's mistaken for a mountain. Around the same age, I read about the roc in another book about mystical beasts, which said it was a bird large enough to carry off an elephant. What a fantastical thing.

Many years later, I was heartbroken to see wedge-tailed eagles, who'd been hit by cars on the highway, living in a wildlife park. None of them could fly anymore, with broken wings that could never heal to carry their weight again. Their massive size had been their downfall—they come down to feed on road kill, but they take so long to get airborne they are often hit when a car comes—and the reason they could never be released. A bird of prey who cannot hunt would starve to death.

When I saw the theme for Dreaming of Djinn, I immediately thought of the roc, the greatest bird of prey, and those eagles. "Parvaz" is the result.

The Dancer of Smoke

Joshua Gage

Long ago, before the great kingdoms of the world were shattered along their mountains and rivers like a glass pulled from the lehr too early, there lived in the city of Jahrom, a boy named Pahlbod who helped his father and his mother run their restaurant. Each morning Pahlbod accompanied his mother to the market to watch her haggle with vendors over their vegetables and meat, often carrying the heavy sacks of rice for her, sometimes even the carcasses of goats or chickens for his father to butcher.

Nightly, white *sofrehs* were spread across the tables, heavy with plates of spicy *kebabs* and *polows* with aromatic crusts, steaming bowls of thick *aash* flavoured with coriander and mint leaves, and platters of flat *taftan* loaves, warm from the stone oven, golden with saffron and cardamom. Long plates of his mother's famous *halwa*, smelling of rose oil and sprinkled with almonds or pistachios, was served for dessert, and guests, often traders from as far away as Pteria and Sardes, stumbled back to their hostels and tents, heads dizzy with *mey* and bellies filled.

After the last guest left, Pahlbod snuffed the oil lamps that flickered shadows across the room, gathered the long *sofrehs* to be washed, then unrolled his sleeping mat and lay down beside the warmth of the stove. His parents tallied the accounts, gathered coins in a small green chest, and made plans for the next day's meal.

Some nights, guests overflowed the tables, and Pahlbod scurried amongst them carrying baskets with fresh loaves of *tafteh* or *naan* and jugs of *mey* or clearing the dirty plates to make room for another guest. Some nights moved more slowly, only a few tables full. These nights, his father and mother stepped from the kitchen, often joining the patrons in the meal, his father telling jokes and stories with the men while his mother gossiped with the women. Pahlbod would curl into a corner, belly warm with food, and fall asleep to the voices and laughter that enveloped him.

In the way that a desert will slowly creep its sands across an oasis until what was once lush with water and trees becomes no more than rock and dust, so too did the caravans slowly move, taking their traders and their goods away from Jahrom. They stopped at Susa at the end of the Royal Road, or continued to the richer markets of Persepolis. Pahlbod's market visits with his mother were shorter and the sacks he carried lighter, until there were days when they did not go to the market at all. There were fewer *sofrehs* spread each evening, and Pahlbod helped his father rearrange the tables, pushing some against the wall, and clustering only three or four in the centre, allowing for a cosier atmosphere, also saving on lamp oil. Eventually, Pahlbod and his father stopped putting out the *sofrehs* altogether, and his mother stopped going to the market more than once or twice a week. The three of them sat at a lonely table in the middle of the room, eating what little dinner they had. Pahlbod helped clean the few dishes that had been dirtied then fell asleep on his mat with his stomach rumbling.

One night, when the moon was full, snug in the night sky like a fresh egg among a nest of clouds, while his mother was making dinner and Pahlbod and his father occupied their time with cleaning corners that were not remotely dirty, a stranger opened the door to the restaurant. His beard was peppered with grey curls, and clothes so sun-bleached and sand-worn as to be more hole than colourless cloth, clung to his near-skeletal frame. His only possession seemed to be the round drum that he carried under his arm. Pahlbod had, of course, seen a *tombak* before. His parents had occasionally hired musicians to play for the crowds in the restaurants on holidays, like Nowruz or Sizdah Bedar, but he had never seen such an intricately carved one. It was as though the drum itself were a prince or caliph in a royal chariot, gilded and encrusted with amethyst and lapis lazuli, drawn from place to place by the lonely horse of the beggar.

The man stepped in. "Please," he said. "I'm hungry. I don't have much." With this, he proffered a few coins from his belt sack and held them out to Pahlbod's father. "All I ask is some bread, and maybe some wine. Please." The coins in the man's hand were barely enough to pay for a ladle-full of water in the market, let alone bread or wine.

Pahlbod's father stood. "Stranger, in your travels, have you met many Bedouins?" The stranger nodded. "Then perhaps you are familiar with the idea that a Bedouin's wealth is not counted by the number of camels or horses in his flocks, but by the number of guests who eat beneath his tent each evening." His face softened as he took the stranger's hand in his and gently curled the fingers over the coins. "You, my friend, are the first person to have stepped through that door asking for food since before the last full moon. I have no tent, but tonight you are a guest at my table, and I thank you for your company." With that, he clapped his hands loudly. "Pahlbod, light the lamps. Set the table." He shouted loud enough for Pahlbod's mother to hear, "A guest will be joining us!"

Pahlbod's mother stepped from the kitchen holding the green chest that held their savings. "I have ears enough to hear what happens beneath my own roof without you yelling at me. We will need more food," she said, and tipped the few coins from the box into her husband's hands. "Go. One or two of our neighbours will have something put away, a lamb's leg or a chicken, and half of their wives usually buy more vegetables than they know what to do with. Tell them it's for me, an emergency, and you will get a fair price. Go, hurry, before our guest starves waiting on you." With that, she shooed Pahlbod's father out the door. Then she turned to the guest and bowed slightly. "We are honoured with your presence, sir. Please forgive us. It's been so long since we've had guests that we've forgotten how to behave. Pahlbod will bring you some wine, and I'll be right out with something to tide your hunger over while we wait for my husband to return."

Pahlbod hurried into the kitchen and returned with an earthenware carafe of wine and goblet for the stranger. "Here you are, sir," he said, bowing before he began to pour. Remembering his manners, he quickly added, "With thanks from our family."

"You seem like a bright child. Pahlbod, was it? Tell me, have you ever seen one of these?" the stranger asked, showing Pahlbod his drum. Pahlbod stared, and slowly nodded. The man laughed at Pahlbod's shyness, then, cradling the *tombak* under his arm, beat out the quick rhythm of a *bandari* with his hands. Pahlbod began to rock and sway with the beat, as though the sound resonating from the drum was an intoxicating spell cast by a magus on his body, forcing it to dance. Still laughing, the man stopped his playing and offered the drum to Pahlbod. "Would you like to try?"

Pahlbod's father had always insisted that guests want children to carry food and wine and to clear dishes, not to pester them with questions of their travels or rumours from far away satrapies, and Pahlbod was often left to cling like a flea to the conversation, sucking what little information he could from the half-heard voices. But here was a guest talking to *him*, offering to play music with him while his mother cooked. Pahlbod nodded and cautiously took the drum, attempting to hold it like the man had, but the drum was heavier than it looked, and Pahlbod struggled to encircle its weight with his arm. Once he had it secure, he brought his hand down upon it, stinging his palm with the smack.

The sound was dull and flat, like a pestle falling into a mortar's seeds. The stranger shook his head, and clucked "No no no. This is an instrument, a thing of poetry and music, not a donkey to swat into submission. Tell me, have you ever eaten a pomegranate?"

Wondering how such a poor man ever afforded such a delicacy himself, Pahlbod nodded. "Once, on Nowruz, I was allowed a few seeds."

"Good. Good. And do you remember how you ate those seeds? Did you squeeze them beneath your fingers like a beetle until they burst?" Pahlbod shook his head. Even the feral beggars on the streets, children who only tasted a pomegranate if they were lucky enough to steal one from a distracted merchant, knew that the seeds must be plucked gently from the rinds lest they explode, staining the skin and nails crimson. "Good. Now, the *tombak* is just like that. You must coax the sound out of it in the same way you pull a seed from a pomegranate. Play it from here," he said, indicating the tips of his fingers, "not your hand." Pahlbod tried again, this time tapping the centre of the drumhead gently with his fingertips.

"Excellent," the man clapped. "Well done. Now, once more, but this time with some feeling, like you're tugging at the sound, pulling it from the drum with a rope. Keep your fingers together, so that they all hit at once." Pahlbod tried again, his fingertips striking the drumhead squarely. Almost before he heard the sound, he felt it winding its way through his body. It echoed in the room, rich and deep, and the stranger yelped with delight. "Yes," he shouted. "Perfect. Well done! Well done! Now," he said, taking the drum back from Pahlbod, "there are four sounds every drummer must know. The first, which you just learned, is the *tom*." The stranger hit the head quickly in the centre, resulting in that deep, resonant tone which rumbled through Pahlbod's belly. "Like I showed you, four fingers, cupped, and a sharp strike in the centre with the fingertips.

"The next sound is the *bak*," said the man, who then struck the edge of the drumhead with his fingertip. The sound was sharp, bright, like a chirp from a small bird announcing the sunset. "One finger, quickly, on the edge, almost as though the beat is the natural response, an inhale to the *tom*'s exhale.

"After that is the *pelangue*." The stranger snapped his fingers against the drumhead, producing a sharp, resounding pop, almost like a twig snapping in two. "This is a useful sound, but one that can be overused quickly, so play it with care. It's simple enough to make, though. Just snap your finger into the drumhead.

"Finally, there's the ornamental *eshareh*." The stranger rippled his fingertips across the drumhead, first one hand then the other, producing a vibration that rumbled throughout the room like the waves from sea crashing into shore. "The trick to *eshareh* is the wrist. Keep the wrist strong, and make sure your thumb and pinkie strike at the same time to illuminate the rhythm.

"Four sounds—*tom, bak, pelangue, eshareh*. Pluck these properly from the pomegranate of the *tombak*, and you will be able to assuage the temper of kings, enchant gifts from the djinn in the desert, and even," he said with a conspiratorial wink, "entice a dancing girl into your bed."

Before Pahlbod could gasp at this stranger's boldness or the talk of such things with his mother so near to hearing, the stranger began to play. The rhythm fell over Pahlbod like rain over the parched desert, each leaf and blossom in him spreading itself wide before the downpour, their roots soaking up what nourishment they could before the song ended. Pahlbod felt his body caught up in the drumbeat like a boat in a storm at sea, pulled through the darkness on the exhilarating waves, every second expecting to shatter.

The drumming stopped short, and Pahlbod fell out of his trance. The stranger stood and bowed before Pahlbod's mother, who was carrying a tray with a steaming bowl of *haleem*, which filled the room with aromas of garlic, pepper and coriander. "This should keep your bellies full until my husband returns with the rest of our meal," she said. "Now, may I be so bold as to ask the name of the guest who will be sharing this meal with us?"

The stranger bowed again. "My name is Narin. I am a traveller in search of the truth, what you in this land might call a pilgrim, but might call a beggar."

"Well, Narin," Pahlbod's mother said coyly. "Whatever your occupation, you are welcome at our table and your music is welcome within our walls. I assume you are hungry after your travels. Please, eat." And eat he did. The *haleem* was completely gone by the time Pahlbod's father returned from his friends' houses carrying a few chickens, a sack of vegetables, and more. Having heard that it was an emergency, their neighbours had been generous. There was *joojeh kebab* with chicken, grilled onions and tomatoes, a bright saffron-yellow cake of *polo zafarani*, long green rolls of *dolmeh barg* bursting with chunks of lamb and rice, filling the room with odours of mint and tarragon. Throughout the meal, Narin told stories of his travels, fascinating Pahlbod with the different people he had met, from Egyptians with their beast-headed gods to the towering gardens of Babylon, which overflowed with green vines and bright blossoms, where water flowed up hill at the command of the priests to nourish all the plants.

After the meal was finished, and the plates had been cleared, Narin stood to leave. "Before I go," he said, pulling a glass phial the size of a small apple from his belt pouch. "I would like to offer you a gift for the kindness you have shown to a stranger and the generosity you have shown to a beggar." He walked to an oil lamp in the far corner and quickly blew it out, swirling the glass jar over the wick to capture the smoke. This he did to each lamp in the room, until only the lamp on the table remained. Palhbod, his mother and his father watched from the halo of its soft glow as Narin capped the phial with a cork and shook it a few times, agitating and condensing the smoke inside. Then, he uncorked it, placed it on the floor, and clapped twice.

The smoke rolled from the phial in luxuriant curls, weaving and coaxing their way across the floor, winding up the table legs and across the *sofreh* like a sleek cat. Once it reached the centre of the table, it spiralled upward until it whirled itself into the shape of a woman with a long billowing skirt and a series of veils spiralling from her shoulders and arms like the wide wings of a *faravahar*. Narin began to clap, a slow steady rhythm, which Pahlbod immediately took up, followed by his father and mother. The woman of smoke began to move her shoulders and arms, stepping back and forth, swaying like a river reed in time to the sound of their hands, scarves whipping out and streaming around their heads with the rich smells of cinnamon and sandalwood. Slowly she floated from the table to the floor, body constantly moving and bending with the rhythm of their clapping, then stepped and swirled towards the phial. Narin snapped his fingers twice, and the visage of the woman began to melt and dissolve, almost as though she was folding herself into a cloud of grey dust, which whirled its way back into the phial. Narin replaced the cork, then handed the phial to Pahlbod.

"I need you to watch over this for me until I return. Remember, two claps to release the dancer, two snaps to call her back. Treat her as you would your sister, and guard her. Let no one touch her. Can I trust you to be responsible? Can you do this thing for me?" Pahlbod nodded eagerly and took the phial gently with both hands. Narin bowed to Pahlbod's father and mother, and stepped out into the night.

The next night, Pahlbod's mother sent his father out to invite the neighbours, who had so graciously given of their kitchens, into their house for dinner. "It will do well to thank them," she insisted. "In case we have another emergency in the future." The feast was simple, but filling, and everyone praised, as they had so often in the past, his mother's cooking.

Once the meal was over, everyone stayed to gossip while Pahlbod cleared the tables and began to extinguish the extra lamps. While he was doing this, one neighbour, a round, sweaty man whose tongue had been loosened by too much *mey*, guffawed, "So, what was this emergency that sent you begging last night?" Pahlbod's father stood, embarrassed, but Pahlbod quickly ran to get Narin's phial.

"Watch," he said, "but do not touch." He pulled the cork, and clapped loudly two times.

As it had last night, smoke began to pull from the phial, creeping across the floor like fog rolling in from off the sea. It billowed together into the dancer, who began to move to an unheard music, as though she was listening to the rhythm of their breathing and the counterpoint of their heartbeats, mirroring them with her translucent body that at times seemed to dissipate into nothing more than a twisting tendril hinting at the mere outline of a woman, only to condense upon itself into a voluptuous white cloud, thick with curve and contour, every indication of a real human being dancing before their eyes.

Mimicking Narin's actions the night before, Pahlbod began to clap, a slow, deliberate rhythm the dancer immediately responded to, hips casting slow figure eights while her shoulders and arms pulled thin veils of smoke in arcing sweeps. Pahlbod's father smiled at him, and took up the clap, followed by a few of the men who had been to enough cabarets to know how to act in the presence of a dancer. The smoke figure, as though encouraged by the audience response, began to move more intensely, her back arching as her arms propelled her veils into billowing circles around her, her whole body spinning, almost lifting off the floor.

Almost instinctively, Pahlbod snapped his fingers twice, and the dancer slowed and began to melt, uncurling in long wisps which twisted across the floor and back into the phial. Pahlbod quickly corked it and returned to its place in the kitchen. All the guests applauded, cheering the performance and babbling their awe.

The next night, the restaurant was full. Their neighbours' drunken tongues and market gossip had spread the secret of the dancer of smoke. Pahlbod was so busy filling goblets with *mey* and returning plates to the kitchen that he almost forgot to bring out the phial until his father reminded him. His father also made a brief announcement, silencing the room and asking his guests to enjoy the show, but to treat the vision they were about to see with the dignity and respect they would afford any woman.

Pahlbod uncorked the phial and clapped his hands twice, and the room immediately silenced before the figure of the dancer swelled across the lamplight like an eclipse of the moon. Pahlbod began to clap, and the guests took up the rhythm. The dancer snaked delicately between the tables and standing bodies, veils spread in intricate patterns, now the wings of an eagle silhouetted against the sun, and now the delicate body of a butterfly clinging to a stalk of birthwort. The perfume of cinnamon and sandalwood saturated the room, to the point that all the guests were deliriously dreamy by the time Pahlbod snapped his fingers, returning the smoke to its phial. Still entranced, they stumbled out into the night, minds still ensnared by the dancer's spell.

And so it went, night after night. Pahlbod watched and waited as guests filled his parent's tables, enjoying luxuriant plates of spicy *kebab bareh* and *morasah polow*, steaming bowls of crimson *korescht bamiyeh*, tart with fresh lime juice combined with okra, and sweet plates of the crunchy pastries *shirini khoshk* baked with diced pistachios.

Pahlbod's father made his customary announcement, and the meal itself was almost entirely forgotten with two claps from Pahlbod, which released the dancer, enchanting every person in the room. Even Pahlbod, who was in charge of the entertainment, was mesmerised by the visage of smoke, the ebb and flow of her body that all but disappeared in the crowd only to coalesce in a flurry of veils. Pahlbod was so entranced by the dancer that he found himself sneaking into the kitchen during the day to smell the small jar of cinnamon his mother kept there, inhaling the fragrance to remember the redolence with which the dancer perfumed the room while she moved. But it was never the same, and every night Pahlbod was eager for the dinner to end.

Even after he led the audience in their clap, he huddled in a corner, tapping out varied rhythms in the dust. He practiced holding his hands around an imaginary *tombek* in the way that Narin had taught him, constantly reminding himself to be as gentle as a man plucking seeds from a pomegranate. He did not mind having to share the dancer with the guests, or even that the dancer wasn't real, but merely a vision in smoke and longing, a beneficent *qarinah*. Even after he snapped his fingers, after the dancer unfurled and curled back into the phial, Pahlbod felt her lingering in the room, as though she had left a hint of smoke clinging to everyone who watched her, like the trace of a beautiful dream that evaporates with the dawn of waking, but enfolds the dreamer in its spell throughout the day.

Soon, word of the magical dancer spread outside the city walls, travelling like a weed through the rich soil of conversation that was the lifeblood of caravan routes throughout the country. People from as far away as Pasargadae were coming to feast from their famous kitchen and become enchanted by the dancer in smoke. Naysayers came to the house to be converted into believers, and believers made the pilgrimage south to be confirmed by this miracle.

One day, a magnificent ebony horse carried a uniformed rider to their door, a messenger from the palace of Ariobarzanes. They were to prepare a private feast for the satrap himself and his entourage, who would arrive the next day at sunset. Pahlbod's father nearly burst with the news, knowing that the fame of such a guest ensured their restaurant would remain filled well into his old age, but his mother was all but panic stricken.

The satrap himself! What could she, little more than a peasant woman, serve to such a nobleman, second in command to the king of Persia himself. To fail in even one dish meant certain scorn and public ridicule, if not the loss of their house and property.

Pahlbod's mother dragged him to the market, emptying the green box, which had been full for months due to the fame of the dancer, determined to serve a feast to end all feasts. Pahlbod's shoulders were laden with two whole lambs, which he carried to his father to butcher, only to be sent back to help his mother carry the heavy sacks of rice and vegetables while she bargained with fishmongers over the price of *hamour*.

When Pahlbod got home, he was set to making the room presentable, polishing the oil lamps until they glistened even without the flames on their spouts, spreading the crisp white *sofrehs* across the tables, carrying platters of juicy *chenjeh koobideh kebab* heavy with mint and coriander, steaming bowls of scarlet *gheimeh badenjan* flavoured with turmeric and smoked paprika, the small wedges of fried eggplant floating like fishing boats on a sunset dyed sea, bright green mounds of *sabzi polo mahi*, the fresh scallions and diced dill and parsley in the rice mixing with the salty grilled hamour.

Each table was a feast in itself, but the main table featured crunchy *polo tahdig*, the crispy rice glistening in the lamplight like a plate of amber, a full rack of lamb saturated in an orange and saffron marinade, cooked rare enough that the meat was still plump with juice and begging to be torn from the bone, deep brown bowls of *khoreste fesenjan* with chunks of glazed duck floating in the nutty stew of pomegranates and walnuts, and a creamy bowl of *mast o musir*, the diced shallots golden in the spiced yoghurt, and the flat loaves of fresh *khubz* in a basket on the side, just waiting to be torn open.

As the sun grew heavy in the horizon, Pahlbod ran outside to watch for the satrap and his entourage. Neighbours hung out of their doorways, whispering and waiting. Finally, Pahlbod heard the horns, deep and haunting, accompanied by a heavy rumbling, almost as though a herd of *shadhavar* were stampeding down the narrow streets of the city. Then he saw them, two lines of men blowing long *karnas* accompanied by two lines of men pounding on *dohols*, clearing the streets for a stretch of horses. The riders wore glistening tunics and plumed helmets, and each one carried a long shield and heavy bow. Behind them, on a magnificent white stallion, rode the satrap himself, Ariobarzanes. Pahlbod had no doubt that it was him, as the image on the coins was accurate in almost every detail—the billowing hair gathered at his shoulders, the tightly trimmed beard, the long, narrow angle of the nose. His armour radiated, accents of jewels and gold catching the remaining beams of sunlight and reflecting them in every direction so that Ariobarzanes was not so much a king but a veritable being of light itself, to whom everyone bowed, including Pahlbod. The entourage came to a stop at their front door and saluted, waiting for Ariobarzanes to dismount and enter the building.

Once inside, Ariobarzanes made the obligatory speech, blessing Pahlbod's parents for their hospitality and generosity. To Pahlbod, he seemed quite honest in his thanks and praise, and his soldiers, the elite guard and high-ranking generals of the army, were certainly more than eager to devour a homemade meal as opposed to their usual military fare. The feast was indeed magnificent, and every man in the room exalted his mother and the spells she wove in her kitchen despite their apparent ignorance of decorum at the table, as they all tended to snatch whatever was in front of them, at times almost coming to blows over the scrapings of a dish.

Despite this gluttonous impropriety, it was clear that they were all waiting, hungry for something more. From the lowest drummer or horn blower to Ariobarzanes himself, they were waiting to see if the stories were to be believed, if there truly existed a magic dancer of smoke under this humble roof in Jahrom.

Soon enough, the meal was over, and Pahlbod's father made his perfunctory announcement while he hurried Pahlbod into the kitchen to retrieve the phial of smoke. With two claps of his hands, Pahlbod once again sent the dancer reeling into the crowd of anxious soldiers, who began to hoot and cheer at the mystery before their eyes. Once again, after the dancer had improvised over the rhythms of the crowd's eagerness for a few minutes, Pahlbod began to clap his slow, steady rhythm, which the dancer immediately took up, each of her veils slicing a crisp arc through the air like a dagger opening a thief's throat. The soldiers and generals immediately took up the clapping, and even Ariobarzanes began to clap, laughing at the marvel before his eyes. The dancer continued to move through the crowd, billowy and luxuriant as a ship's sail, but as steadfast and tangible as a midsummer breeze. Pahlbod worked his way to the back of the room, sick and nearly faint with the way the men in the room whistled at the dancer. They leaned forward, trying to touch her or catch her off guard, each of them a ravenous wolf eager to taste the juiciest morsel of the flock, only to find it herded away at the last minute in a flurry of veils and the lingering scent of cinnamon and sandalwood.

Stepping into the kitchen quickly, Pahlbod put his head between his knees, trying to slow his lungs to long, deep breaths so as not to pass out and leave the dancer alone and helpless before the brutes that were treating her no better than the meals they had just finished. Looking around, he grabbed the first thing that he saw, an iron pot that his mother used when cooking large quantities of rice. He quickly returned to the dining room, where many of the men had clambered to the centre of the room and surrounded the dancer, all of them reaching and grasping at her, trying to pull her close to them, all the while shouting and fighting amongst themselves to be the first to handle such a marvel.

The sound of Pahlbod's fingertips hitting the bottom of the

pot was not the soft, coaxing sound of a drum, but a loud brash resonance that immediately drew the attention of everyone in the room. Pahlbod tried desperately to ignore the stares, the horror on his parents' faces as though he had just spit in the satrap's goblet, the shock on the faces of the soldiers at this impetuous boy interrupting their fun. Instead, he looked right at the dancer, who also had stopped suddenly, at the shadows that contoured the smoke and what seemed to be a set of grateful eyes looking back at him. Pahlbod began to beat a rhythm on the bottom of the pot, holding it at his side by one of its handles. It was a simple rhythm; it sounded dull and monotonous to him as the pot could not hope to imitate the lush sounds of a drumhead, but it was just complex enough to seem authentic, to remind everyone of the manners involved when dealing with a dancer. Soberly, the men retreated to their seats while Pahlbod continued to drum, adding slight variations to his rhythm so as not to break its spell, while the dancer began to spin and whirl again. Pahlbod was so focused on the dancer and maintaining a rhythm that he did not notice the front door of the restaurant open and close, and was surprised when the sensual, vibrant sound resonated through the room, matching his simple rhythm perfectly.

Looking across the room, he found himself staring into the kind eyes of an old friend. Rags still travel-worn and dangling from his limbs like flesh to a skeleton, *tombak* crooked beneath one arm as though it were a weapon waiting to be hurled at some oncoming enemy, stood Narin. Pahlbod watched as Narin quickly took up the rhythm from Pahlbod on the *tombak* and stepped towards the centre of the room.

The sound from the drum echoed off the walls of the house, reverberating through the bodies of everyone present, stilling them to mute, almost timid, observers. Narin stepped closer to the dancer, who seemed to grow taller with the beat of his *tombak*. The rhythm grew in complexity from the basic monotonous pulse that Pahlbod had begun, to a layered, luxurious medley of alternating sounds, the low sound of the *tom* accented by the quick pop of the *bak*, here accentuated by a trill of *eshareh*, and there by the sharp snap of the *pelangue*, until it seemed as though there was more than one drummer in the room, feeding and nourishing the dance with the sound of their playing.

Through it all, the dancer moved closer and closer to Narin, her veils now triumphs swelling through the shadows, her motions completely fluid and uninhibited. It was as though she was dancing only for Narin, and everyone else in the room felt privileged, but embarrassed, to watch. Looking around, Pahlbod saw many of the men, a few of whom had previously been attempting to grasp the dancer, averting their eyes, almost in shame at their desecration of such a wondrous mystery.

Narin continued to play, until it seemed as though the dancer were dancing through him, her veils catching all his awkward angles, getting hooked and unwound on the sharp corner of his shoulder or the blunt end of the *tombak* until they were all but figments of veils, mere unbroken curls of smoke lacing through her diaphanous fingers. Pahlbod found it increasingly more difficult to keep his eye on Narin, as the dancer's body and remaining wisps of veil had now almost mummified him in their cobwebs.

Still the drumming became more and more complex, the basic pulse of the *tom* and *bak* buried beneath a flurry of *esharehs* and syncopated *palangues*, until the accents of the rhythms became almost a speech, the hurried patter of women haggling in the marketplace or men bantering over their *mey* in a small bistro. The haze of smoke around Narin grew thicker and more indistinct, to the point that Pahlbod could barely make out the dancer's body or any of her features, or distinguish where the tumultuous veils around Narin's body began and ended. The drumming was so rapid and complex that it was little more than throb and cadence resonating through the aching bodies of those who listened, and the dancer was merely a spiralling plume of smoke that almost licked the ceiling and accented the underlying beat of the drum with patterns of light and shadow pulled from the lamp flames.

Suddenly, without any warning or adumbration, the drumming stopped, and scrolls of smoke rushed out the door and up into the cloudless night.

In the same way the cotton of the sacred *sudre* is bound snug by the cord of the *kusti*, so was the silence in the room bound by the heartbeats and breaths of those who witnessed the spectacular departure. After what could have been no more than a few moments, but what seemed like hours to Pahlbod, Ariobarzanes stood and politely bowed to Pahlbod's parents, and without saying a word, withdrew himself from the building, followed by his escort of benumbed ranks of soldiers and generals.

Pahlbod watched as his mother slipped into the kitchen, unsure of how to proceed but knowing that there were dishes to be cleaned, followed by his father. Pahlbod walked deliberately to each table, removing the *sofrehs*, then to each oil lamp, which he snuffed until only the moon illuminated the room. Pahlbod walked to the centre of the room and lifted the intricately carved *tombak* from its place on the floor. He fingered the drumhead gingerly, cradling it beneath his arm. Then, he bent again, retrieved the perfectly ripe pomegranate which remained there, and placed it in his pocket.

Afterword

"The Dancer of Smoke" began, as do all my best stories, with my children. When my son was four, I found a used copy of Molly Bang's The Paper Crane *at a bookstore. Now that my daughter is a toddler, I am going through all of my son's old books, and rediscovering the tales. Bang's book is a retelling of an ancient Chinese myth about the Yellow Crane Tower, in which a stranger draws a crane of the wall with an orange peel to attract customers. Bang updates this myth by relocating it to Japan, the stranger in her tale creating an origami crane with a napkin. What is fascinating about this tale is that, unlike other myths and folktales about magic gifts from strangers, it is the gift itself that receives attention. Still, it carries forth the theme of some of my favourite fairy tales and folktales—when one gives to the lowest, the poorest and the most needy of people, one is rewarded.*

The reason I relocated the tale to Persia is because I wanted to write a story in a richly mythic setting, but one which the women had equal, if not more, power to the men. In ancient Persia, women could own property, have careers, etc. While certain trades were "off limits" to them and patriarchy was still rampant, there is a sense of power which they held that has since been stolen. Despite the face that the story is told from Pahlbod's point of view, the women in this story, Pahlbod's mother and the dancer herself, are the one's who have the power and command the attention of the men. I am also fascinated by the concept of exotic dance and its balance of power. As opposed to Western stripping, the dancer is respected and revered as an artist, and though possibly objectified, is seen as somehow commanding or controlling the attention of the men in the audience. I hope that this balance of power comes through for the reader in the story.

The Belly Dancing Crimes of Ms Sahara Desserts
Or
For The Love of Pudding

Angela Rega

I was about to make my veil entrance into the cushion room at Divan's, when a terrible shriek and a clanging of pots rang from the kitchen and the lights went out. I stood in the darkness, one bare foot wedged between the doorway of the pantry cupboard that was my makeshift change room and a room full of disoriented diners.

The lights flickered back on and the voice of Murat, the restaurant owner, boomed across the room of half eaten mezze platters and embroidered red cushions. He patted his shirt smooth over his potbelly and waved his hands in the air as if he was shooing away flies. "Is no problem. We have dancer for you in five minutes."

A second later distorted music belted out and Murat bellowed, "And now, best belly dancer in Sydney! Sahara!"

The regulars cheered as I made my Salome-style entrance. In all the commotion, Murat had put on the wrong CD. I didn't know when all the accents would come in, but I'd ad lib. I tried to readjust my belt that cut too tightly into my hips. They had expanded more than a centimetre or two since I started working at Divans, thanks to Latafat, the chef who had fast become the father I never had, feeding me his speciality, the sweet milk pudding *muhaleebi*. Anyway, I wouldn't have to do this anymore to earn my living once I became a chef. Don't get me wrong: belly dancing is better than working a call centre job, but by the time you hit thirty and your body starts to wobble in places you don't want it to, and you can't stand hands diving too deep in your coined belt when a customer tips you—well, you do need to think of another profession.

As the old cliché went, 'the show must go on,' so when the wrong music belted out, I thought I may have imagined those shouts, Arzu slamming the kitchen door shut and Murat grinning maniacally.

There was always disorganisation at Divan's: nights with no music, dancing to hand clapping and wolf whistles; double bookings of belly dancers that ended in hair pulling, death threats and arm scratches (well, that only happened once and it was definitely Electra Blue's fault); bruised legs from climbing on customers' wobbly tables to dance; and never enough Iskender kebabs. The disorganisation was one of the main reasons I liked working here and had been the resident belly dancer for so long. Long enough that Selver, Latafat's thirteen-year-old daughter, and as sweet as the desserts her father created, had made a fabric doll in my likeness, complete in belly dance outfit. She was displayed in the front window under a fuchsia neon light that flashed my name: *Sahara Desserts*. Bad taste, I know, but it just added to the atmosphere of red velvet, fake palms and hanging Turkish lamps. The temptation of more money at ritzier Arabic nightclubs didn't sway me; at least at Divan's, there was always a sense of fun amidst the chaos.

Obviously no customer had seen anything untoward out the back. I sashayed around the cushion room then hip-dropped on the spot while toothy Tariq, a regular, shoved a twenty-dollar note down my coined belt.

The shriek I'd heard, was it Selver? She was mute, had never spoken a word since her arrival in Australia. My performance smile spasmed a little at the thought.

I shimmied on the spot while casting furtive glances at the kitchen. Murat was plastered across the width of the kitchen door frame, his arms stretched out in a barricade. I layered my shimmies with mayas and reverse undulations then stood still for the finale body freeze. This always got the audience clapping and I had more than enough of a belly these days to make an impact.

I recognised in the music what could have been interpreted as a finale riff. At last! I wrapped my veil around me and spun back to my pantry cupboard but the door was locked. I struggled with the doorknob until Murat grabbed my arm and led me to the kitchen where my change of clothes had been stacked neatly behind the tins of chickpeas. His wife, Arzu, was rolling the pastry for *gözleme*; her face blotched and red, like she had been crying.

Arzu cooking? Instead of Latafat? The last time Arzu cooked, the restaurant was closed for two weeks because of food poisoning. Now I knew that something was wrong. Selver sat next to Arzu, her face white as flour, drained of any life. She sat as if in a catatonic state, mouth open, dribble trickling down her chin.

"Where's Latafat?" I hugged Selver and held her tight; her wet eyelashes were cold against my sweaty skin.

"In the pantry cupboard," Murat answered.

"What's he doing in—?"

"Shhhh!" Murat lowered his voice and leaned towards me. "He's dead. By fire."

"Fire?" Nothing looked charred or burned but I knew that something really had happened to Latafat. A tear rolled down my face. "We've got to call the police!" I said. How could Murat be so calm? My sobs came out like hiccups.

Murat frowned. "No police! We are family! We look after him." He slid a trifle Latafat made towards me so that it stopped on the workbench in line with my belly. "He made this today for you. Family."

I dipped my finger in and tasted it; the sweet icing sugar fizzed on my tongue with the saltiness of my tears.

"We must talk about Latafat and the recipe."

"The recipe?"

"Shhh!" Murat insisted. I wasn't going to find out anything until the last customer had gone.

I went behind the chickpea tins to get changed, picked at my big toenail where some tabouli had gotten stuck and cried silently.

Latafat. Gone.

The kitchen felt bare without Latafat's deep laughter and the delicate aromas of his *muhaleebi* orange flower and rosewater essences, and of course, the wishes that came with his desserts. A secret ingredient went into his recipe, making customers queue at the door; a magical component that made Divan's a favourite in the Sydney restaurant scene.

Latafat would ask customers to write their wishes on post-it notes. The wishes would then be pegged onto a clothesline that stretched over the heads of everyone in the kitchen. No wish could have monetary value and each *muhaleebi* was baked with the customer's wish inside.

Many customers said their wishes had come true: Leila's lover finally left his unhappy marriage and Courtney got pregnant naturally after many failed IVF attempts.

"How do you do that? Make a dessert of wishes?" I asked Latafat. He would kiss me on the forehead and tell me that was his secret. He was the sole keeper of that recipe.

At the end of the clothesline hung three sealed envelopes. They were Latafat's wish, Selver's and mine. I didn't let him look at mine; I'd sealed it up with superglue.

"I don't need to read your wish, Sahara. You just eat the dessert."

Now only empty envelopes hung; like the recipe and his life, they were gone, too. I undid the zipper on my skirt and a small rip appeared underneath it. I should have wished to eat as many sweets as I liked without gaining weight.

I sighed. Even magic had its limits.

• • •

When the last customers had left, Murat, Arzu, Selver and I sat around the red laminate table in the kitchen drinking Turkish coffee.

Arzu swirled my cup around in one hand. In the other, she held her pipe. Usually, I crossed my legs, waiting patiently for the oracle to proceed and make wild predictions about the shapes in our cups. Tonight, I was bursting with impatience.

"Sahara." She moved closer to the table; the crevices in Arzu's face were dark, like they had been filled in with charcoal.

I sat back inhaling Arzu's smoke; the desire to light up making my skin itch. There was nothing like apple tobacco smoked out of a *nargile*. Instead, I grabbed for my other weakness at the table, Turkish delight. Arzu slapped my hand away. I was trying to give up those, too.

"Fire!" Arzu slammed the cup back down on the saucer. Murat banged his fist on the table and Selver burst into tears.

"Show me!" I snatched the cup back from her pudgy hand and peered inside.

Arzu pointed at the little person inside the cup. "You see that people?"

"Person?"

"That one."

"Kind of."

"That's you."

"Me? Am I going to be in a fire?"

Arzu twirled the cup on the saucer. "No, no, no, no—you no listen, you no look properly. See?" She pointed back to the figure in the cup. "Sahara, concentrate!"

I squinted. And then I saw it.

In the cup was a silhouette of girl, her arms up as if to protect herself from flames. The flames were shaped like a torso with long arms, stretched out to grab her. I drew back from the table, almost toppling off my chair.

"You see! Djinn: the spirits of fire. You must fight with the bad spirits to revenge Latafat and get recipe back."

I broke into nervous laughter and snatched the Turkish delight from the plate.

"You no believe me?" Arzu exhaled smoke into my face. "We see."

"Djinn in Bankstown?"

"Djinn everywhere! He are mean spirits with fire in their blood."

Arzu snatched the Turkish delight out of my hand and put it back on the plate. "Stop eating desserts or you lose job! Murat say you too fat for working dancing."

I sucked in my belly and shot an incredulous look at Murat.

"Is true, Sahara," Murat's cheeks reddened. "You too fat."

"Can we talk about Latafat? He's not just overweight! He's dead!"

"Latafat was a djinni," Murat said after a moment.

"Yeah, right!" I thought of Latafat's body stuffed in my change room. "We need to contact a funeral director. I can't believe we've had to wait until all the customers left to deal with this!"

Murat shook his head. "No, we must put him back home."

"You're going to send his body back to Turkey?"

Arzu sucked on the long stem of her pipe and spoke so that smoke came out of the corners of her mouth. "We come from land of djinn. Good djinn live with bad djinn. We escape here. Our Turkey no exist on map, Sahara. We can't go back."

"So now you're djinn, too? But Murat said you have to take his body back home."

"You listen to what I tell you in coffee cup?" Arzu asked me and exhaled smoke through her nostrils with an angry snort. "You revenge Latafat in djinn land, get recipe back."

"And his bottle, for djinn burial, too, otherwise he just stay in pantry cupboard can't go back to spirit." Murat added as he took the pipe from Arzu.

I shook my head in disbelief. The idea of djinn in Sydney was crazy and there was no way that pot-bellied, Santa Claus Latafat was going to fit into a bottle.

"Selver?" She would never lie to me. She looked up at me, her large brown eyes wet with tears. She nodded.

I thought about the wishes hanging on the clothesline in the kitchen—sometimes with Arzu's large, hand washed underpants hanging between them. Customers swearing their wishes had come true.

Wishes in desserts.

Djinn.

Latafat dead. And the recipe for wishes stolen. The ground felt liquid beneath me.

"Why didn't you tell me?" I clung to the table in both shock and a sense of betrayal. Arzu handed me the pipe.

I sucked on it, letting the smoke make my head spin before I exhaled.

"Because we are not djinn anymore," Murat whispered.

"I don't get it!" I pulled out the genie plait hairpiece I wore for my performance, and threw it on the floor.

"After fall of Ottoman Empire, we sold magic for passport here, now forbidden to go home. You must go for us." Arzu wiped her eyes with the corner of her sleeve.

"If you can't go back, how can I?" I said pointing to my small empty coffee cup. "How am I supposed to get revenge, a bottle, and a recipe back from a place that doesn't exist on a map?"

"Like this!" Murat opened the wall cupboard directly behind him and dragged out a garbage bag wrapped around a long roll. With one fingernail he ripped the bag open, letting the bundle unravel with a thump to the floor. It was a deep crimson, silk rug, with floral and geometric designs around the border. In the middle, stitched in gold thread, were words written in what must have been some kind of ancient Turkic script.

"Hand woven rug from magic carpet weavers of Golden Age when djinn live side on side with mortals," Arzu said.

"You mean side *by* side."

She ignored me. "The spell on carpet, you see? In middle. It is written in language of my people, the djinn."

I didn't like flying in a plane and now I was going to go to a place that didn't exist on a map on a flying carpet? I grabbed for another piece of Turkish delight.

"No!" Arzu said. She pushed the nargile in front of me.

"Less sweets better for flying carpet," Murat said.

"What do I tell my Aunty Tia?" I asked. I had no other family and she expected a dinner visit once a week.

"Tell her," Murat answered, excitement growing in his voice, "you have belly dance job in Istanbul for two weeks. Good pay. Good travel."

"She knows I hate flying. She paid for my Fear of Flying Course, remember?"

"So it was money well spent."

"What about cash?"

"In land of djinn, pleasures of life are love, food and dance."

"I don't get it! Why me?"

Arzu poked me in the shoulder and grinned at me, revealing the gap between her two front teeth. "Djinni good one and bad one love belly dancer. She is favourite of djinn. They like to see you shake it." Arzu sensed my uncertainty and shoulder shimmied at me. "We are traitors to djinn left behind. You are only non-djinn girl we trust, to go back for us. You are daughter, like Selver, to us."

— 67 —

Murat kissed his hand and pressed it against my forehead.

"We love you, Sahara. We have nobody else," Arzu said. "If you don't get recipe, maybe next time they come and kill all of us."

I had to go. Fear of flying and djinn aside, I loved them too. Besides Aunt Tia, they were my family. Now, they had trusted me with their secret.

"You pack change of dancing costume."

"My veils and cymbals, too I suppose?"

"And your sword," Murat added.

"Especially sword." Arzu eyeballed me.

"I can balance one on my head but not fight with it, if that's what you mean."

"Sword is for you to fight djinn," Arzu said and I saw Selver's eyebrows rise.

"*Fight* with?"

Arzu sucked on her pipe, making smacking sounds with her lips. Unlike the usual pleasant-smelling apple tobacco, this one was pungent, smelling like a mixture of cow dung and coriander. Her eyes rolled back in her head as if she was in a trance.

"You are djinn warrior of Seventh House of Osman. You know fly carpet. You know fight sword. You know get inside Gathering Place of djinn at Topkapi Palace—old home." Arzu's voice was hypnotic, and her body convulsed.

The room began to swim.

"Help . . . " I squeaked.

Selver put a small, gentle hand on my shoulder to still me. It seemed the room had become almost liquid, and the words on the carpet swirled like a sandstorm of letters. I closed my eyes while Arzu muttered words in a language that I didn't recognise as Turkish.

No sooner than it began, the room stopped rocking and when I opened my eyes, Arzu sat still sucking on her pipe as if nothing had happened. Selver lay on the rug, asleep.

From Selver's pantaloons, Arzu whisked out a scroll and unravelled it with a flick of her wrist. It was a hand-drawn map of the Inner Palace of Topkapi Palace, the Grand Seraglio in Istanbul.

"So it does exist on a map!" I frowned at Arzu.

"You go inside djinn meeting place. This is doorway to our world. Find djinn kitchen. Get recipe and revenge."

I shook Selver but she didn't stir. "Selver?" I lightly slapped her face. "Selver!" I panicked but Arzu shushed me and clicked her tongue.

"Selver is djinn warrior. Her skill now in you. She sleep. You come back—Selver wake up."

"Hurry, time is soon. You must go," Murat said twiddling his moustache.

"What's soon?" I didn't get the sense of urgency after they'd let Latafat sit squashed like the okra in the pantry cupboard all evening.

"It is the Şeker Festival, the sugar festival. The week all of Turkey and djinn, too, celebrate everything sugar and sweet. Who stole recipe, who killed Latafat, wants crown for best dessert. You will find recipe there."

"Go now," Arzu agreed. She picked up a pair of her underpants that had been soaking, wrung them to dry and hung them on Latafat's empty line. "I send you with the powers of the good djinn."

"And if I get these things back—revenge, the recipe—"

"And Latafat's bottle," Arzu interrupted.

"Selver will wake up?"

"Yes! Yes! We give Latafat proper djinn burial, his body change back to spirit and go back inside bottle. Selver wake up. You learn to cook with recipe."

"What if I don't make it back?" I looked at Selver's sleeping body curled up on a pile of purple cushions.

"You must come back." Arzu said matter-of-factly. "Or Selver never wake up."

• • •

Travelling by magic carpet is nothing like flying in a plane. It's worse.

Up.

Down.

Up, up, up down.

Dip.

Side swish.

Even a shimmy.

I kept my *kilij* sheathed and strapped around a pantalooned thigh and my hair in a tight plait tucked through my belt to keep it from flying about—a wise idea from Arzu, as vomit in hair stinks.

Finally I sailed a gentle wind. I relaxed as a soft breeze caressed my face and soothed my stomach sickness.

Just a couple of hours ago, I was an overweight belly dancer at Divan's pushing time until my belly rolls were bigger than my undulations. Now I was flying the night skies under Arzu's protection and with Selver's hidden skills. I was a djinn warrior and in control of my own destiny—even if I wasn't in control of my travel sickness.

The carpet plunged, tilting to the right so that my legs were suspended in the air. I gripped at the fringing. My destiny, like Selver's, was precariously linked to chance. The thought made my head spin as much as the turbulence.

The view made me soon forget the dangers of night flight. Down below, the shah-blue sky contrasted against the shimmer of white sugar lights that were Istanbul and the Bosphorus by night. The minarets twinkled as if stars were lodged inside their windows, and labyrinthine street patterns shifted in front of my eyes like a kaleidoscope as my carpet began its circular descent. Istanbul: the city that lay between two continents, between East and West. Topkapi: the gateway to a world of djinn and magic. My ears popped and my tongue caught in my throat at the sight of the monumental building I had only seen in travel books: the Topkapi Palace. The Grand Seraglio.

According to Arzu's map, I'd landed in the second court inside the Imperial Gate. I rolled the carpet, tying it with my hair ribbon as I hoisted it over my shoulder like a satchel. There was something to be said of Arzu's magical ability. I'd mastered all the skills that had once been unassuming Selver's when she was a young djinn warrior preparing to become a refugee, but the thought of Selver in eternal sleep didn't let me enjoy it.

The smell of damp stone and decay reminded me the palace was now a museum. And at this time of night, closed to the public. My footsteps echoed the hollow emptiness and I followed the smell of orange blossom water to the kitchens. Funny that there should be the smell of cooking essences here, brewing in what was now a museum. Then I remembered the Şeker Festival. The whole of Istanbul would smell of rosewater and honey and burnt sugar.

Two rows of long, wide chimneys, tall like towers, marked the presence of the large kitchens. There were three doors, but

I didn't hesitate, the smell was coming from the middle door. A cold wind whistled past me as I opened the door. In front of me was the shadow of an elderly woman stirring a large pot. I froze, not expecting anyone here at this time of night. She twitched her nose as if she smelt me, then turned and stared, her glowing red eyes burning through mine. My knees shook. Her jowls sagged to her chest. You could brew black tea with the dark bags under her eyes. She put down her ladle and faced me. There was the sound of a slow, wheezy inhalation as she opened her mouth and breathed in. I felt a hot wind of foul breath suck me into the maw that had been her mouth.

Dance for her. Shake it. It was a voice inside my head I didn't recognise, the voice of a young girl, with a strong Turkish accent: Selver!

The thought of Selver speaking made me smile and I danced. The jingling of my coined belt startled the old ghoul. She closed her mouth to smile and began to clap but it made no sound. I shimmied and smiled. At least I wasn't going to be eaten by her, while I danced.

Attack! Now! Selver's voice again.

I pirouetted, drew the sword from its sheath and decapitated her with one swift slice. Thwack! I dropped the sword and grabbed at my cramping shoulder. Selver may have been tiny but she had some strength! The ghoul's head disintegrated into hundreds of glowing red eyes that plopped into the pot. "Gross!" I clenched my jaw and closed my eyes in disgust. I had Selver's skill and strength, but obviously not her stomach.

With the old shadow's ladle I pushed the red eyes under the bubbling stickiness. A handful of little bulbous eyeballs popped back up to the boiling surface and blinked at me.

"I hope that none of the sweets Latafat made me had such ghoulish ingredients," I muttered to the blinking eyes. I left the tray there and closed the large wooden door behind me.

• • •

I was hardly inconspicuous. My coined belt jangled as I crept down the twisting corridors and past the grilled windows. Hearty laughter, followed by belches, resonated from the end of the corridor. If only Selver had invisibility powers for me to draw upon!

"Who goes there? You'd better have brought me something sweet to eat," an angry, male voice said. A cloud of fine particles spiralled under my nose and a djinni appeared.

I coughed and spluttered; the smoke was thick and pungent.

"What did you expect? For me to come in a *nargile* pipe?" The djinni asked. He was obese, with narrow almond shaped eyes, long black hair, and a handlebar moustache.

"No, I, I . . . "

"What are you seeking?"

"I've come for entrance to your land, to find the recipe of *muhaleebi* and—" I stopped short, not sure whether to tell him about Latafat's death.

"*Muhaleebi* recipe! So you have come for the bottle of Latafat! He must be dead. Good riddance to bad rubbish, I say! The djinn that fled at the fall of the last Sultan sold their magic for mortality, so death was inevitable! Let him be buried in the ground like you common mortals. He has become one, after all. " The djinni crossed his arms and then looked me up and down. "Aha! But what have we got here! A harem costume! Can you do the dance of the Seven Veils?" He leaned closer and his breath dusted my face making my eyes water. It was hot like a combination of fire and chilli.

"I can."

He looked me up and down approvingly until he reached my bare feet. "You must wear shoes when you dance. With heels!"

"I can't dance in high heels."

"So don't dance so much!" The djinni appeared annoyed at my faux pas in costume. He clapped his hands once as if it was an order. "You've got to show yourself!" He tapped at the sheathed scimitar strapped across his shoulder. "Or else I will hack you into tiny pieces and there will be seven times the seven veils dancing about." He laughed at his own joke.

A snap of his fingers and we were in a large hall with emerald green rugs, and mosaics of multi-coloured crushed glass carpeting the walls. Fat eunuchs with feathered wings sat cross-legged on cushions playing *ouds* and *neys* and the djinni pushed me into the middle of the floor.

"Shake it, Shake it."

So that's where Arzu got the term from. I had thought it was her broken English.

I unpacked my rolled rug and clothes in a corner of the room. Standing in my ruby red costume, I wrapped one of my veils around my head from which to balance my sword.

The fat djinni reclined on a chaise lounge and slapped his naked belly twice. A siren woman appeared; her face was olive toned-and exquisite, but it was hard not to recoil at the sight of her bird-like extremities. Black wings sprouted from collarbone to shoulder blade, their fine,feathered tips reaching mid-thigh, where arms would have been. Instead of feet, she had spiny talons. She rubbed her head on the fat djinni's potbelly and cooed softly. He stroked her wings and blew kisses at her as if she were some kind of exotic pet.

"Shake it, belly dancer!"

"It's Sahara."

"And I'm Mustafa. It has been a long time since we have seen such a thing. Such entertainments left with the last Sultan in 1923. Now it's just crowds of tourists who don't know the arts of pleasure. Dance!"

"If you promise to return the recipe and Latafat's bottle to me."

The siren woman and the djinni shrieked with laughter. "You will stay here with us; entertain us with your dancing."

The Siren flapped her wings together trying to clap at his cleverness and then stamped her foot. She shrieked like a parrot and stamped her taloned feet. "Wretched wings!"

I swallowed at the thought of Selver in eternal sleep and Murat and Arzu waiting at the restaurant for my return. Were they going to keep me a prisoner? I bowed low to the djinni and his siren, then to the dwarfs and the music began. I did what I always did in a crisis. Since there were no sweets in my vicinity, I danced.

Slowly, sensually, balancing the sword on my head, I swayed my arms like serpents, circled my right hip in figure eights, and sashayed across the floor. The djinni lay back against the cushions and stroked his siren's wings. "Ah, beautiful."

I danced about him in circles stroking his bald head with my hands and the siren began to cry.

"What's wrong, Seren? My love?" The djinni stroked her feathered wings but she pushed him away.

"I want to dance like that! How can I dance like that when I have talons for feet and wings for arms!" And she howled like a child.

I knew how she felt. I remembered the words of my boss before Murat. *"Your body a bit fat, Sahara. But nice moon face. Moon face is beauty in Perfumed Garden. You read this book? It the manual for love. Maybe I read it to you."* He ran a massage parlour as well as the restaurant and thought my talents were better served there. I knew what it felt like to be seen as . . . well, not quite right and full of imperfections. I danced towards her to give her my veil.

"Get me her sword and I'll cut off her arms and legs and give them to you, my love," Mustafa replied.

Fight! Selver's voice again. Luckily, I was warmed up from the dancing. Selver's orders had me in a full bend back to whip the sword off my head and into my hand. Then, a flip up, and a lunge forward so the point of my sword pressed at the roll of fat on his neck. "Why can't you grant her a pair of legs? You're supposed to be a djinni!"

Smoke flared from Mustafa's nostrils. "So you are a warrior as well as a dancer?" A sword appeared in his hand.

Clang! I hitch-kicked his hand and his sword fell to the floor. *Whump!* I pivoted to the side and delivered a kick with my heel to his stomach. Unarmed, he fell backwards onto his cushions. I pressed my sword above his collarbone. "So grant your love her wish and let me take back mine!"

"I only have limited magic now. I lost my ability to grant wishes."

"Latafat, Murat and Arzu defected. You could have done the same thing!"

"Pah!" Mustafa spat phlegm that sizzled where it landed. "I stayed here only to lose my magic too and watch my home become a museum."

He snapped his fingers and a mirage appeared. It was of Selver sleeping soundly at Divan's on a row of cushions in front of the pantry door with my Latafat inside.

"I loved Latafat." I said, trying not to let my voice wobble and keep the point of my sword against his skin.

I thought about Latafat's *muhaleebi* recipe that made people's wishes come true. I looked at the djinni and his mistress; Mustafa cooed at his love, while she nervously plucked feathers from her wings with her teeth. Arzu had said I would fight evil djinn but how could this one be evil if he knew love?

"You didn't kill Latafat." I knew it to be true but kept my sword firm.

"No, but I did steal the wishes—"

"The wishes!" I remembered our own missing from the kitchen clothesline.

"I wanted to give Seren hands and feet. I took the wishes and the recipe, hoping I could make her the sweet with her wish inside. But the djinni who did kill Latafat stole it from me."

"Take me to him."

The djinni laughed nervously and pushed my sword away. I didn't resist.

"*She* is the Bee Queen. The hottest sting and the sweetest honey. With one breath she could burn you; with one sting, she could kill you or envelope you in sticky sweet honey and turn you into part of her Turkish delight recipe."

I thought about Latafat stuffed like a sardine in the pantry cupboard, never to transform into spirit form unless reunited with his bottle, and Selver without a voice in eternal slumber.

"Take me to her." I slid my sword neatly back in its scabbard.

"She's back at the kitchens." Mustafa answered. "The Bee Queen is the Queen Djinni of Sweet Indulgence. And you Sahara Desserts, with a fondness for sweets, she is your weakness!"

Back down the cobbled lane way and into the towered kitchens I went. My neck was stiff and thigh muscles ached. I was not used to using my body this way. The temperature had risen and droplets of sweat trickled down my spine. I wasn't sure if it was the heat from the ovens or my anxiety. Probably both. Who was this Bee Queen? I wanted to ask Selver but she only gave fighting commands.

It was her perfume that reached me first. She smelt of rose water, hot honey and melting sugar, a fragrance that made my stomach rumble and my mouth water in anticipation.

"Aha . . . " a voice drawled down one of the chimneys in the kitchen. "So, one has come from the traitors at last."

A spiral of smoke swirled down the chimney circling me, and the most exquisite woman materialised. She was dressed in a sapphire blue chiffon belly dance costume that matched the colour of her eyes. Her revealing outfit showed a toned belly and firm bare legs that were a deep amber-gold, as if she had been dipped in a honey pot.

Then I recognised her.

Electra Blue. The belly dancer who stole my jobs. The girl who had provoked and perpetrated the hair pulling, arm scratching and death threats over double bookings.

It was *her*.

She saw the recognition in my face and flashed her perfect white teeth. "Latafat is dead. But why is that strange? You are a mortal, death follows your footsteps."

"I want his bottle and the recipe back."

"This musty thing?" She dangled a green glass bottle in front of my face.

I snatched at it but she lifted the bottle high above my head. "Not so fast. We will let the eunuchs decide. You have come for the Şeker Festival, I see, when all vie for the position of Sugar Queen. She who serves the best sweets shall be crowned Queen of Desserts. Take that chance from me, I will kill you."

I remembered when she'd almost killed my career. Electra Blue had walked into Smyrna's where I was dancing. The owner looked me up and down, and then at her honey coloured beauty, and without even seeing her dance, said, "I pay you double what I pay her to dance." That blow did wonders for my self-esteem and my comfort eating.

Now she had taken our Latafat away and she had his recipe, too.

Electra clapped her hands again and a dozen eunuchs appeared cross-legged on my carpet.

"Hey, that's my carpet!"

"Now, now—I thought you were more generous than that, Sahara Desserts. Let's dance a little first before I beat you with *my* recipe and become the Dessert Queen."

The music began. I didn't know who played it but judging from the way Electra danced, she knew it well—every accent, every beat, every rhythm. But I had danced at Divan's—five star restaurant of human error and dancing to the wrong music. I matched each shimmy, each syncopated hip drop. My pirouettes were graceful and my veil followed in circular motions above my head so that the eunuchs gasped and whispered about my proficiency.

Electra Blue stopped, a look of jealousy burning across her face. She clenched her fists then yanked two sticks out from behind a corner cushion and breathed on them. Fire appeared on both ends. "I'll turn you into buttery baklava before the night is over and serve it up to my servants and be crowned Şeker Festival Queen!"

Especially the sword. I remembered Arzu's words.

I unsheathed the sword and the eunuchs retreated to the corner. With a movement quicker than a djinni's magic, I sliced the air, knocking the sticks from Electra's hands. Their flames extinguished as they hit the ground. From the corner, the eunuchs clapped.

"You think that will frighten me?" she hissed.

"It frightens your friends over there."

"They do not fear your sword—their most sacred parts have already been hacked off!"

"Give me back Latafat's bottle and the recipe."

"He stole the recipe from the Djinn Cookbook. I will be queen of the Şeker Festival. I will win! The recipe is mine!"

"Was his life yours, too?"

"He chose mortality. I just made the end come sooner."

I looked in her eyes. Unlike Latafat's, filled with kindness and love, her pupils were little reptilian slits. I remembered Arzu's words: good djinn live with bad djinn. I wanted revenge. "You will pay for Latafat's death," I said.

She laughed at me. "Death already follows your footsteps, mortal. I could quicken his journey. "

She spat fire at my skirt. I danced away, a line of flames trailing behind me. The backs of my calves stung as her spittle blistered my skin but I kept running. Through the dank stone corridors I ran back to the kitchens. I was sure it was the best place to start looking for Latafat's recipe.

Szpah! Her flames reached my hair and the ends of my plait started burning. I yanked until it fell away and heard her screech in frustration. I cracked a grin: there had to be something advantageous about wearing hairpieces. Panting, with a stitch in my side, I pulled at the handle of the kitchen door and slammed it shut. *Must find the recipe.* I rummaged through the drawers.

She was not far behind. A coil of smoke crept up from under the door and the voluptuous honey-coloured Electra fleshed out in front of me.

She winked. "Say your prayers to whatever God it is you believe in. None is more potent than me."

"My God is the God of Sweets—hence my name, Sahara Desserts."

"*I* am the queen of all things made with honey and sugar. My sweets are better than Latafat's. This is *my* festival. You've come at the wrong time. I have the recipe now and I will be crowned the Queen! She dipped her finger into the pot of syrupy blinking eyes and licked it clean.

"Your sweets are not better than Latafat's. But mine are," I mocked, pointing at the pot of toffeed eyeballs.

"His Excellency, the Exarch of Djinn, Şeker himself will be the judge. I'll cook Latafat's wish-granting *muhaleebi* and grant the eunuchs their desires and Şeker will crown me Festival Queen not just for the year but forever! Then I won't have to live in this dump anymore but will ascend to the skies, cooking for the highest order of djinn. I will eliminate you if you dare to compete with me."

Of course the eunuchs would wish for their manhood back; that was a wish only djinn could grant. They would probably help her finish me off. I had to think fast.

"Let me help you," I said.

"Why would you do that?"

"A swap. For the bottle and the recipe," I said matter-of-factly. She put out her hand. "Hand me the ladle."

I did, and she whacked me over the head with it. "I knew you would submit to me eventually!"

"Ouch!"

She spat orders at me, lighting the ovens with her own breath. I followed instructions, chopping vanilla beans and grinding cinnamon. It gave me time to think. Soon she had several large trays filled with buttery, honey-soaked pastries and Latafat's *muhaleebi.* "Now I must rest before the King of Djinn, Şeker is served my sweets. Guard the *muhaleebi* with your life; if I am crowned we may strike some deal."

I curtsied to her. Better for her to think I was passive, so I could take the recipe and the bottle later.

The halls were quiet except for the sound of my stomach gurgling at the aromas that wafted from the trays. I couldn't resist. I could hear Latafat's *Hayir Na Na!* each time I reached for my second helpings, but sweets were my weakness. I took a small spoon and had a taste from the corner of the tray.

— 78 —

The milk pudding melted in my mouth. The combination of rosewater and hot butter made the insides of my cheeks soften and my tongue curl. I took another spoonful. And another.

When I looked down I realised that I had eaten half the tray. Footsteps approached. Flustered, I put the tray in the oven and closed the door. It was Electra.

"Where is the tray?"

"I'm keeping it warm until his Highness arrives to taste it."

"Very good." She nodded in approval. "There is something I want from you while I wait."

"What's that?" I gulped, hoping that there were no crumbs left on my lips.

"Your sword."

"My sword?"

She put her hands on her hips. "Do you want Latafat's bottle or not? I want to practice that trick you did when you hacked at my fire sticks. It can't be that hard if you can do it."

I unsheathed it from its *kilij* and handed it to her without argument. She lifted it above her head and smiled.

Expecting an attack, my shoulders tensed. Instead, she walked away, the sound of the sword swiping at the air. I wiped my sticky lips and pulled the tray back out of the oven. At that moment, I felt a hand on my shoulder. I'd been caught. I held my breath.

"What have we here, a shake it girl? What a lovely costume!"

I wiped my mouth, fearful of any crumb residue, and turned around to see a handsome man with gentle brown eyes and a long black manicured beard. A gold ring circled the point where it tapered. A fine tattoo in bottle-green ink lined his wrists in serpents, and his teeth flashed white and straight. I curtsied and blushed. "Sahara Desserts."

He laughed at my name and kissed my hand, his smile dazzling me. "Sahara Desserts is a name fitting for a Queen of Sweets, don't you think? I am Djinni Şeker and I've come to judge the belly dancing Bee Queen's desserts."

I trembled at the thought of handing him the half eaten tray. He was by far the most enchanting man I'd ever met; he exuded kindness and obviously loved sweets. I trembled at the thought of humiliating myself in front of him with my guzzling of the *muhaleebi*.

The sound of Electra whipping my blade through the air echoed through the corridors to the kitchens.

"What is that?" he asked.

I curtsied. "Djinni Şeker, the Bee Queen is sharpening her sword skills to kill you."

He laughed. "Why, with one breath I could smite her. Surely, she isn't that stupid."

I nodded fervently. "She told me she wishes to usurp you. She wants your position of Şeker Festival Judge."

"Does she?"

I leaned closer to him and whispered into his ear, "What's more, this is not her recipe. It belongs to someone else. She took the life of my dear friend, Latafat, for this recipe."

There was a moment of silence as if he could taste the truth in my words, then he flew into a rage.

"No cheat and murderer should dare aspire to be Queen of the Sugar Festival!"

Flames spat through his nostrils, his face elongating to become a golden-scaled fire-breathing *illuyanka*. Shimmering wings sprouted from his shoulder blades and he flew down the corridor.

Electra burst into the kitchen, Şeker not far behind her.

"Where is the *muhaleebi*?" she screeched.

"In here." I opened the oven.

She ran towards the hot cooker. I spun, and with a butterfly kick into her behind, rammed her into the cooker before slamming the door with a heavy hip flick.

Fight fire with fire. It wasn't Selver's or Arzu's wisdom but my own, fuelled by will, stronger than any wish a djinni could grant.

There were muffled screams and a ferocious banging as she fought to open the oven door but it kept firmly shut. I knew she was melting when honey dripped out of the corners and hinges of the oven onto the stone floor.

"Don't step on it!" It was the voice of Şeker behind me. "You must not step in her honey, or she will cling to your life force and take these back." The djinni handed me back some paper folded into the shape of paper cranes. I knew better than to open the first two. I recognised my and Selver's wish.

The third showed Latafat's writing: the *muhaleebi* recipe. Seeing his handwriting made me teary.

Şeker then handed me another. It was black paper bordered in gold, folded into the shape of an *illuyanka*. "Don't open it."

"I understand." I secured the paper dragon with a bobby pin into my hair.

"Who grants the wishes of the djinn? Perhaps you, mortal, will be the one to grant my wish. I knew Latafat; He was a good djinn and a good chef."

I looked up at his handsome face. "Thank you. But I need one more thing."

"What's that?"

"His bottle."

Şeker laughed. "I could grant you anything your heart desires and you just want Latafat's bottle?"

"My heart desires his bottle," I answered.

He snapped his fingers and a green bottle with a long narrow neck appeared. It was stuffed with sweets wrapped in silver foil. "You may eat all of those," he said. "Sahara Desserts."

He was gone with a puff of smoke and I was left clutching the bottle and a longing not too different from my desire for sugared sweets. But I didn't belong here. This was not my home. Divan's was. Selver was sleeping and Latafat needed a proper djinn burial. I needed to find my rug and get back home.

• • •

The trip back on the carpet was not as turbulent but my heart was so heavy that I couldn't enjoy it. I had avenged Latafat by killing the Bee Queen. I had rescued the recipe. I had procured Latafat's bottle. But there was something about the Şeker Djinni that left me with a longing. I slapped the side of my head to rid myself of romantic thoughts that would lead nowhere and to think of more pressing matters. Would Selver wake up? How would we bury Latafat?

The sky was thick with cloud and heavy with the promise of rain when the carpet circled down to the rooftop of Divan's. My heart swelled at the thought of returning home, too. I loved the familiar narrow streets, the shop fronts all nestled one on top of the other, the concrete yards, and of course my djinn family. I stood up in the centre of the rug, this time with perfect balance, and descended.

Sitting on milk crates on the rooftop were Arzu and Selver. Selver waved up at me, a happy smile on her face.

"You're awake!" The excitement made me lose my balance. I rolled forward and clutched the fringing just in time to haul myself up. I strained my neck in the forward roll, my pudgy knees feeling the full force of the ground. I rubbed my neck; her powers were obviously returned to her now she was awake.

"Sahara!" Selver ran towards me. She put her arms around me and squeezed tight.

"You spoke!" I pressed my face against hers, emotion caught in my throat. My cough broke into a cry.

Arzu hopped from one foot to the other and clapped her hands. "My Sahara back." She grabbed my hands to kiss them. "How you say, revenge was sweet?"

Selver rolled the carpet up and tied it with the elastic from her hair while I clasped Arzu's neck and hugged tight. "How about some Turkish delight?" she asked cheekily and put out her hand to me.

"No sweets. Smoke better." Arzu warned and handed me the pipe.

"No thanks." I pushed the pipe away. "Revenge *was* sweet, Arzu," I said and kissed her on the cheek. "I'll take the Turkish Delight."

• • •

The wishes were back on the clothesline. Selver and I had new ones and the Şeker Djinni's wish joined ours, perfectly sealed. It hung, pegged, as tempting as any sweet, but I knew better than to open it.

After I baked my first *muhaleebi* using Latafat's recipe, I received my original wish. Now, the new relief belly dancer, Samara, gets changed behind the eggplants and okra in the pantry cupboard and I'm busy working as the cook in training at Divan's. And we always have enough Iskender kebabs.

Saturday afternoon; I was busy skewering lamb, when a strange wind outside sent dandelions spores fluttering into the kitchen and the back door slammed shut. There was a sharp knock. Arzu must have been locked out.

"Coming!" I wiped my hands on my apron and opened the door.

There he was, Şeker, the Dessert King of Djinn with a bunch of dandelions and a tray of baklava.

"Welcome!" I said surprised.

He laughed and pointed to his wish on the clothesline. "I have come for you to bake that wish of mine in a dessert."

I smiled and ripped my second wish off the line. It had come true.

Afterword

"The Belly-Dancing Crimes of Ms Sahara Desserts" is an homage to my two loves, the art of Raqs Sharqi, (bellydance) and folk and fairy tales.

I first fell in love with the dance because of two aunties. One had been a bellydancer, while the other migrated, to Australia from Egypt. They would wrap tea towels around our hips on Sunday afternoons and we would dance about the lounge room. The love of this art form took me to studying the dance and performing with a troupe.

In my twenties and early thirties, I worked in Turkish restaurants and Lebanese night clubs performing a cabaret style of the dance. I loved every minute of it: the tabouli caught in your toenails from dancing on tables, the coffee cup readings, becoming part of a secret, inseparable family with the waiters and kitchen staff and the lifelong friendships I've made with other women that have loved this dance form.

As a daughter of the Mediterranean, with migrant parents from Sicily, I grew up being told tales, some of which, I have discovered to also be in the Arabian nights. Fairy tale and folk motifs are ageless and shared in many cultures. They are like the water we drink—recycled and renewed and vital for our story intake. These tales, wherever their origins lie, like the dance form, entertain us, and take us on an adventure of the imagination.

I wanted "The Belly-Dancing Crimes of Ms Sahara Desserts" to be a romp and a fusion of my two loves. I wanted to make the words dance and the dance tell a story.

On A Crooked Leg Lightly

Alan Baxter

The *hashishin* moved like smoke, but Amalia saw him as he melted into one shadow and emerged from the next. His movement was hard to follow, clearer if she looked away, like stars on a misty night. He personified everything she didn't have: power, freedom, grace. There could be no question that he was a terrible threat to the palace.

He moved away from her family quarters, towards the guest wing. Mosaic walls reflected wan moonlight and the occasional candle. Wisps of incense swam fragrant from censers hanging off the arched pillars of the corridors. Amalia should have raised the alarm; the daughter of the Sultan would surely not allow this invasion of her most sacred home, but fascinated, she followed. More quickly and quietly than her deformed left leg would suggest possible, withered left arm held crooked, close to her chest, long thin fingers hooked like a claw, she held her breath and moved. She was nothing like the spectre ahead of her, but she made almost no noise. Almost.

In one deep shadow, the *hashishin* sank away and did not re-emerge. Amalia stifled a gasp and froze, trembling in a shadow of her own. She felt eyes on her, certain he watched. She shrank deeper in to the darkness of the corner, tiles pressing through her gossamer silks to cool her buttocks and back. She stared at the last place she had seen him. *Don't stop!* she silently pleaded. Something in the air changed, the sensation of being watched slid away.

Amalia didn't move her gaze, waited patiently. She relaxed, let her peripheral vision see everything, hoping for the slightest hint of movement . . . and there, nearly at the end of the hallway, a silhouette, barely distinguishable from the blackness of night, moved and slipped through the doors to the guest suite.

Where the visiting merchant king and his retinue were staying.

Where they rested before the morrow's talk with the Sultan about trade routes.

Where it was likely to be decided, Amalia had heard, that the Silk Road would become the purview of the merchant king to tax. The Sultan's dealings with Bin Allali, the self-styled merchant king, were the talk of the markets. Amalia hated to hear the way they insulted her father, even though she knew he was a corrupt man.

She hurried along the hall, paused at the door. She pressed her ear to the heavy, intricately carved wood, but heard nothing. Carefully, so very slowly, she eased it open.

The chamber was dark, but for shafts of silver light splashed across the coloured tiles of the floors and the ornate hangings of the beds from three tall, open windows. The heat of the night drifted in on a sultry breeze. Amalia's eyes roamed the beds and she clasped a hand over her mouth to hold in a scream at the sight of Bin Allali. His rotund belly rose from the mattress like a mountain, but his face hung backwards, his mouth wide, and beneath it his throat cut so deeply that his head was almost severed. Blood soaked blackly in the shadows across the sheets. His retinue slept on, oblivious.

Shivering with shock, Amalia tried to breathe and another cry almost escaped as her eye fell on a shadow in the window. Perched on the sill, framed by moonglow, the *hashishin* crouched. He looked directly at her, nothing visible beneath his dark grey clothing and hood, except his eyes, black and intense. With a slow hand he reached up, slipped back the hood, and winked. A scar ran across his handsome face from just below his hairline, barely missing his right eye as it divided his eyebrow and snaked down the side of his nose to end at his upper lip. That lip curled in a soft smile, white, even teeth catching the moonlight, and he was gone. Amalia didn't see him move; he simply wasn't there any more.

With a knot of excitement in her stomach battling the horror of the killing, she closed the guest suite doors and hurried away. Her almost silent, limping gait carried her through the corridors and back to her rooms where she stared wide-eyed at the ceiling until dawn, when the palace exploded in outrage and shock.

• • •

Amalia watched the commotion from a dispassionate remove. She knew more about it than any of the people running around in near panic, but was, as usual, ignored. Beautiful though broken, adored though unimportant. No one would believe her anyway. It had been that way since the accident, the horse stumbling, falling. Her mother's scream cut short as her neck snapped on impact and Amalia, holding tight behind, but not tight enough, thrown free and dashed into rocks. Her left arm and leg shattered, beyond repair. The adorable Sultan's daughter, suddenly a motherless, damaged flower.

She didn't remember the accident, only three years old when it happened, but she had been told many times. Had only ever known life with two good limbs and two crooked and difficult. Every day since she had been treated as though she might break in the slightest breeze, regardless of how often she proved herself capable and valuable.

And here she was, in possession of knowledge everyone needed and no one asked her anything. Every person in the palace, from the lowliest servant to the Sultan himself had been questioned by the vizier. Every single person but her. Because she was beautiful young Amalia, twenty four years old, but so fragile, like a child, so sad, look upon her with your most pitying gaze and smile. You brave, brave girl.

But she had to try. Loyalty was an important virtue. She found her father deep in conversation with his vizier and advisers. A guard looked awkwardly between Amalia and the royal group as she stood defiant in the doorway.

"He said no one was to disturb . . . " the guard started.

"You truly dare to bar *my* way?" Amalia demanded. Her voice belied her slight frame and the guard flinched. Casting his eyes to the tiles, he stepped back.

Amalia strode into the high-ceilinged room, head held high, her limp barely noticeable. In her left hand she held a heavy, leather-bound book. She had no need of the tome, but a weight in her damaged hand helped to keep her arm straight and her hand from its occasional random jerks. The less obvious her disabilities, the more people paid attention to *her*, to her mind.

The Sultan's eyes darkened as he saw her approach. "Beautiful flower, we are very busy."

"I know, Father. I thought I ought to talk to you about last night."

The Sultan cast an apologetic glance at the gathered dignitaries and Amalia's anger blazed. "You mustn't be scared by the events of last night," he said, crouching to speak with her, even though she stood mere inches below his standing height.

She looked down at him, ridiculous squatting before her. "Scared?" she asked through gritted teeth.

"The palace guard has been doubled, my sweet. The evil man who infiltrated these walls and committed this heinous crime will never be a threat to you, I promise."

Drawing a deep breath, Amalia tried to ignore his pitying eyes. "Father, last night I saw a man in the corridors leading to the guest quarters."

The Sultan smiled. Smiled! She couldn't believe it. "Dreams, my gentle girl," he said. "Please, don't be afraid. You're quite safe here."

"Father, I am not a child! Will you not listen to me?"

His face clouded and he stood. "This is not the time, Amalia, I am very busy. We'll talk later." He turned his back, addressed the advisers. "My apologies for her. Now, where were we?"

My apologies for her. Their entire relationship summed up in four words.

Amalia ground her teeth and left through the immaculate, fragrant gardens, towards the markets. Her anger boiled as she stalked between rose gardens and herb beds, wanting only to be alone.

She enjoyed time in the grounds, at the river, in the hills beyond town. But most of all she liked to be alone in the crowds of the bustling bazaar. The noise of hawkers and camels, children and laughter. The smells of roses and spices thick in the air with dust and heat and sunshine. She wrapped herself in a full, yellow silk, covering her crooked arm, and removed the jewelled strings that tied her hair, to let it fall loose, a thick, shining mask about her face. Then no one cared about her limp as she drifted among the stalls, listening to gossip, soaking in the depth and diversity of humanity.

But today all these things she loved were blighted, shaded by the knowledge she carried like a rock in her chest. That strong, handsome, scarred face. That wink. What did it mean? Her mind wandered and she imagined those silk-covered hands drifting across her body, that proud face smiling down upon her.

It was unspoken but clearly assumed within the palace that she would never marry. Who would have her? Except through pity, and the Sultan would never allow that. Instead he would let her grow old alone, kept safe in the palace like a rare artefact behind glass and she hated him for that.

Her needs were strong and she had sated them many times. Handsome young men in the markets and the travelling caravans were only too willing to look past her damaged arm and leg, to see the smooth and wonderful curves of her. To lose themselves in her wide, deep eyes. She had known and enjoyed lust many times, never admitting to those transitory men who she was. But she wondered if she would ever know love.

Love? Why did she think of that now, with the image of that scarred *hashishin* in her mind? Sadness descended again. Because he represented the antithesis of everything she was. A distant cry drew her eye upwards to an eagle riding a thermal, a hundred yards above the striped roofs of the stalls, flying free. A tear crested her lashes as she let her gaze fall back to earth and she looked right into his eye.

The scar was less obvious in the light of day, without the night's shadows to mark it out. Dressed in plain linen, he was unremarkable, though his strength and power were still apparent. His lip curled in a half-smile and he turned away, moved among the crowds with ease.

Amalia followed, her strides barely hindered by the limp she had carried for so long. The *hashishin* ducked left and right, never looking back, appearing to travel at random through the throng. Was he testing her? She emerged from one line of vendors as he disappeared between the bright and noisy stalls of the next. A man led three camels directly across her path and Amalia stumbled, cursed aloud. The man and his animals passed and she hurried forward again, the *hashishin* lost. The end of the next row gave way to a tea-shop square, where dozens of people sat smoking *nargileh*, sipping from small glass cups, talking, laughing. The sudden open space and crowds disoriented her and she stopped, chewed one side of her bottom lip as she scanned. He could be anywhere.

Her eyes fell on the back of one man's head, his black hair short and neat, his shoulders broad as he sat on cushions spread across a russet-coloured rug. A small, wiry man with long hair and a scraggly beard served him tea in a brightly painted glass.

Amalia watched, waited. It had to be him, the shape, even the demeanour of his position. When the serving man moved away, she stepped lightly across the rug and stood before him, her book held before her like a shield. His scar creased as his smile broadened, revealing straight, white teeth.

"Well done." He gestured at the cushions. "Join me?"

Amalia looked about herself, nervous as she sat down.

"You're tenacious, I'll give you that," he said and sipped his tea.

"I could turn you in. There are palace guards throughout the bazaar and they would heed my word."

The *hashishin* smiled. "But they would be able to prove nothing. Do you think your word against mine would result in anything?"

Amalia scowled.

The *hashishin* held up a placatory palm. "I recognise your skills, would never doubt you. You saw me last night, you tracked me then and again today. You're a very capable woman. But would *they* think so?"

Amalia sighed, looked at her hands atop the book in her lap. "No."

The man sipped in silence, his face gentle. He seemed to be waiting.

"You wanted me to follow you," Amalia said. "Why?"

"You were curious about me."

"Yes, but why let me follow you? Find you?"

"I was curious about you too."

"Why?"

His smile slipped away and he sipped again from the bright glass, said nothing. The silence grew heavy.

"You have magic," Amalia said eventually. The *hashishin* shrugged. "You do. I saw it. The way you move through shadows."

He sipped, smiled and said nothing.

"Is it djinn-gifted?"

"My skills are hard-earned," he replied softly. "It takes a lot of training to do what I do."

She nodded. "But you're helped by things that couldn't be trained."

"Possibly."

Amalia took a deep breath, nerves fluttering through her chest. "I want what you have."

The *hashishin* looked her up and down. He gestured at her leg, her thin arm revealed where the silk had fallen aside. "You think djinn-gift could remove your . . . injuries."

Anger burned hot and fierce through her heart. "No!" She lifted her crooked arm, pointed bent fingers at her left leg. "This is me. *All* of this is me, and always has been. You think I want a cure? There's nothing wrong with me. Why does everyone think I desire to be *repaired*?"

He tipped his head, expression curious. "My apologies. What did you mean?"

"I want your freedom."

He laughed at that, a deep and genuine mirth. "You think me free?"

"Aren't you? You get well paid for what you do, yes? You take whatever jobs you choose and live a life beholden to no one."

His laughter drifted down into a sad smile and he shook his head. "You romanticise my life, princess."

"Don't call me that!"

He lifted a hand again. "Apologies once more. What should I call you?"

"My name is Amalia. And yours?"

He thought for a moment. "Call me Ben for now."

"All right. Ben. And how, exactly, do I romanticise your life?"

"We are all beholden to someone."

"Oh? Who holds your destiny?"

"Why don't you figure that out? Then maybe you'll know what to do." He stood before she could say any more and disappeared into the shadows of the tent behind them.

Amalia jumped up and followed, knowing he would be gone before she could cover the two yards to the cool interior of the tea shop. She was right.

"Can I help you, miss?" the scraggly shopkeeper asked.

"No, thank you." Brow furrowed in thought, she made her way home.

• • •

The palace was still buzzing with nervous energy. Amalia passed the Sultan's chambers, dared the guard with a look and stepped inside. The Sultan and his vizier sat listening to the representatives of the recently deceased merchant king, their faces serious, eyes dark. There was anger and the promise of retribution in the tones directed at them. She was not surprised when the Sultan stood, angry himself. He would not be spoken to like that.

A new political climate had manifested overnight, but some proprieties remained. He yelled about apologies made, recompense offered. When he caught sight of her in the doorway, he gestured furiously with one hand, waving her away like he might bat at a troublesome fly.

She sighed and made her way to her father's extensive library and the educated sage who resided there, curating the gathered knowledge.

"Tell me about the *hashishin*," she said to Fahim.

The old man raised an eyebrow. "Events in the palace got you curious, eh?"

"Maybe."

The old scholar placed the book he held on a desk and gestured to cushions in a large bay window. They sat where they had hundreds of times over the years and he leaned back, closed his eyes to think. Amalia was comfortable, in the company of one of the few people who valued her mind, her personality, her whole being. She had endeared herself to him as a curious child and he had willingly taken on the role of a kindly uncle.

"The *hashishin* are as much myth as truth, Amalia; that much you should know first. Most killers for hire are simply that. Men who would risk their own lives for coin at the expense of another's. But the *hashishin* are different. They claim a higher calling. They have skills beyond those of normal men."

"Djinn-gifted skills?" Amalia asked.

The old man chuckled. "Well, so the legends would have us believe. But there are many things that legends would have us believe."

"And which djinni is it they serve for their gifts, Uncle?"

Fahim smiled softly at the use of the familial honorific, though kept his eyes closed. "Not just any djinni, my sweet, but a *marid* of immense power. The myths say that a person beseeches this *marid* for the killing they want done and, should the *marid* see the killing is justified, he will send a shade in human form to take that life. At a cost."

Amalia's eyes narrowed. "A shade in human form? But aren't the *hashishin* human?"

"Did the human become a shade or did the shade become a human? Does it even matter?"

"And this *marid's* name?" Amalia asked.

Fahim opened his eyes, a flinty gaze to make Amalia jump. "Khalid Maalik," he said softly. "Why would you want to know this?"

"I'm just curious, Uncle. Surely none but a shade could have breached these halls and killed the merchant king while all of us slept."

Fahim's face remained hard for a moment, before softening with a smile. "This is dangerous knowledge, child. But it's always been the dangerous things you've liked the most."

Amalia jumped up and kissed the old man's cheek. "You know me too well. But it's the stories I love, Uncle. Just the stories."

Fahim laughed, flapped one hand at her. "Surely. Run along, enjoy the day. There are books here about the *hashishin* legends if you wish to know more." His eyes hardened again. "But think hard on that name and what it means."

Amalia stopped at the door, looked back. "What it means?"

"There's always a cost," the old man said softly. "For all involved."

• • •

Moonlight bathed Amalia as she sat on her bedroom floor. Musky incense burned. Honey and wine sat in cups before her as offerings, rose petals were scattered around, bright against cool white tiles.

"Khalid Maalik," she whispered. "Hear me."

Her heart beat hard against her ribs. She needed to believe, needed this to be real. Why else would the *hashishin* in the bazaar have said the things he did?

"Khalid Maalik, hear me."

A breeze rose, lifted the curtains and made them dance. The zephyr carried the scent of sulphur and cinnamon.

Amalia trembled, closed her eyes, wished fervently to be heard.

"Khalid Maalik, hear me. Come to me!"

The breeze became a gust and something crackled in the air. A presence filled the room. She kept her eyes tightly closed, suddenly terrified.

A heavy, even breath sighed gently. "You risk much, princess."

The voice was deep as night, and sonorous. It rumbled through Amalia's chest, made her heart race ever faster. She opened her eyes. Above her hung a beautiful man, ebony-skinned, thickly muscled, long haired, naked and shining in the moonlight. Wisps of smoke drifted around him, seemed to caress his limbs. He looked down at her with an unreadable expression in his eyes of jet.

Her mouth was dry. "You came."

"When the call is genuine, I come."

"You listen to the requests of people who would have someone killed, yes?"

"You require someone removed?"

Amalia smiled, though her lips trembled. "Actually, I wondered if perhaps I might offer you my services. You gift men with the magic to carry out your wishes, yes? Do you gift women too?"

The djinni tipped back his head and laughed, long and loud. "You were right," he said.

"Who are you talking . . . ?" Amalia stopped the question with a jump of shock at the sight of the *hashishin*, Ben, perched on her windowsill. Had he been there all along? His hood was down, his scarred face amused in the moonlight.

"I told you that's what she would ask," Ben said. "She has . . . strength, this one."

Khalid Maalik sank in the air, his smooth legs crossing as he sat before Amalia, still a foot off the floor. "You would do my bidding?"

She pointed towards the *hashishin*. "I would have his skills."

"Your injuries have never slowed you down, have they?" the djinni said.

"Never. And they never will. Some people are too short to reach a high shelf, or too tall to fit comfortably beneath a low roof. They learn to live quite normally. I am no different." She gestured with her crooked arm, indicated her difficult leg. "These things have nothing to do with my request."

"You can still run and climb and fight?"

"Of course! I don't run as fast or climb as well, perhaps, and I may not look very graceful doing it, but I do it still."

"And you would be my instrument?"

"I've been forced to live my life in the shadows. I choose to embrace them."

"Do you really understand what you ask?"

Amalia took a deep breath and nodded. "I know the meaning of your name. I looked it up in the oldest books of our library. Eternal Possessor."

The djinni drifted closer, his presence intoxicating in such proximity, the aroma of cinnamon and sulphur almost overpowering. "You would be truly alone. No one and no thing held to you. Just you, the night and the work."

"I am alone among crowds already. My father treats me like a fragile bird. I'm too much a princess to have common friends and too broken to be truly accepted by royalty. I've been alone since my mother died."

"If you were to serve me you would be tested. Requests are never far apart and I would assess your conviction *thoroughly*."

"I seek freedom from my life here. At any price."

"Any price? Very current events still draw my attention."

Amalia's eyes narrowed. She suspected she knew what he meant. "*Any* price."

"You could take no family, own no lands or goods. Otherwise, you could do with yourself as you please, but whenever I call, you *must* answer. Whoever, wherever I say."

Amalia sensed the possibility of success. It emboldened her. "I need no family, but . . . " She leaned to look past the djinni, caught Ben's eye. "But I could still enjoy love, couldn't I?"

Ben smiled and Khalid Maalik laughed. "You could do with your life as you pleased as long as you make no commitment but to me. I am a jealous master."

Amalia turned her eyes back to the djinni. "Then I am yours to serve."

• • •

Distant sounds of insects were all that broke the deep, dark silence of the palace. A waxing moon cast soft light across the corridors. Amalia, swathed head to toe in charcoal silks, stepped on a crooked leg lightly into shadow. The night swallowed her and she moved through it, passing to the end of the hall without stepping on any space in between. A guard, one of many in the doubled security detail, stood by a tall window at the corner of the passageway. He saw nothing as Amalia slipped into a shadow behind him and emerged from another several yards away.

A razor-sharp, wickedly poisoned blade pressed coolly against her palm as she quietly turned the handle to her father's bedchamber and slipped inside, one task away from freedom.

Afterword

I've always wanted to write an Arabian Nights inspired story. The settings and people are so richly developed in what has come before and it's a delicious playground to jump into. I hope my addition to the oeuvre does it justice. One of the things that has always fascinated me about these tales and the associated mythology is the idea of djinn and how they seem to come in every form, from the truly benevolent to the utterly malicious. As I'm a dark fiction writer, I always find myself considering the consequences of things. A djinn with great power would almost certainly exact a great price for his gifts, and what kind of people might be prepared to pay those prices? This is the question that formed the seed of my story here.

I also wanted to write about assassins in palaces on balmy nights, and who else might be in those palaces. Once I started thinking about that, the character of Amalia came to me, and I instantly fell for her and wanted to explore her life and situation. I hope you enjoyed what I came up with.

The Saint George Hotel

Thoraiya Dyer

The St George Hotel is virtually next door to a Porsche dealership.

Young Arab men in clouds of cologne gather to goggle, or to brag that their father is buying them one, but Baasim's eye is on the Mercedes moving slowly towards him along the promenade road.

Dressed in branded beachware and boat shoes, he looks like he's headed for the hotel's glittering, heated pool or perhaps the St George's Yacht Club, but the heavy backpack pulling at his shoulders does not contain towels; the sweat on his brow is not from the warmth less February sun.

His heart counts down its final seconds.

Bism'Allah, al-Rahman, Al-Rahim, he thinks.

Everything about his life is cold and empty, heedless of the seasons. Dying mother in the squalid dark. Baby brothers with bellies full of worms and nothing else. No free hospitals to take her to. No free bread to feed them. Uncles fled. Father dead. Baasim worked in his cousin's pet store for only a few weeks before the boa constrictors and pythons he'd been in charge of had started dying and he'd been kicked out of the shop.

God is my real father.

Baasim walks away from the dealership. He intercepts the Mercedes in front of the hotel, gives the switch in his hand a quick flick. There's a pause before the explosion.

Time stands still. The world is an indrawn breath.

Flame. The Mercedes lifts off the ground. The façade of the hotel swims through the orange curtain towards him.

Flame is everywhere.

But Baasim isn't dead.

Or is he?

He feels no pain.

Fear shrinks him to a black speck surrounded by fire; God, his true father is not pleased with him. Killing the faithless former Prime Minister was not the right thing to do.

Baasim's punishment will begin any moment, now. When he does feel the bite of flame, it won't be fleeting, but forever.

Pain, forever, in Hell.

The speck that is Baasim squirms.

Then it's dark, and a clumsily woven, coarse quilt stuffed with stinking sheep's wool is being pulled over him.

"I have you," croaks a cracked and ancient voice, but it's not the voice of Satan. "Be calm. Be still. I have you."

At least, Baasim doesn't think it's Satan's voice. His shaking body is naked beneath the greasy, scratchy blanket. The backpack and its promises of instant oblivion, the lie of the Western clothes and the terrible flames are gone.

"Is that you, father?" Baasim manages. Slivers of floating light tell him he's in a wood-slatted hut. His bare buttocks rest on a dirt floor. This cannot be paradise.

There were supposed to be flowers and fountains.

"I'm certainly not your father, boy," the old woman says. "But I've brought you into this world, so you may as well call me 'mother'. The spell was more powerful than I ever expected, so don't get too attached to me, for I may die of it quite soon. They gave me no choice, though. I'm to be fed to the dragon in the morning."

Baasim pulls back from her, his eyes straining to adjust. He sees a warty, white-whiskered, female face beneath a pale green headscarf, and hands as big as a man's reaching to wipe the tears of shock from his cheeks with the dangling green corners of it.

"Where am I?" he asks. "Where are my clothes, Mother?"

"You are outside the village of Lod, boy. Your clothes are where you left them. It was you alone that I called for. You that I needed.

A dragon-slayer from the future world. Sorry to drag you back. You must have been famous. You must have been loved."

Baasim realises her error. His jaw drops.

It is the former Prime Minister who is famous.

It is the former Prime Minister who is loved.

Baasim was to be blasted into a million pieces when his bomb went off. Nobody was to have even known he was there.

He was not to be famous.

He was not to be loved, except by God, his true father, who was to have gathered his spirit and brought him home.

But he is not home and his spirit has not been gathered. His naked body has been gathered instead by an old witch who wants him to save her from a dragon.

"You robbed me," he says. "God will fetch me home."

"Your God can't fetch you home," Mother mutters. "Not even the Roman Gods can do that. Slay the dragon, though, and you will be a hero in the village of Lod. They will give you camels and horses. They will take you anywhere you want."

Baasim doesn't tell her that he's never slain a dragon. He's not the hero she was after.

It doesn't matter. He isn't afraid.

When the dragon kills him, he'll be with his father, who can undoubtedly find him even in this strange time and place.

"God," he says again, "will fetch me home."

Mother gives him a yoghurt drink and begins tailoring some men's clothes to fit him.

"They left me 'til last," she says, threading her needle by touch. "Because my spells kept their livestock safe and stopped their women dying in childbirth. Now I am the only virgin they have left. For eighty-three years have I guarded the precious source of my powers, only to end an idiot sacrifice to an overgrown green worm."

Baasim says uncomfortably, "I know this story."

"Oh? You do? Tell me, serpent-slayer. How does it end?"

"I don't know. It's a Christian story, isn't it?"

"Is it, indeed?" She laughs and laughs. "That means there are Christians alive in your time to tell it. That will comfort the Roman soldier who stands by the lake and entreats the good citizens not to appease Satan's puppet with the lives of the innocent. You must stop to visit him at his parents' home. It is about half way between here and the lake where the monster lives."

• • •

The man stands with his back to Baasim, his head bowed over his parents' graves.

"Georgius Gerontius," the gardener says, kneeling. "This boy, Baasim, brings a message for you from the Council."

When the gardener is gone and there's no sound but the bees in the oleander and wind-borne soil sliding over the stones, Baasim says, "The Council didn't really send me. That's just what the witch told me to say. She says they're going to feed her to the dragon tomorrow morning, so I'm to slay it tonight."

Georgius has a thin, long-jawed face and sad eyes. His sandals and cloak and helmet make him look like an actor from an old movie Baasim saw once.

Nodding, he says slowly, "You'll be needing a sword, boy. I'll see if I can find one for you."

"Thanks, but I don't know how to use one. I'm just here to tell you that there's lots of Christians in the future. Millions and billions of them. She thought you'd be happy to hear that."

The soldier's eyes meet Baasim's. He feels hypnotised. Moment by moment, Georgius's gaze grows fiercer and more joyful.

"It's a sign," he stutters at last. "I came back to the village of my birth to consult the spirit of my father. Instead, it's a stranger with a vision that has been chosen as God's messenger. I will go to Nicomedia and renounce my Emperor's edict. I will declare openly my worship of Christ, even though that path leads to death."

All *paths lead to death*, Baasim thinks. *Better to meet my true father in Heaven than stay here on Earth with false fathers who say they will protect their sons but die in agony instead.*

The Christians even say that Christ died in agony.

But the one true God cannot die. None of these sinners can touch him. He can never be defeated. He can never be torn down. By submitting to him, I become safe, forever.

"Please show me the road that leads to the lake," Baasim says calmly.

"I will walk with you," Georgius smiles. "Tell me how you plan to slay the dragon, with or without a sword. Many soldiers have tried. They died."

The road is paved with stone. Small, well-tended fields lie to either side of it. Beans grow in tidy rows. Cloth covers the apricot trees to protect the fruit from birds. Fat-tailed sheep bleat from woven pens.

"I don't know," Baasim says, shrugging. "The old Mother called me serpent-slayer. She gave me these clothes. Do they repel fire?"

"The dragon does not breathe fire. It is a water-snake. It waits for its enemies to enter the water and swallows them whole. Take this sword. Please."

"If you're good with a sword, why don't you kill the dragon?"

Georgius hesitates.

"If I am honest with you, boy, I don't believe the monster can be killed. Lances bend and break against its hide. Sword edges glance away. The village must be abandoned and the sacrifices must stop. Only a holy man can defeat this Devil. If they had not fed it for so long, it would not have grown to such invincible proportions."

"If you think I'm going to die, why are you showing me the way?"

"You can change your mind, boy," Georgius says kindly. "You can turn back. That is precisely my purpose, here at your side. What kind of man would I be, to send a boy alone to his destruction?"

The lake, when they reach it, is soccer stadium-sized.

It's late afternoon and there are no waterfowl colonising the reeds; no creatures drinking at the shore. There are no footprints at all in the silt exposed by the receding water's edge.

"Where is the dragon?" Baasim wants to know.

"On the bottom of the lake. It does not need to breathe often. You are brave, Baasim. You have come fearlessly this far. Now return with me to my parents' home. In honour of your bravery, I will give you the deeds to it. I cannot take treasures with me to the next life."

I am not brave, Baasim thinks. *I just know more than you do about the next life. I've seen it in my dreams.*

My true father will protect me.

Some bundled sticks are propped against a nearby low, stone wall. Baasim cannot swim. He gathers the bundles and launches them into the water, takes a running jump onto his makeshift raft as Georgius cries, "No!"

Baasim floats further and further from shore. Georgius starts cursing the witch.

"Are you a virgin, boy? She did not send you to slay the dragon at all. She sent you as sacrifice! But the fool villagers will not spare her!"

Then Georgius is forgotten. Water before him is erupting.

A tidal wave.

Teeth.

A dark hole, like a tunnel through the souk. A fetid smell, overpowering.

Water is everywhere.

But Baasim isn't dead.

Or is he?

It's dark and he feels the length of his body clamped by a tube of muscle, the powerful rings of it squeezing him, but his head and shoulders are surrounded by bundles of sticks, the collapsed remains of his raft, and they are obstructing the dragon's throat.

The monster thrashes, unable to close its mouth.

It cannot submerge itself, or it will fill like a water balloon; instead, it thrashes some more and the rings of muscle squeeze sequentially, trying to force Baasim and the sticks deeper into its gullet.

But some of the sharp stakes are stuck sideways and though slime begins to coat everything and the convulsions become more desperate, neither the sticks nor Baasim move any further down.

The dragon lays its head on the shore. Night falls outside. Baasim stops being able to feel his feet.

He falls asleep, but wakes when slime accumulates in front of his face. His arms are trapped by his sides, but he rubs his face on the sticks until he has room to breathe again.

The dragon breathes heavily. It has long since stopped straining. The slime it produces is capable of dissolving the timber. Baasim sees this when the sun rises again; his face feels inflamed, and the wood is pitted, as though acid is eating through it.

He hears the distant, horrified cries of villagers at the edge of the lake as they lay eyes on the monster, fully exposed to daylight.

I wonder what they are seeing. I never got to see it from the outside.

Father, will you come for me now?

When he opens his eyes a final time, he sees large, bloody blisters on the inside lining of the dragon's stretched and traumatised throat. They aren't the same as the wounds made by the sticks.

Strange, Baasim thinks blearily. *They look the same as the bloody blisters that the boa constrictors got in their mouths while I was working at that pet shop.*

The snakes all died.

My cousin threw me out.

I was so hungry. They told me that God was my true father.

Then Baasim is being cut from the dead dragon's body by Georgius, who is crying, filthy with lake mud and the monster's blood.

"Baasim," he weeps. "You are holy. Bless you. Forgive me."

His sword clatters to the ground and he lifts Baasim in his arms.

My father is here, Baasim thinks, before the sun stabs his sensitive skin. He howls and writhes as Georgius washes him in the waters of the lake.

Pain.

Pain everywhere.

But Baasim isn't dead.

• • •

He wakes in the hut of the witch.

Candlelight reveals the candle and almost nothing else. There is the smell of cooked lamb and spices. Cool dressings cover the skin of his face and hands and feet. He is no longer in pain.

That does not change the fact that he is naked, again, with his buttocks in the dirt and the scratchy, stinky wool quilt around his shoulders.

"Mother," he calls. "Is that you? You're not dead?"

Mother laughs and laughs and her warty old face looms in front of him, kissing and kissing his cheeks.

"You wonderful boy!" she declares, stopping her kissing to spoon boiled bread into his mouth. "You have saved your old mother, you wonderful boy!"

She seems to be making a sliding, scuffling sound, and Baasim sees that her veiny, clotty old legs are withered like a pair of blackened bananas left out in the sun.

"I lost my legs to that spell," she whispers, feeding him the last of the gloopy contents of the clay bowl. "But I'm still here, and so are you. Georgius brought you back here, after they tried to make him King of Lod for killing that dragon."

"Georgius," Baasim says. "Where is he?"

"Oh, he's gone to the Capital to face his accusers. That old Emperor's going to convert him into a proper Roman, you see. Make sacrifices. Kiss the stone feet of Jupiter. Anyone who admits he's Christian is going to be tortured."

"Georgius won't kiss the feet of Jupiter," Baasim says with alarm. "He thinks I'm a sign. He's going there to die."

"A waste of a good man."

"Where are my clothes, Mother?"

He can change his mind. He can turn back.

"You left them inside that rotting dragon carcass! I can't keep making new clothes for you, boy!"

My father cut me out of the insides of a dragon.

"Please show me the road that leads to Nicomedia."

I will not leave him to die in agony.

"You've seen my legs. I can't show you any roads. Besides, it's late at night. There are hyenas. There are lions."

Baasim stands up with the scratchy blanket over his shoulders, the dressings slipping from his bare feet.

"My father tried to protect me," he says.

"Which father? What? Sit down. You can't walk naked to Nicomedia with burned feet and a blanket."

"Maybe I can't," Baasim admits. *Maybe my birth father could not protect me, as he wished.* "But I think that what I will be judged by is whether or not I try."

Mother eyes him for a long while before grudgingly bringing a pair of soft shoes and a ball of white cheese from the dark corners of her dwelling.

"Take these, dragon-slayer," she says. "Nicomedia lies at the end of the north road."

Baasim walks down the road. He does not feel the cold.

❀

— 104 —

Afterword

My father left Lebanon for Australia to get an aeronautical engineering degree in the 1970s, never expecting he would fall in love, marry, have children or become an Australian citizen.

The Lebanese will tell you that St George's dragon-slaying actually, historically took place in Beirut. Rafik Hariri was an independently wealthy Lebanese Prime Minister who pretty much single-handedly rebuilt Beirut after a 15 year civil war. In 2005, Hariri was assassinated outside the St George Hotel. It was first thought to be a car bomb, but recent continuing investigations have indicated a bomber might have been involved. Some unknown person's DNA turned up at the crime scene, but 1000kg of TNT tend to make a person vanish like they never existed.

Who was that person? Where did they go? Fodder for fiction. And I find it interesting that Saint George, a religious figure and a martyr, is remembered today as a legendary hero, while the self-titled martyrs of another religion are (rightly!) condemned.

The Sultan's Debt

Barb Siples

The landscape changed as we fled. The magnificent palace gardens of Atolan became orchards. The fruit trees gave way to bamboo thickets, the green stalks to oak groves and birch sinks. These became thick forests of fir, became scraggly pines, became a nightmare landscape of tortured rock and sage and juniper. Two broad shoulders in front of me, a callused hand gripping a curved sword. That was my constant. That, and fear.

The howls of the feyatin pursued us. Hard to believe they had once been men.

"Azad," I said to the man riding through the dust ahead of me. "Azad, stop."

My bodyguard stopped at once, turned his stallion to join me in the shade of a boulder.

"I'm tired and I stink and I'm thirsty," I said. My throat felt too tight, clogged with royal anger, royal grief. "At home I'd call for chilled wine and sesame cakes—"

"We have water." Azad passed the skin. He wasn't even sweating. "Finish it, your majesty."

"Am I, still? Am I still Hadid son of Umar, Sultan of Atolan, Lord of the Fifteen Emirates and Heir to the Thousand Year Throne?"

Azad regarded me in silence, patient as the sky. We had been boys together and from boyhood to manhood he had stood at my elbow as tradition demanded, learning to serve and guard his master. He knew who I was. He watched me lift the battered vessel to my lips and swallow the water, swallow my pride.

We returned to the trail in silence. Sunlight glinted from the steel rings sewn to Azad's leather tunic. I closed my eyes and clung to my saddle horn, recalling our frenzied gallop through the gates of Atolan until a sick lurch jarred me from my drifting thoughts. The horse I rode shuddered and collapsed beneath me. I sat in the dirt and stroked its white neck while it died. No creature so pedigreed deserved such a fate.

I climbed to my feet and peered up at Azad where he sat perched in his saddle, waiting for him to tell me that he had no reason to linger. That he would ride on without me. What possible reason could he have left to serve me?

But Azad bent and reached and I swung up behind him. I put my arms about his waist, pressed my chest to the rigid column of his spine. I felt his strength as plainly as I felt the bite of ring mail through the tattered silk of my shirt. I remembered the glory of the once-turquoise fabric, the fall of my hair over the collar, oiled to a glossy black, the admiration in the eyes of the ladies who thronged the sultan's court and populated his harem. My wardrobe hung in tatters about me, barely recognisable as white damask coat, cloth-of-gold pantaloons, rose-coloured cummerbund.

And yet I still had my famous good looks. Poets compared the magnificence of my grey eyes to the flash of steel on the battlefield, the proud straight line of my nose to a javelin. Songs equated the smooth, golden power of my limbs to the graceful saunter of a hunting lion. It wasn't mere flattery either, not all of it. I could tell the difference.

Snug in our shared saddle, I squeezed Azad close and laid my cheek against his shoulder. I knew his weakness, his secret, had felt the change in him as we left childhood behind. Had felt his eyes linger. "Never abandon me," I whispered in his ear.

My bodyguard pressed his knees to his horse's shoulders and the unfortunate thoroughbred shuffled forward.

When the setting sun painted the horizon orange and red we dismounted and assembled our meagre camp, the few items we'd snatched as we made our hasty escape. I surveyed the desolate landscape of sand and rock, sky and shadows. Twenty nights and more we had slept beneath the wheeling stars.

"Azad," I said. "Do all things happen for a reason?"

He didn't look up from the cactus he was peeling. "Almost always."

"Do you think . . . Did they suffer much, do you think? My father and mother?" It wasn't what I'd intended to say. A thin, breathless quality strangled the words.

"Your majesty?"

I lifted a hand and swallowed down my grief. When I could speak again I said, "The Thousand Year Throne will be restored to me, I promise you. I'll set the world on fire if I have to."

Azad went still, the motion of his knife arrested. "And then, your majesty?"

"What do you mean, 'and then'? And then everything will return to how it was. I'll be home in Atolan, in my rooms at the palace. My father's rooms, I suppose. But lamps will shine in the courtyards again, like stars stolen from the heavens. Wine will flow and music will ring from the alcoves. Can you see it, Azad? The veils of the dancing girls will make the night giddy with perfume."

Azad offered no opinion of this vision.

I said, "I'm well aware that the idea of dancing girls doesn't appeal to you. I'm not deaf to court gossip, you know." He flinched and looked away. "Nor am I blind to the way you sometimes look at me. There's no cause for alarm, I'm not judging you. I myself admit to a certain curiosity." That snapped his gaze back to mine in a hurry. "I've had some lovely adventures in the harem, but never that one. Someday, perhaps."

What I'd said was true . . . but calculated. Absent wealth or titles, I had nothing to barter for Azad's allegiance save the use of my body. It served me to plant the seed of the possibility of intimacy in his mind. It might induce him to serve me a little longer.

"They say it's against God," Azad said. "What you're talking about."

"I hardly think He'd mind." I stretched out my hand and Azad handed me the morsel he'd been preparing. I popped the spongy green mess in my mouth and tasted bitterness. I'd eaten worse crossing the badlands. Hunger can make even carrion appetising. "We should have a fire tonight. They're a long way behind us."

"A fire would be dangerous, your majesty."

"I'm tired of the dark."

Azad got to his feet and went to collect tinder.

They came in the night, of course they did. Four of them, the vanguard. I saw them by starlight, by the glow of the embers. The feyatin had once been men, and they retained their human form. But their humanity slept behind their unreasoning purpose, their stiff limbs and a shuffling gait, behind mottled faces, red and black and veined with purple. White filmed their eyes but they followed our movements with precision, a gift of the King of the Djinn's contagion.

"Don't let them touch you," I hissed.

"It's you they're after," Azad said. "Keep behind me."

My hands pressed his back, a shield of flesh and sinew.

Two of the four feyatin carried weapons. One held a crude stick—a tree branch—but the other brandished a nasty little dagger.

Azad gripped his sword with both hands, swung the curved blade over his head in a silver arc. I heard his grunt as the steel slid through the nearest feyatin's spine. The thing's head tumbled to the ground, greasy hair collecting dust as it rolled to a stop. The only way to kill them.

Again Azad's blade swooped up and around. Another scabrous head flapped through the air before landing with a *splat* at my feet. Two remained standing.

The dagger-wielding feyatin advanced, slashing clumsily. Azad danced away, but not quickly enough. Blood laced his arms from the cuts. Rallying, he hacked off the feyatin's wrist, stabbed its face. A pale ichor spurted from the broken skin, reeking of sewage. Azad shouted as he kicked the creature's legs out from under it, as he chopped the head from its shoulders.

"Azad!"

The last standing feyatin crunched its heavy branch into Azad's forearm. A hoarse shout burst from my bodyguard's throat and the sword flew from his hands. He rolled out of the feyatin's reach and I scrabbled along the ground after the sword. I came in from behind, on my knees, and slashed at the monster's calves, gagged at the stench that dribbled from the wounds. The creature roared and whirled toward me.

I held up Azad's curved blade.

The feyatin's branch smacked the steel from my grasp. I watched the weapon spin a silhouette across the stars and squeezed my eyes shut.

Azad?

The first thing I saw when I opened them was a slobbery grin. Just the grin. The top half of the feyatin's face sailed through the air.

"Move back," Azad grunted. He stood behind the monster, clutching the grip of his sword in one hand. I hadn't seen my bodyguard recover his blade, but of course he had.

His next swing went through the feyatin's neck. I scrambled to my feet and danced out of the way. The body toppled like a felled tree to the ground where I'd been kneeling, the branch still clenched in its fist. Azad and I stood panting, regarding each other over the carcass.

"No more fires," I whispered. Azad winced and slid to his knees.

I watched him crouch in the dust, his left hand clenched over his right forearm, chin tucked to his breastbone. After a moment I said, "Is it broken?"

"Fractured, maybe."

I looked around at the lumps of flesh lying on all sides of us. "They reek," I said. "The horse ran off."

Azad dragged himself upright. He wiped clean the blade of his sword, took what had once been a turban from our hastily assembled baggage, deftly tied a knot in the silk with his good hand and his teeth. He slid the faded fabric over his shoulder and tucked his battered arm into the fold. The cuts from the feyatin's blade stood out on the skin of his forearms, raw and painful. How long before Azad realized I wasn't worth his life?

He shouldered our pack and walked into the dark away from me.

"Azad?"

My bodyguard turned and gave me a tired smile. "Let's go, your majesty."

• • •

Toward late afternoon the badlands gave way to straggling pines and the blessed relief of shade. "Will there be water?" I asked.

"Yes, your majesty."

"How close are we, do you think? To the Ufasi?"

Azad slipped through the trees. Branches slithered over his shoulders and tugged at the strands of chestnut hair that fell to the middle of his back. He no longer bothered to bind it.

"Azad?"

"Not close."

"Do you really think they'll help me?"

"Yes, your majesty." It was what he always said. I craved his assurances.

I asked for the hundredth time, "But why should they? Why hand over something as sacred as the Sceptre of Aram, just because I ask for it? The brotherhood of the Ufasi was created to keep talismans of power away from people." People like me, I realised. "Will they really just hand it over?"

"Yes, your majesty."

"We have to reach Salida first, but how far is that? Will they even understand our language? We'll need to hire a boat. And a guide, to take us to the Isle of the Wise. How will we get there, with nothing to pay?"

Azad said, "We'll get there."

In late afternoon we came to a stream. When we had sated ourselves I asked, "Is there nothing to eat?"

"Sorry, your majesty."

Azad thumped his back against the smooth bark of a poplar, slid down the trunk. He leaned his head back and laid his curved sword on the ground beside him. I stepped across the silver ribbon of the stream, sat down on the grassy bank opposite and pulled off the ruin of my embroidered slippers. The cold water made the blisters on my heels sizzle.

I watched Azad's almond-shaped eyes slip shut. His brow cleared, his lips parted. He looked almost as young as his twenty-four years made him. He had fought and killed four feyatin that day, for my sake. I listened to the play of the stream beside us, the chirring of insects, and studied him as if he were a stranger and not my companion since boyhood. His family's dedication to mine was legendary. So were the titles, treasures and grants my father had bestowed upon Azad and his relations. The royal archive that recorded all this generosity lay in ruins.

Pondering this uneasy thought, I drifted into memory. My mind took me to the moments before disaster arrived, moments of light and anticipation, unfolding in the grandest room of my father's palace like a drama from Lyzantium. I recalled how the heat had prickled my skin beneath my damask coat, how the sun shone fierce and hot into the audience hall. In ordinary circumstances lemon-coloured draperies screened the open portico, but servants had secured them. My father the sultan wanted the Emir of Iznik's arrival—and his imminent humiliation—to be well marked by his court.

Indeed the emir was difficult to miss. Tall and skeletal, Musa Rahoudi strode at the fore of his train as if he led a funeral procession, his spine bowed, his bearing tragic in his plain white robes. His only ornament was a fiery blood ruby, fixed at the centre of his turban. He clutched my father's tribute gift in his bony fingers as if the painted cask were his last hope and not an admission of his recent military defeat.

I don't recall the words exchanged. I remember watching my father from where I lounged on the dais, the hard, private smile he exchanged with my mother. Musa knelt and opened the lacquer box to present my father with his vassal's token. Silk rustled as the assembly leaned forward to see what treasure of Iznik the emir would offer. I strained with the others to peer into the box—

I would not do so again, not now, not with night falling. I trained my eyes on the stars beyond the motionless pine boughs and waited for morning.

It was still dark when Azad shook me awake. A wedge of a moon cast shadows among the tree roots. "I was home in my own bed," I said, breathing the memory of scented silk. "Wrapped in a down coverlet."

My bodyguard made a helpless gesture. I recognised the howling in my ears as the calls of the creatures that hunted me. I struggled to my feet and followed Azad through the trees, the broad shoulders, the curved sword, the calloused hand that gripped it.

"Do they sound closer?" I asked.

Azad picked up the pace. Branches whipped past.

"They are definitely closer," I said.

Azad said, "Run."

Footsteps smacked through the leaf mould beside me, behind me. The underbrush began to shiver.

"Azad! They're all around us!"

"This way."

I followed blindly, ducking and weaving through the foliage. A great howl broke from the wood, very close, joined by others. Like the baying of dogs when they scent their quarry. "Here!" Azad called. "Over here!"

"Wait," I called, struggling for breath. "Don't leave me."

A torch flared in front of us. Half a dozen men stood limned in its light. It was to these men that Azad had been calling, not me. I ran toward the flame, burst from the tree line.

"I am Hadid, son of Umar, Sultan of Atolan," I said in a garbled rush. "Heir to the Thousand Year Throne. I demand refuge and protection."

The young man in front of me stepped back a pace. His eyes were wide beneath a modest turban of dyed cotton. A badge of parrot feathers at his ear announced that he was someone of station. "You're who?"

"Sultan Hadid of Atolan," Azad said at my side. "Your overlord."

The stranger's jaw opened and closed. "I am Sogut son of Ghazi," he said at last. "What's making that awful racket?"

"The feyatin, Lord Sogut," my bodyguard told him.

The young man swallowed. "My father's fortress has walls of stone."

I closed my eyes and took a deep breath. Azad had saved me from the feyatin once again.

. . .

The pergola where we rinsed the sand and sweat from our bodies was built from the same dusty red rock as the rest of Lord Ghazi's fortress. Now and again a white blossom drifted from the laden trellis overhead. Steam rolled from buckets of heated water waiting nearby and towels made a heap next to the folded pile of clothes Ghazi had provided. Azad sat with his back to me on a low wooden stool, knees to elbows, and slapped a foamy scrap of cloth across his neck and shoulders. His movements made the puckered scars dance across his olive-gold skin.

"Keep the soap out of your eyes," I advised him. "It stings. Have they really got nothing better?"

It felt like a dream that I should be standing in this wretched hinterland stronghold at all. I should be greeting the day on my private balcony in Atolan, the morning prayer rising from the countless minarets pricking the rosy sky, the marble tiles smooth against the soles of my feet, spiced coffee cooling on the tray behind me while servants laced my bath with scented oil.

"Is there no one to wait on us?" I said, flinging the wretched soap into a basin. "Where is everyone?"

"They mean to give your majesty privacy," my bodyguard said, vigorously scrubbing his chest with the hand of his uninjured arm.

"Rustic fools. They have no notion of what it means to serve."

Azad turned toward me, foam dripping from his hair. "Not many people do, your majesty."

"You do," I said and looked away. My glance caught the circle of punctured skin decorating Azad's left thigh, a mark the size and texture of a walnut. The tip of a lance had pierced his leg there, one of several failed assassination attempts of which I had been the target. The spilled water at his feet turned the red stone the colour of blood and made the memory vivid.

I drew my gaze from the floor to discover Azad regarding me intently. And why should he not? I stood naked and flawless before him. My wet skin shone slick and golden in the dappled light and flower petals shimmered like stars amid the ebony strands of my hair. Even so, there was nothing lascivious in his gaze. Quite the opposite, in fact. I didn't know what to make of the flat accusation in Azad's stare. Suds trickled slowly down his shoulders as he looked up at me.

"What?" I demanded. "What is it you want from me?"

"Nothing, your majesty," he said and turned back to his bath.

We dried ourselves and dressed in silence. Azad preceded me across the courtyard and into Lord Ghazi's fortress, down an echoing corridor to a vast hall supported with gargantuan white columns. Ghazi waited in the midst of his household retainers and officials, a man of expanding girth, of middle height and years. Upon seeing me, he threw himself full length to the painted tiles and kissed the tip of my borrowed sandal.

"Rise," I said, delighted by this evidence of civilisation. Ghazi's obeisance was almost enough to allow me to forget Azad's insolence. "On your feet and lead me to your table."

Lord Ghazi stayed where he was.

"My house is loyal," our host declared to the tessellated floor, his voice nervous as a bridegroom's. "We've done nothing to offend your majesty, not knowingly, I swear—"

"Right now you offend my groaning belly. I hope you've prepared a feast, my lord."

Ghazi's eyes—round and rimmed with the white of alarm—peeked up at me from beneath the folds of his turban. "The sultan has not come to punish?"

"I've come in desperation," I said. "I'm being tracked by the feyatin, as you well know."

"Forgive me, your majesty. My son Sogut told the wildest tale. I assumed he had mistaken your purpose here—"

"Lord Ghazi. Kindly remove yourself from the tiles."

"An honour, your majesty, an honour!" Our host rose with effort and hovered at my elbow, blustery with nerves. "Sultan Hadid, Pearl of Atolan—all that I have is yours for the taking. Please, sit down and break your fast. And Azad, son of Attar the Invincible. Be welcome. Eat."

Ghazi waved away his retinue and bowed us toward a low table, richly set. I chose the nearest of the striped cushions littering the floor and heaped my plate. Azad waited until I'd taken my first bite and followed suit. I began to feel like myself again, like a man of measure and importance. Like the Heir to the Thousand Year Throne.

A flurry of garish colour and a rustling of veils announced the arrival of Lady Turhan, Ghazi's wife. She knelt at the head of the table and poured coffee into brass cups, darting anxious glances at me the while.

"Speak," I commanded Lord Ghazi around a tartlet stuffed with lamb and a wealth of garlic. "I perceive a thousand questions behind your bearded lips."

"Forgive me, your majesty," said Ghazi. "But what tragedy sees our sultan—may God speed your father to Paradise—afoot in the dark, without retinue or servants to comfort you?" He exchanged a glance with his wife. "How can it be that you travel with only this one man to protect you?"

"You've heard nothing of Musa's rebellion?" I said. "Of the sorcery that opened a door into our world for the Demon Lord?"

Lord Ghazi shook his head. "News from Atolan is overdue, your majesty."

"It won't be coming," I said.

Emir Musa's lacquer box sprang to my mind. I watched in memory as he freed the lid. His words burned in my ears. *The people of Iznik will not be slaves, Sultan of Atolan. Not to you, not to your heirs.* He flung his tribute at my father's feet. A gasp rose from the court at this insult and my mother stood up in outrage, bangles clashing. All went quiet.

My father's hall fell into shadow, as if the sun faltered. We watched in shocked silence as a small flame blossomed in the empty box, which was not empty after all. The blaze died, flared, died again. Without warning a column of fire leaped at my father's face. The sultan screamed—or I did—and Azad seized my collar and dragged me out of reach of the conflagration, down the steps of the dais. I sprawled on the marble floor below the throne and watched the sudden inferno consume all who remained: my father, his favoured courtiers, his viziers and effendi.

My mother.

In a moment a mountainous pile of ash and smoking wood stood where my father's royal chair had been. Azad yanked me to my feet. I remembered the awful contortion of his face as he shouted at me, his words drowned by the panic of the court. I wrenched free of his grip and took a step toward Musa's treachery, toward the charred ruins of the Thousand Year Throne on the platform above me.

I noticed a vague stirring, then a trembling, then a mighty quaking at the heart of the blasted pile. Powdery ash shook and shifted, giving birth to a monster. Muscular limbs struggled free from the smouldering mound and stretched to their full length, black as the void between the stars. Hands glittered with talons at the end of each bulky arm. They reached in unison between the emerging scorched shoulders and plucked forth a horned head. It swivelled toward me. My breath caught in my throat. Eyes the sharp colour of embers, blood rubies, found me. Recognised me.

"Your majesty?"

I cleared my throat and met Lord Ghazi's gaze. "The Lord of the Djinn is in the world and he has recruited a foul army. They are on the march. Looking for me."

"The feyatin," whispered Lady Turhan. "Save us."

Returning to memory, my appetite fled, I recalled how the Emir of Iznik scrambled up the steps of the dais and fell to all fours before the abomination he had summoned, but not in worship. Even trapped in the horror of the moment I recognised his intent. Musa scrambled after his enchanted box, the lid already secured in one hand, his other reaching with long fingers, an incantation on his lips. But he could not capture what he had freed. The Lord of the Djinn leaned toward him and set his talons against the emir's turbaned head. He held them there for a moment, a dark blessing.

I said to Lady Turhan from a distance, "The master of the feyatin can only mock life, not create it. Whomever he touches is consumed by evil purpose, forsaking any loyalty to those he knew and loved. The one affected will spread this evil in like manner. And so the army of the Lord of the Djinn grows." I drew a breath. "I've seen it."

In my memory, Musa staggered upright from the master of the feyatin's touch like a marionette, stiff and awkward. The skin of his face flushed a mottled red, a foul purple, and began to darken. His slippered foot slid from the dais and one of his viziers caught him by instinct. At this contact the advisor's skin bloated and flushed like his master's and his limbs began a spastic jerking.

"How does it happen?" Lady Turhan's cheeks gleamed pale. "Your majesty?"

I saw mottled faces, shuddering limbs, eyes blazing with a white fire—

I swallowed hard and shook my head, a wall of stone to either side of me. "Hatred consumes those the feyatin touch, like a contagion. It makes them hungry for death. But they can be killed in turn. A clean swipe must sever the head from the shoulders. If one touches you, though, you're lost."

I thought of the lost, in their thousands by now.

"They are hunting you alone, your majesty?" Lord Ghazi said. "What will happen if they catch you?"

"They won't," Azad said.

"But you say the emir raised the King of the Djinn to wipe out the sultan and his line," Ghazi insisted. "If the task is accomplished—may God forbid it—will the feyatin disperse? Descend into whatever Hell awaits them?"

Azad scowled. A column of white fire burned in my mind's eye.

"And what of Atolan?" Ghazi said. "What of her army? Who keeps the peace among the lords and emirs?"

"Atolan is overrun," I said.

"The lords must keep their own peace," Azad said, his voice thin as a blade.

"Is there no hope?" wailed Lady Turhan.

"Only one," I said. "The Talisman of Aram." I glanced at Azad. It had been his idea, after all. Theology isn't my strong suit. My time at court had been spent idling with visiting musicians, learning the latest songs so that I could sing them to other men's wives.

"The Talisman of Aram," breathed Lady Turhan. "Of course. Only the holiest of relics can prevail against the lord of demons." She leaned forward, her kohl-lined eyes deep. "You journey to the Isle of the Wise, to petition the Ufasi."

Lord Ghazi nodded sagely. "The saints will restore your majesty to power." He stroked his greying beard and the jewels winked on his fingers. "If you can manage to reach them."

"Oh, but how could this happen?" his wife moaned.

I felt a sudden fierce regret on behalf of Lady Turhan. There she sat in her outdated veils, clothed in provincial notions of courtliness, a busy woman with a duty to her household, servants who depended on her for direction, a husband, a grown son. "Curse Musa's treachery," I hissed. "It's all his fault."

Azad cast me a look I failed to decipher.

• • •

In very little time colourful maps covered the table in the cavernous hall and Ghazi's advisors occupied the cushions around the low board, eager to plot the next stage of my journey.

"No need for you to attend the council, your majesty," Lord Ghazi informed me, the very definition of a solicitous host. "You must rest and recover your strength. And those famous good looks. My servants will massage your limbs and ply your hair with oil. The best grapes in the region grow here on my—on your majesty's lands. You must honour me by tasting our wine. I would very much like to discover your opinion."

"If you insist," I said, hardly wanting to appear rude. "Azad will join me."

I favoured Lord Ghazi by inviting his son to share the day with me as well but Sogut had left on some errand. I soon discovered that Azad had likewise made himself scarce, out scouting the landscape or selecting our horses or some such thing. I felt uneasy with his absence, as if I had lost some vital thing I should never be without, something as close to me as my skin.

My distress dwindled in the hands of Ghazi's servants. My opinion of their quality improved with every cup of the heavy wine I drained. In late afternoon my host ended his meeting and called for a meal. All had been decided.

"Tomorrow I will dispatch messengers, your majesty," he told me as he nibbled an olive. The maps had been whisked away and a splendid repast had been set upon the low board. "All the lords in these lands bow to the sultan. I will call on them to send men. A great host will assemble at my door."

"Excellent," I said. "An honour guard to see me on my way."

"Just so," Ghazi said, nodding and smiling. "Just so."

"Impossible," Azad said, stepping through the archway that led into the hall. A vapour of dust hung about his borrowed cotton shirt as he approached between the white columns. "We leave tomorrow, your majesty."

"The Sultan of Atolan requires an escort," Lord Ghazi protested.

Azad shook his head. "We leave at first light."

"But it's been decided," I said. "We wait for Ghazi to assemble an honour guard."

"We need horses and provisions, not men."

"Nonsense. I am Heir to the Thousand Year Throne and I will travel as befits my station."

"Stealth is wiser, your majesty," Azad said, his eyes flashing. "A large party will attract the feyatin."

"There is safety in numbers," Ghazi assured me. The learned men sitting around the table murmured in assent.

"Yes of course," I said. "If you'd been here, Azad, if you'd attended Lord Ghazi's council, you'd know that. You're being foolish. Besides. I'm tired of running."

"Remember the fire, your majesty? You were tired of the dark—"

"Foolish and offensive. Enough."

Azad's face flushed an ugly shade of red. "Lord Ghazi is—"

"Enough," I said. "You embarrass me. And yourself."

The muscles jumped along Azad's jaw as he stifled his next comment. He bowed stiffly from the waist, turned and strode through the soaring archway.

"Azad!" I called after him. "You dare walk away from me?"

"Your servant has grown too familiar," Ghazi said. "Command it, your majesty, and I shall throw him in my deepest dungeon."

"What? No. That's the last thing I want." Alarm cramped my belly like bad wine as I realised the truth of my words. Azad would leave me at last. Not for an hour or a morning or a day, but forever. I scrambled to my feet and chased after him.

I found my bodyguard in the tower room Ghazi had appointed, shoving his ring-mail shirt into our pack. "What do you think you're doing?" I demanded.

"Someone has to reach the Isle of the Wise. It's clear you won't. Your majesty," he added bitterly.

"Stop that," I said. "Stop packing."

He ignored me and began balling up his bedroll.

"I command you to stop that. I command you to stay."

Azad's shoulders jumped as he tightened the straps over our gear and secured the buckles.

I crossed the room in three hasty strides, spun him about and moved him with force until his back pressed the tapestry hanging against the wall. Our eyes were inches apart. I had one strategy left.

"You want me," I said, low and urgent. "You always have. Since we were boys, training together in the palace yard. Tell me it's not so." Azad stood frozen. "You can have what you want. I give myself to you. But only if you stay."

I attacked him with a savage kiss.

A moment later I lay on the wool carpet, ears ringing, jaw throbbing from the blow Azad had dealt me.

"Don't go," I said dully, flat on my back. "I'll give you anything you want."

Azad looked down at me, chest heaving. "Anything?"

"If you stay with me, I'll rule Atolan again. Jewels, land, titles, anything."

"I don't want those things."

I braced myself on my elbows and looked up at him. "What do you want?"

Azad drew a shaky breath. "I want you to answer a question."

"Ask," I said, sitting up, clutching my stomach to hold in a pain that had nothing to do with the thump I'd received.

"How are you different from the master of the feyatin?"

"What?"

"You, your father, all the sultans of Atolan. How are you different?"

"I don't know what you mean."

Azad stood with his back against the wall, his hands balled into fists. "What do you think it's for, your majesty? Being sultan, I mean."

I looked at him blankly.

"Fancy soap? Rich food? Dancing girls? Is that your answer?"

I shook my head. Azad said nothing for a long moment, head bowed, hair veiling his expression from me. I rose to my feet, sick, sore, and stood in front of him.

He said, "Why do you think the Emir of Iznik rebelled in the first place? Why do the rulers of Atolan go always under guard? Why do you fear your own people? Can you answer me that?"

Cicadas keened from the sugar pines just beyond the tower walls. Azad stared at me, patient as the sky.

"How is the Sultan of Atolan different from the King of the Djinn?"

"I'm not the master of the feyatin," I told him. "My touch isn't death."

Slowly, very slowly, I raised my hands. I wove my fingers through his hair and leaned close. The scent of sage rose from his skin.

"Let go of me," he whispered.

"I'm not a monster," I breathed. "Let me prove it to you."

My lips moved over his slack mouth and the stubble of his beard scraped my bruised chin. His chest felt hard where mine was hard, his body tense and unyielding. A sense almost of falling took hold of me. What I did was forbidden, regardless of rank or title. I didn't care enough to stop.

"My touch isn't death," I said again and slid my hands under the smooth cotton of his shirt. My fingers found the curve of his spine, the rigid plane of his back, his shoulders. I ran my palms over the flare of muscle at his breast and down to frame the cage of his ribs, the tight skin of his belly. Azad's breath began to stir the hair at my neck, coming quick and vital. My touch could do more than take. My hands could give as well. I proved it to him, to myself.

Azad abruptly took possession of me. His arms, even the bad one, clamped me tight to his labouring chest as he returned my kiss with a vengeance. He swung me round so that it was I who fetched up against the wall, I who felt his hand knotting in my hair. His mouth pressed mine as if he would devour me and his broad body struggled along the length of mine.

I was astonished to discover Azad had a talent for kissing. So many do not. With whom had he been practising? Whoever it was proved an excellent tutor. I concentrated on that delicious sensation and the other things—that this was my bodyguard Azad, that I was afraid, that what I did was most vehemently against all the laws of God and men—all this fell away. Desire began to take hold of me. The days of running, of unspeakable horror, faded into the distance. My hands tightened on Azad's shoulders. My mouth worked against his. What I felt now was need. Clutched together, we made our way to the mountainous bed.

"You'll have to show me what to do," I managed to say, sounding like the most pathetic of virgins, and he did.

• • •

Dawn came as a pale wash, gilding the edges of the furniture. Azad stirred, lifted a hand to his face, stopped with a wince and came fully awake. He rolled onto his back and cradled his arm across his bare chest, rubbing it absently as he gazed toward the ceiling.

"Azad?"

He flowed from the bedclothes and plunged into the limbering exercises of the *ak keme*, the ancient martial discipline of the Memluks. I got up and scrubbed my face at the washbasin. My eyes burned. I had spent the night staring into the dark, thinking.

Azad didn't look at me. I dried my hands on a cloth and said, "You're leaving, aren't you? What's happened between us changes nothing."

My bodyguard moved in a graceful gyration that showed me his back.

"Listen," I said. "I'm going to surrender myself to the feyatin."

Azad stopped short in the middle of his pose and turned to face me.

"You asked me what it means to be Sultan of Atolan," I said. "That's my answer."

"You would do that? Give up your life?"

"Yes," I said, staring steadily into his eyes. I was well versed at telling lies.

"Why?" he said, clearly suspicious.

"You heard what Ghazi said. There's a chance it will end this horror."

"There's a chance it won't."

"I know."

"Then why?"

"Because it's what you would do," I said. "It's why you follow me and defend me and fight for me. It's not for some reward, you said so yourself. And I know better than to think you do it for me, for Hadid son of Umar. Desire's not the same as love, is it? So why stay? Why not abandon me at first opportunity?"

Azad regarded me keenly, on the verge of belief.

"Because it isn't me you serve at all," I said. "You serve your idea of what's right. And in following your own honour, you serve the people of Atolan."

My bodyguard said nothing. He appeared to be holding his breath.

"So that's my answer. I'll give myself to the feyatin."

Azad stepped close and set his good hand on my shoulder. "Don't do it, your majesty."

"No?" I said. "I have it wrong then."

"Not wrong. Not wrong at all. For the first time, maybe." Azad dropped his hand and stood regarding me in silence.

"What should I do, then? If not surrender to the King of the Djinn?"

"What does your conscience tell you?"

"My conscience?"

"Your heart, then."

"I want to come with you," I said. "If you'll let me."

"Let you, your majesty? It's not my place to—"

"Don't pretend to be my servant now," I said. "Can I come or not?"

I watched my bodyguard's eyes grow bright.

"Yes," Azad said. He shook his head and cleared his throat. "It's a long way to Salida, your majesty. There's time for breakfast before we leave."

He turned before I could answer. I stepped wordlessly after him. My little charade had worked and I would have my way. Where then was my sense of triumph? Instead I felt sick and strange and soiled by the pretence.

Lady Turhan met us in the hall. She gestured to the low table groaning with dishes. The muffled figure of Lord Ghazi sat at one end of it.

"Please excuse my husband, majesty. He's feeling poorly. Sit no closer than you must, though I'm sure it's nothing."

Azad guided me to a spot a safe length from Ghazi, who had wrapped himself in blankets and dabbed his throat with a cloth. His face was red, and swollen. Azad and I exchanged a glance. "It's nothing, I assure you," Ghazi insisted, waving the loose end of his turban in my direction. "Please. Eat."

Azad and I dropped to the cushions and helped ourselves. Our host sputtered and hacked at the end of the table. I looked up from my plate, looked around at the gauzy draperies, the sunlit hall.

"Your son, lady," I said. "Where's Sogut?"

Turhan's eyes widened before she looked away. "You are kind to inquire, your majesty. I'm afraid he's abed. He met with . . . an accident. He took some of the boys into the wood yesterday, to see for himself what threat followed you." Azad sat bolt upright. Ghazi coughed in the distance. "He came back late, disturbed some animal in the dark. A mongoose perhaps. It bit him, on the hand—"

Azad's cushion careened across the floor as he scrambled to his feet. He drew his curved sword in an easy, deadly motion. "We're leaving, your majesty. Now."

"What about breakf—" The word froze on my lips at what came next: a long, low howl rising from some distant cranny of the fortress. In answer Ghazi staggered upright, jaws slavering, eyes shimmering the glossy white of the feyatin. The howl came again.

"God is great! What is that?" demanded Lady Turhan.

"It's your son," Azad said. "That was no mongoose." He backed away from Ghazi, herding me along with his shoulder. "The stairs," he told me.

Lady Turhan stood rooted in shock, staring as her husband staggered toward her.

"Run, lady," I shouted, but his groping hands reached and clutched her to his chest, smothering her, infecting her. While she struggled he threw back his distorted face and let loose a howl, long and low, that sent ice shooting through my veins. His son answered him. So did a chorus from the pines outside.

Azad whirled and chased me to the stairwell. We took the stairs three at a time, our footfalls battering our eardrums. I ran past an open doorway and checked when Azad shouted for me to stop.

Doubling back I found him stalking across a shadowy tower room, quite like the one we'd shared. He flung his sword onto a settee and stepped to a shuttered window. I could hear shuffling footsteps on the stairs, pursuit from both below (Lord Ghazi) and above (his son, no doubt, and whomever of the servants the young man had infected).

"We're trapped," I cried.

Azad ignored me, working the latch on the shutter one-handed until it clattered open. He leaned over the sill, nodded, and walked briskly past me to kick the door closed.

"Calm down, your majesty. Help me move this." In a matter of moments a chest of drawers and a trunk blocked the doorway.

"Now what?" I panted. In answer, Azad took hold of my sleeve and shoved me toward the window, onto the sill and over it. I clung to the frame—my feet dangling in empty air—and stared at him in bewilderment.

He raised his eyebrows expectantly. "Climb down the tower. Use the ivy."

"Ivy?" I peered past my dangling toes. Vines fanned across the red stone.

"Climb down. Go, your majesty."

"Right."

The toes of my sandals found purchase in the thick, green tangle. Hand over hand and the hardy vines held my weight. The sound of bodies crashing against the chamber door grew fainter. Almost halfway to the ground. I glanced up to gauge Azad's progress. There was no one above me. "Azad!"

He appeared immediately in the tower window, sword in hand, the other peeking from his sling.

"What are you doing? Come down."

I was near enough to see the expression on his face. A wistful smile, a trifle condescending. He raised his sling into full view. "Can't. But I can still swing this sword, your majesty. I'll buy you some time."

"Don't be ridiculous," I snarled. "Get down here." When he shook his head I began climbing up again, hot with fury. But my foot slipped on the waxy green leaves and I slid a long way down before I could stop my fall. "Damn it!" I yelled at him, conscious that the noise would attract the feyatin. "Climb down! Now! I command you. As your sultan I command you!"

Azad watched me from the window. There was a long pause.

"Southwest," Azad called down to me at last. "Remember that. The Port of Salida. Find passage to the isle. The Ufasi will help you." He turned away, hair flying, to monitor the strength of the door.

"No." I felt the first stirrings of hysteria. "We go together."

Azad leaned over the sill and smiled down at me. "Sorry, your majesty."

The blade of his curved sword flashed in the sunlight. All at once I gripped an unravelling skein. Azad had cut the vine.

• • •

For a long time after that I kept counsel with the dark, with despair. Nights were the worst. Nights I burrowed in the muck of some deserted canal, or sat hunched in the bole of a tree, shivering while the howls of the feyatin savaged the hillsides. Fear gripped my chest. Hunger squeezed my belly. I sat in the dark and wept for Azad.

But dawn followed dusk. Each morning the glorious rays of the sun broke across the vast plateau stretching before me and transformed the rocks and grasses to silver. Each morning, on the strength of Azad's memory alone, I rose from whatever tenuous shelter I had made to withstand the darkness. On rising I set one foot in front of the other, my face turned south and west. The feyatin lost ground behind me. One day the wind smelled of salt.

Soon the plain sheered away to my right and gave way to the pounding surf. I scrambled down basalt cliffs to rob the nests of the seabirds that made their home in the crags. Picking my way southward along the coast, I plucked oysters from their beds, swallowing them whole with brine for sauce. A fisherman broiling his lunch on a wide sandy beach of white sand shared his meal with me and showed me the road to the harbour city of Salida. Footsore, unkempt and rail thin, I reached the final port before the Isle of the Wise.

Stories can't do Salida justice. Here the holy men strip themselves naked and smear their bodies with ash. You hear their chanting from every corner, where they hover in midair, heads thrown back in ecstasy. The beasts of the field run amok in the narrow streets, their hides and horns decorated with paint, garlands girding their necks, and they speak with human voices. Whenever I looked up, the gilded spires of the maharaja's palace rose above the tidy shops and tea houses and many-storied dwellings of the inhabitants.

A grand roadway of white marble led up to the palace. I trudged toward the royal residence, perceiving the domed roof and intricate windows and potted palms with a pang of sorrow for Atolan. Azad's trust pricked me forward, propelled me up the roadway toward a stately archway spanned by an iron gate and warded by two armed soldiers. They came forward as I climbed the steps to where they stood.

"I am Hadid son of Umar, Sultan of Atolan," I said, my voice creaking with disuse. "I bring grave and terrible news to your master. Let me pass."

I took a step forward and the soldiers clashed their spears together, barring the way. I stared up into their impassive faces, the calm certainty of duty that lived in their eyes.

"I knew a man like you," I said. "If he were here he'd speak for me."

The eyes did not waver. Only the plumes on the soldiers' helms waved in the flower-scented breeze. A crowd began to gather in the streets below to watch the ragged foreigner confront the palace guards.

The soldier on my right said, "Beggars may petition at the temple for a meal and shelter for the night. By the maharaja's grace, none are turned away."

"I'm not a beggar," I told him, knowing it for a lie. I had come to beg a ship from the raj.

"Nonetheless," said the man to my left. "You will not pass these gates."

I took another step forward. Hands seized me and flung me down the steps. I rolled to a stop at the feet of the people who stood watching.

"Fool," someone said from the crowd. "They could have run you through. And rightfully so."

I picked myself up and brushed the dust from my already filthy clothes. A new rip appeared in my sleeve at the elbow. The people of Salida parted to let me pass, shaking their heads. I limped over to a fountain, sat on the rim and put my head in my hands.

"What do you seek in the palace?" said a strange deep voice, close to my ear.

I looked up to meet the gaze of a young white bullock. Paint striped his horns with red and blue and green and a string of marigolds looped his sturdy neck.

"A favour from the maharaja," I said, too defeated to dissemble.

The bullock gazed at me with his great liquid eyes.

"This favour," he said at last. "Is it for you or on behalf of another?"

"On behalf of others," I said.

"Follow me."

"Where?" I said and staggered to my feet.

"Through the palace gate. By the custom of this land, none here may bar entrance to me or my kind."

I made haste to step to the side of the marvellous beast and lay my hand on his shoulder. The heavy muscles slid beneath the pale hide as we climbed the stairs to the palace. The plumed men threw the gate wide to let us pass, then bowed deeply to the bullock as we crossed beneath the arch and onto the royal grounds. Me, they ignored.

My guide led the way through a rose garden to the doors of the palace proper. These too were opened for us. We stepped into a majestic hall of gold and alabaster. The bullock's hooves rang against the jet tiles tessellating the vast floor. Far ahead a cluster of men and women wrapped in silk and bedecked with jewels waited upon a figure seated upon a shining throne.

"There before you sits the Maharaja of Salida," the bullock told me. "Step forward."

"Will you come?"

"It is not I who has business with his majesty."

I adjusted the sleeve of my torn shirt and smoothed the dusty coils of my hair. I didn't like to think about the tangled horror that sprouted from my chin. Gathering my resolve, I straightened my spine and strode the length of the columned hall. The voices of the courtiers ebbed as I drew near.

"Your majesty," I said, stopping a respectful distance from the slender, nut-brown young man who sat upon the golden throne. "Forgive this intrusion. I bring news from far away, urgent news."

A white-beard standing at the raj's shoulder made an exclamation of alarm. "Who dares approach the Maharaja of Salida in such a manner?" he asked, rushing forward. "On your knees, scoundrel, and pay homage to our lord."

"Peace, Mustafa," the maharaja said, rising to his feet. "One king does not bow to another." He swept past the older man to stand before me, adjusting the folds of ivory silk slipping down his shoulder. "You will forgive my advisor. He did not recognise you."

"How is it that you do?"

The young man smiled, a flash of white in his rich brown skin. "The burden of your rule is obvious to me. To anyone who cares to look beyond grime and tattered clothing." He laid a hand on my shoulder. "I can see that you have a long tale to tell. Let my servants bathe you and robe you, and when you have sated yourself at my table we will hear what news you bring."

"Your majesty is gracious," I said, struggling against the image that had lodged itself in my mind, a vision of hot water streaming from silver ewers. "But I cannot rest until I have asked my boon and you have granted it."

The maharaja frowned. "You had best explain."

A servant brought a deep cushion for me to sit upon, and another for the ruler of Salida. I told him the whole tale and never faltered. When I came to Azad's sacrifice in Lord Ghazi's tower room my eyes swam and overflowed but I scraped my cheeks with the back of my hand and finished my narration.

"And that is why," I said at last, hoarse from talking, "I must beg you for a ship to convey me to the Isle of the Wise."

"Where you will seek the Ufasi."

"Yes."

"And convince them to deliver to you the Sceptre of Aram."

"Yes."

"And then you will return to Atolan and challenge the King of the Djinn for the Thousand Year Throne."

"Yes," I said. "Definitely yes."

Mustafa, the raj's advisor, came forward to kneel beside his master. "Your majesty," he said. "Your loyal advisor understands your susceptibility to compassion. But the Sultan of Atolan asks too much. To plunder the royal fleet for so doubtful an enterprise . . . I simply cannot condone the expense."

The raj crossed his arms over his chest and gazed up at the lofty ceiling, considering. When he looked down again and met my gaze he said, "Why?"

"Why?"

"Why must you fulfil this quest? Does the tedium of rule appeal to you so much? Let me extend another option. Stay here in comfort as my guest. The lands of my realm are immune to evil and all are safe who dwell here. Spend your days at your leisure. There are many pleasures to be enjoyed at the maharaja's court. Surely that is better than the danger ahead, even if you were to reach the Ufasi and convince them of your need."

I tried not to consider the offer and failed. The days ahead stretched thin with hardship and misery and the chance of defeat. Azad had been wrong to place his trust in me. I thought of his face peering down the tower at me, the flash of his blade as he cut me free.

After a long moment I said, "There's a debt I owe to the people of Atolan, your majesty. A debt that's a thousand years old. Help me or not, I will repay it."

The raj nodded gravely. "I will help you," he said. "You will have your ship. And a crew to sail her and whatever other assistance you may require."

I closed my eyes and breathed deeply. "Thank you, your majesty."

The raj rose to his feet and stood looking down at me. "Should you defeat the King of the Djinn, the feyatin will threaten Atolan no longer. But those whose bodies were used for this foul army are likely lost. You understand this?"

"Yes," I said.

The raj extended his hand. "Azad son of Attar will not be restored to you."

"The possibility hadn't even occurred to me," I said, reaching for his outstretched fingers. "I wouldn't have dared to hope."

"There is always hope," the maharaja said and raised me to my feet.

Afterword

Some people count sheep. I spend a pretty intense period of time watching made-up movies in my head before I drop off to sleep. On this occasion, a self-centred king and his ethical bodyguard wandered onto the screen in my mind's eye. According to my semi-subconscious stage directions, the two young men were alone in the tower room of an isolated fortress, in dire straits. Their relationship was complicated by the fact that the servant was physically attracted to his master.

On subsequent nights I put the story together by asking myself: How did they get in that room? Where is that fortress? Where were they before they got there, and Where are they headed and why? The fact that I was reading a history of the Ottoman Empire shaped my answers to some of these questions. Once I got the situation mostly figured out, I wrote a draft and asked some generous people to read it and give me feedback. I got some fantastic advice and made a number of revisions, and Hadid and Azad's story is ready to be told at last.

Street Dancer

Pia Van Ravestein

Thoren looked up from his sweaty hands and tracked the arc of silver smoke left by a megajet. The smell of the bazaar—ten storeys below—wafted up: frying game-birds, spices, teas and breads, and behind it the honey-dark smell of spoiled meats and rotted fruits dropped and stomped into the ground. It was not yet two in the afternoon and already the merchants were busy cooking up for the night's revels. Voices rehearsed pure and impure notes, instruments were tuned, an impromptu solo on the tabla entwined lovingly with the mechanical clicks of old-world camels with their rusted, splayed hooves and humps filled with treasures: gold, silks, sweet, fresh water.

Underneath Thoren's elbows was the grit of the rough-hewn stone sill. Lacquered but never polished, it prickled at his skin. This high up, he had a clear view to the horizon.

From just outside the walls, came the click-click-click-whirr of the old-world mechanical cat. He wasn't much of a prize. A low-grade facsimile of the felines they used to have before the virus got to them, so long ago the legends say the original cats never had ears that long. His parts grated and one of his eyes no longer glowed. He'd turned up, and Jeremiah had refused to make him leave or worse, take his power source from him. Jeremiah said that the creature "livened up the place". Thoren had drawn the line at giving the thing a name.

"My gears, my gears, they hurt today," the cat whined in its programmed accent, hard on the 'r' and faintly masculine.

"Repairers don't work for free," Thoren said.

"I'll catch a bird. I'll catch a bird, Thoren. Then you'll fix me," the cat said, and paused, tilting his head.

Thoren couldn't even summon a reply. This was a conversation they'd been having for years. He wondered if the electric impulses in the cat's power source would ever adapt to their meagre income. For a stray cat, he was pretty demanding.

"I'll catch a bird . . . " the cat said again, and turned away, jerking his segmented tail from side to side.

There was a yawn to his right, and Thoren turned to see Jeremiah stretch and rub at bleary eyes.

"Is it nearly festival?" His sleepy voice soothed the room, despite the babble of shouts heard from below.

"Not for another few hours," Thoren said.

"Is it nearly sunset?"

"The sun's not even low in the sky." He looked back at the tan sun and lifted his elbows off the stone. As he made his way to the bed, he picked his way over costumes and clothing, sequins and transparent scarves that oozed vibrant colour even in the gloom of the apartment.

"How are you feeling?"

"M'tired." Despite fourteen hours of sleep, there was a lax scratchiness to Jeremiah's voice. Thoren was finding it different to tell the difference now between exhaustion and pain, sure that Jeremiah's wound hurt him constantly.

"Should you even go to the festival?"

"I'm the market's greatest dancer. Why would they come to the night markets at all, if I'm not there?" Jeremiah's voice, deceptively soft, could turn catty the moment Thoren tried to convince his partner to stay. But he had to try.

"You're ill."

"Just a cut."

"You're sleeping all the time."

"Like a vampire. A djinni." He chuckled and rolled over, brown eyes boring into Thoren's. If he flared his nostrils, there was a smell.

"I'm poisoned aren't I? They'll take my leg off . . . "

"Yes, love, they likely will," Thoren said.

"I'd rather die."

Thoren exhaled and felt his stomach contract.

"Yes, love, I know."

"So I'll die, then?"

"Whatever you wish."

There was a murmur of approval and Jeremiah turned away. Soon heavy breathing filled the air and Thoren went to stand back at the arched window. Frustration was a pull like indigestion in his chest. They couldn't afford the milky-chalk medicine to stop his reflux, either. A short while later the cat returned without a bird and stared at him, while he stared at the sun. Click-click-click-whirr.

• • •

Later that evening, Thoren watched his partner dance while he sipped cinnamon tea in the shadows. The cry of wolves in the background haunted him, but they were only those who wanted Jeremiah, to take that curling figure home. They watched as he swayed and offered a portmanteau of ritual steps and seductive shimmies, undulating his hips in figure eights, removing veil after silk veil before letting them flutter to the ground as though they were worthless. Thoren smirked to himself; take off that final gauzy veil and what was left? Once—what seemed years ago now—a beguiling nudity and an educated, privileged wit. Once, Thoren had considered himself humbled that Jeremiah had chosen him, because he was nothing by comparison and they'd all known it. Now all they would see was the heavy black mark on their dancer's left calf, a wound left by jagged metal. The oozing smell of putrefaction.

But his partner didn't live for those who howled and howled; his partner lived only for the dance.

So he danced.

Instead of the consecutive hours of dancing Jeremiah was famed for, he only managed a meagre two before he fainted.

• • •

As the terracotta brown of dawn signalled the coming sun, Thoren supported Jeremiah's weight. A megajet zoomed overhead and left its silver trail in the sky. Thoren bit the inside of his lip. He tasted blood, swallowed it down, hoped the wound would close again soon. His partner was light: he had lost too much weight.

This was the first evening that Jeremiah couldn't simply dance through the pain. The memory of his collapse on stage, the surrounding cries of shock, haunted him; though it had only happened an hour ago, it seared into his brain. Jeremiah floor-bound, once gracile, now graceless, the silks of his costume garish and gauche. Thoren had hated running out from his darkened corner onto the stage, into the spotlight. Those forced lights with their yellow glare made a mockery of his haggard, thick-set features. Awkwardly, he'd lifted a limp Jeremiah and they had left without pay.

"Thoren . . . " Jeremiah's voice was sleepy again, it lurched towards unconsciousness.

"Yes, love?"

"I don't understand how I can feel no pain when I dance, but now . . . " he moaned into silence.

"Because dancing is your only love," Thoren said. He swallowed the bitterness of that statement.

"Thoren, you know I love you."

"But you never—"

"Just . . . just take me home. It's time to go home now."

They passed a loud ensemble of cheerful drummers. Five minutes later, invisible cymbals still clashed in his ears. His head rang like a gong. He kept his mouth closed, tasting blood, and dragged the limp Jeremiah up ten storeys home again.

• • •

He had nothing to take with him to the Magus, and the Magus knew it. He glowered over his heavy mahogany desk, pursed lips and steepled knotted, clever fingers while vials of sparkling liquid glittered around him. Thoren wondered if one of them, any of them would help Jeremiah. He could just steal one, and when they used the Punishing Knife to sever his jugular it wouldn't matter, because Jeremiah would be saved, and Jeremiah only loved the dance anyway.

"I'll do anything." He heard his voice and wanted to scrape out his own throat for sounding so desperate.

"Jeremiah is a rich man, he could—"

Thoren laughed and laughed. The Magus' brow narrowed in distaste, and then finally he frowned in disgust. Thoren found that he didn't care anymore, and the truth spilled upwards and out of him.

"How do you think he got so injured in the first place? He takes drugs. Anything at all. The more expensive, the better. But I'll protect him better if you help. It was an accident. He doesn't deserve to die for an accident. I'm good with my hands, I can—"

"No," the Magus said. "I don't want you. You're not even a Repairer."

Thoren had begged and threatened and then finally seized two of the vials and turned to sprint away, but it was stupid, because he had pitted himself against a Magus. It only took a few jolting bolts of magic for him to drop them and try and hold himself together while his body tried to shake itself to pieces.

The Magus had touched him with a stern finger under his chin, lifted his bowed head. Thoren couldn't tell what the man was thinking, sure he was hallucinating the softness in his eyes.

"You'll be nothing, when he dies," the Magus said, his voice brittle, and then made his new-world guards escort him out.

• • •

The cat was curled on the bed, powered down in hibernation, whirring softly. Broken eyelids hung lopsided over its eyes, giving it a demented appearance in sleep.

"'Miah, what happens when you die?" Thoren hated his weak voice.

"To me?"

"To me," Thoren whispered from a chair covered in costumes. Beads dug into his thighs. The cruel weight in his stomach tasted entirely of acid. The wretched smell was so pervasive now, it was like they'd dragged a carcass home.

"To you," Jeremiah purred softly and coughed. "Well, you go on. The market and my patrons, however, will be devastated."

Thoren rested his chin on his naked leg and his eyes travelled sideways to the umber moon. It was dim, but there nonetheless. Below, the shrieks and booms of the festival drifted in the harsh night winds. No patrons had offered to pay for what would now be an expensive healing. Only a Magus could cure the blood poisoning. Thoren felt he was drifting between worlds. He knew no one else in this town in a meaningful way. He had no family.

"Does it hurt, Jeremiah?"

"Only while I'm still breathing," Jeremiah said, and Thoren could hear the pained smile in his partner's voice.

"What should I do when you die?"

"Mope, I suppose."

"Jeremiah," Thoren said, swallowing down bile.

"I have something for you, but it's a Death Present. I can't give it to you now. So you'll have that, at least," Jeremiah said, his voice weak. "It's so pretty," he added.

"Because I've always looked so good in silk," Thoren mumbled.

"To me," Jeremiah said, and Thoren could almost believe him, if the man hadn't refused to see a healer or a Magus in favour of the drugs and the dance. If he hadn't made his choice and danced himself to death.

"It's in the third drawer down," Jeremiah gasped. Thoren smiled ruefully, that was where all the special camisoles were kept, the fragile ones. It made sense that Jeremiah would leave him the clothing that marked his most momentous performances.

The cat clicked and buzzed as it awoke from hibernation mode. It stood slowly, sensitive to its own rusts and weaknesses. It attempted to stretch and then aborted the movement and tottered up to Thoren.

"I hurt. I need help, Thoren," it whined. "My gears, there's something wrong with my gears. I tried to get you a bird. You said. You said you'd get me a Repairer."

Thoren wanted to say something, to say that he had never said he would get that damned cat a Repairer, but instead he just rested his forehead on his knees and took deep breaths. One after the other. Like he was suffocating.

"'Thoren can you get me . . . get me some fruit?" Jeremiah now, voice so thin.

"What?"

"I have a craving."

Thoren shifted and placed both of his feet on the floor. He looked hard at the still figure in the dimness. He could hear Jeremiah's harsh breathing, wheezing. Tiredness licked at Thoren, coated him with a sticky fatigue. He had not slept for two nights.

"Can I just lie next to you instead?"

He waited, breathless; Jeremiah had forbidden him from sleeping in the same bed for three nights, because he had violent dreams. Thoren still bore furrows across his stomach where his partner had flailed spasmodically, sharp manicured fingernails burrowing trenches into his skin. Thoren had bled and tried to hide the injury, but eventually Jeremiah noticed the pain and found the cause.

Thoren had not been allowed near Jeremiah since.

But he hoped. He hoped he might be allowed. Jeremiah seemed too weak to flail and kick and fight him in his sleep, now.

No answer came.

Wrapped tight in fear, Thoren crept closer to Jeremiah. His eyelids had settled peacefully against a face that glowed with sweat. His brown lips were cracked and red from ochres and blood. His cheeks were heavily stained with the rouge that the dancers of higher status had to wear. Jeremiah was sleeping.

Thoren reached a shaking hand out to touch his partner's forehead. He stopped before he made contact. Even there, hovering a small distance above skin, he could feel the heat radiating. The reality of death broiling in his partner's blood.

Thoren swallowed and his hand jerked into a tight fist. Jeremiah's breath rose and fell in uneven jags, the sickly scent of pus drifted from somewhere beneath the filthy blankets. In the drawer by his ankle lay a Death Present. Still, Thoren refused to think about how final it all was.

He turned and sifted through the many glimmering colours of the costumes on the floor to find his own dusky brown clothing. He pulled it on in the humid darkness and then reached into his trouser pocket to see what was there. He felt small, almost worthless coins.

He nodded, an absent movement.

It was time to buy some fruit.

• • •

Thoren returned some time near dawn, bearing a basket of unripe bananas and one ripe plum from the stallholder who had said We missed him last night, hope to see him soon! The dark sky was giving way to a salmon pink pre-dawn light. The moon had set. Soon the sun would take its lonely place, a dull brown disc in this region that had once—according to the stories—been brightly coloured.

He climbed each step slowly. At the fifth floor he took the plum from the basket and bit into it, purple skin breaking, a tangy, sweet flavour filling his mouth. He savoured it, sucked at the juices to stop them from running down his chin, and continued the rest of the climb slowly.

He passed through the door and the cat skulked in by his ankles, keeping its one yellow eye firmly forward, its leather ears unhappily back. Thoren watched it stalk over to the corner and sit on awkward haunches. He continued across the soft tread of discarded clothing to the bed. He took a few deep, shuddering breaths, the smell of decay a constant thickness in the back of his throat. He stared down at the still body covered in blankets. A few minutes passed before he placed the basket down gently where he used to be allowed to sleep.

Without looking at the figure, he moved to the chest of drawers and opened the third one down, and reverently drew out each precious camisole and thin costume and placed them one on top of the other on a bare patch of floor near a bowl of congealed cream. When he reached the simple black purse, he paused. Air stuttered out of his lungs.

It was larger than his hand, and when he tested it, it was surprisingly heavy.

"No," he said.

He opened it and looked at the contents. He saw only gold. For a moment he thought he could smell it; rich and mellifluous. Only gold coins, more valuable than silver, which was more valuable than copper, which was more valuable than iron. More than enough to buy and furnish his own apartment, to live richly in a good district.

Certainly enough for a Magus to perform an impossible healing. Which Jeremiah would have known.

"No," he said again, voice breaking.

He clutched the purse in his left hand and stood, aware of the weight pulling at his arm. He turned to stare at Jeremiah's peaceful face. He did not bother to check whether the chest was still rising and falling. He could hear nothing. No wheeze, no rasp of lungs. The dancer's chest was already still. Thoren swallowed and looked at the fruit basket on the bed. The colours were muted in the ambivalent twilight of almost-morning.

He looked his fill of Jeremiah until his face and neck were itchy with dried salt. The mechanical cat approached him, cocked his head, stared.

"My gears, Thoren. My gears need a look. Will you look?"

He turned to look at the cat that had diligently—if intermittently—brought them pigeons for two years now, all in exchange for the same repetitive conversation.

"We'll . . . " Thoren began, and then took a deep breath, "I mean, I'll . . . I'll get you a Repairer. I'll even give you a name, if you like."

"Oh, please," the cat made a rickety, clattering noise, and Thoren realised it was his crude attempt at a purr.

"You can be a Jeremiah too, if you like. You'll be as good as new."

"But there's no money, Thoren, there's no money."

"Come on," Thoren said, rubbing at his eyes before they could produce tears. "Come with me and we'll get you a Repairer."

With his eyes turned determinedly forward he walked silently through the door, away from the arched window showing streaked silver trails from the megajets, and the first glimmer of the dusky sun. He half-stumbled, half-walked down the stone stairwell, a clickety black cat haunting his footsteps, the black purse a burden in his pocket.

Afterword

"Street Dancer" is a prequel to the character of Thoren, who is part of an ensemble cast I'm exploring in a series of steampunk novels in a semi-arid world which still relies heavily on spice trails and barter, alongside magic and Magi. The core meaning for 'djinn' translates to that which is hidden from sight. I decided to explore characters who would hide things from each other in their relationship, as many people do, and what consequences that might have for both of them.

I wanted to occupy a world where bellydancers and market dancers were as often male as female. Where it is normal for men to wear colourful silks and kohl, while moving masterfully to the beat of the tabla. "Street Dancer" is set in a magical world, but it deals with a normal relationship where each partner is trying to deal with their conflicts as best as they can. It remains one of my favourite themes to examine in writing; bringing the mundane into the magical, thereby making the magical accessible and the mundane fantastic. And of course, who isn't a fan of a talking mechanical cat?

Harmony Thicket and the Persian Shoes

Havva Murat

Harmony Thicket loved shoe shopping.

Her abundant curves and voluptuous, hourglass figure (some reckoned it more like a tumbler) barred her entrance to the hip and flashy couture establishments of Melbourne's upmarket shopping precincts, but her dainty, size six, regularly pedicured and fuchsia-toenail-painted feet were her inner fashionista's saving grace.

By renaissance standards Harmony was a veritable goddess—or so she reminded herself as she caught a glimpse of her silhouette in a shop window and straightened her back.

It was a shame she couldn't yet find a man who could appreciate this theory.

"Oh well, at least my Mary Janes look great!" she told her reflection as she shook out her strawberry blonde curls and kept moving.

There was only one thing that Harmony loved more than general shoe shopping and that was shopping for *vintage* shoes. The sight of them made her pulse thump and so it was that she found herself trudging down High Street towards her favourite vintage store, *Yesterday's Treasure,* early one Saturday morning, braving the Melbourne fog to get her shoe-fetish fix. The promise of digging up a glorious pair of vintage pumps or peep toes and giving them a new lease on life buoyed her spirits like nothing else. She almost didn't mind that the vintage coats and precious lace dresses wouldn't stretch to encompass her abundant bosom.

She could trust in the shoes.

Her heart pitter-pattered as the shop came into view, its lace drapes and embellished scroll-work on the front window drawing her in, whispering fulfilment. But today, there was a new sign taped to the mint-green front door.

UNDER NEW MANAGEMENT

Harmony's shoulders sank as she read the sign. *That's weird; Jillian never mentioned she was leaving* . . . Jillian had become a great ally in Harmony's shopping crusade over the last two years, always digging up interesting and hard-to-find vintage shoes for her.

Whatever would Harmony do now she was gone?

And, as if in answer to her question, the front door to the shop swung inwards and the scent of cardamom and jasmine wafted out to tickle her nose.

Harmony sneezed like a cat. Once, and then again, digging through her huge leather handbag for one of her cambric handkerchiefs. The smell emanating from the shop wasn't unpleasant, but it was very different from its usual worn leather and musty odour.

"It is good luck to sneeze." A thickly accented voice made Harmony look up in surprise.

"What?" She jumped, dropping her bag.

The woman stood in the doorway, her kohl-rimmed, almond-shaped eyes sweeping over Harmony as she stooped to pick up her bag, shoving her wallet and perfume bottle back inside.

"It gives others the opportunity to bless you. Would you like to be blessed?"

"I guess so . . . " Harmony shrank further backwards, feeling completely naked under that frank, skin-penetrating stare.

"Then, come inside . . . " The woman's lips took on peculiar smile as she stepped aside, gesturing for Harmony to enter. Scheherazade had nothing on this enigmatic goddess.

Harmony straightened her skirt and blouse, and, sucking in her stomach, stepped past the mysterious woman who was a great deal taller and much slimmer. Even the woman's choice of a loosely fitted, embroidered, silk shift couldn't hide her lovely form.

"You are wondering where Jillian has gone? Yes?" The woman turned to Harmony, leaning on the counter behind her.

"Well, yeah. She didn't tell me she was leaving and I come here all the time . . . " Harmony looked around the familiar racks and shelves stuffed full of vintage coats, hats, dresses, shoes, wallets and frippery. The shop seemed darker, almost sinister, without Jillian's sunny face.

"And you do not feel comfortable with me in her place?"

"Am I that transparent?" Harmony had the feeling it was better to be straight up with this exotic wisp of a woman.

"You are honest—it's a rare quality these days." The woman's ruby lips split into a smile that revealed beautiful white teeth.

"Well, I'm yet to meet a man who displays the quality, so you must be right."

"So, finding good men is a universal problem, then?" The woman smiled again before holding out her tanned hand with its long, tapered fingers. "I am Houri. I met Jillian while she was travelling through Iran last year. She visited my antiques store in Esfahan."

Harmony took the long fingers in her much shorter ones and pressed them. "Harmony Thicket." She had no exotic story to add to her name so she simply shut her mouth and deliberately glanced away. The woman was mesmerising; it almost hurt to look at her.

"Ah, so *you* are Harmony?" The smile travelled to Houri's eyes. "Jillian and I have swapped shops for two months, but do not worry, for she has left me strict instructions to take care of you."

"Jillian is great." Harmony felt herself relax at the knowledge that Jillian hadn't just disappeared off the face of the earth. "Swapping stores sounds like an awesome idea."

"Now that *you* have arrived, I believe it *will* be awesome. You are my first customer for the day." Houri picked up an ornate silver dish from the counter and pulled the lid off. "Iranian candy. Please, take one."

"Ah, thanks, but I'd better not. I'm on a new diet." Harmony turned to busy herself with the nearest basket of scarves, pulling crumpled satin and knitted wool out to inspect.

"A diet . . . " Harmony heard the lid clink back onto the silver dish. "Every beautiful woman is on a diet. Your problem is not what you eat." Houri came to stand before her.

"If you're about to launch into a lecture on the benefits of exercise, don't bother. I'm allergic to the gym, and the reason I spend forty-five minutes on the train, this early on a Saturday morning, is so I can shop without being judged by skinny, couture-clad bitches." Harmony felt the shameful burn spread down her neck and rubbed at her prickly skin.

"Then you've come to the right place. No skinny, couture-clad bitches in sight." Houri laughed as she looked faux-surreptitiously around the store. "And, what I was about to say, *was,* that your problem is not what you eat, your problem is the way you perceive yourself."

Harmony dropped the scarves, shocked that this stranger was trying to psycho-analyse her this early on a Saturday morning. "What are you? Some kind of Eastern spiritualist or something?"

"Perhaps . . . " Houri's tinkling laugh filled the darkened room.

"Well, I might love myself for at least a few hours today if I found a new pair of vintage pumps to wear tonight. Jillian usually has some fantastic 1950s stuff and I can't leave until I've bought *something.*" Harmony's eyes scoured the racks.

"Ah, yes, she told me about your shoe obsession. I think I might have something very different for you." Houri's eyes twinkled as she moved towards the back of the store.

"If they're pre-war heels I'll wet myself." Harmony squeaked, as she watched Houri disappear behind the silk drapes that separated the storeroom form the rest of the shop.

"Pre-war, no." Houri called over the drapes.

"Oh." Harmony deflated, although she knew it was almost impossible to get anything that old, she had hoped that maybe this eastern goddess was able to weave some magic.

"But how does nineteenth century Persian sound?" Houri's glossy black head popped back through the curtains, eyes gleaming as she held a jewelled pewter chest before her.

"*Nineteenth century Persian*? How on earth did you get something that old?" Harmony's voice rose in wonder.

"I deal in antiques. Everything in Persia is for sale if the right price is offered." Houri smiled, somewhat sadly.

"But, if they're antique, there is no way I could afford them! Besides, won't they fall apart?"

"It's not a question of money or age—it's a question of whether the shoe fits." Houri placed the pewter chest onto the nearby antique sideboard.

"I've never had a problem with finding a shoe that fits before." Harmony chewed on her bottom lip.

"Well, I'm sure your luck will continue today. Go ahead, open it." Houri gestured at the chest.

"Okay." Harmony's fingers trembled as she clasped the lid of the pewter chest and slowly lifted it. The lid swung backwards with a creak and the scent of worn leather and some strange spice she couldn't place filled the air around her. "*Wow . . .* " was all Harmony could utter as her eyes fell upon the jade-green leather heels lying in a bed of royal-purple silk. Her fingers froze on the edge of the chest.

"You *can* touch them," Houri giggled.

"I'm almost too scared to; they're so *amazing.*" Harmony took the right heel gently from its satin cocoon and held it up to the light. The green leather was embossed with a peacock feather pattern and tiny pearls were stitched around the top edge of the shoe.

"Yes, they are, but that's not all. Turn it over." Houri's eyes twinkled even brighter.

"Turn it over?" Harmony darted a confused look at Houri, but did as she was told. Faded blue ink was scribbled across the tan sole in what looked like some eastern script. "Wow, what is it? Is it a spell?" Harmony's pulse thrummed at the sight of the ancient words.

"It's Persian, and if you consider *love* a spell, then yes, it is."

"*Really?* But, what does it say?" Harmony's fingers tingled as they traced over the words. It was like running her hands over the warm skin of a lover.

Pointing to the inscription, Houri translated:

"*The dust under your feet is brighter than the dust of the stars.*" Her voice was a low hum. "And, under this one, the inscription continues." She reached for the second shoe, turning it over in her hands. "*I would give my life for the dust beneath your feet.*"

"That's beautiful . . . " Harmony exhaled, wistfully. "But, who wrote it?"

"It's signed by the shoemaker—see, here . . . " Houri pointed to three characters scribbled beneath the others. "These shoes were made for his princess. He was the royal shoemaker and she, his most influential patron. He once said that his life began the moment he slipped these shoes on her feet. Imagine being loved like *that* . . . " Her eyes took on a far-away look.

"If only I could." Harmony put the shoe back into its silk cocoon and turned away to hide the loneliness that had crept into her eyes.

"Love like that is rare, Harmony. If you wore these shoes, you might be able to imagine what that feels like."

"But, I can't possibly wear them. They're too precious—too old!"

"These shoes were made to be worn and cherished, not to sit in some box rotting away. This leather remembers what it was to be worn by a Persian princess two hundred years ago who was loved by a shoemaker." Houri stroked one of the shoes, reverently. "I'll loan them to you for the weekend. Try them on." She kneeled down to place the shoes on the floor and then placed a chair behind them. Holding the back of the chair she waited for Harmony to sit down.

"Okay, I'll try them, but they look a little small, even for my feet." Harmony sat down on the edge of the chair and leaning forward, sucked in her stomach as she reached to unbuckle her Mary Janes. Slipping them off, she stretched her toes, and shuffled on the chair as Houri slid one of the Persian shoes onto her left foot. Somehow the delicate leather stretched, moulding to her foot. It was softer and more comfortable than anything she'd ever felt before.

"It fits!" Harmony beamed, jumping up to look at her foot in the floor-length mirror that leaned against the opposite wall.

"I knew they would! They once fit a princess and now they do, again." Houri smiled.

"I don't know about the princess thing, but I do feel pretty amazing! They're just magic!" Harmony couldn't take her eyes off the shoe. "Can I try on the other one?"

"Of course." Houri handed her the other shoe. "Shoes *are* magic, Harmony. They can turn you into someone else; all you have to do is slip them on."

"And you're sure I can have these for the weekend?"

"Please do, I'm heading out of town later and I won't be back until Monday, so just bring them back to me next week."

"Thanks, so much!" Harmony gushed. "I've got just the place to wear them. I work for a newspaper and we've got our annual bash on tonight at the National Gallery. I can't wait for the advertising girls to see me in these!" She felt triumphant already.

Let them keep their designer heels—she had an ancient love story on her feet and they looked amazing. Hell, she could even make the front page of her paper with such an incredible story.

"Then I expect to hear *all* about it next week when you return." Houri smiled and handed the pewter chest to Harmony who was still staring at the shoes on her feet.

• • •

"Well it's about time!" Harmony's work colleague, Eva Lopez, rolled her eyes as Harmony appeared in the foyer of the National Gallery of Victoria later that night.

"You didn't have to wait for me out here; you could have gone in." Harmony fiddled with her black satin wrap dress, adjusting the bow on the side.

"Like hell. Every office bitch and perve is standing on the other side of those giant glass doors and I am *not* facing them alone." Eva paused to run her eyes over Harmony. "There's something different about you tonight. Have you had surgery?" She narrowed her eyes.

"What? No! When the hell would I have found time to have surgery?" Harmony stopped fiddling with her dress to look up.

"Well, *something's* different. You look fresher . . . almost sparkly. Did you get some kind of tan or something? Is it that new Spanish product?"

"No. You know I don't do tans or surgery. I haven't done anything, *really*." Harmony wrinkled her nose.

"Oh my God, you've met someone! Is that why you're late?" Eva's eyes were huge.

"Well, I did meet someone—but it wasn't a man—she gave me these shoes." Harmony lifted the bottom of her silk and tulle skirt to show off her borrowed Persian shoes.

"What, she just *gave* you those shoes?" Eva's eyebrows shot up.

"Well, technically I'm just borrowing them for the weekend." Harmony shrugged.

"And what do you have to give her in return?"

"Nothing, I just have to return them Monday. Houri is Iranian, kinda strange, but really nice—and these shoes are nineteenth century Persian. Aren't they *amazing*?"

"I guess so." Eva shrugged. "But I need a wine in my hand while you carry on about yet another pair of shoes. Let's go in."

Ignoring Eva's dig, Harmony followed her friend towards the gallery's main exhibition hall, but froze before a glass display cabinet just outside the doors. "Oh . . . My . . . God!"

"Shit, Harmony, not *more* shoes!" Eva threw her hands up.

"But they're *Georgian* shoes." Harmony's eyes devoured the three pairs of satin and brocade heels that shimmered beneath the display lamps.

"They're clunky and ugly." Eva rolled her big brown eyes.

"Are you *crazy*? They're gorgeous!" Harmony tore her gaze away from the shoes to glare, but the giant shoe poster plastered to the wall above Eva caught her attention instead. "Eva, there's more upstairs!" she squealed.

"*Harmony*, you can come see them anytime. We're here for work, remember?"

"Come on, Eva, you know I *have* to look. I'll just be ten minutes. No one will even notice I'm not there." Harmony wrung her hands as she pleaded with her friend.

"Oh, whatever, I'm tired of waiting. I'm sure I'll find better company at the bar anyway." Eva spun on her stilettos and disappeared through the giant glass doors into the undulating crowd.

Feeling slightly guilty, Harmony picked up her skirt and carefully walked up the flight of stairs that would lead her to the shoe exhibition. Her guilt melted away as thoughts of the treasures awaiting her danced through her mind. She couldn't believe she hadn't heard about this sooner—a travelling exhibition of shoes from across the globe and from multiple centuries? It made her palms sweaty as she approached the smaller exhibition hall. Taking a deep breath, she grasped the handle, pushed the door inwards, and entered nirvana.

"Sweet God . . . " Harmony breathed in the scent of leather and antiquity. The wall sconces emitted a soft light that gave the interior an otherworldly glow. Glass cases were lined up along the walls and through the centre of the room, each containing a new and different pair of shoes. Harmony floated amongst the cases, exclaiming and sighing as she looked upon shoes from every decade of the twentieth century along with *babouches* from Morocco, *kabkabs* from Syria, Chinese silk shoes, *padukas* from India, nineteenth century sandals from Brazil, reconstructed *caliga* sandals from Ancient Rome, Venetian *chopines*, and more damask Georgian creations.

"This is sooo awesome . . . " Harmony came to a stop before the last glass cabinet that held a pair of Persian silk, embroidered shoes within. She felt a magnetic pull to the Persian creations and bent down to examine them more closely.

"My thoughts exactly." A smooth male voice interrupted her reverie.

"Shit!" Harmony jumped back as she spied a pair green eyes staring at her through the glass case. "You scared the life out of me!" She blushed as her eyes swept over the rest of the stranger's tanned face and tousled, dark hair. He was lean and had a bookish look about him enhanced by his Armani reading glasses and grey suit that melded to his frame.

"I'm sorry. It's not often I see someone so transfixed by my exhibition; I did not want to break the spell." He flashed an infectious smile and cute dimples at her. His voice was accented—a mix of something Eastern and European, but she couldn't place it.

"*Your* exhibition?" she squeezed out.

"Well, technically, the shoes aren't *all* mine, but I am the curator and I have travelled with the exhibition from Germany."

"So, you're German? You don't look it." Harmony stared closer at him before catching herself and turning away with another blush.

"So, it's not only shoes you study." She heard him laugh. "I'm Amr Husseini." He held his hand out as he stepped around the display case.

"Harmony—Harmony Thicket." She trembled as she grasped the offered hand. She'd never met anyone as ridiculously gorgeous as this shoe god and she dropped her eyes to their clasped fingers.

"*Harmony* . . . That's a lovely name. And to answer your question, I'm Persian."

"Shut-up!" Harmony exclaimed, biting down on her tongue as she watched a surprised expression cross his face.

"Well, I've never had *that* reaction to my heritage before." His thick, dark eyebrows rose.

"I'm sorry, I didn't mean any disrespect." Harmony stepped towards him, wringing her hands. "But you're the second Persian person I've met today, actually, you're only the second one I've met in my *entire life*. This is so weird!"

"So, we've made an impression on you? I see you're quite taken with the Persian, pointed shoes here." He grasped the edge of the glass case and smiled down on the treasure within.

"They're fantastic. I love shoes! It's all I ever buy. In fact, only this morning I was given some new . . . " Harmony was about to tell him the story behind the shoes Houri had given her, but thought better of it. Museum people could get quite funny about items of cultural heritage. What if she got Houri in trouble? And, quite frankly, she didn't want to be forced to give the shoes up yet—they made her feel confident and alluring.

"Some new . . . ?" Amr prompted her.

"Oh, never mind. How on earth did you get such a fantastic job?"

"I studied art history at university. The shoes in this exhibition are some of the finest artwork I have ever seen."

"Oh, I agree, they are definitely works of art!" She forced herself to breathe. Her head was spinning. She had never dreamed of a meeting a man that understood the allure of shoes the way she did. She hoped to God he wasn't gay.

"There is a story behind every pair in this exhibition, I could share them with you, if you like?" His green eyes were magnetic as he stared at her.

"I would love that." She swallowed, loudly. "But I have to be somewhere. Actually, I have to be downstairs; my newspaper's having a thing. I'm meant to be there." She darted a nervous look at the door.

"Your newspaper?"

"Well, not *my* newspaper, I just work there. I'm a journalist." She played with a strawberry curl that had come loose from her upswept hairstyle.

"Do you write about shoes?" Amr took a few steps towards her.

"I wish! Mainly I write about boring stuff like kidnappings and road rage."

"Oh!" he laughed. "Well, if you go to dinner with me tomorrow night I could help you write an article about the shoes in this exhibition . . . "

"You want me to have dinner with you so I can write about your exhibition?" Her face fell. She was stupid to have hoped for more. This guy must have a whole harem of women from here to Germany hanging on his every word.

"No, I want you to write about my exhibition so I can have dinner with you." The warm smile played across his handsome face again and Harmony felt her stomach hit the floor.

"Well, okay, if you're sure. I mean, as long as I'm not dragging you away from your work or something." She grabbed the glass case to steady herself.

"Of course I am sure," he laughed. "And you would be a welcome diversion."

"Oh." She swallowed again. "Well, where should I meet you?" She began backing away towards the door, not trusting herself to remain vertical in his presence for much longer.

"I'll meet you here, say, around seven? That way you can take some photos of the shoes for your story."

"Yep, the story—good idea." Harmony fiddled with the clasp on her evening bag.

"Well, 'til tomorrow, Harmony." Amr dipped his head and held his hand over his heart.

"Sure—and thanks."

"For what?"

"I'm not sure yet, but I've got a good feeling about this story." She gave him a wobbly smile before turning and running from the room.

• • •

"It's the shoes, I tell you! They must have some kind of weird energy field all of their own. I can't *believe* he asked me out to dinner! He's like something from one of my *English Patient* dreams!" Harmony gushed into her mobile the next evening.

"Wow, that's really saying something, knowing how obsessed you are with that long, excruciatingly boring film." Eva was her usual cynical self on the other end of the line.

"And, it wasn't just him! I had this other guy asking for my number on the train ride home—he wasn't my type, blonde, sporty looking—but still, that *never* happens to me." Harmony panted as she power-walked towards the museum for the second night in a row.

"Why didn't you tell me all this last night? No wonder you were missing *forever*!"

"I couldn't believe it had happened and I thought if I told you, you might accuse me of just making it all up."

"It does sound a little too weird to be true. But hey, weird is your thing," Eva chuckled.

"Shit." Harmony pulled up short as the museum entrance came into view.

"What? Did split your skirt again?"

"No, you cow!" Harmony dashed sidewards to hide behind one of the old trees that lined the road. "He's waiting for me at the front door. Oh, God, I don't think I can go up to him!"

"Don't be an idiot! For the first time in your life a hot man has asked you to dinner. If you don't go, I'll put on my highest stilettos and go to dinner with him myself!"

"Keeping your stilettos away from him is all the motivation I need. Wish me luck!" Harmony squeezed her eyes shut and tried to slow down her breathing.

"I don't need to. You've got your genie shoes on—break a leg." Eva hung up.

Gathering her fledgling courage, Harmony looked down at the Persian shoes and felt her determination peak. She was going to go out with Amr and she was going to take full advantage of the edge these shoes gave her.

Good-bye frumpy, vintage girl. Tonight she was a Persian goddess!

Willing her new goddess legs to move, Harmony stepped out from behind the tree and walked determinedly towards the crossing where she waited for a break in the traffic. Catching Amr's eye from across the road, she smiled weakly at him as his dreamy eyes travelled down the length of her jade green dress. The smile that lit his handsome face reassured her that last night hadn't been some weird delusion. He looked just as dashing tonight in his charcoal suit and Middle Eastern patterned scarf draped expertly about his neck.

Unable to tear her eyes off him for a second, Harmony moved with the other pedestrians as they surged forward, failing to notice the steep drop onto the road below.

"*Shitttt!*," she squealed, as she landed painfully on her knees. She only hoped that someone would run her over and save her the humiliation of facing the gorgeous man who had just witnessed her ungraceful demise.

"Harmony, are you okay?" Amr pulled her to her feet before quickly gathering the purse and coat that had fallen beside her. "We must move." He held her arm as she limped to the other side of the crossing.

"My shoe . . . " Harmony panicked, looking around frantically as she felt the bitumen bite into her bare left foot.

"I'll go back and get it. You sit down." Amr guided her to a bench outside the museum before dashing back to the other side of the road where Harmony's discarded shoe lay in a puddle. "I'm so sorry, it is wet," he apologised as he returned, holding the shoe before him.

"It's okay. I don't mind; I'll wear it anyway." Harmony's anxiety built as Amr studied the shoe, turning it over to inspect the bottom.

"Was there an inscription here?" He looked up at her, a question in his eyes.

"What do you mean, *was* there?" Harmony snatched the shoe from him and felt her stomach burn as she looked at the bottom. The ink of the shoemaker's inscription had smudged, the words now completely indiscernible. "Oh no, it's ruined!" Harmony wanted to cry even harder now.

Was the spell broken? Would Amr now see her for the boring, fat girl she really was? She couldn't risk it; she couldn't go to dinner with Amr now that her magic shoes were ruined.

"Where did you get these shoes, Harmony? I swear I have seen these before. In the museum in Tehran?" He reached to take the shoe back from her.

"I have to go—I'm sorry." Harmony backed away from him, ignoring the pain that shot through her grazed knees and the tears that were threatening to spill.

"But you just got here. You are hurt." His face showed real concern as he noticed her limp.

"No, I'm just an idiot. I ruin everything. I'm so sorry," she apologised again, pulling the other shoe off her foot so she could make her escape.

"Harmony, don't go. At least let me drive you home! When will I see you again?" Amr called after her.

"If you're lucky, never." The words caught in her throat as she hobbled away down the street in her stockinged feet, feeling more foolish than she ever had in her life.

• • •

The windows of *Yesterday's Treasure* were dark when Harmony arrived just after eight on Monday morning. She hadn't been able to sleep all night, alternately dreading the moment when she would have to return the damaged Persian shoes to Houri and picturing the look on Amr's face as she fell flat onto hers.

He must think her a total freak.

"Well, he'd be completely right," Harmony sighed as she collapsed on the stoop of the vintage store and hung her head.

"What would he be completely right about?" The Iranian woman's throaty voice startled Harmony.

"Houri!" Her head snapped up. "I'm so sorry. I am the world's *biggest* klutz!" Harmony's eyes filled with tears as she looked up at the Persian beauty.

"I don't believe that for a second, but I think you should come inside and have some mint tea while you explain why you look so miserable." The woman smiled kindly as she unlocked the front door. "Come." She tugged gently on Harmony's hand.

"I think you might want to pour some weed killer into that tea after you've heard what I've done." Harmony held the chest with the damaged shoes tightly to her bosom as she followed Houri inside.

"You didn't kill Amr, did you?"

"What? No." Harmony's distress turned to confusion.

"Well then, no weed killer is necessary," Houri giggled.

"But wait—how do you know Amr?" Harmony put the chest down on the front counter, momentarily forgetting about the shoes.

"Are the shoes in there?" Houri ignored her question and moved forward to open the chest and take out the green leather heels with their beaded edge and inscribed soles.

"Oh God, Houri—I have never been so sorry about anything in all my life!" Harmony's voice shook. "The left shoe, it fell in a puddle last night. I didn't notice the drop down onto the road and I fell flat on my face like a big buffalo, and the inscription, it washed off! Well, actually, it got all smudged after the shoe fell in the water . . . " Harmony sucked in a deep breath and grasped her trembling hands together.

"It smudged?" Houri turned the shoe over to look underneath. The poetic Persian inscription had turned to a faint blue stain.

"I know! I can't believe it. I have successfully destroyed a piece of your country's heritage and possibly the evidence of the most romantic love story in history! If you want to use that weed killer in my tea now I will totally understand . . . " Harmony winced as she waited for the torrent of abuse she was certain would come.

"Well, I guess we will have to fix them." Houri's left eyebrow arched.

"Of course, but how?"

"A dash of ink and a little more faith is all that's needed."

"What?" Harmony laid her fingers over the tear tracks that ran down her cheeks. "I don't understand—actually I haven't understood anything that's happened to me since I first saw those shoes."

"Do you remember I told you that Jillian and I had spoken about you before?"

"Yeah, so what? What does that matter? I've ruined your shoes!" She tugged at a lock of hair, which had come loose from her ponytail.

"I brought these shoes here for *you*, Harmony."

"Why? Why would you bring shoes for me? How could you even know that you would meet me?" Harmony's head swam as she tried to make sense of what Houri was saying.

"When Jillian spoke of you I knew intuitively that you would benefit from these shoes. I also knew that Amr would be here at this time." Houri looked proud of herself.

"But what has Amr got to do with any of this?" Harmony felt her cheeks burn as she used his name. She felt blasphemous speaking it aloud.

"He has got everything to do with it. You like him, don't you?" Houri smiled, knowingly.

"Shit, he's not your boyfriend, is he? God, I should have known it was too much of a coincidence running into two gorgeous Iranians in one day, especially when they just *both* happen to have ancient

Persian shoes at their disposal—I'm such an idiot!" Harmony had to sit down in one of the empty wicker chairs.

"He's always been beautiful . . . "

"I swear I'll never go near him again! He's yours—I'm not that kind of girl!" She held her hands out before her.

"You don't have to do that, I am very fond of Amr, but not in the way you imagine." Houri's tinkling laugh filled the quiet shop.

"He's not your boyfriend then?" Hope blossomed in Harmony's chest before she firmly shook her head. "It doesn't matter anyway. I can't ever see him again. Not after I nearly broke my neck in front of him the other night! The only reason I ever agreed to go out with him is because I thought those shoes had some sort of love spell over them." Harmony pointed at the offending green shoe that Houri still held.

"Jillian and I thought as much . . . " Houri's long lashes dropped as she took out a bottle of ink from a drawer in the front counter and a nibbed pen.

"What are you doing?" Harmony jumped to her feet and leaned over the shoe, afraid to touch it but needing to be closer.

"I'm restoring the spell."

"But you can't just write the words back on there. It doesn't work like that." Harmony was horrified.

"Doesn't it?' Houri smiled.

"My God, you wrote the spell on there in the first place didn't you? There's not any magic love spell at all . . . " Harmony's shoulders drooped. She wanted to cry.

"Now that I have restored the ink inscription." Houri put down the pen and held the shoe up to blow over the glistening characters. "Now comes the part where we need a little faith, Harmony."

"Faith?"

"Yes, faith. On Friday night you believed these shoes had a love spell on them and they led you to love didn't they?" Houri reached a hand out to caress Harmony's cheek lightly.

"Well, yes . . . "

"So who's to say what is real and what is not? If *you* believe it, then that is all that matters." She smiled and turned to place the shoe back in the pewter chest.

"But, did the Persian shoemaker and his princess really exist?" Harmony held her breath.

"Yes, these was once a princess who was loved by a shoemaker. He made her a beautiful pair of shoes that looked just like these ones and inscribed them with words of love. You can see them at the museum in Tehran if you ever go to visit my country."

"Good," Harmony sighed. She was relieved to know that it hadn't been all a lie. "So, now what?"

"So, now you believe in yourself. Believe that you are worthy of being loved without any magic shoes on your feet." Houri winked at her as she picked up the chest and headed towards the curtain that separated the back of the store.

"That's a lot to believe." Harmony's voice was shaky.

"Well, you better start believing it very quickly. Amr is only here for another few days and he liked you without knowing anything about your shoes."

"But, how can I just show up at the museum again when I made such a fool of myself the other night? He'll think I'm crazy."

"Do you really believe you can stay away from a love like that?" Houri's beautiful smile played across her lips as she turned to look back at Harmony.

"I guess not." Harmony's heart felt like it would break right through her ribs as she thought of Amr. "But, I'll need a favour . . . "

"Name it," Houri eyed her, carefully.

"I'll need an impressive new pair of shoes. He is a shoe curator after all."

Afterword

Writing "Harmony Thicket and the Persian Shoes" was a complete delight. A natural inclination for all things eastern and mythological lead me to stumble upon a photo of 19th century, inscribed Persian shoes while on the internet late one night. Such an incredibly romantic pair of shoes demanded their story be told and it wasn't too much of a stretch to create a bumbling, kind-hearted girl who would fall under their spell as I had. And who better for the shoes to lead her to than an enigmatic, Persian museum curator? Blending the ancient with the contemporary is what I love to do and so the world of Melbourne vintage shopping collides with the magical courts of Persia in this story.

The Green Rose

Cherith Baldry

Lord Sabir, Chief Eunuch at the court of the Immortal Soldan, carefully poured water into the alabaster pot, and watched as the dark earth soaked it up. The rose tree lifted up fresh green leaves. The flowers were no more than slender buds, the sepals spiralling to a point. Their blooming was still many days away.

Lord Sabir touched one leaf with a fingertip, and drew back sharply at a sound behind him, from the archway that led into his courtyard garden. He turned to see Barrakar, the Court Enchanter, stumping towards him across the paving stones, prodding with his staff at the boy in front of him.

He was a tall youth, all knees and elbows and a shock of reddish hair, casting terrified glances around him as he stumbled forward.

The Court Enchanter poked him with the staff and grunted, "Kneel, offspring of pigs."

Lord Sabir sighed. With slender fingers he plucked a spray of jasmine and held the sweet smelling flowers as a shield between himself and the reek of fear and sweat and onions that was rising from the boy sprawled at his feet. "What is this, Barrakar?" he asked mildly.

The Court Enchanter grinned, his teeth white in the midst of a wild tangle of grey hair and beard. He poked the boy again with his staff. "Sing."

The boy stayed on his knees, giving the Court Enchanter a look of wild incomprehension, as if he had said, "Fly."

In a rustle of his silken robes the Chief Eunuch sat on a stone bench beneath a rose trellis. The Court Enchanter—vile old man!—was no doubt playing some elaborate joke, though what the purpose of it was, or who was to be the victim, Sabir could not tell. In the same quiet voice he said to the boy, "Stand up. There is nothing to fear. If you can sing, do so."

Darting nervous glances at him, the boy scrambled to his feet and stood with hands clasped behind his back, like a small child reciting a lesson. The Court Enchanter settled himself on another bench, resting plump hands on his knees.

"What would it please you I should sing, lord?" the boy asked.

Sabir waved a hand impatiently. "Do I know your songs? Sing what pleases you."

The boy took a breath. Sabir was prepared to be bored, even disgusted, but what came out of the boy's mouth was pure music, purer even than the cadences of the fountains in the arbours of the Immortal Soldan. The clear treble held Sabir motionless as twilight began to gather in the garden. His own stillness seemed to spread to the trees and flowers around him. There was not even the rustle of small creatures in the shrubbery, or the song of birds. *Nightingales*, Sabir thought wryly, *would not dare.*

At last the boy's song ended and he stood looking expectantly at Sabir. Sabir spoke to the Court Enchanter. "Is this one of your tricks, Barrakar? Some sorcery?"

The Court Enchanter chuckled and shook his shaggy head. "No tricks, Sabir. I heard him in the marketplace, singing for coppers. And selling onions, may He Above be merciful! Good, eh?"

"Indeed. Boy," said Sabir. "You shall sing for the Immortal Soldan."

The boy looked even more terrified, glancing from side to side as if he wanted to escape. Lord Sabir clapped his hands, and a servant appeared, bowing low.

"Take this boy," Sabir said, "and have him washed. Thoroughly. Burn his rags and give him clothes fitting for a page of the Household. Then feed him and find him a place to sleep, and bring him to me in the morning."

The servant bowed again and motioned to the boy to follow him. Hesitantly, he obeyed. Before he disappeared through the archway, Sabir halted him. "Boy." The lad turned. "Tell me your name."

"Mahar, lord."

"Have you a family, Mahar, who will be looking for you? Do you wish to send a message?"

The boy's face suddenly split into an incredible, illuminating smile, assaulting Sabir like a blow. "No, lord," he said cheerfully. "There's only me."

Momentarily unable to speak, Sabir waved him away. Barrakar, unfortunately, was not so easily disposed of. Clasping his hands over his paunch, the Court Enchanter said, "You'll need to have the boy cut, Sabir, and soon, if you want that voice to last."

Sabir gave him a look of controlled distaste. "Are we barbarians?"

The Court Enchanter let out an derisive chuckle. "It hasn't done you any harm, Sabir, with your silks and jewels and your fine garden."

A pang went through Sabir, though he kept his face impassive. Choosing his words carefully—for he would preserve courtesy, even for this old goat—he said, "My father became . . . politically inconvenient. If I had been given the choice, who knows?"

Barrakar shot him a glance that was unexpectedly shrewd. "There is no choice, Sabir. Only the will of the Immortal Soldan."

"The Immortal Soldan is too ill to make his will known," Sabir said austerely. "So I must interpret it for him. The boy may prove unsuitable."

To his surprise, Barrakar suddenly doubled over in a fit of snorting laughter. When he could speak again, he said, "I like you, Sabir. You'll do anything before you admit that you're a decent man."

Sabir made no reply. When the Court Enchanter had shuffled out of the garden, still chuckling evilly, he wandered down to the courtyard pool. The water under the sky of evening was a silver sheet where Sabir could see himself mirrored: the thin face, pale and disdainful, the sleek, dark hair, the jewels in his ears. He reached out as if he could smash the image; his fingers dipped into the water and the ripples banished it. Behind him a soft voice said, "Sabir."

Sabir turned and fell to his knees as he saw the slender figure, swathed in dark veiling, who stood before him. "Lady Amalia."

White hands put back the veils to show a face, no longer young, not beautiful, with dark hair beginning to silver and quiet dark eyes.

"Don't kneel, Sabir," she said, smiling. "No need, for such old friends as we, and here alone."

"Lady, you should have sent for me," Sabir said, rising and taking her hand to escort her to a seat.

"But I wished to speak to you where no ears could hear us. And to see your beautiful garden." She paused beside the rose bush in the alabaster pot. "This is new, isn't it?"

"Yes, lady." Eagerness touched Sabir's voice. "A new cross. I shall not know if I have succeeded until the first flower opens." Hesitantly, he added, "When it does, it shall be yours."

She smiled again and sat under the trellis which was already covered with heavy swags of blossom, pouring their scent into the night. As Sabir, at her gesture, took his seat beside her, she grew suddenly more businesslike.

"Sabir, the Immortal Soldan is dying."

Lord Sabir took a painful breath. "Blasphemy, lady?"

Lady Amalia's lips tightened. "Sabir, spare me the court cant. The Immortal Soldan is a man like other men. Should I not know, being his wife for so long? He is old and he is dying, and I doubt that he will be mourned."

Fear surged over Lord Sabir, so that he could not prevent himself from reaching out as if to lay his fingers across her lips. What she had already said could mean death for both of them. Lady Amalia took his hand and clasped it briefly. "Sabir, I need your help. The Soldan must name his heir."

"He has not done so?"

Lady Amalia shook her head. " He has listened too long to his flatterers. He does not believe that he can die."

Sabir sat silent, his hands gripping hard together in an effort to still the sudden racing of his heart. He was unsurprised by what the Lady Amalia had told him. But he was unprepared for the rush of mingled fear and hope that the news brought him.

"Then someone must convince him," he said. "He must name Karrahir."

Karrahir. The Soldan's only son, and Amalia's. She leant towards Sabir in a whisper of gauze draperies.

"Sabir, we have worked for this day, for so long. We have taught Karrahir what he must do, what he must be, when he succeeds his father. We must not fail now. Not now when we have the hope of right rule here at last."

Right rule, Sabir thought hungrily. Good government, by a Soldan who did not believe himself a god and greater than a god, who did not look upon his city as no more than a pot to feed his own swollen appetites.

May He Above grant it, Sabir prayed silently, knowing that it would take a miracle from Him Above to set Karrahir on the throne if the Soldan did not name him as his heir. Instead of the order Sabir craved, there would be chaos as each of the provincial governors tried to assert his claim, and the city would go down in fire.

"I cannot speak to the Soldan myself," Amalia said. A gleam of humour appeared briefly in her eyes. "For I am a woman, and who would listen to a woman's vapourings? Karrahir cannot ask for his own inheritance, or they might say that he murdered his father. And the Soldan's courtiers tell him only what he wants to hear. Sabir . . . "

Fear contracted Sabir's heart as if he stood in a cave of ice. His voice shook for all his efforts to steady it. "There is no one else."

Amalia reached out and laid her hand over his; it was all Sabir could do not to cling to it in sheer terror. "Dear friend, I know what I ask of you. But it is for Karrahir. And for all the city."

Sabir thought, *No; it is for you*, but did not speak the thought. Instead, he murmured, "He has not sent for me in many days. His guard may not admit me."

Lady Amalia rose, her draperies brushing at the trellis. A few pale petals detached themselves and drifted slowly to the ground. "Leave that to me," she said.

A moment more and she was gone, her veiling melting into the gathering night. After she had disappeared, Lord Sabir sat long in the rose arbour, oblivious of the chill of the night dew.

• • •

The next morning, Lord Sabir was seated at his desk when a shadow crossed the light and he looked up to see Mahar. His brows rose appreciatively. "Now that is much more satisfactory."

The boy was clean, and wearing a plain linen tunic. Someone had shaped his hair into a cap of short chestnut curls. He looked taller than Sabir remembered. Under Sabir's scrutiny, he shifted his feet uncomfortably and began to scratch.

"Will you scratch yourself in the presence of the Immortal Soldan?" Mahar reddened and snatched his hands behind him. "You will not." Sabir sighed. "I can see there is a great deal of work for both of us to do before you are fit to stand in the Immortal Presence."

He put aside the letters he had been writing, and began to teach Mahar the ways of the court. He had duties enough, but the extra work helped him to put out of his mind the summons that must come soon, if it came at all, to the deathbed of the Immortal Soldan.

In the days that followed, he taught Mahar the reverences proper to himself, to the provincial governors, to the Lady Amalia, and the prostration he must perform before the Immortal Soldan. He taught him the proper forms of address. He taught him how to pour wine and how to offer a dish. Sighing frequently, he accepted that Mahar would never be graceful, but he would at least be correct.

Each day, towards evening, Sabir took a lute and accompanied Mahar's singing. He was a fair musician, good enough at least to teach him courtly songs to take the place of his market ballads. And in the last hour of the day when the sun went down, they worked in the garden.

The buds of the rose were swelling. Lord Sabir stared greedily at the tiny wedges of creamy white that were beginning to force their way out of the constricting sepals.

"Will it have scent, lord?" Mahar asked.

"I don't know." Sabir carefully tipped water into the pot. "I don't know."

• • •

The summons came towards the end of the fourth day. Sabir had considered and honed a thousand speeches, only to reject them all. There was no safe way to tell the Immortal Soldan the truth of his own mortality; perhaps there was no way at all.

Terror gripped him, but Sabir made sure he showed nothing of it, as he summoned his servants and had them bring him the formal robes, heavy with embroidery, proper for an audience with the Immortal Soldan.

As he set the jewelled clasps in place, with fingers that he prided himself on keeping steady, Mahar said, "Shall I attend you, lord?"

Sabir waved away the servant with the mirror. Mahar was looking worried. Though Sabir had told him nothing, he was not stupid, and he could not help but know what was going on. Sabir hesitated, unwilling to involve Mahar if he was going to his ruin, but realising that he had a practical use for the boy. And—he pushed the thought away as he led Mahar through the passages and courtyards that led to the Soldan's apartments—there was something comforting about Mahar's presence.

"Wait here," Sabir ordered him, when at last they stood outside the Soldan's doors. "If . . . if there should be trouble, take word to my Lady Amalia."

Mahar nodded. He was grave and quiet now. He sank down on a bench, gripping it with both hands; his eyes stayed fixed on Sabir's face.

"May He Above go with you, lord."

Out of surging terror, Sabir managed a dignified nod. "My thanks, Mahar."

The guards outside the Soldan's suite raised their spears for Sabir. Servants pulled back the carved sandalwood doors. As Sabir crossed the ante-room, one of the concubines from the Immortal Soldan's harem slid past him, her eyes downcast as she clutched torn draperies around herself. Disgust warred with Sabir's apprehension.

At the entrance to the bedchamber the heat and stench hit Sabir in the throat. Lamps burned in intricate brass housings, sending up a smoke of incense that hovered in a gauzy canopy below the ceiling. In a far corner something bubbled and reeked in a copper dish over a brazier. Nothing masked the foul stink of corruption flowing out from the bed in the centre of the room.

Courtiers huddled and whispered in the shadows, and the Court Enchanter Barrakar muttered over his charts. They all turned to stare at Sabir as he stepped inside. He performed the ritual prostration with the measured grace of long practice and approached the bed.

It was a low circle carved from ivory and jade. Filmy white hangings surrounded it, ghostly in the lamplight. Within the hangings, a mounded shadow heaved and sank back.

The Immortal Soldan's physician stood at the head of the bed, beside a table strewn with pots and potions. He was a scrawny, white-bearded man, barely able to contain his fear. *With good cause*, Sabir reflected.

As their eyes met, the physician shook his head slightly, and with one hand swept back the gauzy hangings. Sabir stepped forward.

The Immortal Soldan was a huge man. Sabir remembered when he had been tall, muscular and commanding. Now he lay wallowing among silken cushions, arms spread wide. Rings were embedded in the flesh of the white fingers that snatched feebly at the coverlet. Restlessly he turned his head, caught sight of Sabir and peered vaguely at him.

"Sabir?" The voice was a wet sound in the Soldan's throat.

"My lord, you sent for me?"

The Soldan looked puzzled. If he had given the order, he had forgotten. He shook his head, raised a hand as if the weight of it exhausted him. Sabir was suddenly afraid that he would speak the words of dismissal. All his carefully prepared speeches went out of his head."My lord, you are dying. You must name your heir."

A choking gasp came from the elderly physician at his elbow. A listening silence fell on the whispering courtiers. *At least*, Sabir thought with tart satisfaction, *I have said what none of them would dare.*

An arm thrashed out. Clammy fingers closed round Sabir's wrist and pulled him with surprising strength down to the side of the bed. Sabir sank into the piled cushions, their stale scent rising around him. The instinct to struggle free was almost too much for him. The Soldan heaved himself up and brought his face close to Sabir's.

"I am the Immortal Soldan. I cannot die. This ailment will pass. My physician has promised me."

The old physician, trembling violently, bowed so low that his head almost brushed the pillows. "I swear it, lord."

Sabir barely glanced at him. "My lord, you are a man as other men, and you are dying. You must name your heir."

"You are lying, Sabir. I will have you staked out in the desert for the vultures and scorpions."

"Have I ever lied to you, lord?" Small eyes peered suspiciously at Sabir out of rolls of fat. One part of Sabir's mind, cold and controlled, answered his own question. *Yes, old fool. I have lied to you, and lied again. I would lie now, if it would serve me, but it will not.* He made his voice come out steadily. "You are dying, my lord. If you have no heir, there will be war."

As he watched, a change crept over the Soldan's face. Terror glazed his eyes. His grip on Sabir's wrist slackened. He pawed feebly at Sabir, the scrabbling fingers catching in the heavy embroidery of his robe. "Life ... life ... Help me, Sabir, help ... "

Sabir held still against the crawling touch. "My lord, there is no help now, save for the mercy of Him Above."

The Soldan flopped back against the scented cushions, whimpering like a small child.

"Your heir, my lord." Sabir's voice was steely now.

"My heir ... Karrahir, that feeble boy ... " Sabir drew in his breath sharply; the name had been spoken; it was enough. "He will sit in my place, he will rejoice ... all of you will rejoice ... " The Soldan broke off, and a look of craftiness replaced the terror in his eyes. He groped for Sabir's hand. "Sabir, you will go into the city and take the head of each household—fathers, eldest sons—and have them slain at my funeral. Then all the city will grieve at my passing."

He broke into cackling laughter that gave way to coughing and retching. Spittle drooled from one corner of his mouth.

"My lord, you cannot do this," said Sabir.

"Cannot?" The word was choked out. "No, Sabir, you will do it. You and Karrahir." He broke into weak laughter again, only to gasp for air, clawing at his chest. "Pain—too much pain ... " The voice died away into breathy sobs.

Sabir felt a hand touch his shoulder and turned to see the Soldan's physician, holding a cup out to him. "Give him that."

Sabir had to overcome all his revulsion before he could touch the dying man, but as he cradled the Soldan's head and tilted the jewelled rim of the cup against lips that sucked greedily at oblivion he felt the last thing he had ever expected to feel—compassion. Once the Soldan had been a child, bright with hope. Innocent, eager for life. It was power that had done this.

When the cup was empty and the Soldan had collapsed moaning against his pillows, Sabir withdrew. Head erect under the bored, contemptuous gaze of the guards, he stepped outside the doors and took a few paces down the passage. His vision was swimming as he lost his tight control of his own fear and revulsion. The heavy, formal robes weighed him down and the floor felt uneven under his feet. He knew he was going to faint, but not even shame could marshal his scattering senses.

Then a hand touched his arm and he made out Mahar's face looking down anxiously into his. "Mahar—why..?"

"You told me to wait, lord." The words clanged out from an unimaginable distance.

"I—I'd forgotten . . . "

He felt himself sinking, and Mahar's arm suddenly tight around him. Grey mist covered his eyes.

• • •

When he came to himself again he was lying on cool grass with the scent of flowers around him and air moving over his face. His robes were torn open, the jewelled clasps tossed aside on the grass. Mahar was dabbing his forehead with a wet handkerchief.

"Lord?" His illuminating smile appeared. "Lie still, lord. You'll be better presently."

Sabir sat up and bowed his head into his hands. It throbbed painfully. No one saw him like this—weak, dishevelled, bereft of all dignity. Never. Not even in the hell of the Immortal Soldan's bedchamber.

Looking up, he saw a long, narrow pool, bordered with paving stones. Moonlight glimmered on the quiet surface. Branches heavy with blossom arched over his head and scattered petals over the grass and the disordered folds of his robe.

"This is the Immortal Soldan's garden," he said. "We shouldn't be here, not without leave."

Mahar shrugged. "Who's to know?"

"There are always eyes in this court, boy." Though perhaps they were turned elsewhere just now. Sabir remembered that when Mahar first came, so few days ago, he had imagined that he might stand here and sing, for the Immortal Soldan and his courtiers. No longer. Mahar should sing—yes, Sabir decided, he should sing for the first time at the enthronement of the new Soldan.

. . .

That night Sabir dreamed of the Soldan's bedchamber, of those fleshy hands dragging him down to suffocate in scented cushions. He woke gasping, bathed in sweat. Moonlight was pouring through the lattice, and Sabir thought he saw Mahar, sitting cross-legged on a reed mat near his door, his lips parted in a murmur of song. He slept again, and when he awoke the next morning he wondered if that too had been no more than another dream.

Sabir felt as if a fever had shaken him. He lay face down among the silken pillows, as powerless to move as if some vast weight were pressing on him from above. But his head was clear. Cool air breathed into the room from the garden; Sabir could hear birdsong.

His door crashed open. He turned his head to see Mahar panting on the threshold. His rebuke died as the boy gasped, "Lord, the rose!"

The weight vanished. Sabir sat up, reaching for the silken bedgown that Mahar thrust into his hands. He felt shaky as he stood, but Mahar put a hand under his arm to steady him.

The garden was netted with mist and dew. Sabir sank down into the grass beside the pot. One bloom had half opened. The petals were cream coloured, waxy, with a green glow down in the depths of the flower. The scent was thin and piercing, and reminded Sabir of mountains, or a melody in a minor key. He knew that he was weeping, and felt briefly ashamed that Mahar should see.

"It's beautiful," Mahar breathed.

They sat together, looking, until the sun rose over the palace rooftops, setting every stem and leaf to glittering. Sabir shivered at dew soaking through the thin silk of the gown. He rose to return to his apartments, summon his servants, and robe himself for the day ahead.

Only then did Mahar tell him that during the night the Immortal Soldan had died.

. . .

At first Sabir could not face the turmoil of the court. This private room, leading into the garden, was precious to him, and he gave orders he was not to be disturbed. He sat at his desk and began to make notes for the ordering of the late Soldan's funeral, and the enthronement of the new Soldan. He tried not to think of the Soldan's final, monstrous order

The morning was well advanced when there was a tap at the garden door, and Mahar came in, with earth from the garden on his hands. His eyes were wide, and his voice held a barely suppressed excitement. "Lord, the Lady Amalia . . . "

Sabir brushed past him. Not only Amalia was waiting for him in the garden. Karrahir was with her. Sabir touched head and heart and held out open palms in reverence, and out of the corner of his eye was aware of Mahar doing the same. Not the prostration yet; that would come after the enthronement.

Karrahir was a tall youth, no more than a year or two older than Mahar. Superbly handsome, with bronzed skin and curling black hair. He nodded gravely to Sabir; it was Amalia who spoke. "Sabir, we have need of your wisdom."

He could see pride in her as she looked at her son, yet not the joy he had expected. She was agitated. Sabir guided her to the rose arbour; Karrahir seated himself beside her under the arching blossom.

"Sabir," Amalia said. "There is talk of an order that the Soldan gave before he died."

Sabir grew tense. Absurd to suppose that no one would have spoken of it. He said, "The order was vile. There can be no compulsion—"

Karrahir had plucked a rose, and began meditatively stripping off the petals. "Yet I would not have it said I denied my father his rightful mourning."

Though the sun shone, Sabir felt as though a cold breeze crept through the garden. What was Karrahir, that he would even contemplate the slaughter the Soldan had commanded? Had he and Amalia made a fearful mistake? Mentally, he shook himself. It was youth and inexperience, no more, and the piety that a son should show his father. Drily, he said, "My lord Karrahir, what will they say of you, do you think, if you slay the head of every household in the city?"

"Lord!" The exclamation, outraged, came from Mahar. "You can't do it!"

Sabir winced. Karrahir's eyes narrowed, but his voice was quiet as he said, "Sabir, your gardener forgets himself."

Sabir said, "He is not my gardener, lord. Mahar, leave us. You—"

Mahar ignored him, and spoke directly to Karrahir. "Lord, with so many dead, who will work for you? How will their families be fed? Lord, I know the city. I beg you not to do this."

Karrahir rose; the two boys measured each other. Sabir waited for Karrahir's order to call the guards. Instead, he asked, "If he is not your gardener, Sabir, who is he?"

"His name is Mahar, lord. He is a singer. He will sing at your enthronement."

Karrahir hesitated, and then a smile touched his lips. "I shall await that eagerly, Sabir." He pointed to the grass at his feet. "Sit, Mahar. Tell me of the city."

With a sidelong glance at Sabir, as if belatedly realising that he should have kept his mouth shut, Mahar sat. As Karrahir began to question him, Sabir exchanged a glance with the Lady Amalia. She was flushed a little; her eyes shone. Sabir smiled, and called for servants to bring wine and sweetmeats.

When they had come and gone, Karrahir and Mahar were still deep in conversation. As Sabir approached again, Karrahir glanced up and waved a hand carelessly at him. "Sabir, you may leave us."

Sabir felt as though someone had struck him. Impassively, he bowed and withdrew. As he closed the door behind him, he heard Lady Amalia's voice through the window lattice. "Karrahir, this is Lord Sabir's garden. You should show him courtesy."

A breeze rustled the rose leaves outside the window. Shadows danced over Sabir's robe, his hands. Karrahir said, "I do not like these half-men. They spy and creep in corners. They are not like us."

Lady Amalia's voice grew sharper. "Karrahir, without Lord Sabir your father would never have named you his heir. You will sit on the throne of the Immortal Soldan because of him."

Shadows traced patterns on the marble floor. Sabir shivered.

Laughter, and Karrahir's voice again, infinitely kind, infinitely condescending. "Maybe. But Mother, we do not need him now."

Sabir moved away from the lattice, and sank down among the silken cushions of the bed. He felt cold. He could still hear the murmur of voices from the garden, but now he did not even try to make out what they said.

He was not sure how much time passed before the door opened and Mahar came in. Sabir had a thousand questions for him, and somehow he could not utter one of them.

"Lord?" Mahar looked puzzled. "Lord, are you angry with me?"

"No." Slowly Sabir got to his feet, grasping desperately for self-control. "What did the Soldan Elect say to you?"

Mahar grinned. "Lord, there'll be no slaughter. He'll give a dole to every family in the city, as a memorial to the old Soldan."

And to buy favour for the new Soldan, Sabir thought sourly, and was at once ashamed. He beckoned to Mahar. "Come, I have a task for you."

The green rose that had opened that morning was in full flower, at the first moment of its perfection. Sabir took a pruning knife and severed the stem. He gave the rose to Mahar.

"Take that to the women's quarters," he said. "Have it delivered to the Lady Amalia."

Briefly Mahar hesitated, staring down at the rose, his face unusually troubled. "Sir, are you..?"

Lord Sabir drew himself up. "You know what I am. And she is the widow of the Immortal Soldan. Take the rose."

Meeting Mahar's eyes, he was startled to see tears there. Reaching out, his fingers brushed the hand that held the rose, and though it would have taken little for him to weep too, he managed a wry smile.

• • •

While the city still reeked with the old Soldan's burning, the new Soldan was enthroned. The elaborate temple ceremonies took all day; as night fell Sabir was already weary, but he still had to oversee the feasting. Knowing that every courtier in the palace would be flaunting himself, he chose austerity: a robe of heavy ivory silk, entirely without ornament.

For Mahar, he had ordered fine linen, equally plain, and examined him with approval when the boy reported to him at the start of the festivities. He could not deny a stirring of pride as he saw the tall, upright figure, the shining copper hair, and the confidence with which Mahar held himself. I made this, Sabir thought, from that grovelling little onion seller.

He smiled. "No wine at supper, Mahar. There'll be time for that later, if you wish. Someone will send for you when the Soldan is ready."

Mahar nodded, and clasped Sabir's hand. "Thank you, lord."

As Sabir turned away to his duties, he still could not repress the glow of pride.

· · ·

The feast itself was drawing to an end. From end to end of the vast, painted hall, the Soldan's courtiers sipped wine, gossiped, and waited, bored, for the entertainment to begin. Karrahir caught Sabir's eye and nodded; Sabir despatched a servant to bring Mahar. As he saw the boy appear from the ante-room, followed by his accompanist with a lute, he murmured to himself, "Let's see if they're bored now."

Into air heavy with perfume and the reek of wine, Mahar's voice fell like rain. The babble of voices and the clatter of wine cups sank into silence. Guests sprawling on the silken cushions were suddenly still. There was nothing in the world but pure music, the voice intertwining with the complex cadences of the lute. Sabir thought he could almost see it, a silver exhalation rising to the heavens.

When it was over, a low murmur swelled among the guests, and the pattering of hands slapped in appreciation against the paved floor. Mahar bowed, and looked uncertain for a moment until Sabir signed to him to withdraw.

A group of musicians took his place, breaking into a sinuous, wailing melody. A troupe of dancers glided into the central space, their veils floating. Sabir sighed a little as Mahar's magic dispersed.

He saw the Soldan beckoning to him, and went to kneel before him. The boy was smiling.

"Mahar pleased you, lord?" Sabir asked.

"Indeed." The Soldan twisted the great ring that had been placed on his hand during the ceremonies that afternoon. "He pleased me greatly. So fine a voice must be preserved. See that he is cut, Sabir."

"Lord?"

As Sabir's shocked eyes met his, the Soldan's smile grew cruel. "I thought to reward you, Sabir," he said. "Isn't that what you wanted?"

To Sabir, the rest of the feast seemed to drag out for an eternity. He could not forget the pleasure in the Soldan's eyes as he gave his order. He understood Karrahir all too well. Before he was enthroned, he had been wise enough to tread softly, but he would not forget Mahar's presumption in the garden. And if he thought himself indebted to Sabir, to the eunuch he despised, he would clear the debt in the way that would hurt most.

And yet . . . Sabir could not deny temptation. Karrahir had seen what he wanted, when he had never put words to it himself. When the order was carried out, Mahar would be his. No, Sabir told himself, for what was left afterwards would not be Mahar, but something twisted, a life wrenched out of true. Something such as Sabir knew himself to be.

• • •

At last Sabir's duties were done, and he could escape to his garden. Lady Amalia waited there for him, as he had known she would. No need to ask whether she knew what her son had ordered.

She ran to Sabir and caught at his hands. "Sabir, he is a monster. And I placed him here, may He Above forgive me!"

"I aided you." Sabir's voice was bleak. "We placed him here together."

"What can we do?" Amalia asked.

"I don't know."

He wrenched away from her and stood staring down at the rose bush. Half a dozen flowers bloomed there, from fully open to just emerging buds. As Sabir looked down at them they stirred in a faint breeze, as if they were dancers awaiting their music.

"So beautiful . . . " Amalia breathed.

"They will die." Sabir could feel nothing but a rising disgust. "Everything dies."

Amalia laid a hand on his arm, as Mahar came striding into the garden.

His smile was expansive, his arms spread wide. "They liked my songs!" he said. "All those fine lords and ladies, and the Immortal Soldan himself. Lord, it was wonderful!"

Feeling sick, Sabir forced himself to say, "They liked you too much."

Mahar's smile faded. "What do you mean, lord?"

"The Immortal Soldan ordered you cut." When Mahar still looked bewildered, Sabir added more explicitly, "He will make you as I am."

He knew he would take to his grave with him, seared on mind and heart, the look of fear and revulsion that Mahar turned on him. His gaze locked with the boy's.

"You knew!" Mahar's voice was hoarse, and roughened back to the accents of the marketplace. "You must have known what they would do. Right from the start."

Sabir made a helpless gesture. "At first . . . the old Soldan would have left it to me. And I would not have ordered it. Now . . . " His voice shook for all his efforts to speak with his usual precision. "I believed that all the old ways were over and done with."

He could say no more. The rustle of Lady Amalia's gauzy veils roused him as she laid cool hands over his own. "Peace, dear friend." She turned to the rose trellis, and Sabir saw there for the first time the Court Enchanter hunched on the seat beneath the arch. "Barrakar, can you spirit the boy out of the palace?"

Barrakar raised his head. "I can. But who will tell the Immortal Soldan he is gone?"

"I will." Amalia drew herself up. "I am his mother."

"The danger . . . " Sabir protested.

"Sabir, if Karrahir is such a thing that he would turn on me, do you think I care about danger to myself?" Imperiously she gestured to the Court Enchanter. "Do it. Now."

The old man heaved himself to his feet and shuffled forward until he stood in front of Mahar. "I will cast a glamour over you," he said. "No one will see you until you leave the Palace."

"On me also," Sabir said tersely. "I must lead him to the gate."

The Court Enchanter nodded and raised one hand. Sabir had a second only to think how curiously commanding the old villain looked, before his eyesight blurred briefly and he thought he discerned a single note of music, high on the edge of hearing.

The Court Enchanter lowered his hand. "It is done. Go quickly."

Sabir turned to Mahar. He still could not speak to the boy, but he beckoned to him to follow, and led him out of the garden.

Swiftly they paced along corridors, through the halls and ante-rooms of the palace, through other courtyards and gardens. At this hour there were few people to see them, and those there were ignored them as they moved under the Court Enchanter's charm.

At last they reached a little used gate, kept by a single guard. He was a young man, lolling against the gatepost with a bored expression on his face. His eyes never flickered as Lord Sabir and Mahar drew near.

Sabir pulled off a ring and pressed it into Mahar's hand, making him take it even though he sensed the boy's reluctance.

"Go to another city," he advised. "Sell that there. Change your name. And find another trade than singing."

He turned to unlatch the gate. When he turned back, Mahar caught him awkwardly into his arms, and hugged him hard.

"I'm sorry," he said.

With an effort Sabir would not have thought himself capable of, he kept his face impassive and his tears unshed. "Go now," he said. "Go safely. And may He Above be with you."

And then Mahar had slipped like a shadow into the shadows of the street outside, and the gate was closed again, and it was over.

• • •

Sabir threaded his way back through the courts and terraces more slowly. The Court Enchanter's charm had faded; late working servants reverenced him as he passed. Gradually he began to relax, and by the time he reached his own garden again he felt fit to face the world.

Amalia hurried swiftly to him as he entered through the archway. "Is he safe?"

"Yes."

She breathed a blessing, pressed his hand briefly, and was gone. Sabir looked after her for a moment. She still had her part to play, and it would need more courage than his own. But Lady Amalia had never lacked for courage. Even Karrahir would see that, and see the fury he would unleash on himself if he turned on his mother.

And there was still the rose. Lord Sabir crossed the garden and knelt in the cool grass beside the pot. The flowers glimmered pale in the twilight, exhaling their faint, unearthly perfume.

Sabir's momentary revulsion had left him. In a few days, he thought, when the first blooming was over, he would take cuttings, graft them on to good root stock, and grow new bushes for next season. He would give a pair of them to Lady Amalia, to stand one on either side of the entrance to her bower in the women's quarters.

"Notice anything different?"

Startled, Sabir looked up. The Court Enchanter, looking like a bundle of abandoned rags, was still sitting in the rose arbour. He was grinning hugely.

"No," Sabir said.

"Nor should you. But it is different, all the same."

A chill gathered around Sabir's heart. "What have you done?"

"Can you guess?"

Coldly Sabir said, "Don't play games with me, old man."

The Court Enchanter looked offended. "You said it would die. So I laid a charm on it. It won't die now, ever. It won't ever look any different from how it looks now."

Sabir knelt very still, gazing at the rose, his fingertips delicately touching the very edge of a petal.

The rose would never die. It would always be beautiful. But for that it would be sterile. There would be no cuttings, no new bushes, no gift for the Lady Amalia.

"What's the matter, Sabir?" Barrakar asked. "Is something wrong? I thought you would be pleased."

Sabir wanted to scream at him, to rage and weep. But Lord Sabir, Chief Eunuch of the Immortal Soldan, could not allow himself such self-indulgence. He made himself rise, and turn.

Barrakar was gazing up at him with an eager look, on the edge of hurt, as if he guessed he had done something wrong, but could not begin to guess what it was.

Sabir sighed. "No, nothing is wrong. The rose is beautiful, and I thank you for it. Come in with me now, Barrakar, and let us drink a cup of wine together."

Grinning widely again, relief banishing his momentary anxiety, the Court Enchanter hauled himself to his feet, and stumped along happily as Lord Sabir led him indoors.

Behind them, as moonlight filtered through the trees of the garden, the rose bush lifted its eternal flowers to the sky.

Afterword

The story started with the rose. I saw it in a huge floral arrangement on a pedestal for a church wedding. It was so beautiful that I wanted to keep it, but it wasn't mine, and anyway, flowers fade after a few days. So the only way I could preserve it was in a story.

Music is important to me, and many of my stories contain music in one form or another. I also like to write stereotyped characters in an unstereotypical way, and as a fantasy court's Chief Eunuch is always evil and manipulative it seemed interesting to make him a good man.

After I'd written the story I discovered that the name Sabir means 'endurance'. I like that a lot.

Oleander: An Ottoman Tale

Anthony Panegyres

I.

Chrisaphina waited on her *stroma*, fingertips running over Stephanos' soft baby shoes. She'd sneaked them from *Baba*'s chest. Her brother was a boy when collected for the Janissary Corps: a boy with a gummy gap where his last adult-tooth sprouted. He'd be a man now—with a new name. Perhaps he remembered her pinching his cheeks, perhaps he now realised she'd purposefully fumbled her knucklebones whenever they played or perhaps he'd ceased to remember her at all?

On hearing the *clip-itty clop* of horsed Ottomans, Chrisaphina resettled memories of her brother into their burrows. Black slippers on, she sprang from her room and out on to their low-lying balcony where the setting sun painted the sky the colour of pomegranates. She leaned over the railing and imagined that she could smell the rose petal jam in the bags of Greek pedestrians in sky blue hats and black slippers; the salty *bastourma*; or the horse sweat as the Ottomans rode by, not just horse manure awaiting the night sweepers.

A burst of emerald. His turban was always sharper than the other greens. Thank God (or Allah) that he never wore the sickly yellow favoured by some Turks. His apple-round face possessed an alien beauty, skin pale as sleet, eyes young and glinting like spearheads—unlike the sorrowful eyes of the Greeks and Armenians. His freely given smile was a forbidden gift for her. *Baba mustn't ever realise.* She tamed her face, glanced down, keeping her own smile closed.

Once he passed, she dashed inside. Would his voice be stolid and earthy or a mellifluous purr?

Baba sat at the table. She kissed his out-held hand, tasting of the sea, and served plates of salted cod with *skordhalia,* and *horta* with lemon juice and olive oil.

"Arabs in town," he said, chewing. "Real Arabs—not the dirty thieving local kind. You should see the port, Chrisaphina. Carpets flying this way and that. Oil lamps shining as brightly as stars."

"Why are they here?"

No response—and he was often generous when it came to sharing anything he knew. "Prepare my *narghile.*"

She did. Water, tobacco from the Americas, now grown throughout the Empire, and then the coals, lighting then poking them around until they glowed. She presented it to her father who dragged from the serpentine tube's nib and blew smoke plumes around the room, watching them as if he created something more whimsical than stealing moisture from her eyes and throat.

"They tried to rob me blind in the boat yard today. I ended up with my price though. But these Arabs—there's an indefinable twinkle in their eyes and their beards are as rich as molasses."

"You always say that Arabs are so dirty soap is wasted on them." Chrisaphina loathed these talks. She never warmed to her father's view of the town: Greeks were cunning; Turks dogs; Armenians short tempered; Arabs untrustworthy. She willingly chatted with everyone in the port, whether they were Armenians with their navy hats and violet slippers or Jews in their yellow skull-caps and blue slippers or even the rarer Arab traders with their perfumed wares. All could be cunning, all could be dogs, all could be untrustworthy.

"These are different. Money too. Proper wares."

Chrisaphina stayed quiet. If *Baba* could accept them—Muslims—then maybe a thread of possibility existed. And if she tended the thread it might strengthen into rope.

That night she was woken by a heavy, syrupy perfume, like a myriad of rose petals pervading the room. Where could it have come from? Her door was shut and the shutters closed.

By morning and then throughout the day, the room smelled as always: odours of wood and plaster and the *stroma* she slept on.

Clip-itty clop, clip-itty clop and she was outside. Would he smile again? She married herself to the railing, thirsting to be serenaded with *kantades* like they did in Smyrna or the distant Ionian isles. Afterwards, he would scale the low balcony, lose a boot in the process, and they would wind themselves together.

As his horse walked past, he tossed up a lemon-coloured tulip. She caught it and turned sharply; shutting him out of her vision, hoping he hadn't caught her blush. She waited until the hooves vanished before smelling the flower, trying to summon visions of last night's perfume. The reluctant tulip delivered a scent like stale water.

Where could she put it? Possibly under the *stroma*? But her father might see. She needed to be rid of it. But how do you rid yourself of a love's first gift? She removed the stem first and dropped it over the balcony, then pulled off the petals and watched each individually float down. Soon she had the last in her hand. She wanted it with her, this large petal. Chrisaphina bit and chewed. Green and peppery and wrong. She spat the remains over the railing.

Dinner was meant to be the lentil soup she'd already prepared but her father arrived with a rare treat, a spatchcock. She stuffed it with breadcrumbs and chopped livers, pine nuts, currants, crushed cloves and butter before sewing it up for roasting.

"Change into your church wear," he demanded.

"Are we going to an evening service?" She noted the worry beads in his hand. He never used them and his stodgy fingers moved among the beads far quicker than other more relaxed digits did in the town squares and taverns.

"No. But you must look your best."

"But—"

"Hurry along."

His lips tightened. In moods like this he was impossible to digest. She changed and came back, anxious that when they eventually ate, spraying juices from the spatchcock might stain her dress.

Chrispahina had never witnessed her father lay a table but there they were—three plates set with three serviettes.

A knock on the door and *Baba* directed her to sit. She obeyed—she liked to please *Baba*, especially since Mama had passed. Chrisaphina wished she could remember her mother differently from how she had left them: flesh-eaten and hollow cheeked, her skin like tanned leather.

Baba patted his clothes down and spread his fingers through his snowy moustache. As he walked to the door, he seemed somehow straighter, somehow taller, like a young soldier. He made a theatrical show of welcoming the stranger, all his market skills on parade. "My house is your house, Effendi. You sweeten it with your presence."

The Arab entered and she should have been impressed. Broad with a glistening beard, a turban of violet silk and a fierce raptor nose. He sat, his jewelled fingers clinking against the oaken table.

"Ziyad. My daughter, Chrisaphina," said her father.

"She is as beautiful as you claimed. Skin like honey and eyes of cinnamon."

Cinnamon and honey. Do you plan on eating me for dessert? What was *Baba* planning? The man was Muslim. A Muslim whose eyes—she conceded—were dark and beautiful like large beads of polished coal. Not the Muslim she wanted. Not her emerald-turbaned Turk.

The guest and *Baba* chatted of trade and Ottoman rulers. Ziyad told tales of the East, of flying carpets and lamps with soulless djinn and new delicate sweets coming from Persia, where sugar could be turned into silken thread. Now and then they spoke in Arabic and she was lost in its many 'h's and 'wa's and 'l's; only garnering snippets and phrases.

At the end of the night, after the *kafes* and a piece of *galaktoboureko*, Ziyad bowed, turning back at the door to Chrisaphina. "Share a carpet ride with me tomorrow as the sun sets."

She lifted her head, motioning *no*. Chrisaphina may have been curious, maybe even seduced by the notion, but she knew better. Even in richer Arabian lands, she had heard of the many falls. There was little riskier than clinging to a rug, high up battling the elements. In the end, the apple-faced Ottoman blinkered her to all other men.

Baba unfolded his palms. "She is afraid of heights. Please, grace us again soon."

Her father wheeled on her mutely after the Arab left, his silence marred by a flurry of hand gestures. She bit her lip to refrain from shouting *how dare you sell me off?*

With a beseeching whisper for the Lord and the Heavens to help he brought over two waters, spooning a sticky scoop of *vanilia* into both.

Sugaring things. He wants me calm.

He reached across and laid a hand over her arm. Chrisaphina yanked hers away, cautioning herself—*be careful, there is only so far you can go.* He was rarely brutal but like most fathers in the Ottoman Empire he could deliver a stinging cheek-slap when he felt justified.

"I lied yesterday," said *Baba*.

Chrisaphina didn't reply. Confessions came easier without commentary. They stirred the globule of *vanilia* at the base of their glasses, licking it now and then from their spoons, only ever sipping the water, making it last.

Her father breathed her name, "Chrisaphina," before his words spurted out: "I never received my price yesterday like I told you . . . and today was a ruin. Other merchants still manage to compete, but I can't—not now the Arabs are in town. They're ruining me."He pressed his palm on to the table. "People are saving their coin in hope of flying carpets and the really wealthy for lamps. Ziyad's brother has a stall with lamps—and carpets that quake as you watch. How am I to compete with live carpets?"

"You'll be fine, *Baba*. We always find a way. We did our best for Mama. We recovered when they took Stephanos away to become a Janissary." Had she ever really recovered? She saw her brother's face on every homeless boy. That look, eyes pleading, that indescribable stare of being less.

"I spent all I had on that chicken," said *Baba*.

"What about *Theio* Nikolaos or your other brother, Eleftherios? Surely they will help." She knew that they could not.

"All have young families with many mouths. Their charity would deprive them of food."

"Things will be fine. We'll eat pulses and greens and bread." They would not be fine. She could sweeten her words too.

Strange that her father had hosted the Arab. In Asia Minor, she supposed other places too, desperation led to values changing in a flash—even in the more 'civilised' quarters. She thought of leaving the table, escaping whatever scenarios her father would suggest. She lingered though, scenarios were unavoidable: they would hang on to her like leeches as long as she lived in the house.

"Marry this Arab. He will take care of you. You'll live well. Your children and grandchildren too one day. No son will be stolen for the Janissary corps. You'll never suffer what we have."

"*Baba*, you know I'll have to convert by Ottoman law. Your grandkids will be 'dirty Arabs'." In all this nonsense, she saw hope brighten. Her father might weave some logic here that would lead her to an emerald turban.

"Survival and family are all that really matter. I've been wrong in my mutterings. All believe in the same God: Greeks, Armenians, Jews and Muslims. Thousands of Christians convert through marriage. What's more important? Your health and future—or the past?"

"You must be unwell." She gulped down her water and took the spoon of *vanilia* with her to the bedroom, not turning back to see if he followed, ready to strike. Once inside she released a gush of relief, collapsed onto her *stroma* and licked the *vanilia*. *Elope with the Turk,* she reminded herself.

A taste woke her during the night. She poked her tongue around. Nothing. No texture except her gums and the roof of her mouth, teeth and fleshy cheeks. But the taste held, rich and honeyed like communal wine, with more: cloves and fig jam and cinnamon.

Like the previous night, the scent of roses swept through the room.

2.

The following sunset, as his horse trotted by, her Ottoman called out: "I am Murat!"

She mouthed her own name, common enough in the town, in reply, hoping he could read lips.

His words were few, three to be precise. But what gift is more beautiful and lasting than a name? A strong name too: sharp and solid. A name that suited her emerald-turbaned man.

Baba did not arrive for dinner. She covered his bowl of bean soup and went to bed.

Midway through the night she woke to sounds near the door. "*Baba?*" she called out. "*Baba?*" Her voice more timid this time as she spoke into the blind dark. She gripped her sheet as if it were a shield against a night stranger. The same aroma imbued the room; the same taste in her mouth. The flavours should have delighted, but now, accompanied by unseen sounds, she was afraid. Chrisaphina heard breathing and the slip of shoes over the floor. She squinted but could not detect the source. She pulled the sheet over her head and hid. Concealed, although she knew it was idiocy, she felt safer.

The breathing drew close, as if the spectre were bent low next to her. Chrisaphina squeezed her legs to prevent herself pissing. She held her breath and counted numbers in her head to quell the fear.

A voice shattered her attempt.

"A palace. I can take you to a palace on a hilltop from which you can watch the ocean; take you on sail-crafts down the Nile, to bazaars that are beyond your wildest imaginings, or far away temples and cities carved into mountainsides. I can give you all this."

The voice sounded like the aroma, the taste of sweets. Yet the floral cadences did nothing but terrify her. She recalled her Mama's advice about the Lord's Prayer. Although she doubted whether she believed, she began to chant, whispering the words over and over, out from the armour of her sheet.

"I will return. Whatever you desire, that is all I am here for."

Chrisaphina did not *desire* anything—outside of her father's business improving and Murat's lips on hers. Lips that would be supple and considerate yet strong like his name. Thoughts of him obscurely calmed her to sleep.

3.

As soon as day broke, Chrisaphina left her room. *Baba's* bowl on the table from the previous evening had been emptied. He'd departed earlier and she had no doubt that he'd return later again.

She took the long route to the markets. Along the way she saw a few sooty barefoot kids nipping around. When adults looked at them, their faces slumped like whipped stray dogs. Survivors too, Chrisaphina noted, as one pilfered a cheap *koulouri* bread from a stand. '*Xypolytos,* barefoot,' her father would snarl as if there

— 187 —

were no lower rung than an orphaned gypsy. But to Chrisaphina, the images mirrored Stephanos. If she could reach out, take them home. *Baba*'s brow would scrunch, affronted by any suggestion of taking a child in.

At the markets, among people bargaining with colourful gestures and varying tones, a few Arabs boldly flew around on carpets. She wondered if one was Ziyad or his brother—the lamp and flying carpet salesman. There were new wares for sale. Glittering lamps that cost a home and more with 'Djinn' printed on signs by them. The carpets she saw with her own eyes but the notion of soulless djinn imprisoned in lamps was another thing altogether.

Once home, she prepared egg-and-lemon fish soup, using cheap fish heads for stock. Sucking on a white fish eye, she headed outside. She would not wait in her now-dreaded room for the sun to set. Time crawled by and, tired from the nightly interruptions, she dozed.

When the hooves sounded she was awake, up and leaning out over the railing. Her eyes unashamedly sought their quarry. There Murat was. He stopped the horse beneath her and the others were forced to manoeuvre around.

"Chrisaphina," he called. "Let me come up."

She desired that but she knew what was required. It was clear in all the stories. *Porni* was a word brandished around too easily and it tainted longer than the word's brevity. "Sing for me," she said. "And tomorrow we'll see."

Murat's head swivelled as he waited for the last three horsed Muslims to pass. He cleared his throat and began. His singing voice was girlish and weak and missed the low notes, which had her giggling. He sang a Greek song too, about a lover as white as snow and as red as fire, like the marble in The City.

Once finished, he bowed awkwardly from his horse. Chrisaphina wished she had a handkerchief to drop from the balcony. Instead she clapped briefly.

"Can I come up?"

"Tomorrow, perhaps. But you'll have a wall to scale."

He blew a kiss, and she smiled at him before withdrawing inside. His airy kiss made her buoyant. She floated about the kitchen as she covered the soup, two fish heads and an obligatory chunk of bread. She tried to sit and failed; instead she sang the song she had been serenaded with, and all but skipped through the room.

Later, she nearly forgot her fear of the bedroom. She said the Lord's Prayer just in case and then fell asleep dreaming of Murat's lips on hers. Somewhere in the midst of her sleep she heard the relieving creak of the front door—*Baba* was home.

Rose petals in the air, honey-spiced wine in her mouth, whispered promises. She woke and froze, as still as mortar and brick. The bedroom door whined open. Pronounced steps crossed the floor to her *stroma*. In the shadows of the colourless night her sheet was pulled away. Her eyes caught it aloft before it glided back to the floor. A moment later, depressions moved along the base of her *stroma* and then up near her side. Breath on her earlobe made her shiver, then a touch, light and warm and wet, on her neck. She wanted to scream, and opened her mouth, but fright had stolen her vocals. She urged her lungs to sound. Nothing.

"Shhh. Calm. Enjoy the offerings," an accented voice whispered.

The breathy kisses continued and she felt a light touch of fingers around her neck that soon trickled under her night-wear just below her throat. Gentle trills of fingertips still made invasive fingers. What ghost was haunting her? What sin had she committed? Was it her love for a Muslim?

The fingers continued feather-like across her breasts, followed by warm breath on her chest and stomach. It was not her Murat. The hands firmed around her thighs. A warning? A sob shook her. She pushed out with her entire body and this time the ethereal arms were iron pincers.

She kicked but hands anchored her. The *lick* of a lapping tongue. She thrashed but the spirit was immoveable. *Lick*. She wheezed, shaking her head from side to side. *Lick*. And Chrisaphina found voice, for a line or two she did not realise that she was muttering lines aloud: *hallowed be thy name, thy kingdom come* . . . When she understood, she called louder and louder in an ensuing crescendo. "*Baba*!" she screamed. "*Baba! Baba!*"

Her door flung open. Amber light from her *Baba*'s oil lamp illuminated the room, vanishing the demon like a tallow's flame in a gush of wind.

Chrisaphina was panting. Her father turned his back. *He had seen her.* She tugged at her nightgown.

"*Baba*," she said as normally as she could. He turned as she said his name. She would not cry in front of her father. She had wept when Stephanos was taken; she had wept in front of *Baba* at Mama's funeral. Since then she had never shed tears before him.

He appeared pallid and bleached.

He sensed something too. What did he see?

"Come here." His voice quivered. Two strides and she buried her head into his comforting chest. He stroked her back and hair. "Come," was all he said when he released her. He gathered her *stroma* and they moved to his room. She slept by his feet at right angles, burrowing her head under the sheets, her tears hidden: silent and unheard.

4.

Before sunrise, she felt her father's moustache prickle her cheek with a gentle kiss goodbye.

Chrisaphina arose only after the door sounded his leaving. From the corner of her eye, she noticed something covered in velvet cloth. *Baba* trusted her implicitly. The secret was to be covert: cover things exactly as they were found. That way he never realised that she knew most, if not all of the house's secrets: where he kept Mama's wedding ring; the tiny shoes that Stephanos had worn; the story of Ysmine and Ysminias; the icon of Athanasios that he displayed on a whim; and his leather water pouch that was filled and emptied every two days with aniseed spirit. The velvet had two folds and an inch or two covered the floor on one side. Easy enough work though velvet could be tricky. She unveiled the object: a sparkling oil lamp, engraved in Arabic script, possibly lines from the Koran. Meticulously, she replaced the velvet.

Chrisaphina went into the kitchen and wrote a letter to her father.

She continued with her daily ritual as though there was no letter, as if things weren't going to be ripped and torn.

Chrisaphina made the sign of the cross as she left. Outside, she felt adrift, stained, damaged. She looked downward as passers-by called out in greeting, and feigned not seeing people she knew when she reached the markets. On glimpsing her great-aunt Antigoni she abruptly turned and—realising her auntie's bandy legs were incapable of catching her—hurried to the far side of sacks filled with pine nuts, walnuts, pistachios and sesame seeds. When her neighbour Eleftheria saw her, Chrisaphina strode straight past, pretending to stare at some dried currants in the distance. Usually she enjoyed this part of the day. The open stalls, many on wagons, full of fresh produce and loud haggling and calls of *Fresh!* and *The finest!* and her favourite, *Still living!* which was how any edible sea creature was described to imply its freshness. Today's fish—out of her price range—had crystal ebony eyes, not the blurred cataracts of those a little older.

She did not haggle for fear her voice would break. She listened to the calls. Watched the signs. Found the cheapest goods. Chrisaphina soon had chicory and *vleeta* and bread.

She went out of her way to go by the port. From a distance she saw *Baba*, possibly for the last time, his face furrowed as he haggled with an Armenian. Chrisaphina had not come for him though. She was where she needed to be: the Arab merchant. Lamps with palatial prices; a few carpets, woven from the sapphires and crimsons of Persian silk, with knots so thin they were invisible. One carpet's ends wriggled on its own accord, as if seeking the air, as if masterless.

The Arab sat cross-legged on a cushioned carpet in front of his wares. A stallion of a man, the same stock as Ziyad who her *Baba* wished her to marry. If it weren't for his lighter chestnut eyes she may have thought it him.

In no mood for conversation, she stood a few yards back and watched; trying to force herself forward.

The Arab's eyes laughed. He gestured her closer with his hand. She approached, staring at the few lamps that shone brighter than the rest. Their inscriptions were in Arabic. All stood on cloths of velvet.

She darted out a hand to pick one up. Quick as a striking viper, he slapped her arm away.

"Those are not to be idly touched."

She let a hint of her inner confusion out on to her face and waited.

"A thousand apologies. But these are not any old lamps."

Djinn. "Have you sold many?"

"They may be a little above your range."

"No doubt," and she let her lower lip quiver ever so slightly.

"About seven—eight if you include my brother's."

"And if I rubbed a lamp, like in the tales. Three wishes?"

"No, an answer only—if they know it. The owner is the sole person who can tell a djinni what to do and even then—"

It was all too cryptic; she could let a tear fall if she wanted to. But could she then stop? What had she to lose?

"No tears. You have too much pride to cry in front of a stranger."

How do you know?

"A fragile carnation weeps. A thorny rose acts strong but cries as it burns under the sun. You are the beautiful oleander who survives all hurt."

It almost made her teary. *Oleander,* she would remember that. It warmed her to the man. Overflowing with thoughts, confusion and hurt, Chrisaphina let all out in an avalanche: the nightly visits, her father, the Arab suitor. The only thing she withheld was her Turkish suitor.

"Djinn," said the Arab calmly. "Do not sleep there tonight or he will be fully fleshed."

"Fully fleshed?"

"The soulless ones take a while to solidify."

But what had her father done? How could he throw all their earnings away? Fish heads and beans and pulses. For what?

"Do they bring wealth?" *Baba would like that.*

"No money. A djinn cannot carry things back to his lamp. It's control, power, prestige. In the East they keep women content in the harem. In the West they are used as guards. In both the East and West they keep tabs on those around the house and streets nearby.' His mien stiffened, 'But the owner needs to keep eyes on them in turn. The lamp has to have been close to you or they could not materialise at all and then . . . As you've seen it takes time. Possibly the djinn was exploring the house and has taken a liking to you. Or—"

"What?"

"Someone could be commanding it. I know this hurts, but your father or my brother—"

"Your brother?" She knew the obvious as soon as she'd spoken.

He nodded. "Yes . . . Ziyad. Or someone else close by in the neighbourhood."

The casualness of it all had her swimming.

She spat, not caring about the Arab's gaping response. Then she fled.

Her purchases banged awkwardly against her legs so she dropped them. Somehow, close to home, she lost herself in a back alley. She turned in circles until the world rotated and spun. Covering her head in her hands, she sat down on someone's step. A shoeless street urchin, dark and grimy, came tentatively towards her, a bag in his hand. She reeled as he drew close. He stank putridly, like a tanner.

"Yousef," he said introducing himself.

"I have nothing to give you, gypsy." She said *gypsy* derisively—like her father.

"Please, I have something for you."

"Are you deaf as well as filthy? Run back to your family."

"I have no family. But I have—"

"What's that matter to me? I said go!"

The boy slunk off but abandoned the bag behind him. She sat, face in hands, once more. Eventually, she looked up at the bag. Her *vleeta* and chicory and bread. "Yousef!" she called futilely. "Yousef, Yousef!"

Chrisaphina raced out of the alley, "Yousef!"

The sun would set shortly. She asked the first stranger—a young black clad widow—for directions. Her home was only five blocks away. All the way she called for the gypsy boy, but he did not reappear.

On arrival, she scrambled into *Baba*'s room and put his lamp into a carry bag. Then she tossed the letter to her father, along with the groceries, on the kitchen table and ran through her bedroom and on to the balcony. Sweat made her clothes cling but she was just in time. The sky was beautiful, like stone fruit: all apricots and peaches. The musical *clip-itty clop* arrived although the sun had not quite set. Still, she looked over the railing in hope, but rather than her Murat, it was the Arab merchant. He swung up a leather pouch.

"One question only, Oleander. Then bring it back to me, quickly. That way nobody will know." She opened the bag and there was the lamp from the Arab's shop, gleaming. "I could never live with the shame of it had Ziyad misused the djinn to test you, or worse." His horse trotted off as the sun set. She returned the lamp to its leather pouch and it joined the other in her carry bag.

Murat came soon after, bounding down from his horse and securing it. He tried leaping at the wall to scale it, and fell heavily on to his back with a muffled grunt. Chrisaphina gasped but he was back on his feet and already gripping his legs around the corner where the walls met. He steadily made his way, almost like climbing a palm tree. Once up, he clambered over the railing and bowed low.

"Take me with you," she said. Her lips hurried to touch his but met a turned cheek.

"It is bad luck before an Ottoman wedding," he said, a little flushed.

As they fled through the house and reached the entrance, Chrisaphina turned, "Wait here."

She slipped away into *Baba*'s room to withdraw Stephanos' baby shoes. She kissed them, holding them, etching them into her mind. *I'll bring them with me*, she thought, but instead returned them to her father's storage chest.

While they walked, Murat leading his horse, Chrisaphina knew she had to ensure she was no stranger to Murat; that she was more than a tale. So she partially explained her story of the Arab suitor; and the recent events with Yousef: how she hurt the boy and how, with that hurt, she tarnished memories of her own stolen brother. "I would like Yousef to have a place to stay," she said with finality. If she was nervous, her face, held high, did not show it.

Murat heartened her. "He is welcome to live with us." He also tut-tutted on hearing of Stephanos. "Not all Turks agree with the way the Janissaries are formed."

Chrisaphina took his free hand—the one not looped about the reins—and curved it around her waist and they semi-embraced, careful that their mouths did not touch. His chest and back felt steady, dependable.

Not once did she mention the lamps.

5.

In six days they were to be married. His home had a plump garden, ripe with tulips, that led onto fields. Her future mother-in-law's face was round and sweet like her son's.

Everyday Chrisaphina learned things about Murat. Most she liked: he kept fit wrestling, put things away, always had fresh flowers in a vase, treated his horse with tenderness and spoke to her as a friend. A few she didn't: he wouldn't touch almonds or pistachios and he read little outside of the Koran.

Each morning, Chrisaphina, with Murat's support, searched the streets for Yousef. She pestered merchants until many called out on seeing her—*Not seen him, You again? Back already?* and others waved her on with disdainful flicks of their hands. She questioned people in the markets—*A boy, so high*—brushing off their indignance. She asked any homeless child she saw, shouted his name down alleyways until she was hoarse. Yousef's face mingled in her mind with that of Stephanos.

And every evening—after Murat and she sipped the last of their steaming *salep*—Chrisaphina explored her new home. Every inch she made sure she knew. Every *narghile*, every Turkish rug, every Ottoman vase.

On the fourth evening, Chrisaphina inspected the storage shed, a jumbled mass of bulbs and shovels and trowels. She paused behind a box hidden behind some rusted tools. She took it inside and stood before her mother-in-law.

"Please, could you open this?"

"It's locked." Her mother-in-law held her hands and kissed her cheeks, her breath pleasant like sugared apple tea. "You'll be happy here. Murat will take care of both of us."

"And Yousef."

"Your gypsy boy too. Now put it back where you found it."

Chrisaphina dropped the box into her carry bag with the two lamps and made for the port.

Near a small jetty, long abandoned and partly lost to the sea, she smashed the lock against stone on top of a pillar again and again until she heard a satisfying crunch. With trembling hands her fears crystallised as she withdrew a lamp.

Chrisaphina lay the three lamps onto the faded wooden planks.

The Arab suitor, Ziyad, meant nothing to her, but he might have felt differently.

Her father? There were strands of love there still. They would be wiped away.

Murat? Why hadn't he spoken of the lamp? That didn't equate to guilt—she had not yet told him her story. Her dream would morph into a nightmare.

She sat for a time, watching the lamps sparkle in the twilight. She leant over the Arab's ready to rub it. Rubbing, what a strange concept—there were no stains or blemishes on any of them. *They belong in the ocean, they belong to nobody.* She lifted one up, ready to hurl it out past the waves that lapped against the pillars, then replaced it. Thoughts of the djinn burned and sizzled. This time, in one fluid motion, she snatched the lamp up and flung it into the sea. The next lamp she booted out as far as she could. A searing pain shot through her foot, making her hop and yell and make whirlwinds with her fists. Still smarting, she sat by the splintering ledge, took off her slipper and massaged her foot.

What if it wasn't Ziyad? What hurtful truth would she learn—or would she not ask and remain ignorant, living a possibly fabricated tale? Or could she unearth the recent past by herself—and ask something else altogether?

Chrisaphina picked up the lamp. As she rubbed, it grew warm in her hands.

• • •

He sat in a familiar alley. Dank, discarded citrus peel, and a few white bones, long bereft of meat, lay scattered nearby. A dust-coloured dog licked at his face.

"Yousef?" she said.

He squinted upwards. On recognising her, his head resignedly bowed.

"I am sorry, Yousef. I have something for you," she laid a round sesame covered *koulouri* bread before him.

He kicked it away with a bare foot. The dog sniffed the *koulouri* and wandered off.

"I will come back everyday," said Chrisaphina. She wanted to say more, that she had a home for him. Towels, soap, linen, a fireplace and more tulips than he could imagine. But she refused to buy him that way. She would earn his friendship first if she could.

Oleander knelt down, picked up the *koulouri* and tore it in two, holding one half out to him.

Yousef's impassive eyes never ventured near Oleander's; seemingly more captivated by the fallen sesame seeds on the paving. His twig-like fingers, however, clasped the offered bread.

Afterword

To be honest, the inspiration came from the theme itself and the challenge of writing for an anthology and a deadline. I utilised the genre elements (such as the purposefully flowery balcony opening) and at the same time I endeavoured to subtly subvert genre elements by breaking from convention wherever possible— it was a fine balancing act of both a floral promotion of the genre and simultaneous subversion.

I also have a passion for Ottoman history, so incorporating significant details and thematic issues was important too. Janissaries (at one stage the taking and transforming of the eldest Christian boys into an Islamic crack troop) and segregation via different hat and slipper colours occurred—not necessarily all events were synchronous as in the story (tobacco came later on). There was also a voluntary conversion of many Christians to Islam—a reality that I have no issue with. For specifics, I am seriously indebted to (and inspired by) the magnificent history by Philip Mansel: Constantinople: City of the World's Desire, 1453– 1924 *(although "Oleander: an Ottoman Tale" is not set in 'The City').*

Inspiration regarding food, as always, comes from my youth and all those extended family name days and festivals with grandparents and a myriad of great uncles and aunts.

Above all, despite the story's horrific elements (and I was reminded of soulless djinn via reading nobel laureate, Naguib Mahfouz, last year) and the various threads and themes, the story is still primarily about humanity's true strength lying in compassion and the choices we make.

A Dash of Djinn and Tonic

D C White

Colonel Jonas Watson looked at the officers seated on either side of the longish rosewood table. He was pleased to note that all looked well turned out. There had been a certain amount of scruffiness observed in the Officers Mess of the 151st Regiment of Artillery in recent weeks, and he was keen to nip it in the bud. *British India is no place for sloppy officers*, he told himself. *That's what Australia is for.*

"Gentlemen," he said, sitting up in his special Colonel's chair, "I believe that concludes this week's meeting of the Regimental heads."

"Not quite, sir," Ponsonby the Adjutant began. "There is one small other matter."

Watson frowned. He was not terribly fond of Ponsonby. The man had an attitude. He *knew* things. Colonel Watson disliked clever people on principle, seeing knowledge as proof of ambition. If there was one thing he disliked more than scruffiness and the delaying of meals, it was ambition.

"Fine," he sighed, shifting his not-inconsiderable bulk in his chair.

"We've had a request for assistance, sir."

Ponsonby shuffled some papers in a manner Watson found extremely annoying.

"It's from one of the hill tribes. A Mr Al-Ah-Din. He writes that—"

Watson cut him off. "Honestly, this is what we have you admin wallahs for. If this Alawhatsisname wants to complain that the weekly camel to Islamabad didn't arrive on time then I expect you to deal with it, not hold up important Regimental business."

"Begging your pardon, sir, but this is Regimental business."

"Explain."

Ponsonby did a bit more shuffling. "When the Adjutant's Office receives a complaint it undergoes an extremely rigorous sorting process. This is all laid down in the Regimental Charter. Unfortunately the nature of Mr Al-Ah-Din's complaint demanded it be addressed by the full board."

Colonel Watson found himself mildly intrigued. "I see. Well, you'd best carry on then."

"Mr Al-Ah-Din's tribe lives towards the edge of the Regiment's purview, almost in Afghanistan. They tend sheep."

"How wonderful. Get to the interesting bit."

"Mr Al-Ah-Din says his sheep are disappearing."

Watson began to drum his fingers on the table. "I would have thought that stock theft . . . "

"Rustling, sir," one of the other officers seated at the table piped up. There was some muffled laughter and a muted cry of 'yee-hah' from down the table.

Watson glared his best Colonel's glare. *This place could do with a bloody good clean out. Or a war*, he thought, the latter idea brightening him considerably. "Rustling, as my learned colleague so rightly points out. I should have thought that rustling was more the responsibility of the Colonial Police?"

"Under normal circumstances, yes."

Watson raised a bushy eyebrow. "Am I to take it we are not dealing with a normal circumstance?"

The Adjutant shook his head. "No, sir. Mr Al-Ah-Din claims his sheep are being taken by an ifrit."

There followed a longish pause, during which Watson chose his words carefully.

"An ifrit, Mr Ponsonby?"

"A type of djinn, sir."

"I know what an ifrit is, man," Watson snapped. "I have been Colonel around here for a while, you know." He pondered the matter. "Could it not be said that an ifrit would be more within the remit of the Colonial Administration?"

Ponsonby shook his head. "The Administration wallahs apparently informed Mr Al-Ah-Din that they are only concerned about actual things that really exist, sir."

Watson leaned back in his chair. "And why didn't we think of that?"

"Because of Clause 92, subsection M."

Of all of the answers Watson had been expecting, this was not it. "I'm a bit hazy on the majority of Clause 92," he replied. "I don't suppose you could see your way clear to appraising us all of its contents?"

Ponsonby frowned. "It was found by one of our young lieutenants, a Mr Kirk. He's a new bod. Clause 92 chiefly relates to the finding of artefacts during earthworks and other fortification projects. Subsection M, however, states somewhat more esoterically that *if at any time a new species is found, chiefly of a mythological or a cryptozoological nature, the report must be investigated by no less than two Regimental officers.*"

"Rather an odd clause, wouldn't you say?"

"Yes sir. Records indicate it's a 'Lady Lonsdale'."

As far as Watson was concerned, that was the icing on the cake. Lady Lonsdale was almost a mythological creature herself around the Regiment. The wife of the original Commanding Officer, she had contributed greatly to the formation of the original Regiment, even going so far as to draft much of its Charter herself. While her additions to Regimental lore had been generally sound, there was the odd aberration. This was why the toilets in the Regimental HQ were ritually cleaned on the hour, every hour, regardless of patronage. Any new officers who complained about this invasion of their privacy and dampening of their civil liberties were simply handed a towel, an annotated copy of the Charter, the first volume of Lady Lonsdale's memoirs: *Poise, Style, Grace and Efficiency* and were left to draw their own conclusions.

Watson was a man who drew his conclusions quickly. "So someone has to go and take a look?"

Ponsonby nodded.

Righty-o, thought Watson. "Up in the hills, you say? Northish?"

"Just a bit past Afridi, sir."

Colonel Watson leaned back in his chair. "Now then," he announced to the meeting in general. "We're not wasting any of the Regiment's valuable time on this. I'll go and have a look."

Ponsonby had a sudden fit of coughing. "You, sir?"

"Yes, me. I'm quite capable of dealing with some mad old villager, I can assure you."

"Clause 92 Subsection M clearly states that two officers must be present."

Watson sighed. "Fine," he snapped. "Then you can come with me."

Ponsonby went a bit pale. "M . . . m . . . me, sir?"

"Indeed. Do you good, some country air."

"Begging your pardon, sir, but I am terribly busy. Paperwork, you know."

"Nonsense. What paperwork?"

"Yours, mainly."

Watson assumed this was correct. He had a severe aversion to paperwork, believing the proper role of a Colonel was to be outside shooting things.

"Who else wants to come then?" He looked down both sides of the table. There was a distinct lack of volunteers.

"If I might be so bold, Lieutenant Kirk seemed quite keen," Ponsonby ventured. "Very big on exploring up north. Puts his hand up for everything."

"Capital!" Watson declared. "Now then gentlemen, if there's no further business, I declare this Officer's meeting of the 151st Regiment of Artillery closed."

He stood. "Fetch me this Kirk," he told the Adjutant, "We've got a date with an ifrit."

As he headed out the door he remarked, "Oh, and does anyone know if they still have that bakery in Afridi? The one that does those delicious sausage rolls?"

• • •

As a mode of transport the elephant has many advantages. Firstly, it has a certain undeniable gravitas which comes in handy when dealing with recalcitrant locals. Secondly, it's hard to bring one down, which is even better when the locals' recalcitrance turns ugly. And third, it's good for shooting at things from the back of, once you compensate for the boat-like rocking.

Colonel Watson squeezed both triggers on his Purdey and shook his fist in triumph as a small bird exploded to their right. "Got the blighter!" he cried. "Come on Kirk, your turn."

Lieutenant Kirk lay at the bottom of the wicker howdah, looking slightly green. He'd been there for the better portion of the trip so far. A thin young man, in stark contrast to the older, larger frame of Colonel Watson, Kirk did not seem to appreciate the wonders of pachydermal transport. *In fact*, thought Watson with a frown, *he looks like the sort of chap who doesn't enjoy much at all.*

Watson had little sympathy for those not of a sporting bent. "For heaven's sake man, anyone would think you were seasick."

Kirk gave a little "Yes sir" and crawled shakily to his feet, only to be nearly knocked over by a hearty slap on the back by the Colonel.

"There," Watson roared, completely oblivious to the lieutenant's discomfort, "what did I tell you? A bit of fresh air, that's all you needed."

There was a pause as Kirk vomited over the side. Watson peered over the howdah's wicker brim. "Oh dear," he said. "Don't worry, we'll get one of the sepoys to scrape it off later."

Kirk groaned in response. Colonel Watson was already thumbing shells into the shotgun's breech. "I heard Lieutenant Jaredson bagged a leopard last week. In his pyjamas. Mind you, what it was doing in his pyjamas no-one was quite certain."

Kirk remained biliously silent. Watson scowled. "For heaven sake man, snap out of it. I shan't waste any more jokes of that calibre on you if you're not going to appreciate them. Ha! Calibre, get it? And we're out hunting." He chuckled.

Getting no response, he decided to ignore the man and get on with shooting. Colonel Watson was a hunter of the old school, who held that everything in nature deserved to get shot unless it could run away fast enough. Watson sighted along the thick twin barrels of his prized Purdey. *There is something comforting about looking down at open sights*, he mused. *Although I suppose the pleasure is mostly mine.* In vain he swung the barrel around, looking for something to blast away at. Unfortunately, they were at the entrance to a long, deep and animal-less ravine.

"I say, bearer," he cried to the native chap leading the elephant. "Isn't there any game around here?"

There was no answer, and Watson began to feel as though something was wrong.

"Kirk," he said. "We've stopped."

"Thank God," the lieutenant mumbled in a voice that Watson noted as grounds for disciplinary action later on.

Watson scanned the tops of the ravine. "I think the bearer's done a runner. Does that strike you as odd?"

To his credit Kirk seemed to pull himself together quite quickly. He undid the button on his holster-guard. "Indeed, sir," he replied.

Before either man could say more there was a gunshot, and a bullet hole appeared in Kirk's pith helmet.

Watson eyed the helmet coolly. If there was one thing he drilled into his regiment it was the requirement for not getting shot. "I say Kirk, do you realise there's a hole in your helmet?"

Kirk nodded. Watson saw his training kicking in as his eyes beginning to scan the left hand ridge above them. "Indeed, sir?"

"Dashed inconvenient, what?" Watson's eyes scanned the right.

"It's only just arrived from Horsnell and Co." Kirk nodded very slightly to Watson.

Watson nodded back. "I'd say some rotter's about to catch hell for that, wouldn't you?"

At the signal both men dropped behind the wicker hide of the howdah. Watson's shotgun tore through the silence of the ravine twice in quick succession. Kirk's service revolver boomed as he began to pick off targets amongst the figures who had appeared along either side of the ravine. Several screamed as they were shot, tumbling over the cliff.

"Last one under the elephant is a rotten egg!" Watson cried, grabbing his ammunition case and leaping over the howdah's edge in a move which was surprisingly sprightly for a man of his bulk and years. Several seconds later he was crouched under the pachyderm with a slightly soiled Kirk. Watson looked him up and down. "You've only got yourself to blame. Should have gone over the other side."

The lieutenant's resolve seemed to waver. From above them came the sound of gunfire being poured into the canyon. Most of it sounded as though it was hitting the top of the elephant, but some slammed into the ground nearby, throwing up chips of dirt which made Kirk flinch. "What do we do now?" he yelled.

Watson was shocked. "Mr Kirk," he replied. "Pray remember you are an officer in Her Majesty's 151st Regiment of Artillery. The requirement for a stiff upper lip does not evaporate the moment you find yourself huddled for cover beneath a vomit-covered elephant."

"Terribly sorry sir, but we're trapped." He patted the elephant's leg. "Nellie here is not going to last forever. What are we going to do?"

Watson grinned. For the first time in years he was in combat and he was determined to enjoy every minute of it. "One doesn't get to be a Colonel without learning a trick or two." He put a hand on the straps that fastened the howdah around the elephant's stomach, and indicated that Kirk should do the same. With his other hand he pulled an orange out of his ammunition case. The case he then hung from his belt, while the orange he placed between the elephant's front legs.

He pulled out his service revolver, looked over at Kirk and said, "Now hang on."

Watson shot the orange, or rather, he shot the dirt directly behind the orange. The fruit in question leapt forward in front of the elephant who, having been bred for hunting parties in which rich people fed it cake, galloped off after it heedless of the shots from above. The bullets had reduced the howdah to matchwood but so far had failed to penetrate the elephant's hide.

Beneath the elephant, somewhat predictably, chaos reigned. Colonel Watson had to admit, as the dust flew and he was nearly jolted out of his uniform, he hadn't really thought this through. Despite all his boasting to Kirk he had made this plan up on the fly. Of course he was damned if he was going to admit that to the young lad anytime soon. Instead he concentrated on his next shot, trying with a superhuman effort to steady himself as he lined up the orange again.

• • •

The elephant was perturbed. She didn't like canyons at the best of times, and now her back was sore and there was an orange, an orange she rather wanted, but it kept running away. She remembered when she was smaller than she was now, and one of the small pink monkeys had tried to make her move by holding a carrot on a string in front of her. After the first few steps she had figured out what was up and had simply walked to the nearest water hole, gathered up a trunkfull and blasted the little chap until he ran away howling. The resultant punishment had been enough to convince her, with the advice of the older elephants, to play dumb. She had been satisfied to wander about all day while people rode around on her shooting things. She was resigned to her lot in life. Now, however, she hadn't had lunch, there didn't seem to be any cake in her immediate future and there was this orange that wouldn't keep still. She kept running after it and it kept running away. So focussed was she on the job at hand she failed to notice the canyon narrowing up ahead.

• • •

Things had been going well for a bit too long as far as Colonel Watson was concerned. After several shots he had managed to not actually hit the orange, which would have spelled disaster, or at least the loss of the apple he was keeping in reserve for afternoon tea. He was lining up the next shot when he heard Kirk shout from the other side of the furiously swaying pachyderm stomach.

"I say, sir, look up ahead!"

Watson looked up and saw what he didn't want to see: the canyon narrowing. He holstered his revolver, reached over, grabbed hold of Kirk's tunic and pulled them both directly under the elephant. "Assume crash position!" he cried.

"What's the crash position?" yelled back Kirk.

Before Watson had a chance to elaborate further, the elephant, which had been travelling at some speed, became too wide for the narrowing canyon. Two large protrusions on either side of the canyon walls seemed to grab hold of her flanks, almost as if the canyon were a slip fielder and the elephant a badly-placed cricket ball.

The elephant thundered into the gap and stopped very suddenly. The moment it was stuck, there issued forth at speed from between its front legs a pair of red-coated British military officers. They hit the ground and rolled to a dusty halt.

Colonel Watson sat up, brushed at the dirt on his uniform and tried to get his bearings. They were, as far as he could see, at the end of the line. Beyond the bit filled with elephant the canyon widened to form a natural amphitheatre. The only way in or out was blocked by the elephant who, despite her predicament, was still at full stretch, her trunk quivering with effort as she strained to reach the orange, dusty but whole, which still lay tantalisingly out of reach. Watson was the sort of man who thought of himself as kind to animals, or at least those animals he couldn't shoot at or eat in some fashion so he picked himself off the ground, and handed the fruit to the elephant, who immediately ate it. Job done, he walked over to the recumbent form of Kirk. "Lieutenant!" he barked. "Get up, man! They'll be here soon. I'll not have a stay-a-bed sluggard in my regiment!" He nudged Kirk with his boot.

Kirk groaned, face down in the dust. Standing up, he spat the greyish powder from his mouth. He steadied himself for a moment, then saluted. "Reporting for duty, sir."

"Ah, formidable. It's my sad duty to inform you, Mr Kirk, that we appear to be trapped."

Kirk looked around. "Indeed, sir."

"What's more, you've lost your hat. And I don't think it will be too long before those bandit chappies show up, either. When they do they'll hold the high ground."

Watson heard a noise above them. Looking up he saw a large man on a mule looking down. His hand instinctively moved to his holster but it was empty, his service revolver lying at the end of its cord some feet away. *Damn thing's probably out of shots anyway.* The thought didn't comfort him, especially not when he heard the cruel, mocking laugh from above.

"Well well, Effendi," the big man yelled down through several layers of dirt and beard, "You do seem to be in a, what do you say? A bit of a spot."

"Oh, I shouldn't worry about us," Watson replied in a voice as pleasant as he could muster. "I'm sure we'll muddle through somehow."

While he spoke, both Watson and Kirk slowly backed away, trying to put as much distance as possible between them and the rim of the canyon. "When we get to the opposite wall, look for cover," Watson whispered.

They kept their eyes fixed on the bandit, who kept grinning. "I not worry about you, Effendi. Ali will be here soon, and he will be very angry with you."

Watson found himself slightly affronted by this. "The bloody cheek!" he declared, "The bugger was shooting at us. A man's allowed to run aw . . . make a strategic retreat!" He hoped no-one noticed his little slip.

The bandit roared with laughter. "Ali will not be angry that you ran, redcoats," he told them. "Ali will be angry you found the location of his treasure cave."

Before Watson could respond, Kirk coughed politely and stepped forward. "Begging your pardon, but this Ali you speak of. He wouldn't be Ali Baba, by any chance?"

The bandit nodded. "The very same. Ali comes from a long line of bandit chiefs whose beginning is lost in the mists of time."

"And this is where his treasure cave is?"

"It is almost directly behind you, Effendi. But do not bother to look for it! The entrance is sealed fast by a terrible magic. Only Ali knows the password."

"*Iftah yah simsim!*" yelled Kirk.

Watson jumped as behind him the wall of the canyon parted with a great grinding of stone. Behind it was a cavern, almost totally dark.

"What . . . what . . . what did you do?" The bandit's unshaven face gaped at the sight.

"Thanks awfully, old chap," Kirk said, before running inside.

Watson thought it best to follow quickly behind.

When they were both inside, Kirk yelled, "Close, *simsim!*" The canyon walls seemed to flow as if they were liquid, sealing up behind the two officers and making the cave as black as night.

Watson was not perturbed by the dark, but Kirk clearly was. "Colonel, may I borrow some matches?"

"Of course not."

"Why not?"

"I don't smoke, for a start. And for another start, I'm not doing anything until you tell me what the bally heck is going on here, Kirk. What's all this Ali Baba business? I thought that was just an old nursery tale."

"I thought you knew, sir."

Watson took a dim view of people who expected him to know things. "It seems you were misinformed."

"Remember when I arrived, sir? I had an interview with you while you were shouting at the polo match."

Watson did recall something along those lines, although he wasn't about to admit he hadn't been even slightly paying attention. "Quite, quite," he muttered. "Well, that explains it perfectly."

"No, sir," Kirk explained. "Remember I told you about my time at Cambridge, how I studied ancient Persia and Araby, and that's why I'd requested a posting to the northernmost-stationed regiment in India?"

"It's ringing a bell."

"That's why I brought you the message this morning. I knew something must be up. I mean, Mr Al Ah Din? Really? Aladdin? Sweet Fanny Adams could have seen something was awry there."

Watson was glad it was dark as it prevented Kirk from seeing the astonished look upon his face. "Quite, quite," he said. "Still, I expect you were jolly relieved then when I decided to come along to sort things out."

There was a small, polite pause.

"Of course, sir. Although I will admit to being a little perturbed when you decided to take only one elephant and one bearer."

"Strategy, Mr Kirk, strategy. I find it's always better to be underestimated."

"It certainly seems to have worked, sir."

Watson glowered and decided the best strategy in this case was a change of subject. "Never mind that," he said. "How are we going to get out of here? Does this cave have a second entrance?"

Kirk's voice seemed to come from further away, as though he were moving out into a large, open space. "The legends all agree on only one entrance, sir."

"Well that's no good. We can't climb the canyon walls with those chappies shooting at us, and the elephant is blocking the way back up the canyon. Of course, it's blocking their way in, too, but they're sure to get it unstuck soon and then we'll be in it up to our neck."

"In what, sir? The elephant?"

"Don't be facetious, Mr Kirk. I suggest your time would be more profitably spent finding a way out of here."

Kirk's voice sounded farther away still. "I agree, sir," he replied. "And what will you be doing?"

Watson felt he was on firmer philosophical ground here. "I shall locate a weapon and wait here for this Al chap to open the door, at which point I'll bean him."

"Ali, sir."

"No, it's a door. Damned strange door, granted, but a door."

Kirk said no more, and Watson resolved to keep his little jokes to himself for the time being. *The man obviously has no sense of humour,* he thought.

Watson's foot brushed something, and he picked it up. "Here's what we need!" he declared. "A lamp. Mind you, it feels a bit grubby. Wait on, I'll just give it a quick rub. Soon have it looking like a new pin."

Colonel Watson, if asked, would happily admit that he was not a scholar of middle-eastern folklore. However he would also happily admit that even if he had been the Dean of Folklore at the University of Baghdad, he would still have given the lamp a rub. People like Colonel Watson were born lamp-rubbers, door-openers and sayers-of-things-like "Well, at least it's not raining."

As Watson vigorously applied the sleeve of his tunic to the side of the lamp, he became aware of an eerie blue glow issuing forth from the spout.

"I say, Kirk," he declared. "What do you make of this? Rum show, what?"

The glow grew as the smoke wreathed its way into the middle of the cavern. It began to be bright enough to see by.

Kirk came dashing over. "Sir!" he cried. "Put it down! Put it down at once."

Watson's voice was deceptively mild. "That almost sounded like an order, Lieutenant."

"I'm sorry sir, but that lamp really is terribly dangerous."

"What, this old thing? Nonsense. I expect it's just marsh gas or something."

"It's a djinni!"

Watson regarded him coolly. "I think we're getting into the realms of fantasy here, Kirk."

The cavern had brightened considerably and Watson could now see that they stood on the edge of a massive grotto which was full of gold coins, expensive rugs and tapestries, mysterious suits of armour and weaponry of all kinds. There were chests full of gold, silver and gems which glittered even in the dim blue light. As interesting as these things were, he was becoming more interested in the smoke, which seemed to be forming itself into the shape of a man. Watson watched while the strands coalesced into the form of an Arabian chap in traditional dress, quite stout, with shoes whose pointy ends curled up. The apparition floated in the middle of the cavern, twice as big as a man. It looked down over its folded arms at the Colonel.

"I am the Djinni of the Lamp," its great voice boomed, "and I am bound by a geas to grant whoever frees me from my prison three wishes."

"I was chased by geese once," Watson said, in lieu of anything more appropriate. "Mind you, I was only eight. They're dashed big buggers when you're only a little chap, you know."

"Not geese, sir," Kirk explained. "A geas, a magical enchantment."

Watson harrumphed, mainly because he was sceptical but also because harrumphing a lot was just what a Colonel did and he was down on his quota. "I see." He put down the lamp and rubbed his hands together. "Well, while I don't believe you're anything but a figment of my and Kirk's collective subconscious, first I'd like a bit of light. Can't see what I'm doing around here."

The djinni clapped his hands and the cavern was lit from all sides with a glow of light.

"Mmm," nodded Watson. "Not too shabby for a whiff of old marsh gas."

"Sir," Kirk hissed. "I don't think that is marsh gas."

Watson regarded him with disdain. "Indeed, Mr Kirk. Giant floating chaps? I think not." He pointed up at the djinni, who appeared to be taking it in stride. "This wallah here, while undoubtedly full of local colour and interest, is a figment of our imaginations, Kirk."

"But . . . "

"I expect we'll soon wake up, discovering that the elephant walked too close to a currently-pollinating, rare species of hallucinogenic orchid found only in this location."

For a moment, Kirk appeared to be struggling with some inner emotion, then he smiled. "Indeed sir, I couldn't have put it better myself. However, since we're here, we should make the best of it, shouldn't we? Think of the opportunities."

Watson did. "By Jove, you're right," he said. He turned to the djinni. "I say, you, blue fellow. So I get three wishes then, what?"

"Two," replied the djinni. "You've already had one for the light."

"Quite so, quite so."

"Ask him for all the world's knowledge, sir!" Kirk whispered in his ear.

Watson screwed up his face in disgust. "What on earth would I want that for? No, my good man, I should like you to make me a shotgun, 12-gauge, that never runs out of shot."

This time the djinni didn't even unfold his arms, he just nodded. There appeared before Watson his beloved Purdey. The normally stoic Colonel uttered a wholly unexpected cry of delight. He grabbed the gun, cracked the breech to check it was loaded, snapped it shut, discharged both barrels into the roof of the cavern and cracked it open again. There, nestled in the barrels were two more fully-loaded wax paper shells and caps.

Watson realised he was standing there with his mouth hanging open. He shut it and the gun at the same time. He looked at the djinni. "This still doesn't mean I believe in you," he warned the apparition. "I'm C of E."

If the djinni was at all put out he didn't show it. "What is your third wish?"

"Sir!" hissed Kirk, looking extremely annoyed. "Think of what you could do with your last wish. Please don't waste it."

"My dear fellow, I have no intention of doing any such thing." He addressed the Genie once more. "Righty-o. One last wish, eh? Then what happens?"

"Released from my geas, I shall take my leave of this plane of existence. It is a tiresome world."

"Yes, well we like it." Watson wasn't easily affronted but he wasn't about to have some hobbledehoy of a djinni disparaging the only plane of existence which currently contained the British Empire. He returned to the matter at hand. "I've got no idea," he said at last. "Kirk, is there anything you were after?"

The djinni butted in. "Could you hurry up please? I'd like to be getting along soon."

Watson dismissed this with a wave of his hand. "All in good time."

Kirk looked like he was about to explode. "Well, sir, now that you mention it, there was the matter of all the world's knowl—"

Watson cut him off with a snap of his fingers. "I've got it!" he cried. He turned once more to the djinni. "Do you know, all my life I've wished for a really nice bacon sandwich. No-one ever seems to make them just right."

From behind him he heard the unmistakable sound of a lieutenant falling to his knees in frustration. Watson ignored this.

The djinni did not appear to notice either. "With lettuce?"

"Ooh, yes. And brown sauce. And proper butter."

In front of Watson appeared not one bacon sandwich but a whole tray. "I say, thanks awfully," he told the djinni. "Would you like one?"

"Not for me, thanks, I'm off." He disappeared.

"Well, he was nice," said Watson, munching on a sandwich as he sat on a handy treasure chest. "Jolly good cook, too, for an hallucination." He held the tray out to Kirk where he knelt, his head in his hands. "Have a sandwich, old chap. Do you the world of good."

Watson was not prepared for Kirk to explode the way he did.

"You bloody great fool!" he screamed. "The world does not revolve around guns and bacon sandwiches. I don't believe this! You had it, there in your hands, the key to solving the world's problems, advancing the human race, curing diseases and . . . and . . . and . . . you chose BACON SANDWICHES?"

"If you didn't want one you could have said."

Kirk collapsed to the floor, sobbing. "All my life I've searched for the cave of Ali Baba. I even joined the Army and got myself posted to the northernmost regiment so I could search for it. Then finally, finally I find it and what happens? My one chance is ruined by a fat, priggish, devil-may-care oaf!"

Watson frowned. "Now see here, I may be fat, I may be a prig and I admit I may conduct my affairs with a certain *joie de vivre*, Mr Kirk, but I have something you don't, and that's a ruddy backbone. Look at you. Your life's work gets ruined once and you go to pieces. How many times do you think my life's work has been ruined, eh? I always wanted to shoot a yeti, but the one time there was one sighted in the area, what do you think happened? The bloody Mutiny, that's what. You try hunting possibly-mythological hominids with a load of angry Sepoys trying to cut off your goolies. It's not easy, let me tell you. But did I go to pieces, Mr Kirk? Did I wallow in the dirt and dust and give up? I did not. I shot a lot of people and blew up a camel with an artillery piece, that's what I did. However, I'm nothing if not generous. I'm prepared to overlook this little indiscretion, Kirk, if you're prepared to stand up, grab a scimitar, open that door again and help me clear out these bandits in the manner of an Englishman."

Kirk stayed on the ground a long time. Finally he raised his head. "I'm sorry, Colonel," he said. "It's been a bit of a day."

Watson helped him up and patted him on the shoulder in a manly fashion. "Quite understandable, under the circumstances. Never mind, I'm sure there'll be other lamps."

"Actually I'm pretty sure there won't be."

"That's the spirit," said Watson, not listening. Instead his mind had switched to other things and he walked over to inspect the suits of armour. "I say," he called over to Kirk. "This one has a jolly nice sword."

Kirk had wandered over to the piece of wall which, for want of a proper name Watson mentally referred to as the door. He appeared to be listening.

"Good man," Watson agreed. "Situation report?"

"I can hear some very faint sounds, sir." He frowned. "It sounds like a lot of groaning and some quite raucous trumpeting."

Watson chuckled. "They're probably still trying to get the elephant out." He helped himself to another bacon sandwich. "You may as well sit down and have something to eat. They'll be ages yet."

From outside came the sound of a greased elephant being pulled free from a very tight space.

"Bugger," said Watson. He stood and hefted his shotgun. "Stand back and grab a sword, Kirk."

Before the man could move there came the sound of stone grinding on stone. He ran back to where Watson stood. "Behind me, Kirk!" Watson yelled, a wide grin splitting his face, "Cry havoc, and let slip the dogs of war!"

The wall parted and the bandits rushed in with swords drawn. This was a mistake in the confined space of the small corridor, and one which Watson took full advantage of. The silver Purdey's muzzle flashed again and again. Between the gun's repeated roars and the bandits' horrific war cries the noise was fantastic. Slowly but surely, through sheer weight of numbers, the bandits began to advance into the cavern, forcing Watson to strategically retreat and take cover behind a particularly large chest full of gold coins. Several of the bandits had pulled out revolvers and they traded shots with the Colonel. They pinged around him and he was forced to abandon his cover, retreating further back into the cave.

"Lieutenant Kirk, kindly find some way to make yourself useful!" he bawled over the din.

"Can do, sir!" came a triumphant voice from above his shoulder.

Watson glanced around. There sat Kirk, seated triumphantly upon a carpet which seemed to be hovering in mid air.

"What on earth are you doing?"

"Being useful, sir! Would you like a lift home?"

While it rankled somewhat to abandon the field, Watson was not inclined to argue at this juncture. Instead he fired a brace of shots in the general direction of the bandits then clambered up onto the carpet. It wobbled alarmingly.

"Do you know how to fly this?"

"Yes. No. Well, I'm pretty sure."

"Good enough. Get us out of here, Kirk."

"Righto, sir." Kirk nodded and Watson was knocked off his feet as the carpet surged forward. There were cries of alarm from the bandits as the carpet rushed towards them. This alarm was not decreased by the figure of Colonel Watson sitting splay-legged on the back, firing his Purdey with nothing short of gay abandon. The bandits had to duck down as the carpet passed overhead and out of the cave.

It seemed to pick up speed. "I say, Mr Kirk," cried Watson over the increasing rush of wind. "Don't you think you'd better ease off a little bit?"

Kirk turned his head. There was worry etched in his features. "I can't, sir!" he yelled back. "The bally thing seems to be stuck."

"Stuck? How can it possibly be stuck? The thing's got no moving parts!"

Watson curled his fingers in the carpet's greasy pile. Previously the fastest thing he had ever been on was a locomotive. That had seemed fine compared to floating up over the edge of the canyon with the breeze in his hair and nothing between him and the ground but a thin piece of centuries-old cloth. At least the train had a club car. *Yes,* thought Watson as he tried not to notice how far away the ground was getting, *a dash of gin and tonic would be quite the ticket right about now.*

"Can you at least steer the bloody thing?"

"I don't think so. Which could be a problem."

Watson's gaze followed the lieutenant's pointing finger until it saw the large, black thunderhead ahead. He did not know a great deal about meteorology yet he felt this was bad. He fired his shotgun at the cloud on the grounds that shooting things generally resolved issues to his satisfaction, but in this case the job was a little too big. It did not appear to make any noticeable difference, but it did take both hands which meant he was almost thrown over the side as a sudden gust of wind shook the carpet. He grabbed hold with one hand and yelled at the storm. "Bloody ratbag!"

The storm took no notice as the black clouds enveloped them entirely. The world became dark and wet as the carpet was thrown about, tossed like a dinghy on the rolling ocean, at night, in the freezing cold, with someone throwing ice cubes at it and enjoying themselves altogether too much while they were at it.

Watson clung on for dear life, one hand entwined in the warp and weft of the carpet and the other gripping his beloved Purdey with white-knuckled force. However as the carpet bucked, turned, plunged and soared, it soon became obvious something would have to give. The carpet flew around the sky like a paper kite, buffeted and blown through all possible permutations. Watson felt his grip on the carpet loosening and knew he had to make a difficult decision. With a regret that seemed to boot out all thought he opened his hand and felt the shotgun, with its silver filigree and inlays, its rosewood and copper stock, pass into the ether. He gripped the carpet with both hands with a fervour he would not have thought possible, which was probably a mistake. The carpet was old and had never been made for punishment like this. Its tired fabric began to part where it was forced to support the Colonel's weight.

"Kirk! This thing's falling to bits!"

"Yes sir," cried Kirk. "Happening over here too."

"What are we going to do?"

Kirk yelled into Watson's ear. "I have an idea! Roll towards me!"

Watson was in no position to complain about being ordered around by a lieutenant. Instead, he rolled. The sudden change in weight distribution caused the carpet to nose down but, still buffeted and thrown about by the storm, they began to lose height. Very rapidly.

"Kirk! Slow this thing down at once!"

"I would if I could sir."

Watson peered around him from his supine position on the rug. On the plus side, now that they were heading downwards the clouds seemed to be thinning. On the other hand, this meant he could now see the surface of a lake approaching quite quickly.

"Mr Kirk, I suggest you brace yourself!" he yelled whilst tucking his head down between his arms.

Whether Kirk did or he didn't, Watson was too busy to tell. Rather, he was too busy going from quite fast to stationary in a shorter amount of time than he was really comfortable with. The carpet hit the lake at the right angle, skipping like a stone several times before slowly settling down onto the choppy water. Acting more on instinct than anything else Watson grabbed hold of Kirk's tunic and paddled madly towards the edge of the lake. As luck would have it, by the time he had splashed his way to the shore the monsoon had moved on, leaving Watson to drag the now very soggy lieutenant onto the bank. This was not an easy task and for the first time that day Watson was beginning to feel his age. He heaved the unconscious Kirk out of the water and dumped him unceremoniously onto the sand. He looked around at his surroundings. He didn't recognise them. Gods knows how long it would take them to get back to civilisation, or a reasonable facsimile thereof. His mind flitted to the loss of his shotgun. *Easy come, easy go*, he thought.

Presently the sun came out and he began to dry off. Now that the storm was over, it was really quite pleasant, he decided. He began to wonder when the hallucinogenic spores, or fungus, or whatever it had been would begin to wear off. After a few minutes he began to get the sneaking suspicion that they weren't going to.

"Well, Mr Kirk," he informed him. "This is another fine mess you've gotten me into."

Romance of the Arrow Girl

Richard Harland

No expense was spared for the marriage of Khaan Arash-e Azam and the girl Parisi. The *sofrehaghd*, the ceremonial candelabras and the mirror of fate were all as rich and fine as for the most high-born of brides. The Khaan's married sisters extended a silk scarf above the heads of the couple, while his own mother ground two cones of sugar for sweetness over the scarf. After Parisi had given her consent on the traditional third time of asking, the bride and groom dipped little fingers in a bowl of honey and licked the sweetness from each other's fingertips. Then the clapping and singing began.

Parisi wasn't deceived for a moment. She could feel the hostility radiating from the Khaan's sisters, while his mother would have undoubtedly preferred to drip poison not sugar over her daughter-in-law's head. The priest's face wore a sour expression, and the wedding guests looked on with disapproval. Ambassadors from neighbouring countries, elders of the noble families of Khorasan— only the will of Khaan Arash forced them to play their roles. He had chosen against all precedent and propriety, yet it wasn't in their interest to challenge his choice.

And Parisi was the one he had chosen. He had proved his love for her, and his power was enough to protect her. Already he had imprisoned the head of one dissenting noble family and driven another into exile. Who cared what the world thought?

She glanced at him sideways under her eyelashes. With his proud mouth, broad forehead, black eyebrows and even blacker eyes, he looked every inch a Khaan. *Handsome* didn't begin to describe him. He had a presence that filled the hall. In this moment, he seemed almost unnaturally calm, calmer than she'd seen him at any stage of their courtship. Yet she knew the passion within him, and was glad of it. Tonight she would match it with a passion of her own. She looked away in a hurry as her heart beat faster.

Her gaze focussed on Laleh, half-hidden behind a pillar at the back of the hall. Laleh, her best and oldest friend—and the only person from her previous life here present for the wedding. Her family and friends from her home village hadn't been invited, of course, and not only because they were three hundred leagues away. But Laleh had shared the whole adventure with her, and Parisi couldn't wait to exchange notes about everyone's reactions and behaviour at the ceremony. With luck, she should be able to slip away while Arash stayed on to receive a great many insincere blessings and compliments. She was sure the guests wouldn't feel obliged to include *her* in their formal displays of courtesy.

She caught Laleh's eye, and Laleh responded with a grin and a wink.

• • •

Laleh had always known that Parisi was special. She had no illusions about her own looks, but she had always dreamed of a glorious future for her friend. In the village of Errekan, Parisi was like a swan among geese. Even Parisi's mother, though pretty enough, never stood out with any particular grace or refinement. But Parisi was a born princess.

Laleh had always tried to shield Parisi from the roughest kinds of work—and there was no rougher work than her own part-time occupation. Since the age of fourteen, Laleh had been a battlefield scavenger, collecting arrows to sell in bundles at the Dowalan market. It was a grisly business pulling arrows from the bodies of the slain, especially when barbed arrowheads had to be cut out with a knife. It was also dangerous when victorious soldiers still roamed the battlefield. Yet Parisi had insisted until Laleh finally gave way. They had gone together to the bloody aftermath of the great Battle of Tazakh . . . and there, of all places, was where the village princess had met her prince.

Busy with her scavenging, Laleh hadn't noticed the party of mounted knights riding up. When Parisi pointed, she cursed under her breath. These were no ordinary soldiers, but shining in armour with cloaks flying from their shoulders. Laleh could always run faster than a foot soldier could chase, but men on horseback were a different matter.

"Fight for your life," she told Parisi, and took up a defensive stance, knife in hand.

At the time, she didn't know who they were or who their leader was. She only saw that he was handsome, with his black eyes and square-cut beard. He wore rich red robes under his red cloak, and the helm on his head bore an inscription of two interlocking gold 'A's. Even then, he was staring at Parisi.

"No need for knives," he told the girls. "We are not barbarians. Tell us your names."

Parisi, who hardly seemed to realise the danger, gave their names and explained their scavenging as though they had every right to be doing it. The other knights eyed her like a dish they could hardly wait to taste. Laleh moved to stand in front of her.

"You'll have to kill *me* before you have *her*!" she yelled at them.

She meant it too. Twelve months ago, she had stabbed and killed a robber who had tried to attack her in the back streets of Dowalan. She was good with a knife, and she wouldn't go down without taking someone with her.

The men considered it a joke until their leader quelled the laughter. "This one is not for you," he growled.

"Of course, you have the precedence, sire," one responded with exaggerated civility.

"She is not for anyone except by her own free will."

That started them muttering. "Only a peasant girl, sire."

"I have spoken," he said, and turned his back on them.

It was then that Laleh guessed the meaning of those interlocking gold 'A's. This must be the famous Khaan of Khorasan, Arash-e Azam himself! Yet he continued to talk to Parisi as if they were equals. Was it some game of chivalry? It was a serious sort of game, at least, because he'd asked Parisi— and both of them, when Parisi insisted—to travel to his palace in Nishapur and join his imperial household. In what capacity, Laleh wasn't sure, but he had promised them fine clothes, books, music and private rooms, so they certainly weren't slaves or ordinary servants.

That was how it had begun, and Laleh could have asked for nothing more. For Parisi, she might have wished for a secret love affair with the Khaan, an unofficial but intense relationship. Even her wildest dreams could never have risen to the height of what had now happened. An actual marriage was beyond all possibility!

She surveyed the Khaan's imperial bedroom where she sat talking with Parisi. Parisi perched on the gold-embroidered rug that covered the bed, while she sat on a footstool facing her. All around were silken drapes, painted panels and patterned wall-hangings. A thousand flowers in vases had been brought in for the wedding night: white lilies, desert orchids and purple azaleas. There were also small circular tables piled high with sticky pastries, rosewater jellies, figs, dates and honeyed nuts. Laleh's senses swam with the heady sweet perfumes.

And Parisi deserved it all. Laleh studied the smile that kept plucking at the corners of her friend's mouth. She was so extraordinarily beautiful in her white wedding dress with the kohl around her eyes. Laleh didn't envy her; she couldn't even imagine having that kind of beauty herself.

"I've never seen you so happy," she pronounced. "You're radiant. Absolutely radiant."

Parisi lowered her eyes and seemed almost embarrassed by her happiness. "I still don't really believe it."

"No one else could have done what you did. I wouldn't have had the willpower to hold out on him."

"Because he's so handsome?" Another tiny smile plucked at the corners of Parisi's mouth. "Or because he's the Khaan?"

"Both. How many times did he come to you in the palace? How many times did you refuse him?"

"Dozens. Almost every day."

"And so many gifts he gave you—yet you never yielded."

"Would you have become his concubine?"

Laleh laughed. "Well, a very special concubine. With all the clothes and jewellery and servants of a wife. I'd have cost him plenty! But I wouldn't have expected him to marry me. I wouldn't have had the nerve."

"It wasn't my doing." Parisi grew serious. "He chose."

"But you made him choose. You played him perfectly, until he was out of his head with desire."

"And love. I wanted him to prove what he pleaded. Deeds not words."

Not for the first time, Laleh was amazed at her friend's quiet determination. "What a gamble, though. He could so easily have taken you by force, and then where would you have been? Nothing left to trade. You must've had him worked out better than I did."

"No, I just hoped he was more honourable than most men."

"Same lust but more honour!" Laleh laughed and made an indelicate gesture. "Yes, that's when they're vulnerable."

She had her own theories about men, and would have expounded upon them but for a sudden knock on the door. A servant entered, a round-shouldered, middle-aged woman called Maheen. She was one of the senior servants and had already supervised many of the wedding preparations.

"Time to make ready for the groom," she announced, unsmiling. "He'll be coming soon, and he expects his bride to be at her most beautiful."

Laleh couldn't imagine how Parisi could be any more beautiful than she already was. She gave her friend a kiss on the cheek and left her to Maheen's ministrations.

• • •

With long, slow stokes, Maheen brushed Parisi's hair, separating the strands and fluffing them out in a great dark mass. Only a husband should see the full glory of his wife's hair. Parisi sat motionless, lost in her thoughts and smiling to herself.

Laleh's interpretation of her courtship with Khaan Arash could hardly have been more wrong. *You played him perfectly*—but she hadn't, not at all. Never for one moment had she expected him to offer her marriage. There was no cool calculation to her resistance, only a fear for her own heart. The fact was, she had been hopelessly, stupidly in love with Arash ever since that first meeting on the battlefield at Tazakh. Hopeless and stupid, because he belonged to a different world and might as well have belonged to a different species. But her heart wouldn't listen to reason . . . and her heart would break if he cast her aside after she'd yielded to his desires. Therefore, she must never yield. Once she'd let down her guard, she would never be able to dam back her feelings again. He had power over her, he could force her to his will, but she would never ever *give* herself to him . . .

After the hair-brushing came the massaging with oil and perfumes. Maheen brought out a small camphor-wood chest containing dozens of stoppered glass bottles. She warmed the oil in her palms, then applied it in firm, sinuous strokes to Parisi's feet and calves. Parisi relaxed under her expert touch, though she sensed the woman's antagonism. She had grown used to the servants' hostility in her time at Nishapur.

It had started from the moment when Parisi and Laleh first arrived in the palace. The soldier who'd escorted them on the long journey passed on the Khaan's orders that these newcomers were to be given special privileges, and every servant in the imperial household immediately understood that Parisi was the Khaan's favourite. They respected and feared their Khaan more than they liked him, but nonetheless he was *theirs,* and they resented anyone else cutting in. They took their revenge by telling Parisi horrific tales about his cruelty and tyranny. In their version, he was a terrifying warrior with a fondness for massacres and a taste for torturing prisoners. They seemed to be talking about an entirely different person to the one who had shown such chivalry to Laleh and herself, and she ignored their attempts to frighten her off. When the Khaan came back from campaigning three weeks later, he came back as the person *she* knew.

He summoned her to meet him, and she took Laleh along with her for support and protection. He was pacing the paths of a small courtyard between myrtles and orange trees. In the centre was a fountain, a constant trickle of water playing over a circular basin of bronze.

"Let your chaperone stand at a distance," he said. "We won't stray out of her sight."

So Parisi walked in the courtyard with Khaan Arash while Laleh waited in the shade of the surrounding colonnade.

"How do you like my palace?" he asked

She was reluctant to admit just how much she liked it. With its blue-tiled floors and painted ceilings, its stuccoed corridors and vast domed halls, it was an Aladdin's Cave to her.

"I like it well, sire," she replied.

"You may call me Arash," he said.

"Arash," she echoed obediently.

"And you, little arrow girl . . . you know you have shot an arrow into my heart?"

He put his hand on her arm, and she stared at the rings on his fingers, set with huge cut amethysts. "Ever since Tazakh, I have tried to put your face from my mind," he went on. "Yet still you haunt me. You are the queen of my nights and days."

His words were sweet in her ears, unbearably sweet. She listened as he talked of his sleepless nights, his helpless yearning, his unquenchable need. They passed in and out of dappled shade, inhaling the scent of oranges.

"Take pity on me," he murmured, like some wounded beast that had indeed suffered a fatal dart. "Only you can make me whole again. Only you can give me peace and paradise."

Parisi dislodged his hand gently from her arm. "You want my love?"

"Yes."

"As your concubine?"

He heaved a sigh and said nothing.

"But I shall never be your concubine."

He swung and stepped before her, blocking her way. There was barely a hands-breadth between them, yet she refused to take a backwards step.

"No." She controlled her voice. "You said it in front of witnesses. *Except by her own free will.* No one can have me except by my own free will."

"I . . . when I . . . " His breath was hot on her face, and he was shaking with passion.

"That was your word. Your soldiers might ravish what they cannot win. But you? Would you descend to their level?"

He glared at her with a baffled look in his eyes.

"Everyone would know you couldn't win me," she went on. "Everyone would know you could only take me by force."

"I shall win you." The vow seemed torn from the depths of his chest. "I swear I shall."

Then suddenly he was gone—and Parisi's mask of composure went with him. She took a few tottering steps to the fountain and leaned for support against the metal rim. She had nearly given in, so very nearly!

The temptation never went away in all their subsequent meetings. She wanted him, and it took every ounce of her willpower to hide her desire. He was desperate for more intimate conversations in secluded places, but she took the precaution of always bringing Laleh as chaperone.

Then one morning his mother came bursting into her room. Farinoush, the Mahd-e-Oliaa, was a tall woman with a nose like a hawk's beak and iron-grey hair peeping out from under her headscarf.

"My son is not for you, *arrow girl!*" The way she said *arrow girl* was a spit of contempt. "Who do you think you are?"

"I'm no one," said Parisi quietly.

"No one, and no family." Parisi's quietness seemed to quieten Farinoush too. "Listen to me, girl. Be realistic. Your aim is too high. We are a proud family, and my son is the proudest of us all. Can you imagine the shame if he married a peasant girl?"

"I don't ask him to pursue me."

"No? But you don't stop him either."

"How could I stop him?"

"Let him have his way. He'll soon get over this madness. Let him have his way with you, and you'll be well rewarded. I give you my word. You'll never want for anything for the rest of your life."

Except him, thought Parisi, and held her tongue.

"He's ashamed in himself," Farinoush went on. "He hides it, and he would fly into a rage if anyone dared suggest it. But I'm his mother, I can see it. It is humiliating for a great Khaan to be at the mercy of a peasant girl. You have no idea what you're playing with."

"I'd help if I could."

"I've told you how you can help."

Parisi shook her head. "I have my self-respect."

"Self-respect? You?" Farinoush flared up again. "What does a peasant girl have to do with self-respect?"

She stared deep into Parisi's eyes as if unable to believe her stubbornness. "You know he's betrothed to a princess from Bactria? It was the seal of a dynastic alliance. We need that alliance. Would you stand in the way?"

"I didn't know he was betrothed," said Parisi, still refusing to make the concession that Farinoush wanted to hear.

"Oh, this will end badly," hissed the older woman, and stormed out in an even worse temper than when she'd burst in.

After that, Parisi had another explanation as to why Arash wished to meet in secluded places. Of course, he was ashamed that others might see and hear him. Even when he uttered words of love, he always lowered his voice. Yet he continued to seek her out at every opportunity, and his pleas grew increasingly urgent. Parisi deflected the pleas with something else she had learned from Farinoush.

"I know you don't love me as you say you do," she told him.

"I swear it."

"You already have a love. You're betrothed."

"What?"

'To a princess from Bactria."

"Oh, that. She means nothing to me."

"She will when you marry her. Is she pretty?"

"Compared to you?" He raised the palm of his hand and blew away an imaginary speck of dust.

"You won't think like that when she's in your bed."

He snorted. "What do you want me to do? You expect me to throw over an alliance my ministers have been working on for years?"

Parisi didn't answer. If she set the bar impossibly high . . .

"You *do*!" He gaped at her, thunderstruck. 'You really think that could happen?'

"I don't think anything. But you keep saying how much you love me."

He walked off shaking his head, and stayed away for the next three days. On the fourth day, Parisi and Laleh were watering oleanders in the Green Ibis Pavilion when he strode in, his handsome face flushed with emotion.

He addressed Parisi as though Laleh wasn't there. "It's done."

"What?"

"I've ended the betrothal and broken off the alliance with Bactria."

Parisi was aghast. "Because of me?"

"Yes, you. I've damaged our reputation and put Khorasan at risk of war. All because of you."

She set down her pitcher of water. She'd been keeping her feet on the ground, and suddenly the ground had dropped away beneath her. For the first time, she began to doubt her sense of what was and wasn't possible.

"I don't believe you," she said.

"Ask anyone. The whole court thinks I'm mad."

Indeed, he did seem a little mad in that moment. His nostrils were wide, his eyes narrowed, and he was breathing heavily. Parisi retreated a step as he advanced towards her. He caught her sleeve before she could back away further.

"Now can you see how much I love you?" he demanded.

He bent to kiss her, his arms enclosing and gathering her in. Shock and desire mingled to overwhelm her. Her legs went weak, and a fire beat up in her breast.

"No!" yelled Laleh, and rushed forward to thrust an arm between them. "You can't do that!"

He drew back, his black eyes fixed upon Parisi. "Can't I?" he asked.

Parisi looked down and shook her head.

"Don't you feel *anything* for me?" He sounded hurt. "What more proof do you want?"

Parisi's feelings almost spilled out there and then—but her friend was more practical.

"Try proposing marriage," said Laleh.

Arash continued to address Parisi as though the suggestion had come from her. "Is that it? Is that what you're holding out for?"

He took her silence as a *yes*. With sudden violence, he kicked out at Parisi's pitcher and smashed it to fragments.

"Impossible," he snarled, and stamped off.

Parisi told herself to be realistic, yet instinct told her this wasn't the end of the story. Could it have a fairytale conclusion?

Eight hours later, when dusk had settled over the palace like a black velvet blanket, she was summoned to the chambers of the Mahd-e-Oliaa. Farinoush's face was screwed up with bitterness and suppressed fury.

"My son the Khaan has asked me to act on his behalf," she said in a hard, tight voice. "I am to request your hand in marriage."

Parisi's heart leaped, but her mind remained wary. "Why you?" she asked.

Farinoush recovered a little of her usual condescension. "Marriages in *noble* families are arranged between senior family members. I don't know how it is done in *peasant* families. Since you have no family, I am forced to make the match with you."

"I'd rather your son did it himself."

"That would not be appropriate."

"I'd still like to hear it from him. Where is he?"

Farinoush stamped her foot. "He has matters of state to worry about. He's discussing important plans with his generals in the Hall of Lions."

"His plans for me are important too," Parisi retorted. "If they're true."

"Of course they are—"

But Parisi was already walking out of Farinoush's chambers. She knew the way to the Hall of Lions, in this same wing of the palace.

"Wait!" Farinoush called out. "You can't!"

Parisi strode along corridor after corridor. The Hall's curtained doorway was just ahead when she heard footsteps rushing up behind. As she parted the curtain, the Mahd-e-Oliaa's hand fell on her shoulder. She stepped forward into the room, and pulled Farinoush along in her wake.

The Hall of Lions was the oldest room in the palace, with a ceiling of hammered gold and twenty-four lions carved into the walls. Khaan Arash-e Azam was seated with his generals, talking in a loud voice, banging his fist on the table for emphasis. He broke off in mid-sentence when he saw the two figures in the doorway.

"Well?" he demanded. "Is it done?"

Farinoush shook her head. "She wants to hear it from you."

"What?"

Parisi sensed rather than saw the scornful curl of Farinoush's lip. "She won't be happy until she sees you beg."

The generals scowled and made disapproving noises—directed at the Khaan as well as Parisi. They were the last people to sympathise with weakness over a woman. Arash defied them all.

"Did you present my gift to her?" he demanded.

"She didn't give me the chance," his mother replied.

He sprang to his feet and strode across the room. Farinoush gave Parisi a push that propelled her forward. Arash snapped his fingers and extended his hand to his mother, who passed him a small box decorated with interlocking gold 'A's. He lifted out a precious blue stone on a chain.

"My betrothal gift to you," he told Parisi.

There was a gasp of indignation from the generals. "That's the Qebleh-ye Aalam!"

"Heirloom of his ancestors!"

"Rarest turquoise in the world!"

Parisi could feel the heat of their outrage beating down upon her. She looked at Arash and shook her head. "I don't need your gift. All I need—"

She never got to finish her sentence because he whirled and flung the Qebleh-ye Aalam savagely across the room. For good measure, he flung the box after it.

"How low must I go?" he thundered. "You want me to beg in front of my own generals?" He clenched his fists and dropped to his knees. "Everyone, hear and bear witness! I, Arash-e Azam, ask this woman to be my bride!"

There were cries of protest from the generals. Parisi wasn't sure what was happening, only that it was utterly unthinkable. And still he hadn't finished.

"Am I humble enough for you?" he demanded. "Do I have to kiss your feet now? Or the hem of your dress?"

As he reached for the hem of her dress, Parisi whisked it away from his grasp. "Only to know you love me," she said. "I accept."

Arash jumped back on his feet and swung towards his generals. "You heard. She accepts. The wedding will take place five days from now." He raised his voice as though someone had objected. "Yes, five days. I've waited long enough." He turned to his mother. "Make the arrangements."

The look on his face was more like rage than joy. If he seemed triumphant, it wasn't a sort of triumph Parisi cared to remember. She could have wished that scene out of existence; it would surely have been a very different declaration of love if she had gone to him in private. She had never intended to humiliate him.

Still, he had proved his love beyond question. What could be harder for a proud man than to confess his feelings in front of others? Harder than any fight or quest or act of bravery! Now she could be sure that he was hers as she was his. They were bound together in love as well as law for every day of their lives. She smiled to herself . . . and became aware that Maheen was watching her.

The woman had finished oiling and perfuming Parisi's legs, arms and hands. As she stowed her bottles back in the camphorwood chest, she seemed to be studying Parisi out of the corner of her eye. Parisi couldn't work out the meaning of her expression. It wasn't hostility, though it certainly wasn't a smile. It might almost have been pity.

What? Why? Startled and puzzled, Parisi shook her head . . . and heard the bass voice of her new husband in the corridor. Arash was bidding farewell to someone outside.

Maheen flung her last few bottles into the chest and scampered for the door. Not fast enough—the door swung open from the other side and crashed against the wall. There stood Arash in his ceremonial wedding robes. He caught the old woman by the shoulder and thrust her roughly into the corridor.

"Out of my way!" he commanded. "She's on her own now."

• • •

Laleh wandered round the imperial wing of the palace, restless and excited. She had known desire a few times in her life, but never transfigured by love. The passion of Parisi's wedding night was beyond her imagination. Such utter and everlasting commitment!

By now the groom had surely joined his bride. Without conscious reflection, Laleh's wanderings carried her in the direction of the imperial bedroom. She wasn't the only one; half a dozen servants had already gathered outside the bedroom door, listening with their heads pressed hard against the wood. Even from the far end of the corridor, Laleh could hear small moans and cries from within. The servants weren't giggling or tittering—in fact, they were strangely solemn—but Laleh turned away with a frown. Yes, she had been curious, but not *that* curious.

Still she didn't go to her own room, knowing she would never fall asleep. She continued to wander, and came across more and more servants in the corridors. Their secretive manner suggested they were all heading towards the imperial bedroom.

It was twenty minutes later when she passed two servants hastening in the opposite direction. One was an old male retainer; the other was the woman Maheen, who had come to prepare Parisi for her wedding night. They were talking in worried voices, and Laleh overheard some of the exchange: 'the Mahd-e-Oliaa . . . it's our duty . . . has to be told . . . what will she do?' Laleh stared after them with a sudden feeling of dread. Something was wrong! Something between the young wife and her husband!

She made her way back to the imperial bedroom. A crowd of thirty servants now filled the corridor outside the door, and their expressions frightened her. They weren't just solemn, they were grave as mourners at a funeral. She joined in at the back of the crowd, and strained her ears to catch the whispers.

"Fallen quiet again."

"Is that good?"

"Or bad?"

"She's married to him now."

"I could've seen it coming."

"We all saw it coming."

"Not as much as this."

"Male pride, that's what it is."

"*His* pride. We're not all like that."

"Yes, you are. It's in every—"

"Shh!"

Laleh spun around. The Khaan's mother, Farinoush, was approaching along the corridor, her face very stern and grim.

"What's this?" she snapped. "Go back to your tasks, all of you."

The servants only moved aside, and Farinoush didn't enforce her command. Instead she rapped sharply on the bedroom door. "Arash-e Azam!'"

There was no answer from within. She waited, then flung open the door and marched in. For a moment, the servants hovered in the doorway, while Laleh pushed forward from behind. Then, as if a dam had given way, the whole crowd flooded into the bedroom.

Except for a few vases of flowers overturned, the room looked much as Laleh had seen it before. Khaan Arash stood glowering, clad only in a length of cloth wrapped round his waist, his muscular torso gleaming with sweat. In his hand was a knife with a bejewelled hilt and a curving blade reddened with blood.

There was no sign of Parisi, but the rug had been pulled from the bed and thrown as if hastily over something on the floor. Laleh's heart seemed to stop as utter dread swept over her. She couldn't think, she couldn't speak—she just sprang across the room and dragged off the rug.

Parisi lay motionless, eyes closed, half on her back and half on her side. There was no visible knife-wound, but her naked limbs were covered in welts and bruises: terrible welts from a strap or a belt, dark bruises from fists or kicking. He had killed her!

But then Parisi's eyelids fluttered open. Laleh knelt beside her with a sob of relief. She was breathing . . . barely breathing, but still alive.

"Why?" Laleh demanded. "*Why?*"

Parisi only stared back at her, wide-eyed like a frightened child. Instead, the answer came from Arash in a loud, arrogant tone. "She's my wife, and I'll do whatever I want with her. *Whatever I want.*"

Farinoush shook her head. "You've done quite enough. This does not look well, my son."

"Enough?" Arash curled his lip in contempt. "Enough for a first night."

Parisi's breathing turned into a kind of gasp. She was sucking in air, struggling to speak. "He wants me to suffer . . . the rest of my life. He told me."

Arash tossed away his knife, which fell with a clatter beside a table of sweets and pastries. "Yes, I told her. Every shame and slight and humiliation she put me through—I remember every moment of it. She will pay for it all the nights of her life."

"You acted out of lust, and now you're acting out of pride," said Farinoush. "Do you even know the difference?"

"I am the Khaan Arash-e Azam."

With a dismissive gesture, he spun on his heel and strode from the room. There was a moment's hush as his footsteps faded down the corridor. Then everyone began talking at once.

Laleh was about to cover Parisi's nakedness with the rug when she heard her friend's whisper. "My back. What did he do to my back?"

Laleh bent over and rolled her further onto her side. It wasn't a deep set of cuts, but there was a great deal of blood. Seeing the pattern, Laleh guessed what it was even before she cleaned the blood away with the side of her hand. Two interlocking 'A's! He had cut his initials into the skin of her back!

There was a roaring in Laleh's ears, and everything blurred before her eyes. When she recovered, Parisi had again rolled over onto her back. Laleh couldn't bear to tell her what her husband had done. Meanwhile, the servants had formed up in a line as Farinoush addressed them.

"Listen to me," the Mahd-e-Oliaa was saying. "This has to be kept quiet. It would damage us all if it became public knowledge. As loyal servants of my family, I'm sure you understand. I require a promise of silence from each and every one of you."

"What happens to the bride?" a young maidservant piped up.

"A promise of silence," Farinoush repeated. "Until the wedding guests are gone."

Laleh stared at the woman, at her cold, haughty mouth, waiting for the words that never came. Nothing about saving Parisi, nothing about stopping the Khaan's revenge. He could still do whatever he wanted to do to his wife, every night for the rest of her life!

No one asked any more questions. The servants might disapprove, but they would never rebel. Laleh gaped at them as they held their up hands one by one and swore themselves to silence. They hung their heads, they knew it was wrong, yet they did it all the same. This was the way things worked—in Nishapur, in Khorasan, in the whole world.

Laleh had a sense of absolute helplessness. For every night of her own life too, she would know what Parisi was suffering and be powerless to prevent it. Trapped, eternally trapped . . .

Then her eye fell on the Khaan's knife, where it had fallen to the floor. Mentally, she closed her hand over the hilt and felt the muscular strength in her arm. She still had one last thing they couldn't control. She was good with a knife.

She pulled the rug up over Parisi so that only her friend's face showed out. Farinoush was still looking the other way, still taking promises from the servants. Laleh touched Parisi's cheek, very lightly, and swore a promise of a different kind.

Then, silently, she slid across the floor to the knife beside the table. No one was watching—or at least no one was telling Farinoush. Laleh closed her fingers on the knife, this time for real, and noticed that her hand was already red with Parisi's blood. A good omen? She could almost feel the blow she would deliver, the blade sinking in between the Khaan's ribs, the twist she would give to carve the life out of him.

Now! She sprang to her feet and ran for the door. Voices called out, Farinoush's among them. "Stop her! Where's she going? *Stop her!*"

Laleh ran on down the corridor. They were too late. She would find the tyrant before they could catch her. Her fingers were locked round the hilt of the knife with a grip that nothing but death could break.

Afterword

"Romance of the Arrow Girl" began as a minor element in an entirely different story called "The Town Closes Its Gates". Within that story, it featured as play, where the content of the play had to carry conviction, but didn't matter much in its own right. Trouble was, it carried too much conviction—too much thematic and emotional power to stay as a minor element. It grew and grew, took on a life of its own and burst right out of the original story. Which is why "The Town Closes Its Gates" never made it to the state of a finished, publishable story—and "Romance of the Arrow Girl" did.

But the arrow girl story—which didn't even involve an arrow girl at that stage—was still not fleshed out. It had stopped being a medieval play with a medieval setting, but it hadn't become anything else. I couldn't make up my mind exactly what it needed to be, and I can't write a story until I feel an absolute necessity about it. So I let it languish for a few years, until Dreaming of Djinn came along—and, out of the blue, I suddenly discovered the particular fleshing out that this particular story-seed had been begging for. All the fairytale and romance associated with the Arabian Nights—the perfect context within which to uncover the reality of the Khaan's behaviour!

I'd still call "Romance of the Arrow Girl" a fairytale, because I'd like to believe it has the logic and simplicity and fundamental truth of all good fairytales. But definitely not a happy-ever-after fairytale! It's a terrible story, perhaps more frightening than any story of witches or wolves, because the monster here lives inside *the human heart (and I could say, the male ego). It's not the whole truth—God forbid!—but I do believe it is A truth.*

Many of the details come from the real world and real world history. The form of a Persian marriage service, the royal titles, the names of almost all the towns and countries. Yes, there really was a Khorasan Empire! It was fun doing the research for this story. Only I don't guarantee that all the details converge to a single real place and time . . .

Djinni Djinni Dream Dream

Jetse de Vries

Each man shall be tested thrice, and thrice only.
—Enheduanna's Hymns

In his younger years, Jamal Muhammad—liberator of 434 Hungaria, the Fleet Captain who saved Mars, husband of the genius Ysebeau Scheherazade (the inadvertent creator of the quantum AIs—quais), who mysteriously disappeared after the failed RC-craft Mark II Tests—took part in sensory deprivation tests in escape pods.

In those days, medical systems, powered by body heat, could keep a human alive for about forty-two days with no food and drink. A pilot missing longer than that was assumed dead.

However, pilots had been found after less than forty-two days, and while their bodies were still functioning, their minds had gone. 'Extended Outer Space Isolation Syndrome' was the official term. Most people just called it space madness.

Space pilots were a rare breed: only the best and toughest could make it. On top of that, their training was exorbitantly expensive, so the Space Force hated losing even one. Volunteers were requested to test periods of intense isolation, both with and without a full virtual reality interface, in an escape pod in a low moon orbit. The young Jamal was one of them—this would be the first step in settling his karmic debt, according to the beliefs of his warrior caste—thinking he was made of sterner stuff than those who succumbed to space madness.

In his one-thousand-and-one hours in space, with full VR capability, Jamal figured he should pace himself. He started by studying his ancestors: according to the earliest reliable records, he descended from a generation of fisherman in medieval Persia, around 1000 AD. He researched living conditions, the cultural, social and religious mores of the Buyid Amirates, and was relieved to find that fisherman was a common profession, if not a very honourable one. Toiling, demanding and often quite dangerous. But also rewarding and very satisfying.

When he felt he had done sufficient research with the data available, which was surprisingly plentiful—Jamal wondered if the VR interface extrapolated, or even made things up?—he began building his own virtual reality: to become a fisherman in Siraf in the ancient Amirate of Shiraz. Not only was this a major commercial port in those times, where rich traders lived in luxurious villas, and the place to be when diving for pearls, but also a spiritual congregation with the glorious Jam'eh mosque and its minor mosque brethren spread across town. As it was, the city controlled no less than three ports: Bandar-e-Taheri—the hub for trade with the Arabian Peninsula, India and East Africa, Bandar-e-Kangan—the centre of berths from which the pearl divers took off, and Bandar-e-Dayar—the humble fishermen's abode.

From scratch, he built his own boat: a *daw* like his fellow fisherman used. He actually built four, as the first three had design faults only shown after usage. He made his own nets: not to be underestimated as it took about as long as building the boats.

Then he went out to fish. His first catches were very poor, and he nearly drowned as he needed to learn to sail, as well. He became sea-sick, and slept very badly at night, if at all. At day he sailed and fished, exerting himself to exhaustion, was sunburned, and still caught little.

Finally, more by accident then by design, he chanced upon a way to increase his catch. He began to get a feel for the sea, where to find places where fish were more abundant. He was slowly becoming a real fisherman.

He thought he had closed the deal when he brought in his first good catch, only to find that his troubles weren't over: he had to *sell* his fish, as well. Precious little people were interested in purchasing from a totally unknown fisherman. There was a market mechanism at work where quota and selling rights were already dished out. There was the open market—the bi-weekly seafood bazaar—but one needed to obtain a permit for that. And fast, before his catch rotted away.

Jamal subsequently learned trade the hard way: befriending fellow fishermen, working for them, getting information, negotiating the market place, getting a permit and finally selling his own fish.

It was a seemingly never-ending cycle of learning by trial-and-error, advancing by three-steps-ahead-and-two-steps-back, exploring dead alleys along the way. Fishermen were on the lowest rung of the city's ladder, well behind the daring and glamorous pearl divers and the very wealthy traders. Not that Jamal cared— people, no matter how revered or rich, always needed to eat— and loved every minute of it. This was not a test: this was pure Heaven.

After a while he did achieve a certain amount of success. What first was an exploration was now slowly becoming a routine; what was first exciting was becoming boring. Also, because he had been so very much occupied, Jamal hadn't kept count of the number of daily mental check-ups for the isolation period: surely he had passed the halfway number by now?

He considered courting women, but quickly thought the better of it. These were only simulacra who simply didn't have the emotional and intellectual depth, the mysterious unpredictability of real women. If it was merely sex he was after, then he could have set himself up as a sultan with a harem: but that would merely be virtual masturbation. He preferred the honesty of the real act.

• • •

He needed a fresh challenge, so Jamal reprogrammed his virtual world to incorporate magical elements, but in such a manner that they would come to him as a surprise. Having done that, he set out to sea in eager anticipation.

To his chagrin, nothing much happened at first. In the back of his mind he wondered if he had become a sensation addict, and was losing the virtue of patience? He ground his teeth and kept fishing, something he could do almost blindfolded by now.

While he was surreptitiously looking for something else, his nets become full with catch. There was nothing to it but to reel them in. A very good one: another like this and he had to go back to port. But there was something strange in there: a large, auburn fish he didn't quite recognise . . .

It wasn't a fish, but a copper bottle with a lead seal. A symbol was stamped in the seal: two intersecting up-and-down triangles in a circle forming a kind of hexagram, the spaces outside the hexagram filled with dots. It looked vaguely familiar. Jamal racked his brains: he'd be damned if he simply asked the computer. *Merkabah, the Spirit Wheel? Almost . . . Ah: the Seal of Solomon.*

Which means there's a dangerous spirit inside, Jamal realised. *Well, let's find out just* how *dangerous.* He broke the seal and opened the copper jar. Glittery, purple-gold smoke escaped like an ascending spiral, turning into a demon-shape ghost. The ghost became a bald man with a pointy goatee; the bottom of the smoke settled as his wide, purple pantaloons held up by a blue waistband; the rest of the smoke condensed as gold: necklaces, wristlets, anklets and even a chain around his waist.

Jamal was thrilled. "Who are you?"

"I am Shakahr," the ghost answered. "Thank you very much for freeing me."

"No problem," Jamal said. "It was nothing."

"Nevertheless, I shall reward you." Shakahr bowed and gesticulated. "Please choose the manner of your death."

"The manner of my death? What kind of a reward is that?"

"For a thousand months plus one, I have been locked in this copper jar," The ghost explained. "During the first three hundred months, I swore that I would enrich forever the person who would free me, but no-one came. During the second three hundred months, I swore to bring great wealth to my liberator, but again nobody showed up. The third three hundred months, I vowed to grant three wishes to the noble soul ending my imprisonment, yet still nothing happened. Then I became enraged, and furiously decided, for the fourth three hundred months, to grant the man disabling the Seal of Solomon the manner of his death."

"This is madness: I do not wish to die."

"Everybody dies: I am granting you the mercy of deciding how."

"But I do not know how I wish to die." Jamal said, his mind racing to attempt to outwit the evil ghost.

"You must decide. It is my will."

"But you are only an evil djinni from a bottle." Jamal protested.

"I am Shakahr: the mightiest djinni of all. Solomon is the only one who ever beat me."

"But Solomon is dead."

"As you will be. Now choose."

"I refuse to choose," Jamal said, clutching at straws. "As long as I don't choose, you cannot kill me."

"The coward's way out." The evil djinni sneered.

"Cowards accept enforced choices: brave men refuse."

"You are bound to me by breaking Solomon's seal. I will plague you forever until you make your choice."

"How can you plague me 'forever' if I must die by making a choice?"

"Ah, you like riddles? Then riddles it will be!"

Jamal frowned in disbelief: a plague of riddles?

—it starts out small, looking dafter—

—than sores, becoming an unstoppable force—

—more contagious than laughter—

—running faster than a galloping horse—

"That's too easy. Why waste my time?"

"Answer my riddle, or choose your death."

"A plague, not unlike you."

"Correct. The next one—"

"—No: I shall put you back in your bottle."

"You will, puny human? Then where is your powerful seal?"

"I have the seal of indifference, combined with the seal of contempt."

"No way, I'm sorry to say: you will have to answer *all* my riddles first. And boy do I have a lot. . ."

And they came: an avalanche of puzzles, conundrums, mysteries and enigmas. Unrelenting, seemingly never-ending. At first, Jamal tried to answer them, but simply *couldn't* know the sheer encyclopedic number of them (and yes: he knew where they *truly* originated from). So inevitably, he gave wrong answers. It didn't matter, after receiving a wrong answer, Shakahr posed a new one.

There was a small reward in answering a riddle correctly: then Shakhar would wait half an hour before coming with the next. Wrong answer: the next riddle comes immediately. After a riddle is posed: three minutes to come up with an answer. No answer: next riddle.

He couldn't get rid of the evil djinni, no matter what he tried. The ghost was immaterial: physical violence went straight through it. It just followed him wherever he was, shooting puzzles at him.

Jamal tried earplugs of every type imaginable, but the djinni's words were ghostly, aimed only at him, and just passed through worldly barriers. It went on and on and on: during his work, during meals, in his bed. He only slept through sheer exhaustion.

He tried to drown the incessant riddling out by going to noisy markets, loud theatre plays, wild chanting choirs in the Jam'eh mosque. These proved only a temporary reprieve, and became exhausting in their own right.

Other people couldn't see or hear Shakahr. To his virtual brethren, Jamal came to be known as the crazy fisherman: the one who spoke to the air with nonsensical words.

Deep down in his soul, Jamal knew there must be a way to outwit the plaguing djinni, but the constant chattering made it impossible for him to concentrate. Instead, half the time, he automatically tried to answer.

It was maddening, but he refused to go mad. A stalemate in Hell.

He should just stop: he could order the VR-program to do away with the djinni at any time. But he vigorously hated backing away from a challenge: deep inside his warrior soul, he was programmed to compete, and to come out on top. To never give in, and always fight to win.

Intellectually, he should have known that his limited brain capacity was no match for riddles against a machine that outdid both his memory and computation ability with two orders of magnitude. Like trying to move the Moon with his bare hands, with no place to stand on.

Even halfway through the 22nd Century, computer software wasn't (self-)conscious or even self-aware: you basically got out what you put in, and creativity was not on the programming horizon quite yet. It was just that a truly humongous amount of facts and statistics had been put in, establishing routines that mimicked real life eerily closely. Beyond the mountains of data, though, inventiveness was still in the uncanny valley.

In matters of pure knowledge, Jamal was outclassed. He should have known that his *forte* lay in originality of expression, thought and visionary imagination. But he kept fighting a fight he couldn't possibly win.

On top of that—or rather, at the bottom—there was the persistent undercurrent of the true test: he had to stay sane for forty-two days. That was basically the more important test, and at any point Jamal could just stop his adventure in the VR-world of his choice, and just start another. Any future commander worth his salt should know when to lose a battle in order to win the war.

Still, Jamal didn't pull out. Maybe because his youthful self simply refused to give in. Maybe because he felt he hadn't put up enough of a fight. Or maybe, somewhere in the very core of his being, he thought the virtual test more quintessential than the real one.

He tried self-hypnosis, but Shakahr remained the only spell he couldn't break. He was driven to the edge of exhaustion. When walking past the Jam'eh mosque, he wondered if Allah might save him. But he wasn't a true believer, and figured that before any true god would want to save him, he needed to prove he was worth saving. He was pushed to the threshold of despair. He considered drugs, but a vestigial sense of self-preservation decided against it. He teetered on the brink: I mustn't go mad! I mustn't give in! Riddles kept coming, riddles kept going, while true answers remained elusive. He almost dropped off the edge of exhaustion into the abyss of madness. Looking deep into that pit, it was as if something stared back.

Suddenly, there was a third presence, next to him and the relentless djinni. Someone who looked just like himself, but had a mad glint in his eyes. Yet, his twin brother was dressed exactly like Shakahr: the same wide purple pantaloons, the same light-blue sash and the same bling around his wrists, ankles, waist and neck. A far cry from the dull brown fisherman pants and loose white shirt Jamal was wearing.

"What the hell is happening here?" Jamal wondered. "Am I going insane?"

"Not insane," his djinni-like twin answered. "Merely a bit schizophrenic."

—it looks charming from a distance, but dangerous from nearby—

—at first glance it seems interesting, even fascinating—

—a second look mystifies, but the more you see it, the more it repeals—

—up close and personal, its powers to compel cannot be denied—

The real djinni kept riddling, and Jamal, even in his unbalanced state, had no problem distinguishing it from his djinnied self.

"This refusal to choose the manner in which you will die," the fake djinni said. "Is basically the manifestation of your unwillingness to die for the right cause in battle. Deep within, you are a coward, soldier."

"What nonsense is this?" Jamal's belief that he could not possibly get more frustrated was proven wrong. "I cannot foresee what happens in the future: if the time comes to make a sacrifice it will depend on the situation then, not a stupid, uninformed decision now. This is madness."

"Correct again," the real djinni said. "Next riddle in thirty minutes."

Jamal couldn't believe it: in order to prevent him from going mad another spectre appears? Fight fire with fire?

"What use are you?" Jamal looked at his spectral self. "Now I need to talk to two poltergeists. No time to think at all."

"Wrong," the fake Jamal caressed a goatee the real one would never grow. "I am your sounding board, your mental sparring partner. With me, you can try out answers and scenarios for the only question that truly matters: 'choose the manner of your death', before giving the best one to the evil djinni. Make one mistake with him and you're the sacrificial goat."

Jamal had to admit that made sense. He had already been musing about ways to outwit Shakahr, but the constant riddling kept breaking his train of thought. Maybe, with the help of his gaudy self, he could test his plans. Or at least delay the onset of his madness (if talking to himself was considered sane).

If there was no escape from blathering, Jamal figured he might as well get into the thick of it, and headed for the trade plaza in

Bandar-e-Taheri—the commercial port—where a small fleet of Cushitic traders from the Horn of Africa had just arrived. A lively barter of unlikely goods: large, heavy, almost rudimentary ebony statuettes of forbidding idols were weighed against bright, almost incandescent lapis lazuli, or revered ancestor vases from the Afghan mountains. Intricate ivory carvings were compared with agate and amethyst necklaces from South India. *Maybe*, Jamal thought, *in the howling wind no-one hears you scream.*

Yet an incessant whisper pierced through:

—some say it repeats itself, some say it's different every time—

—winners have their versions, as do losers: which will prevail—

—under fierce scrutiny, it can turn on a dime—

—although often the strongest remain to tell the tale—

"Even I know that one," Jamal's stand-in said. "Truth."

"That's not true." Jamal began doubting his double's usefulness. "It's history."

"In truth," the sly djinni waved a sleight-of-hand. "Fact or fiction are in the eye of the beholder: subject to interpretation."

Jamal disagreed: "History is in the hands of man. Truth is in the eyes of God."

Shakahr supported Jamal: "History it is. Now state the manner of your death so you will join it."

"Is that another riddle?" Jamal II jeered.

"Why should naming the manner of my death be another riddle? What if it is the real deal?" Jamal tried suppressing his deepest doubts, but failed.

"Remember the old adage: 'Be careful what you wish for'?" Jamal's djinni-twin rolled its eyes. "You'll get anything, except what you bargained for."

"Like: 'Sometimes the angels punish us by answering our prayers'? But I didn't pray for anything."

"Are you sure you didn't?" The fake djinni feigned surprise, "Never *ever* wished you'd never die?"

"Of course I did. Which kid didn't?"

"Then you must still be a child: the djinni obviously picked that deep desire off you," said the djinni's advocate.

"I thought you were on *my* side." Jamal experienced new depths of exasperation, just when he thought he'd hit rock bottom. "So what do I *do* about it?"

"Outsmart the ghost," his split-off copy shimmered. "As you're supposed to do."

"What if I say that I want to die the moment the Universe suffers its heat death?"

"That may be exactly what he wants, because then the utmost part of your life—assuming he has the power to keep you alive in that long, cold darkness—you will be living in a deathless Universe, where nothing happens except the immensely slow Hawking evaporation of black holes in the dark void. For countless trillions of years: utter, absolute boredom will seem like the epitome of happenstance in comparison with that."

"Hold on: we're in a VR recreation of old Persia, and after forty-two days I'm reeled back in—even as a failed fish—by the testing authorities. No way Shakahr can keep me alive in the real Universe."

"He may not need to: the way you experience time in this virtual world you created is different. He may keep you alive through what *you* experience as countless aeons, fast-forward the interesting bits and dump you in the middle of an ever-slowly expanding Universe hurtling towards its entropic end point with nothing more exciting than black holes shrinking at an immeasurably slow pace against a dark, bleak canvas and a cosmic background temperature fading from 4.2 to 0 Kelvin."

"That's insane."

"Which you will be, in that scenario. He will stretch it into a virtual infinity."

"Oh well: I need to think of something else."

They wandered through the port of Siraf. Trade was booming: so much that there were craftsman manufacturing plates and cutlery especially for the traders from the Western Chalukyas dynasty in India, reserved for when they returned. Ivory, spices and ebony were brought in from East Africa. Gemstones, fine jewellery and clothing were imported from Western India. There were even emeralds, rubies and sapphires, brought in overland by camel caravans from Afghanistan.

Successful pearl divers tried to trade their wares, as well. In the commercial mêlée, a lone fisherman seemingly talking to himself was easily lost. On the one hand, Jamal hoped that Shakahr's insistent riddling would drown in the sea of voices bidding for barter. On the other hand, the incessant hubbub made it hard to concentrate. He wanted to outsmart that damned djinni, even if it took his last breath, barely realising that this might be exactly what Shakahr wanted.

The straight approach didn't quite seem to work: so maybe he should look into more, well, paradoxical alleys? A choice so inherently self-contradictory that it would freeze up the evil djinni? One such a proposition welled up in his mind, but he'd better spar the notion with his schizoid self. Not before Shakahr fired off another riddle, though.

—*some wish to be this in reality, even if it's a fool's errand*—
—*others wish to attain it through their legacy, so grand*—
—*but as it is, nobody will ever know where they stand*—
—*because that exercise is akin to drawing lines in the sand*—

"Lamaj," Jamal decided the name might as well mirror the situation. "I think I may have a way."

"The way of the warrior," Lamaj wielded an imaginary sword, "or the way of the wizard?"

"I can't physically fight an ethereal ghost." Jamal lamented. "And I'm not into wizardry. I wish to be wise. Lacking that: smarter."

"Let's hear it, then."

"OK, suppose I say: 'I choose to die as a man who is truly immortal'?"

"Crafty one, but do not underestimate Shakahr's wiles. Are you familiar with the classic Fredric Brown?"

"Never heard of him." Jamal then realised: "I suppose you are directly linked to the electronic database, like Shakahr?"

"Possibly. Probably." Lamaj seemed unsure. "To sleep, perchance to dream in the same nirvana. More importantly, in Brown's mini trilogy of *Great Lost Discoveries*, the third was about immortality.

"The protagonist had developed an immortality serum. Yet he was reluctant to use it, fearing its implications. Then he became terminally ill, and used the serum on himself. Not only he, but his disease had become immortal, as well. He lapsed into a coma from which he never woke, but also never died. After a few decades his pragmatic doctors simply buried him."

"So you're saying Shakahr could pull something similar on me: give me a horrible disease first, then make me immortal, and then let me suffer forever."

"It would most certainly not be beneath him."

"Stupid immortality."

"Correct," Shakahr said. "Even if immortality as such is not 'stupid' nor 'smart', per se."

The main port wasn't exactly an oasis of silence even during the lowest of seasons, but the current rabble of excited shouts rising from many throats was exceptional by its own, elevated standards. Like the rest, Jamal had also noticed that the *zaruq* of Captain Shariyari had just entered the port, returning from its long trip to *Cīna*. Admittedly trade ships from China were a rare occasion, but did not rate this unprecedented outburst.

Seeing Jamal's facial expression—both quizzical and irritated—a bystander slapped him on the shoulder. "Haven't you heard?" Jamal shook his head. "Abharah is *al-rubban*!"

"But this is Shariyari's *zaruq*," Jamal said, flabbergasted. "Abharah is lost, presumably perished at sea."

"Captain Shariyari found Abharah in his *mityal* with a water-skin, and thought he had saved him. But in truth it was the other way around, as Abharah actually saved *al-burran* Shariyari and his crew, ensuring a good trade in the process, and becoming captain of Shariyari's *zaruq*." The man said, almost breathless. "It's an incredible story."

As the man launched into the infamous sea story, Jamal was distracted by yet another riddle from Shakahr:

—*for those that don't know, it's something*—

—*for those that know, it's nothing*—

—*for you it depends on everything*—

—*you won't get something for nothing*—

"My life here would be so interesting and fulfilling," Jamal said to Lamaj, "if it wasn't for this ridiculous riddler, this persistent plague on my senses."

"Then get rid of him," Lamaj suggested. "Give him what he *thinks* he wants."

"I'm trying. How about 'I wish to die in a manner unknown to you'."

"Close. He could possibly kill you and then induce amnesia, claiming he doesn't remember how he killed you."

"Let's fine-tune it then: 'I wish to die in a manner unknown to you *before*, *during* and *after* my death."

"Closer. But he could launch a number of killing causes at you: bullets, knives, arrows, canon balls, and more. Then he'd let random chance decide which of the multitude exactly killed you, without him knowing which singular one it was."

"Are you sure you're not related to him?" Jamal threw his head in his hands. "You think just as twistedly."

"Only trying to help you. Nobody said it would be easy."

"It seems nigh-on impossible," Jamal said. "The riddle of all riddles."

"Right again," said Shakahr. "You're getting good at this. Now choose your death wish before it gets boring."

Jamal ignored him. He needed a change of scenery, and walked towards Bandar-e-Kangan: the berths of the pearl divers. The free-diving pearl fishers were exercising in two seemingly diametrically opposed methods: about half of them were involved with slow-motion, zen-like breathing workouts to increase their underwater stamina; while the other half were running around, doing push-ups and other strenuous training schemes to also increase their underwater stamina.

The pearl divers were a small world unto themselves, but not disrespectful: if you let them do their thing, they wouldn't interfere with you doing yours. Live and let live: they performed their specialities and contributed in their unique way to society. Live and let die: unfortunately, only about one in a thousand oysters did have a pearl, and of those only one in a thousand was perfectly round, rather than pear-shaped, oval or otherwise irregular. Inadvertently, by bringing up a ton of oysters for every three or four perfect round pearls, they were minor competitors to the fishermen, as oysters were regarded as delicacies in the wealthy trading classes. Jamal didn't mind: the catches of his fishermen friends (and himself) fed everyone, not just a privileged class. To him, it felt good to be part of the people at large.

—*they are precious, but not from a mine*—
—*claimed as a source of wisdom divine*—
—*careful: don't throw them before swine*—
—*from the deep: in the light they shine*—

"Come on, Shakahr," Jamal sneered. "Pearls. You're slacking off."

The evil djinni acquiesced with a nod that seemed almost demure.

It gave Jamal the idea that he was finally getting somewhere. Inspired, he turned to his gaudy twin. "Try this: 'I wish to die through a bullet that goes faster than the speed of light'."

"In a vacuum," Lamaj added. "As light can go much slower in other media; under some circumstances it can almost be stopped."

"OK: faster than the speed of light in a vacuum." Jamal said. "That should settle it."

"So you trust your life on a theory by Einstein?"

"General Relativity still holds up, to this very day."

"In normal space/time, it does. But you forget that we are in a virtual environment."

"So Shakahr can cheat himself out of this one?"

"By letting a bullet travel in an Alcubierre warp drive: while theoretically possible, there's no such technology yet, but nicely feasible in our VR world."

It wasn't fair. The moment Jamal thought of something (he believed) foolproof, his second self ran circles around it. Too easy in a virtual world; in the *real* world he'd kick Shakahr's arse. On the other hand, in the real world, Shakahr simply didn't exist.

Rationally speaking, he should just let this go. Waste of time, thought space and resources. But giving in to an *imaginary* challenge? How could he ever face a *real* one? He'd rather go insane. Scratch that: maybe he already was. How many Rubicons did he need to cross before this mental torture ends?

In the meantime, Shakahr's riddles kept coming, on time, without fail. Like a clockwork demon James Clerk Maxwell himself would be proud of.

—*a razor-sharp two-edged sword*—
—*it can be a driver and a drag*—
—*hoist you by your own petard*—
—*make you wave the white flag*—

Maybe Jamal should try another approach: gain the moral high ground. Looking at his brighter reflection, he launched his next attempt. "Let's say: 'I want to die from happiness when all the poverty in the world is eradicated'."

"He might kill everybody and give all their money to you: no more poverty." Lamaj said.

"That is truly sick."

"We are dealing with an extremely evil djinni," the faux djinni pulled a faux angry face. "The most formidable in history."

"Why do I have to deal with him?" Jamal tried to suppress his despair.

"Look deeper into yourself," his twisted mirror image said. "You never settle for second best. Burning ambition."

"Hey," Shakahr said, somewhat irritated. "The true coward needs to answer."

Jamal was more than irritated: he wanted to beat Shakahr, kick the shit out of him, torture him, slowly, excruciatingly until he liked it and then stop. But no, he was better than that. It was absurd, like fighting smoke, like chasing clouds. At least chasing clouds was fun.

—it follows no commands or logic—
—it chases dark alleys wilfully—
—fluid, infuriating, elusive, stoic—
—ignoring every rule willy-nilly—

"Try harder." Jamal smirked. "Absurdity."

"You sure?" Lamaj said. "It could be genius, as well."

"Oh no: genius doesn't chase dark alleys, it *lights* them."

"If you know genius so well." Lamaj gestured to a virtual sky. "Then why don't you use it against Shakahr?"

"I'm trying. How about 'I wish to die from an impossible cause'?"

"Tricky one. Define 'impossible'."

"That which cannot exist or come into being."

"Under what rules?"

"The laws of physics."

"Which are, basically, theories." Lamaj postured like a Rodin statue. "Theories which do not apply in this virtual realm. I just explained that your Einstein gamble wouldn't work here."

"But there must be different versions of impossible." Jamal inadvertently grimaced like a Munch painting. "Logical, philosophical, absurdist, whatever."

"All of which are as malleable in this virtual reality as the warped creations in your own mind."

"A logic, an *über-gestalt* independent of the reality in which it is invented," Jamal posited. "Internally consistent, like arithmetic."

"Good luck with that: David Hilbert's second problem. Gödel's incompleteness theorems gave short shrift to that."

"No matter how brilliant Gödel was, they're still theorems." Jamal tried to pierce through the multitude of meta-layers. "If my paradox is stronger than Shakahr's, I'm home free."

"A new type of psychological warfare," Lamaj jammed. "A siege of semantics."

Barely aware of his surrounds, Jamal only noticed that he had walked into the spartan fisherman's quarters of Bandar-e-Dayar when several friends greeted him. Anybody else would have noted the heady mix of fresh seafood—cobia, milkfish, silver pomfret, rabbit fish—and rotting fish innards that nobody ever seemed to be able to clean away.

Up the hill overlooking the fishing port, the joyous mosaics of the Jam'eh mosque were reflecting a cascade of colours in the setting sun. A flock of seagulls set out for their evening catch against a vermillion sky. Mosquitos buzzed and swarmed in the autumn haze.

Maybe his subconscious was willing him to get out to sea. But that would not bring him any rest: he'd be with two passengers instead of one. No, it must be time jump off the deep end.

—*if this axiom is axiomatic*—
—*then what founds the fundaments*—
—*do the knots that weave its fabric*—
—*pull reality up by its own bootstraps*—

"OK. Here's my curve ball," Jamal said. "It proposes: I choose to die from happiness the moment the 'this statement is false' paradox has been conclusively solved with a 'yes' or 'no' answer."

"The Liar's Paradox?" Lamaj smiled. "There are precedences in quantum mechanics, like the wave/particle duality: for example an electron can be a particle and a wave *at the same time*."

"The double slit experiment works only for quantum objects. As such, 'this statement is false' may very well be a philosophical manifestation of a deeper, quantum mechanical truth, a truth that defies common sense. Thus, its solution can then—by definition—not be a common sense solution, but something beyond that. However, in my question to Shakahr, the answer to 'this statement is false' must be common sense ('yes' or 'no') for me to get my chosen manner of death. That is impossible, thus Shakahr cannot kill me."

"You are betting it all on the premise that Shakahr can not find a solution to the Liar's Paradox."

"Nobody's been able to prove nor disprove it, so Shakahr can't. There will be so many contradictions in the database it will freeze him. If not forever, then at least until my time is up."

"Is that not a Phyrric victory?" Lamaj raised his hands. "Don't you want to win in an unambiguous way?"

"I do, and I could if this played out in the real world. Now the best I can do is defy the tricks of the coyote trickster by making it chase its own tail."

"Be Nasrudin's donkey? Rostam the demonic demon-subduer?" Lamaj lifted his right brow, then left brow, vice versa, repeatedly in a mad dash for acceleration until his eyebrows were a blur. "Making it choose its own demise?"

Enough is enough, Jamal decided, and turned to Shakahr. "I have made my choice, evil ghost."

"Finally," Shakahr said with fire in his eyes. "I began to believe you were too chickenshit. Let's hear them, your famous last words."

"I choose to die from happiness," Jamal said, as anticipation and relief flooded his nervous system. "On the moment the 'this statement is false' paradox has been conclusively solved with a 'yes' or 'no' answer."

Shakahr became quiet, and seemed lost in thought. The silence lasted, seemed to stretch into a virtual eternity, when . . .

. . . the sky opened . . .

. . . a voice descended from the heavens . . .

"TIME'S UP, PILOT MUHAMMAD. WE ARE GETTING YOU OUT OF THE ESCAPE POD"

• • •

"You came through remarkably well," the medic said at his debriefing.

"Everything was fine until that damned djinni showed up." Jamal lamented.

"You could have reprogrammed that whenever you wanted."

"True," Jamal flinched almost imperceptibly. "But that would be like giving in. Why didn't the VR throw me some other form of magic: mermaids, evil vizier wizards, even a Sphinx? Anything but that bloody ghost-in-a-bottle."

"The interactivity of the VR-programming gives you more of a certain thing if you respond positively to it. Which you did."

"Positively? I hated that djinni!"

"But you kept interacting with it, which the program interprets as a 'positive' response. You should just have switched interests."

And admit defeat? Jamal thought. "I'll keep that in mind for the next time."

"We certainly hope there will be no next time, Commander Jamal," the medic smiled, slightly exasperated. "We don't want to lose such a fine fighter as you."

"One who never gives up." Jamal couldn't help himself.

"Your schizophrenic self defence: that was something else, indeed." the medic admitted. "I can't wait to share that with our psychologist." When he saw Jamal's expression he added, "Sorry soldier: no secrets in the army. We don't want the officers we have trained so well to bail out on us unexpectedly."

Quickly, Jamal nodded assent. "Then let's just move to the second test?"

"The one where you spend 42 days in total isolation, with no electronics—except life support—working?" The medic was flabbergasted. "You barely finished the first."

"I feel fine, and according to your tests I am fine. So I might as well get it over with." Jamal said. "And after that Riddle-o-matic attack, forty-two days of silence will be bliss."

"Be careful what you wish for," the medic raised his hands. "The military may just give it to you."

Afterword

Basically, "Djinni Djinni Dream Dream" is a section of a much longer piece: a—so far unfinished—novella called "Jamal and the Jinnee in the Klein Bottle". In that novella, I try to explore certain consequences of the development of both new propulsion systems and new types of pilots on the way space battles are fought. Jamal is the principal character: he grew up as a young space pilot with the 'old' ways of space battle, but as he climbs the ranks all the way to admiral he is confronted with the 'new' way of doing space battles, which hugely shifts the balance of power.

The "Djinni Djinni Dream Dream" section—originally it didn't have a name—shows an important part of Jamal's character development: his confrontation with a powerful djinni (I actually prefer to call it 'jinnee'), possibly of his own making, that will come to haunt him later in "Jamal and the Jinnee in the Klein Bottle".

I was (am) still struggling with the final section of the novella when I noticed Dreaming of Djinn's call for submissions. I thought that this particular section might work for the anthology if I made it a bit more stand-alone and expanded it a bit. Well, it grew from a 2600 words section to a 6200 words short story. Not only did I greatly increase the stakes and the philosophical interaction between Jamal and his evil djinni, but also infused the 11th Century Persia in which it was set with a much stronger sense of place and time.

Now, of course, I need to re-integrate it back into the larger narrative, meaning the novella will grow to well beyond 40,000 words, before I can cut my teeth on the final section. In the meantime, I hope the reader will enjoy "Djinni Djinni Dream Dream" (actually, "Dreaming of Djinn" would have been a perfect title, but that was already taken by the anthology at large).

Silver, Sharp As Silk

Dan Rabarts

It is sharp, and beautiful, and awful to watch them burn, but burn they must, wrapped up in dust and flame, writhing and curling and dying, thin hard men who wear cold steel at their belts while trading silk for silver, spices and myrrh. Sometimes, as they cry in anguish before the dust chokes their voices forever, I savour the sound, relishing that it is not I who cries in anguish for that which I have lost—not this time. Over rock, across dunes, between the sleeping canvasses of their caravans and the snorting of dromedaries, I blot out the sky before them, judge them, and deliver my sentence, or my mercy, as I see fit. I come upon them in the brutality of screaming wind and shredding sand, descend on them in a howling rage, summoning the nightmares of their sweating half-sleeps to their eyes, their throats. I swirl and thrash about them, knowing their bright Arabian steel, Damascan gold and Grecian silver will not shine so bright when I am done, when I have blasted the skin from their flesh and the flesh from their bones.

But not the camels, nor the silk, shall I harm, for the camels are without sin, and when at last I settle back in the secret darkness among the shimmer of bloody gold and silver, when I resolve from dust and ash to what passes for flesh on my bones, I will press the silks to my brittle hands, the dune-dry crags of my face, and remember the softness of my children's skin, so long ago. Time and again, I will them once more to breathe, knowing that they never shall. All I have left is my grief, my rage, my shadow against the desert sky.

But it has not always been so.

Once I was a not a shifting form of black sand swelling up along the horizon, a spectre of fear, hot fever spreading on nightmare wings. Once I was a thing of longing and hope and elation, a thing of need and love and song. Once, I rocked my children to sleep in my arms, crooning softly over them in the half-light until their rippling breaths rose and fell in silken tides with the ebb and flow of my voice, rumbling in my chest. Once upon a time I held them close, felt their breathing mingle with mine, and it was all I needed, even when everything else had been burned out from under me.

At those times I might forget the betrayals, the black face of what I was and what we had all become. But the betrayal, the betrayers, would not forget me. And in time, they would even strip away what little remained to me, leaving only my rage; the burning black sand in the white desert sky.

• • •

"You are young. You are a fool."

The merchant set down the small silver cups and poured steaming green tea from a pot only mildly tarnished by sand and salt and age.

Ahmed nodded his thanks and took his cup, sipping thoughtfully. "But caravans pass through here and travel across the Empty Quarter in every month of the year. Why should mine be any different?"

"Because you carry silk." The fat bearded man sipped his tea, as if this explained everything. When Ahmed met his stare with doubt bordering on reproach, he shrugged. "No silk merchants ever arrive by way of the sands; always, they go around. Sometimes, the foolish young ones leave here and ignore the warnings of the wise, and never again do they pass this way. The spice traders, they have no problem, presuming they employ enough guards to keep the Bedouin at bay. But Ar Rub' al Khali swallows silk like the sands soak up water, and those who carry it are swallowed up along with it."

Ahmed set down his cup. It would not do to admit that he did not have sufficient means to pay a cadre of mercenary guards to escort his wares around Mazun and the Arabian coast as far as the nearest city—Moscha, if his memory served him correctly, the city the Greeks called *Cryptos Portos*. He would run out of coin somewhere along the road, and then be forced to face a horde of armed and angry men wanting to be paid. And even if he did make it as far as the Sassanids' hidden port alive, what point was there if he arrived destitute but for a load of finest silk to sell, when those who lived there were little more than fisherfolk, who neither cared for silk nor valued its worth? No, he must cross the great sands, with his silk and his silver both, so that when he arrived on the Gulf shore he might purchase a new ship and carry his wares to Baghdad to sell, as he had intended before the fury of the sea had driven him so far from his course, casting up his wounded vessel on this barren stretch of desert coast without so much as a tree to be seen for the felling and repairing of stricken boats.

Crossing the sands posed its own problems, of course; the Bedouin, for one, and the desert itself, but these were of less concern to him than men grown greedy for the shine of silver. At best, he might barter his way around the nomads with a bolt of shimmering blue, despite knowing that it would be carved up by curved blades to fly as warriors' banners in the stiff desert breeze, or to swaddle pale-eyed maidens on their journey from virginity to womanhood. At worst . . .

"I have travelled many long miles," he told the merchant. "I have walked the Silk Road, passed beneath the high black windows of Petra, crossed the snows and highlands of the Mongols, and eaten rice on the China Sea. There I bought the finest silks, for none make silk so perfect as the Chinese—smooth as ripples on a pond, sharp as the silver moon—and I sailed them back by way of India. Much have I seen, many dangers have I faced. Had my boat not been thrown up on this scrap of land I would have sailed all the way up the Tigris to Baghdad, but I have my life, and my wares, and for that I am thankful.

"However, there are economics to consider." *And the stories*, Ahmed thought. Economics were nothing without stories, and even if all his silver and all his silk were stolen from him, none could ever take his stories. And of those he had many, many indeed. "I have no choice but to cross Ar Rub' al Khali."

"It is no choice at all. You will never reach the Gulf. You will never reach Baghdad. You are young, and a fool, and the desert will eat you alive."

"Because I carry silk?"

The old man nodded, and poured more tea. "You should not go. It would be a terrible waste of fine silk."

Ahmed stepped out of the tent into the light of the louring sun, a bright eye hanging over the scorching horizon, over the souks and bazaars which feigned the shape of civilisation against the inevitability of the creeping sands. Beyond the rocks and scrub, Ahmed trudged to where the waves touched the earth, where his wounded boat ground listlessly in the tide that washed upon the beach.

"*Ni hao.*" Shen's voice, as ever, was like moonlight rippling on autumn waves. She stood on the bow, firm and proud as a mariner embarking unto the blue yonder, not thrown up to wrack and ruin on a foreign shore. Ahmed splashed through the light surf and clambered up the ladder, to wrap her in his arms.

"Well?" she asked. "Will we dare the desert, then?"

Ahmed nodded. "Yes. We can buy camels and load them with our wares, and we will go alone. We can trust these men of sand no more than we can the desert itself. But first, we have a task."

"And that is?"

"We must fashion garments to clothe ourselves, of only the finest of our finest silks, stitched with thread of silk and gold and silver."

Shen drew back, her fingers still twined in his. "What have we to fear of the desert that silk might protect us?"

"There is a story I think you ought to hear. I will recount it for you while we sew."

• • •

I seethe. I surge. I howl relentless, and the desert howls with me.

I subside.

In the dark hidden places I wrap myself in folds soft and cold as liquid, and weep tears of ash and mud. I sleep among the silence of silk and gold and silver and bone. I wake, as always, to the emptiness of my grief.

Alone, enraged, I rise, to darken the sun and torment those who fall beneath my shadow. On this day, I smell the silk from a dozen leagues distant. The sandstorm billows black and choking around me as I descend, a rasping maelstrom. There are but two, a man and a woman and a score of camels, heavily laden. The sweet perfect smell of the silk is thick about them, drawing me in, down. I scream, shrieking rage and defiance at those who dare, who *dare*, to bear silk into my domain and think it is theirs, and not mine.

They scream back.

For a moment, I relish their terror, their pain. Then I hear the scrape of sand on silk and this gives me pause, and in my pause, many things become clear. I realise that they are clothed not in cotton or leather or steel, but in silk, and that in my rage I am hurting it. I am hurting the precious silk.

I also understand, with a sudden dread, that their cries are not merely those of pain and fear, but *words*, words foreign and ancient and powerful, words spoken together, many tongues as one.

By the time I comprehend all of this, however, it is too late. For the first time in more long centuries than I care to remember, I know fear. I gather myself to flee, yet I cannot. The ancient magics bind me, and the silk is hardier to them than the steel armour of those whom I have shredded to the bone in days gone by, for I cannot bring myself to turn my strength against it.

The winds falter and the sands draw me down, into the clutches of the spell, and I howl and curse and grasp at hot dust which can never hide my guilt, or my shame, and which can never fill the emptiness inside me, for it is only sand, and the wind will drive it into the empty places of the world.

• • •

Shen checked the bright silver chains draped across the withered form's limbs, while Ahmed chose robes of finest silk in which to clothe it. They had erected their tent where it had fallen, dust condensing out of the sandstorm into bone and brittle flesh, captured by the words of power Ahmed had learned among Scythian mystics on the fringes of a distant desert a long time ago. The creature's skin was dry and rubbed away at his touch, like a corpse left too long in the sun, *years* too long. Even its mouth was a barren cave, its tongue as rough as old bark.

Shen stepped back, satisfied that the silver wrapped around its wrists, ankles and neck would hold the creature when it awoke.

Ahmed took the silks, deepest blue as the sky over the sea and embroidered with tracing patterns of gold thread—glittering shadows of lotus and tiger and dusk—and wrapped them around the sexless thing where it sprawled in the sand. He considered it a moment, the way its rigid, withered fingers reached out in desperation, as if seeking to bury itself in the sand forever.

Shen brought over the tea; green leaves and Pishacha blood from India, ginseng and ground horn of Chinese dragon, brewed over a flame of burning bird bones, magics of waking and binding. With only a flutter of nerves, Ahmed dribbled the tea down the desiccated cadaver's throat.

"Ifrit," he intoned. "Awake, and know your master."

• • •

I choke on wet sand, gag with the swallowing, like river mud gurgling in my open mouth. From the darkness I try to burst forth but my limbs are powerless. A weight that burns with the fire of a thousand noons presses me down, snarls me in dust and earth, crushes me into submission. I know this pain, this ancient curse. It has been a long, long time since I knew this weight which bears down my arms, my legs, my will. It is a magic I had thought lost under the seas of sand, broken by the tides of time, smashed into oblivion in my grief and rage. Evidently, I was wrong. Even the razing of cities was not enough to drown this curse. Once the words have been unleashed upon the world, they can never be buried back in the darkness from whence they came.

The trickle of sludge in my mouth begins to clear, and I gasp on air. The *saahir*'s brew seeps through me, tying me ever more firmly to the living world, making soft flesh of fire and dust and ash. I strain once more against my bonds but know I cannot overcome the perfect silver flame that shackles me. I am captured. I am defeated.

I am bound.

• • •

"Arise, ifrit," Ahmed repeated.

Behind the creature, Shen knelt patiently. In her arms she held an urn, fired blue ceramic inlaid with silver inscriptions and decorated in a mosaic of shapes and forms which at once suggested and defied narrative. Her fingers rested lightly on the vessel's blown glass stopper, her body poised.

Ahmed lifted his hands and, like a marionette, the creature rose. The silver bracelets seemed to hang towards the sky, as if suspended on invisible strings. The thing opened its eyes, and its gaze was hot enough to melt the flesh from the bones of weaker beings.

"I would not know your name, for I wish no power over you," Ahmed said. "I suspect such a boon would come at a price I am not willing to pay. But I would know the truth of your story, so that we might strike a bargain." He reached behind him and produced a dish, which he slid forward across the canvas spread over the sands. Coarse white crystals spilled from it. "I share my salt with you."

The creature paused, eyeing the dish with suspicion.

"You know what I am, ifrit. I am *saahir*. Ritual is my truth, and my reality. I cannot offer you my trust as a lie. I see your torment. I see how you make the world suffer with you for your loss. With this salt I pledge to you a bargain of peace in return for your tale, for peace is my art and my trade. In return, I wish only safe passage across the Empty Quarter, for myself and my beasts and my wares."

"And should I refuse?"

Ahmed's smile did not change, yet his face seemed suddenly colder. "Then this silver will draw you down into the sand, where you will know only choking torment for the long years it will take for the metal to tarnish and weaken and allow you to escape. Peace is my trade, not a gift. It does not come free."

The creature considered. Then it reached out, touched a wrinkled finger to the salt and placed a crystal on its tongue. Ahmed nodded and did the same, his shoulders easing. He set cups before himself and the ifrit, and poured tea for them both.

"So," growled the ifrit. "My tale."

• • •

"Hear me well, for mine are words of woe.

"We are an ancient race, our history dark and troubled. Long before the races of man found themselves at the pinnacles of empires they were weak, divided like dogs struggling to survive in the harshness of desert and mountain, warring amongst themselves and laying out their dead for the scavengers to feed upon. So tied up were they in their animal beliefs, their myths and stories carved in blood and ochre on smoke-dark cave-walls, that they were easy to deceive into our snares and nets, our primitive fictions. Swarms of locusts, pillars of fire, giants, lights in the sky, all these forms we could take, and take them we did. In their legions humanity bowed down, gave us names that were not our own, called upon us as gods to deliver them miracles and the corpses of their enemies. So it was that their wars became ours, and ours became theirs.

"We grew cruel, and reckless, and vain. I drove my people to build a tower so high it would kiss the heavens, so that they might collect the silver of the stars themselves and paint my temple in their light. But my brothers cared not for my aesthetic diversions, and laid a curse upon my people that they might speak only in a confused garble of tongues. Everything ceased. Men who cannot understand each other cannot work together. Tools were hurled upon the sand in frustration. Families broke apart and the city fell to ruin, my people scattering, the tower abandoned. All I had left were the silk flags that fluttered in the desert breeze. These I stripped from the walls and breathed life into, and thus my children were born, to haunt the empty streets and echoing temples, to play among the crumbling scaffolds of a tower doomed to decay and collapse, an edifice not unlike everything that my brethren had become. For a time, I had only my sorrow, and the songs I sang to my children in the dark.

"But my brothers were not done with me yet. It was not enough to scatter my people. They sent armies to scourge my ruins, bringing fire, breaking walls, and bombarding my tower with rocks and burning oil. But among the armies there were men in dark hooded cloaks who bore a terrible new weapon: words. Words of power. Words of war, and death, and binding. Words born of the curse laid upon my city. Words of magic.

"Did my brothers know that the curse they delivered upon me would become the curse of our very race? I will never know, for they too were soon bound by the very *saahir* whom they had empowered to destroy me. Their wizards spoke their words of magic, and their power shackled me, for a time: a long while among mortals, perhaps, but less so for the ifrits. In time, silver will tarnish and even the most powerful words will echo into silence and be forgotten, or so I thought, and thus it was that my bondage ended, and I unleashed my vengeance upon the world of man. I raged upon them as storm, and plague, and swarm, in the hopes of destroying every last echo of those terrible words. But words cannot be erased entirely, not words such as these, when the hungry and powerful covet them so. They have a power which gives them their own immortality.

"I returned to the place where my city had been, where my children had roamed and fluttered and played, but nothing remained. The foundation stones lay covered in sand, and though I called down a hundred and one raging windstorms to blow aside the detritus of years, no sign of my children could I find. So I drifted from place to place, ever searching, until finally I came upon this empty land, which I chose to rule by the terror of wind pregnant with flame.

"It was among the skulls and tattered canvas of a daring yet doomed caravan that I found it. It was thin, and cold, and did not shift and slide and sweep with a life all its own. It was a single bolt, blue, its edges ragged, but I knew what it had the potential to be. I carried it high into the desert mountains where I could bury it deep in the warm safe earth, far out of reach of the greedy and the treacherous.

"I tried to give it life; I tried, so very hard. I breathed upon it, I willed it to live, like I had willed life into my children back in my doomed city, but all I achieved was my own exhaustion, and an even blacker despair than that which I already knew. I was no longer a bringer of life; the *saahir*'s cursed words had reduced me to nothing more than an instrument of death. So I dwell here alone—far enough from anything my brothers might covet to ensure that they no longer bother me—never knowing the touch of my children, never hearing their soft songs, never rocking them to sleep like I once did, in the shadows of Babel.

"Yet still, I hope. Those who enter my realm bearing silk know my wrath, and I spirit away every bolt of fabric to cross my path, hoping one day I will touch again upon the magic that will bring them to life. And here you are, with your cursed words, and your silver which cuts me as sharp as the touch of your silk, which itself tears me to the core by its very softness, its dead stillness.

"That is my story, that is my sorrow. That is the fire that burns at the heart of this storm. Do you truly have the courage to risk my rage? A rage which has levelled cities and reduced hundreds of mortals to nothing but carrion for the worms and bones for the wind to grind to dust? Would you truly dare?"

• • •

Ahmed finished his tea. The ifrit's cup still sat steaming before it. Its final words spoken, it reached down, lifting the china delicately, and sipped.

"Your story is told, far and wide, in many forms. Some have the right of it, others . . . less so. Such is the way of words, of histories, how they bend under the weight of memory and time and desire. For without desire, a story is nothing."

"So," said the ifrit, placing its empty cup before it. "Now that you have bound me, and you know what I am capable of, what are your commands? Whose walls shall I lay low? Whose temples cast to ruin? Whose fields to ravage and wither?"

"If I give back to you what you have lost, will you allow my caravan to cross your desert, and protect me and mine from all harm along the way?"

The ifrit's body stiffened, creaking like sand scouring rocks in a hot wind. "Give back?"

"The breath of life," Ahmed waved his hand dismissively. "The words of binding laid upon you by the *saahir* of Babylon burned a mark of unmaking upon you, so that you might become nothing more than a weapon to be controlled. The power of making is one that lies beyond the reach of most mortals, but it is a simple enough thing to render unusable. It is likewise a simple task to awaken again. I need but remove the taint, and you will once more have the power to breathe life into your children. In return, you will grant safe passage to my caravans—and my caravans alone— for as long as I need. You will be free, you will have your peace, and I will have my trade. Do we have a deal?"

The ifrit rose to its full height, its face darkening. "You would have me kill all others who try to cross the desert? How does that make you any better than the rest?"

"You need not kill. Terror will suffice. Let word of your awful dominion become greater than the truth of it. Words have such power. And you will see your children walk upon the wind once more."

As the ifrit opened its mouth to reply, the first arrow punched through its chest. It gasped a little, its face contorting with the unfamiliarity of pain, and a trickle of dry sand began to spill from where the shaft jutted between its ribs.

"Bedouin!" Ahmed gasped, dropping to his knees. Shen was already moving, dropping the urn at her feet, her fingers tracing lines in the air as she tossed a handful of sand over her head. Light flashed above them and for a second Ahmed was blind, hearing only the sly whistle of more falling arrows and the crackle of arcane energy. With a sound like summer rain exploding on a bronze shield, the volley of missiles smashed themselves to splinters on the luminous sphere that wavered in the air above them.

"Unbind me!" roared the ifrit. "Prove that you would not control me. Release me from the silver!"

Ahmed scrambled back, knowing that Shen's protective ward would only last for a few heartbeats more. "We have shared the bond of salt. That should be all the proof you need. Do we have a trade?"

"Salt is not silver. I should let the raiders kill you. In death, these bonds will be broken."

Ahmed held forth his fist, presenting the silver ring that girded his thumb. "Then you will never know the touch of your children's breath again. I do not wish to command you, ifrit, but I will if I must. Do we have a trade?"

The ifrit glowered, smoke spilling from its eyes, its mouth, its fingers. "I will make the deal of which we have already spoken, but these raiders, they are a price you must pay. For saving you here, you will owe me another debt."

Ahmed scowled, but he had little choice. Had they been mobile, they could have used all manner of wizardry from across the eastern realms to evade the Bedouin, but tethered as they were to this spot in the sands, they were at the raiders' mercy. And if the ifrit would truly sacrifice the *saahir* to the Bedouin, then their lives were worth nothing, no matter what they might offer the monster. After all, now that it knew the secret, it would only be a matter of time before it sought out another *saahir* to perform the ritual cleansing, and time was something that the immortal had no shortage of.

The globe above them faltered, cracked, grew dim. Shards of glass began to splinter and fall around them.

"Yes, ifrit, we have a deal."

As soon as the words left his lips, Ahmed knew that he had been rash. He had agreed without knowing the other side of the bargain. Such was the nature, sometimes, of life-and-death decisions.

The ifrit thrust out its wrists, the silver jangling. "Unbind me!"

Ahmed nodded, spoke a word, and the jewellery fell away. At worst, they still had the urn.

The ifrit burst forth in an eruption of dust and a swirl of smoke. The roof of the tent disintegrated in a haze of ash and cinders, and the arcane shield exploded outwards as the desert spirit ascended. A cloud of fire and sand twisted out of the cerulean void to wrap the apparition in a cyclone of destruction.

Ahmed and Shen crawled together, squeezing tight their eyes against the screaming sands, and their ears against the screams of dying men. In less time than it took to begin, so it ended. A dusty silence fell upon the desert, as if even the scorpions dared not rattle their armour for fear of the ifrit. Gingerly, Ahmed extracted himself from the wreckage of their tent, helping Shen to her feet. A haze of smoke filled the sky, and in places the sand still burned, hot and black and glassy. Dark shapes lay scattered about, twitching, some lost under drifts of sand stained red.

Ahmed and Shen turned their gaze upward, to where a darker mass circled at the fringes of the smoke cloud. Shen lifted the urn, gripping its glass stopper.

"No," Ahmed touched her arm. "We must honour our side of the bargain."

Shen's eyes did not flinch from the sky, and her voice was thick with scorn. "The bargain you made without knowing the price? In all our years together, I have never known you to make so foolish a judgement. Let me imprison it, so that it can never make its demands."

"It will escape, and it will hunt us down. We have only bargained with it in good faith so far. Let us not taint out intent with malice."

Shen spared him a glance, and even beneath the Arabian sun's smothering heat, Ahmed felt a chill run through him. "It is a being of deceit, and has been so for more millennia than either of our civilisations have existed. You cannot outwit it, just as you cannot defeat it with magic or flee from its wrath once aroused. Our only chance is to seal it in the urn now, while we have the advantage."

Ahmed shielded his eyes from the glare of sun on sand. "It wants only to be a father once again, to love its children. In order to gain *its* trust, we must offer it *our* trust."

"And what of the price of this bargain you have entered into? What if you cannot pay it? You will then be beholden to its will, instead of the opposite, as you intended."

"I never intended to command it, only to bargain for our safe passage. That is all we have done."

Shen's voice softened, if only slightly. "Ahmed, you are too tender of heart. You travel from place to place, learning magics thought long forgotten, gathering stories of ancient pasts and weaving them together in your head to form one great tapestry in which everything makes a kind of wonderful sense to you. You look at history and deceive yourself into believing that the narratives that form out of these stories are some sort of truth. But there is no truth, not like that. There are no heroes, there are no happy endings, only lies in one shape or another, remnants of memories held together in the ghosts of words that one defeated empire passed down to the next.

"The immortals have lived long enough, seen enough truth twisted into deception, that deception is all they can ever see. When everything you have ever known has been proven to be a lie, then all you can ever see are lies. That is all the ifrit will see in you, whatever truth you try to offer it. He will be up there now, trying to decide how you are deceiving it with your promises of peace and freedom, because there is no profit in peace, and nothing to be gained by offering a slave its liberty. It is raw power, and you had it under your control. Only a fool or a very cunning foe would have set it free. So it will return, because it has deceived you into its own power now, as it believes you had deceived it. So you had better be ready when it arrives, and you had better hope that you are the better liar, because your truth will not satisfy it."

Ahmed bit his cheek, and did not argue. He had long since learned that when Shen made a point, she generally had the right of it. Now was not the time to argue semantics. He truly had a battle of wits on his hands, and he was quite uncertain that he was up to the task.

The dark shape descended on a buzzing of wings, and the two *saahir* covered their faces as a swarm of locusts rasped around them. The insects coalesced into a human form, dressed in the silks they had prepared for the ifrit on the shores of the Arabian Sea, only now its skin was smooth and unblemished, the face almost handsome, though if pressed Ahmed would still have been at a loss to say if the being was man or woman. It strode among the scattered dead, kicking at a leg here, an arm there. It stooped and picked up a curved *makhaira* from among the bodies, before looking at the *saahir* where they waited.

"So, sorcerer," the ifrit said, swinging the sword twice, thrice, like a gladiator warming up before entering the arena. "Our deal. You will remove the taint from me, and I will allow you and your caravans unhindered passage across my desert. No others will I let pass."

Ahmed nodded, swallowing hard, trying to ignore the vicious glint of sun on steel. "It is as you say. But first I must see you in your true form, to find the mark of unmaking, so that I might remove it."

The ifrit's smooth, dark skin melted away, revealing the dry husk of ash and sand that Ahmed had conversed with in the tent.

"Come," Ahmed said, gesturing to what little shade remained amongst the wreckage of their tent, and the ifrit followed. It took an hour, maybe less, for Ahmed and Shen to work through the intricacies of the Babylonian curse and strip it from the creature's essence. Blood of basilisk and feather of roc they mixed and ground and boiled, intoning ancient tongues and tracing sigils with their fingers like dancers through the smoke. The sun slid overhead, relentless in her scorching.

"Now," Ahmed said as the ritual ceased. "As a sign of my good faith, I offer you your choice of my silks, to prove my spell is true and complete. Take one, and breathe your life unto it."

A crooked smile crossed the ifrit's face, as its crumbling visage disappeared once more behind the veneer of beauty it chose to wear. It stood and strode across the sands to the camels and began to pull one bolt after another from the beasts, unspooling a few feet of cloth from each, running it between its fingers, rubbing it against its face. The ifrit let a bolt of rich red silk run out in the wind a ways, pouring across the sky like wine, before letting the blade arc and fall. It held the cut section to its face, and breathed. Then it let it drop towards the sand.

But the silk did not fall. It drifted upwards, as if on the wind, then swooped, dipped and dived, like a dragon on the wing.

"We should be moving on," Shen whispered. "Maybe in its distraction with the silk, it will forget the second part of your bargain."

Before Ahmed could answer, the ifrit spun. "So we have made a deal, *saahir*, and you have honoured your side of it. You have your safe passage, and I have my children. But you must know that my protection will not extend to the mountains, the fastness where I hide from the world. Enter those lands, and I will shred you to the bone, silk or no silk, bargain or no. You understand this?"

Ahmed nodded, the sweat now running cold down his spine.

"These men around you; many I watched enter the world, as babes screaming in their mothers' blood, saw them grow to boys, to men, watched as they became fathers. Saw them honour their own fathers, showering them in joy and pride. Some I have observed as they laid their grandfathers upon the pyre, or their fathers, or their sons. These are men I knew, men whom I have watched from afar, whose lives I have lived vicariously, envying them their joys and their sorrows and wishing only that I might be a part of those lives, yet knowing I never could be." The ifrit watched the silk dance and twist, entranced. Then its eyes snapped back to Ahmed, bright like fireside coals. "These are men that, by the bond you placed upon me, I was forced to destroy. Now their sons are orphans, their wives widows, and all for what? So that you might cross this desert with your silks and know happiness and wealth in a distant city, where the struggles of such poor folk as these Bedouin need not disturb your sleep at night?" It cut another length of silk, golden yellow, pressed it to its face, and tossed it up to leap and dive in the sky. "But that is well, for such is the nature of peace, is it not? It must come at a price, and so long as it is not you or I who pays that price, then it is all worthwhile in the end, no?"

The ifrit cut another length, this one green like the jungles of distant Serendib. The blade's song as it sliced the fabric was almost palpable. The silks rose and drifted around them, wraiths of light and colour and whispering folds. "But you will know by now that I am done with taking revenge, for vengeance is pointless. To take a life for a life, this is nothing more than a slow spiral into torment and self-destruction, and I will have no more of it.

You have restored to me my children, and for that I am eternally grateful. I could not abide the shame of having my children see me as a murderer, not even in vengeance. No, *saahir*, there shall be no more of killing.

"But as I watched these men grow," the ifrit gestured with the sword at the corpses where they lay, "watched them fall in love, be wed, and as I watched the babes suckle at their mothers' breasts, saw the love of woman for child, I finally understood that this was the one thing I had never given my children. How could I wish so very hard to be a father, without wishing my children also have a mother? How could I have been so selfish?"

Ahmed's mouth was dry as sand, even as Shen took a step backwards, her eyes flaring with the same sudden dread that flooded him.

"So now, perhaps, *saahir*, you will know the price I demand to complete our second bargain. I will not deny my children their mother."

Ahmed lifted his hand, the silver cold and heavy on his thumb, forming words that might yet bind the creature, as Shen wrenched the stopper from the urn and the hollow echoes of unseen depths howled forth from its neck in a sudden chilling wind.

All of it, too slow.

The ifrit's sword flashed, trailing an arc of red. The pain came a moment later as the meaty part of Ahmed's palm gushed blood into the sand. He cried out, staggering and clutching his hand to his chest, and he was falling, through a cloud of shrieking locusts and swirling dust, even as Shen's cries vanished on a sudden rush of burning wind.

On his knees, pain-wracked and blind, spitting sand from his mouth and wiping it from his eyes, Ahmed lurched toward the place where he thought he had last heard Shen's voice. The dust began to settle, and he saw that he was alone, save for the corpses of the Bedouin and the camels stirring listlessly nearby. He spun around. "Shen!" he cried, but no reply came back to him, not even an echo. All that remained was the bloody glinting *makhaira* and the urn, its dark essences reaching out for its quarry and finding nothing. Ahmed crumbled to his knees under the blistering sun, clutching his hand to his chest and struggling to hold back the flood of sobs that threatened to drown him. He turned his face to the eastern horizon, where a dark smudge hinted at mountains. Against the sky he saw flashes of colour; silk shimmering in the sun as the children followed their father home, to the mountains where he could not go for fear of arousing the wrath of the ifrit.

But Ahmed had walked the Silk Road, and sailed the Indian Ocean. He had smoked with the Scythians and supped with the Mongols. He had stood under Chinese stars watching the dragons spiral through the darkness in their celestial dance. He had his stories, and his magics, and he believed in truth, and in heroes, and in happy endings. Whatever lies the ages may have wrought upon the world, there was power in believing. He wrapped a hunk of linen about his bloody hand and gathered up the urn, replaced the stopper, and slipped it into his satchel. Then he arose, grasping the *makhaira* in his uninjured hand. The desert wind whipped the sand about his ankles, and whispered his name between the rocks.

There was a story in this. For once, he would not be seeking to salvage it from the oblivion of memory, polishing it so that he might slot it neatly into his journals and dwell on its meaning, find its truth, make sense of it.

No. This time, he would *be* the story.

Gathering his camels, he set off towards the distant mountains, the taste of blood and fear and legend on his lips.

Afterword

When I began writing this story, I was spending at least half an hour every evening rocking my one-year-old daughter to sleep, softly singing to her from the repertoire of lullabies I could best draw on: songs by Pearl Jam, Iron Maiden, Pink Floyd and the like. Sounds crazy, but it worked. Call me a sap, but I was right when I thought to myself that I'd miss that feeling when finally she was too big for me to hold her to my chest and croon over her little snoozing form, or when we had to convince her to go to sleep on her own. Because quietly I cherished that very special time, just my daughter and I, time not to be wasted, because it was time that would never come back, and I was determined to make it mean something. And as I sat in the dark, rocking, I dwelt on this, and on what it would mean—how awful it would be—to have that snatched away.

I've always loved the idea of the ifrit, that baleful evil force in the djinn pantheon, and as I wrote this story I thought long and hard on what it might mean to live so long, with so much power, and how such a creature might find meaning in its existence after aeons of omnipotence. And so my ifrit soaked up the fears of a father for his children, the terror of having them taken away, or of being left to raise them alone. I then took this sense of contradiction that such a character must have—the destructive yet nurturing evil spirit—and created Ahmed, a counterpoint to this creature, also woefully contradictory—both genuinely trusting and blatantly deceitful, clever and streetwise yet dangerously unwise in the ways of people, and immortals, and the weave of power that holds them all together.

Because people are contradictory, and power is contradictory, but one thing that is not contradictory, but is real and genuine and honest and soul-quenching, is the soft breathing of a baby in your arms, and it›s that sense of something pure amidst the chaos of people and power and the struggles that leave the world a broken place that I was trying to capture in Silver, Sharp as Silk.

The Pearl Flower Harvest

Jenny Schwartz

Reba Django leaned easily under the weight of the basket strung by a harness from her shoulders. One full basket, distilled, would yield a single drop of the pearl flower oil required for the curse. She picked methodically, stripping the dark green bushes of their glimmering flowers. She'd discarded her shoes an hour ago and the dirt felt cool as she curled her toes into it. The wind blew in from the Indian Ocean, salt and moisture mingling with the elusive scent of the pearl flowers. By dawn she hoped to have finished the harvest. Then she'd distil the blossoms.

The eager attention of the djinn pressed in at the wards around her home. They knew what this harvest presaged. Most years, she let the flowers fall unpicked to the ground.

She sang quietly the songs of the Silk Road. The old language curled around her tongue, its familiarity grounding her and reminding her of the strong bonds of family.

"The winds of the desert . . . hiding, revealing . . . "

There was no desert, here. The south-west corner of Australia was gentle and green. She'd been born in vineyard country and stayed to cook and grow herbs, raise goats and a family, one day. Her brother Jay, on the other hand, was a wanderer. His journalism took him to every trouble hotspot on earth. If he had a talent, it was the pursuit of danger. Reba had stayed to wrap herself in the family traditions. So when a wizard came looking for the family, he'd found her.

Ethan Trent would be flattered to be called a wizard. He was such an average man, perhaps on the pudgy side. But the fact that he'd crossed her wards told Reba all she needed to know of his determination—and ambition. Most human strangers retreated before they reached her house. Ethan had driven straight through the closely planted trees, the oddly carved stones and the bells tied to chime in gentle disharmony.

Light shone from the windows of her kitchen. She hated the thought of Ethan in it. A man didn't become Procurer of the Unwished Wish to a billionaire by having scruples. He'd invaded her life, family and privacy. He was snooping through her world in there, while she picked the pearl flowers.

Of course, his official title wasn't Procurer of the Unwished Wish. He'd flashed his business card at her when he had arrived: Ethan Trent, Executive Assistant, with the logo of the billionaire, Umberto Smith. Different title, same game. Ethan Trent made his living serving up to Umberto treasures to delight a jaded soul.

She didn't waste time questioning how he'd heard of her family's djinn candles. Rumours did circulate through the centuries. Ethan had come prepared with a threat.

"Thank you, Jay," Reba muttered as she flexed fingers that were stiff from plucking the flowers.

Her brother had gotten caught up in some feud in the Sahara. According to Ethan, he'd been thrown into gaol to be tortured and killed, but Umberto Smith had bought his freedom. So now Jay was the prisoner of the billionaire. Not that Ethan had so crudely expressed his demands for a ransom. He spoke of her "gratitude" for rescuing Jay.

"Huh." The video evidence he'd produced showed Jay bruised and bloody in a stark concrete compound. The harshness of the light gave the impression of baking heat. The camera panned slowly, showing guards with guns. She heard Jay start to say something and the film ended.

Jay had gotten out of worse places.

However, the real problem was that now Ethan believed in the existence of djinn candles, he would escalate the threats against her family until he possessed a candle for his billionaire.

Greed was like that.

Which left her without a choice. Family tradition had a rule for this situation. She'd make the candle tonight or—she glanced at her watch—in the morning. Allowing time for distilling the oil, making and cooling the candle . . . Ethan ought to be out of here by mid-morning.

God forgive her.

• • •

Shit. He hated the cute cottagey charm of Reba Django's house. He'd nearly turned back at the entrance to her driveway. The letterbox made of twigs had warned him what to expect—something green and wannabe hippie. He'd overcome his distaste, but his fears proved well founded. The kitchen was Woodstock meets French Provincial with a side order of whimsy. For hell's sake, there was even an owl-shaped teapot being used as a vase.

Ethan slammed a third cupboard door and opened the fourth. It wasn't that he expected to find secrets among the spices. It was more that he could never resist the temptation to learn about someone. The more you knew, the stronger your power over them.

Reba had appeared properly cowed by the threat to her brother, but it never hurt to have a Plan B because no matter what happened, he had no intention of leaving without the djinn candle.

He closed the fourth cupboard door and leaned back on his heels.

The candle.

Ethan considered himself a connoisseur of power. On the streets, violence had been the currency of power; that and possessing the means of supplying addiction. He'd come a long way since the early years of pushing drugs. He'd learned the power of money and presentation, and the still greater power of knowledge.

He'd found mention of the djinn candle in a Latin translation of an old Arabic text. Not that he spoke Latin any better than he spoke Arabic, but there were good translation programs and he used them often in his work. The Arabic text had discussed magic.

The key to reading so-called magic texts was to pick out the truths scattered through the authors' hopes and fears. Truth had its own smell, sharp and vaguely repellent. The story of the wizard with the djinn candle had smelled like that.

Ethan stretched up and began searching the overhead cupboards. Opening one door bumped a string of onions hanging from the rafters and pieces of their papery skins drifted down.

"What are you doing?"

He hadn't heard the back door open. He looked around to see Reba setting down a basket of the strange flowers that grew around the house. "None of your business." He shut the cupboard and walked up to her. He sifted a hand through the basket of flowers. "These stink."

"So don't touch them."

He narrowed his eyes, assessing her mood. "You do remember your brother's freedom and life rest on your good behaviour?"

"Don't worry. Your boss will get his djinn candle. I have to set up the still."

He washed his hands at the sink while she assembled the still from what he'd taken to be random junk in a low cupboard. Her shoulders were stiff with resentment, her movements abrupt but assured. All too soon the scent of the flowers filled the room. He extracted aspirin from his briefcase and swallowed two.

Dawn touched the windows. Reba reached out and flicked off the lights. Without explanation, she stooped and rolled up the circular rug in the centre of the living room. She set it aside and returned to the kitchen to collect chalk from the third drawer down. On hands and knees, she began drawing a pattern.

"Don't you have to refer to a book or notes?" He kept his own knowledge securely encrypted online.

"The ritual is part of me."

Ethan rubbed the back of his neck, annoyed to realise the small hairs had risen at her words. "What is the pattern?"

"Where did you find mention of the djinn candles?" she countered.

"I'm not saying."

She sighed and paused a moment to roll her shoulders.

He got the impression, though he couldn't see her face, that she also rolled her eyes.

"If your unnamed source had known anything of the ritual, they'd know that when a Django calls the djinn, the pattern is new to the time and place." *And to the need*, she added silently. This pattern was a curse. Usually she summoned the playful djinn. This time she had to call one of the guardians.

Her shoulders, arms and hands hurt from picking the pearl flowers. Her lower back ached. She inhaled a steadying breath of the flowers' essence. The closest ordinary flowers to pearl flowers were carnations, but they lacked the intense heat. This was a sweet spiciness that could burn.

She finished the pattern and stood a moment studying it.

It looked like a fractal. To her tired eyes, the lines seemed to move. When she melted the wax in the centre of the pattern, the lines would truly surge with power.

Modern technology saved a lot of time and mess. She placed a butane burner in the centre of the pattern and laid matches beside it. Back in the kitchen, she sliced wax from the lump of beeswax her friend, Aaron, had given her. The trick was to heat the knife blade over the gas hob.

She noticed Ethan shy at her easily handling of the knife. It was interesting that he was nervous of such mundane threats, but not of the major magic she was preparing for. Was he really that ignorant?

The precious drop of pearl flower oil had collected in its copper bowl. She picked up the bowl, using tongs, and set it on its stand above the butane burner.

"Almost forgot." She went back to the kitchen and cut a length of wick from the coil she kept beside the chalk in the junk drawer. She tied one end around a butter knife. It would hold the wick straight as the wax solidified around it. She dug the candle mould out of the back of the cupboard. This wouldn't be a fancy candle. This was wick, wax and magic. The result would be stumpy and ugly, but powerful.

Her hand tightened around the butter knife. She'd never called a guardian before.

Her grandfather had explained the family's situation once.

"Magic." He'd spat in among the rows of broad bean seedlings. "Better call the djinn aliens. It's they who set up this link between the blood of a few families here on Earth and their dimension of reality. They see us as a game. Different dimension, different abilities. Silly to call that magic. But it's our blood that opens the dimension gate—with the help of the pearl flowers. It was all explained when our ancestors agreed. The djinn can enter at our invitation but only if they are tied to an object. It is too dangerous to tie them to one of us. Never do that. Once in our world, they are free to undertake three actions. Three wishes. They're obliging buggers—except for the guardians."

"The guardians keep the balance."

"What did you say?" Ethan was jittering, his fingers tapping the kitchen bench he leaned against. His voice came out too loud.

"I'm starting the ritual." She sat cross-legged in front of the butane burner, lit it and added the wax to the bowl containing the drop of pearl flower oil. As the wax melted, the pearl flower oil eeled through it. Thin threads of red slowly built an echo of the pattern she'd drawn on the floor.

Her breathing quickened as if she'd ascended to high altitude.

When she called the playful djinn, she had to lift the wards around her house before she began, else they couldn't enter. But the guardians were different. They went where they would.

One was watching her, now.

"Aren't there words you have to say?" Ethan stood adjacent to her, just outside the pattern.

She heard, but didn't answer. The oppression of the guardian's power was frightening. So much power.

The wax melted. She turned off the butane burner and reached for a knife.

Ethan swore and stepped back.

She sliced her thumb and squeezed the pad to build the blood oozing from the shallow cut. It stung, but knife cuts were a familiar hazard for chefs. She welcomed the pain. It was, at least, hers. The guardian was stealing even the air she breathed. Her pulse thumped in her ears.

Fear made her clumsy. She concentrated on using the tongs to pour the wax into the candle mould, tipping her thumb so her blood mixed with the wax and pearl flower oil. She almost knocked the butterknife with the wick attached from its precarious balance across the mould. She steadied it with a hand that shook.

"Welcome, guardian."

A tornado of power arrowed down to the mould.

She retreated in a terrified scramble that scuffed the pattern of the curse.

"What's wrong with you?" Ethan demanded. "Hell, don't tell me that damn flower oil is just an hallucinatory. Are you seeing demons?"

No eyes, no body of any kind that Reba recognised, and yet, she knew that tornado of power—endless, obliterating—watched her and was amused. It confined itself to the candle, and the house echoed with the silence of power.

She gulped air.

"Don't crack up on me. I still have your brother."

I, Ethan said. She noted it, sucking in confirmation along with oxygen. The Procurer of the Unwished Wish craved the candle and its power for himself.

"The candle is done." She crawled forward and pulled the candle from its mould using the butterknife. She was accustomed to djinn magic setting the wax fast. Her whole body ached as she dragged herself up and into the kitchen.

"It's cooled already?" Ethan trailed her.

"Yes." She snipped the wick and stared at the candle. The natural beeswax was shot through with scarlet. The red was a promise. A blood promise. "You don't have to do this," she said to Ethan.

But *she* did. This was her family's contract with the djinn. She had to keep the balance, and when someone came threatening, came demanding . . .

"Remember your brother and give me the candle." Ethan held out his hand.

She dropped the fat candle onto his palm.

He turned on his heel, strode across the broken pattern and picked up the box of matches she'd left there. "So now I'll test it." He brought the candle back to the kitchen table and struck a match. The tiny flame reflected in his eyes before he glanced down at the candle and set the match to its wick. "Three wishes; and for my first wish—"

He screamed.

The guardian didn't grant wishes. It took the wisher. Keeping the balance. For the djinn that entered Earth there had to be humans that entered the djinn's world. But unlike the playful visiting djinn, Reba had never heard of any humans returning.

She wrapped her arms around herself and bowed her head as Ethan vanished in the tornado of power.

"One," a great voice boomed.

Reba snuffed the candle with shaking fingers. This was the

— 281 —

bargain. She owed the guardian two more lives in return for calling the djinn into this world.

• • •

The morning wind came from the east, across mining country and farmland to whistle through Reba's garden before losing itself over the Indian Ocean. Dry leaves rustled, lifted and settled in its wake.

She sat on her back step, elbows on knees, chin in hands. An empty coffee mug stood beside her. She'd cleaned the house: mopped away the chalk marks, stowed away the butane burner and still. Only Ethan's briefcase sat on the table, mutely accusing. She'd locked the candle away in it and come out here.

The bantams were out, released from the night's imprisonment in the fox-safe chicken house. They scratched busily for insects and ignored her. Occasionally the wind ruffled their feathers and they ignored that, too.

Reba sighed. Time she stopped ignoring reality.

She picked up the car keys she'd taken from Ethan's briefcase. He'd been—still was, somewhere—a paranoid bastard, someone who believed knowledge was power. He hadn't wanted anyone to know his secrets. He hadn't even hired a car. The old rattletrap was strong evidence he'd bought it for cash. Untraceable. When she drove it into the bush and abandoned it, no one would know or care.

A deep shudder shook her. Would anyone care that Ethan was gone?

For now, she drove the car into the old shed and shut the door. When her brother returned, he could follow her into the bush and she'd ride pillion back from the car on his dirt bike.

That wasn't the only aspect of this mess that Jay would need to help her clean up. There was the candle. *Two more lives.*

She would send it to the billionaire, along with Ethan's business card. Jay could post it from somewhere nicely anonymous, like New York. After all, Ethan hadn't been working alone. His employer's wealth and influence had imprisoned Jay, had held him hostage for the candle and three wishes. Balance demanded the billionaire be presented to the guardian. If Umberto Smith wasn't power crazy and merely Ethan's pawn in this game—Reba snorted. *As if!*—then he wouldn't light the candle and wish, and he'd be safe.

But he wouldn't be able to resist the lure of power, which left the problem of the last life required by the guardian. Who?

Cold ate at Reba's bones.

. . .

"Albert Crapaud." Jay had ridden in on a shriek of djinn laughter just before lunch. His face was raw and bruised, and the cautious way he moved showed he carried other hurts. Still, he ate the ham and pickle sandwiches with enthusiasm and pushed his mug towards her for more coffee. "He's the bastard I was tracking through East Africa. Child slavery, sexual exploitation. Things you can't imagine."

When Jay said things you couldn't imagine . . .

Reba shuddered. "He's the one who organised your arrest?"

"I'd think so." A grin and a wince as his abused face hurt. "Though I did annoy a few other people." The laughter died out of his eyes. "This billionaire you spoke of, Umberto Smith. It took more than money to ransom me from Crapaud. Smith must have managed to scare even him." He sipped his coffee cautiously. "Put your conscience to rest, Reba. Those two deserve everything and more the djinn can throw at them."

She nodded, though the uncertainty of what they faced in the realm of the djinn—what Ethan was currently enduring—tensed her stomach. At this rate, she'd have ulcers.

Jay picked up the stubby candle that held the guardian. It fascinated him. "I can't sense any power in it. With the playful djinn, there's a buzz."

He would know. He'd created his own candle a few years back and wished on it. One wish was instant transportation anywhere in the world. His playful djinni thought it immense fun, scooping him up and sending him whistling through dimensions to land, often upside down, in the requested destination. Jay and his djinni had developed an odd friendship, which was how the candles were meant to work.

The djinn didn't grant wishes because they were cursed. They granted them as a free exchange, as participants in a friendly game.

When she called the guardian, the curse Reba had woven had been for *humans*.

Jay put the candle down. "Did you speak with the guardian?"

Oh, the insatiable curiosity of a journalist.

She remembered the great voice and that ominous single word, *One*. "No."

"Pity."

"If the guardian feels chatty, I'll direct him to you."

A grin. "Do that. So, you got an address for this billionaire?"

"Yes, from Ethan's briefcase." She pushed the slip of paper across the table along with one of Ethan's business cards.

Jay scooped them up as he stood. "Dasher, we've got a delivery to make."

The playful djinni swirled into the room bringing the scent of pearl flowers and sandalwood. The different djinn had their unique scents, as well as unique names—pretty nearly unpronounceable for the human tongue. Jay's djinni seemed happy enough with its nickname.

"Central Park, New York, please."

Her brother vanished. He'd return when he'd wandered anonymously into a post office and despatched the candle. He needed sleep and healing.

She needed sleep, too, but nightmares waited for her. Instead, she cleared the table, changed into her chef's whites and headed for the restaurant.

Heather Li, owner and manager of *Every Taste*, was a friend as well as her boss. Reba wouldn't let her down.

• • •

Reba drove home cautiously from work. She wasn't concerned about hitting a kangaroo; statistically, that was a dusk and dawn issue. It was well past dusk. The car smelled pleasantly of apple pie, left over as Reba had worked overtime on producing comfort food this evening. *Every Taste*'s menu altered with the produce available and Reba's mood. Tonight, all the staff had taken home leftovers and two extra pies were stashed in the freezer—emergency supplies.

Jay had left a light on in the kitchen, which was comforting in itself. He'd phoned her at work to say that the package had been delivered and that he was crashing.

She popped the half pie in the fridge for him to find in the morning, showered and went to bed. She pulled the covers up to her chin and stared at the ceiling. She wouldn't sleep, but her body could rest.

Would Ethan be able to rest in the realm of the djinn?

Reality flickered, edging into dreaming. Ethan's eyes enlarged until he resembled a fly. Every facet of his bulbous eyes glittered with greed. "Give me, give me." His arms flapped like wings. "Me, me."

She shivered, slept and woke to the voice of doom.

"Two!"

4 am. She blinked at the bedside clock and thought idiotically that the American postal service must employ elves. They were fast!

Then reality hit and she scrambled out of bed. She poked an arm through the wrong sleeve of her robe, swore and got herself straightened out.

Jay padded down the hallway to the kitchen. "I heard the guardian." He stretched out an arm to flick on the lights—and hesitated. "Holy hell."

The candle had returned. It sat on the table. It wasn't lit, yet the wax glowed with a fire's fury.

"Put on the lights," Reba said urgently.

In the glare of the electric lighting, the impact of the candle's glow lessened.

Jay circled the table, examining the candle but not touching it. "The guardian brought it back to you."

Ugh. She headed for the fridge.

"It must be part of the guardian deal. You get to choose who is taken."

She slammed the fridge door shut and splashed milk violently into a saucepan. "I'm making hot cocoa. You want some?"

"Reba, you can't just ignore this. I thought I would have to fetch the candle somehow. I was wondering whether to whoosh into the billionaire's office dressed in a ghost costume."

Trust Jay to reduce terror to comic book terms.

She added cocoa, sugar, vanilla extract and cinnamon to the milk and stirred it on the stove top. "There's apple pie in the fridge."

"You can't bury a problem in food." But he left the candle on the table and opened the fridge.

"The sooner this problem is gone, the happier I'll be. Can you deliver it to Albert Crapaud tonight?"

He cut generous slices of pie. "It's not as simple as with the billionaire. Ethan had primed this Umberto Smith to expect a djinn candle and to crave its power. Crapaud has to be presented with the idea."

She glanced across at the candle. Its glow had vanished entirely. "How do you intend to do that?"

"I know a weapons dealer."

• • •

Who can resist power? Certainly not the brutal, who go in constant fear of meeting one more brutal than themselves. Albert Crapaud bought the candle. And lit it.

"Three!" The great voice shook Reba as she balanced on a ladder, clearing leaves from the gutters of the house. The pearl flower bushes shivered in the wind, shivered and shed every last petal. The glimmering white blossom carpeted the garden and as the wind fell, the scent of the dying flowers rose up on the late morning air.

With extreme care, Reba unclamped her hands from the gutter, gripped the ladder and forced her feet to find each lower rung and the next until she was safely on the ground. Then she collapsed, huddling her knees up and hiding her face.

"It is done," the great voice whispered.

"So go," she muttered. She felt like a murderer. Never mind the old commandment, an eye for an eye.

"Melt the candle, Reba." It landed in front of her, the slight thump jarring a dandelion clock. The tiny seed heads puffed away on the wind.

She picked up the candle and it started to melt in her hands. It dripped down and she tipped her hands so the wax—no more than pleasantly warm—pooled in a hollow in the ground.

The red of the pearl flower oil and of her blood swirled into a new pattern. She could feel the guardian using the power of her blood to perform this minor magic.

"Look," the guardian commanded.

The three men she'd sent through the candle dwelt in marble palaces. Their every wish seemed to be being fulfilled, but by ghostly forms, semi-transparent and somehow unreal.

"Everything they wish, we give them—in hallucinatory form."

Their wishes were hideous, appalling. She scooped up dirt and dumped it over the wax. "They live in a nightmare."

"Of their own creation." The sense of the guardian's presence vanished.

A person couldn't live on nightmares. The three men would starve.

Reba shuddered and reached for the rake leaning against the verandah. Clearing the gutter debris could wait. There were pearl flowers to be gathered in.

Afterword

I've been dreaming of djinn for a few years now. For anyone interested in the djinn and in current beliefs regarding them, I recommend Robert Lebling's "Legends of the Fire Spirits". It's a fascinating book. The djinn have a powerful grip on human imagination and storytelling.

Like angels, the djinn can't be proven to exist, but that's not the point. They celebrate the chaotic nature of life, and give it meaning. I've written stories where the djinn are romantic heroes and heroines, but in "The Pearl Flower Harvest" I wanted to explore their "alien" nature; that they belong, and yet don't belong, in our world.

The delight and terror of the djinn is that they don't fear life. They play with it. It's a gift that I hope they grant us.

The Quiet Realm of the Dark Queen

Jenny Blackford

Dumuzi—my beautiful brother Dumuzi, lovelier than the first green shoots of barley rising from the dark mud of an irrigated field—Dumuzi was dead.

Father had not spoken for six days. Not long ago, he'd been a great king in the fullness of his manhood, but now he was hobbling around the halls of the palace like an old grasshopper waiting for death. His hair was grey; his face was greyer still.

Mother was quiet at last. For six full days and nights she'd wailed and screamed on her wide bed of gold, tearing her soft face and her lovely breasts with her nails, pulling great lumps of curled and scented hair from her luxuriant head, berating all the gods for their cruelty to her. The people said that she was no mere mortal beauty but a goddess walking on earth with us, and she did not disagree; but even if this were true, it did not diminish her fury against the other gods.

"My life is nothing without him," she'd screamed again and again. "Why did you not take me instead, or my husband, or my worthless, thankless, useless daughter."

I was the useless daughter, of course. I had failed to save my brother from the demons that hunted him to the Underworld. My mother would never forgive me.

Finally, Mother swallowed enough sweet wine laced with poppy juice and honey from the alabaster cup I held to her lips, to bring merciful sleep. Death would perhaps have been more merciful for her.

As I put down the cup and smoothed her hair, my mother woke herself just enough to hiss, "Far better that you had been taken, daughter, than him, Dumuzi, the beloved of my heart. Why did you not give yourself to the demons instead? Why did you let them take *him*? Why? How *could* you let them take him? *My Dumuzi!*"

And, truly, I understood. My brother Dumuzi had been more than beautiful, when he had walked this earth.

My suitors—brought by my father's wealth and my mother's beauty—had been enthusiastic enough, over the years, until each in his turn had seen my brother. Only a few men are immune to the charms of a pretty boy, and will always prefer the soft roundnesses of woman to a boy's firm flats and hollows. Even those men, those devoted lovers of women, wanted my brother more than they wanted me, once they had met him. But all left the palace disconsolate: Dumuzi had eyes for none but peerless Ishtar, daughter of the Moon, queen of heaven and earth, goddess of love.

• • •

I had not always been in second place. I was the firstborn child of our parents; when I was a toddler, I was my father's delight, my mother's plaything. Father ordered his artisans to make me golden carts with silver wheels, and dolls carved from fragrant cedar with eyes of lapis lazuli and hair of gold. Mother dressed me in tiny versions of court ladies' dresses in blue and purple, fringed with silver and pearls, tinkling with the myriad silver moon-crescents sewn to them. But in my fourth year, my mother's belly swelled again.

Even as a newborn babe, Dumuzi shone tender as the spring sun on a field of emmer wheat. I was forgotten. Kings and wise men came from the ends of the earth with gifts of jewels and spices, merely to gaze on my brother's shining face. The peasants bowed down to him; the slaves openly worshipped him as a god.

But now that Dumuzi was dead, now that the demons had taken him to the Underworld in exchange for his lover, the goddess

Ishtar, no man could bear to look upon my face; they turned their heads in angry grief for my brother. Women screamed and wept, tearing at their cheeks and their clothes. If they had dared, they'd have attacked me with their bare hands.

Even the sheep, which Dumuzi had loved above all other beasts, refused to walk to their grassy fields. The noises that they made were so full of grief that they would have brought sorrow to the heart of the most joyful stranger. The sun was hot in the sky, burning the crops, and the fertile irrigated fields were cracked, dry mud. Only the old vizier came to my room and wept with me for my brother's death. Perhaps the people were right; perhaps it would have been better if I had died, instead of him.

But it was not my fault that Dumuzi was taken from us as ransom for Ishtar, and only the gods knew why the goddess had challenged her sister's power in the Underworld, and been trapped there. I had done my best to protect my brother, as an older sister must, when demons were sent to drag him to the Underworld to take mighty Ishtar's place.

The demons had threatened me with death when they searched for him; they even tried to bribe me with precious water and with fields of grain. But my brother was my river of precious water; he was my field of grain. I could never have betrayed him. It was not *me* who gave him up to the demons, but his childhood companion, his dearest male friend, who took the bribe. But no one cared. They loved my brother Dumuzi so much that they loved his friend for his sake; my less lovely face reminded them too much of my beautiful sibling.

After another night of evil dreams, I could not bear it another moment. A little before noon, I went to the Field of the Winged Bulls.

• • •

The life-sized sculptures of the human-headed bulls that guarded the entrance to the palace, strong golden wings tucked against their massive basalt flanks, made all who saw them catch their breath in fear and awe. Though the bulls' magic protected the city, few other than the members of our family had ever seen the models for those sculptures in real life.

The winged bulls and their mates, in the flesh, were more glorious in appearance and in power than words could tell, but they detested the eyes of human strangers. A plump, bejewelled dynasty of blond slaves from the north tended to all their needs: combed their glossy blue-black hides, polished their golden hoofs, fed them the figs and dates, sweet grapes and honey cakes that they craved; but I was the only living human, other than their slaves, whom they permitted to enter their compound.

The human-headed bulls lazed with their herd in the shade under the date palms, in the vast enclosure that they had requested a thousand years ago, when they'd taken up residence in the city. The huge twin males, rulers of the herd, lay perfectly still, not moving a feather or a shining hair, while the three queen females slowly fanned them with their wide golden wings. Six or seven smaller beasts, close to fully grown, lay quietly around them. Even the frisky calves, their wings mere buds on their shoulders, were relatively placid in the heat, scuffling quietly in the grass for fallen dates.

The two great bulls spoke steadily to one another, their deep voices strange and sonorous to human ears. Their faces looked human, but the sounds that they could make in those deep chests were beyond the reach of any man or woman, or ordinary animal, alive. No human had ever learnt more than a few words of their language. They far preferred for us to speak to them in courtly Sumerian or everyday Akkadian, rather than to hear their ancient, sacred speech distorted and defiled by human mouths.

They would not tell us—not even me, their longtime favourite— where they had come from before they took refuge in our palace, except that it was somewhere long ago and very far away. "You wouldn't understand, child," they'd said when I'd asked them, when I was young. "It was our destiny. It was in the stars. We are here, now. That's all you need to know of where we came from." They'd looked so sad, as they answered me, that I never dared cause them sorrow by asking again.

The deep poetry of the twin bulls' ancient voices as they conversed in their own language was strangely soothing. I stood leaning against the warm stone wall of the huge enclosure listening, not comprehending anything they said, but slowly growing calmer, until they spoke to me.

"You are unhappy, Geshtinanna," one of them said. "Is it your brother?"

I nodded.

"Of course," the other said. "How could things be otherwise, when humans are involved? And the people blame you, though you are surely blameless?"

I nodded again. I did not want to burst into tears in front of the bulls.

The first one said, "Even *we* were powerless to prevent this fate from falling upon your brother. How could your people believe for a moment that *you* had the power to challenge the will of the gods?"

I squeezed my eyes tight shut, but fat tears ran down my cheeks nonetheless.

The three dominant females spoke together for some time, after that. I wiped my tears on the hem of my dress and watched their grave conversation. Their voices were like the sound of great bronze bells, sweet but dangerously strong. The males listened, silent like me, as the massive females spoke, each in her turn.

At last, the largest of the females flicked a golden wingtip against my hand, gently as a kiss, and gave me their decision: "You must go to the wise woman, child. Go to Siduri, the woman who brews her beer and keeps her tavern at the end of the earth, by the shores of the Waters of Death. She will advise you what you must do."

Mother had told me tales of Siduri, of course. Siduri's tavern, with its peerless beer-vat made from pure gold, stood by the fabled Garden of the Gods, full of vines hung with gems, shrubs with jewels instead of flowers, fat gemstones in the place of fruit. Mother described it endlessly, greedily. Perhaps the people were right; perhaps Mother was a goddess in truth, and belonged there in the jewelled garden. Perhaps she would have been happier there. But the place held dangers as well as riches. A single drop from the deep abyss of the Waters of Death could kill in an instant.

"But how do I travel to the ends of the earth, to consult Siduri?" I asked the powerful inhuman creature lying on the grass in front of me. "I am a woman virtually alone, ignored now in my parents' own palace, though I was born a princess here. Even with the strongest men from my father's army, I could not hope to travel through the well-armed kingdoms and the trackless wastes between our city and Siduri's tavern. Even a hero would surely die in the attempt."

The human-faced female who spoke now for the herd spread out her golden wings in a graceful gesture. "You see my children, and my sisters' children, all about you. The oldest of them was born some centuries ago, now, and they are almost full-grown, though still young by our standards. We have taught them all we know: astronomy, astrology, cosmogony, theology, geometry, mythology and more."

I just nodded. What could I say?

She went on, "We will send Kalla with you on your quest, child. She is not much more than three hundred years old, or thereabouts, but she is wise for her age, as you also are."

One of the young winged cows lifted her head, then and looked at me. Her eyes were the hard, pure blue of the best lapis lazuli, but fierce intelligence shone in them. But did her mouth tremble with suppressed fear? I tried to smile bravely at her. I was a princess. A princess might know fear, but she must never show it.

The older female spoke again. "You and Kalla will do well together, we believe." She sighed. "We hope so. This quest could be more dangerous than any that we have attempted for many years."

Fear touched me with its black wing, then, but what could I do? My life in the palace, or anywhere in Father's kingdom, was insupportable. Each moment pricked me to the heart like a sharp bronze dagger. A quest to the ends of the earth and perhaps beyond with a wise, if young, winged beast could hardly be more painful, or more difficult. It was more than likely, I knew, that I would die; but Dumuzi was already dead. What was my life worth now?

"Thank you," I said, not knowing what else to say. Father's elderly vizier had coached me well in diplomatic language since my toddlerhood, training me to be a good queen when the time came, but this was not one of the endless number of situations that he had covered.

"Go now, child," the old female said, "and prepare yourself for the journey. This will be no ordinary journey. Pack a little food and water, yes, but other things too. And return soon. It would be best for you to leave before the sun is low in the sky."

I made a formal gesture of thanks, as the vizier had taught me, and rushed back to my room. To my relief, I reached the room before I burst into flooding tears.

• • •

After I composed myself and packed, I went to farewell my family.

In my mother's room, the chief of her women barred the way to her bed, hissing like a snake in an irrigation ditch.

"Geshtinanna! Who do you think you are," she said, "coming to torment the Queen? You let Dumuzi die, you slut, you useless bitch. Do you think she ever wants to see your face again? Do you think she will ever again call you daughter, after what you did? Go!"

I went, saddened but dry-eyed.

My father, in his throne room, looked at me, then away. The vizier by his side, his hands shaking, pulled at my father's elbow. "It is your *daughter*, my King," he whispered. "It is Geshtinanna. She comes to speak with you." But Father's eyes, and mind, were somewhere else, somewhere not good.

The vizier followed me to the door. "I am sorry," he said. "Your father the King . . . he is not himself, these days. He will recover, in time. The doctors say so. We must wait patiently."

"Yes," I said, then turned to leave.

He looked stricken. "It was not your fault," he said, in a rush. "The gods know, it was not your fault. The people are like silly sheep. Even their leaders are like sheep. *It was not your fault*."

I gave him the formal embrace of sincere thanks which he had first tried to teach me when I was a clumsy four-year-old princess. We were both in tears when I left the room.

Soon, though, I stood again in the Field of the Winged Bulls, this time with all the pieces of my old life that I intended to take with me when I left the palace. Around my neck I wore a necklace that Mother had given me when she still loved me, flat red-gold links with a cow carved from lapis lazuli hanging down from the central point, and from my earlobes dangled crescent earrings covered in golden granulations, also her gift. On my hands were three rings set with hunks of carnelian, sapphire and emerald, all from my father, each given to mark an auspicious birthday. My right wrist bore a bangle of bright beads from the Indus Valley, a gift from Dumuzi, and my left ankle held an anklet of heavy gold inscribed with the signs of the greatest gods, the symbols of the Sun, the Moon, Venus, Mercury and Mars.

There were gold and less precious objects—brooches and pins and other small gewgaws that I could exchange for what I needed on the journey—in a soft leather sack concealed under my dress, and another one, flashier, with less gold in it, tied to my belt. In a bag strapped over my shoulder I had a water-skin, plus soft cheese and juicy half-dried figs; they would last maybe two days. The journey could take months, or never end; I would get more food and drink when I needed it, or not at all.

Kalla was at one end of the compound, alone. I walked over to her.

"You must settle yourself behind my wings," she said, flicking her tail nervously. "I will carry you where the elders say you must go." Her blue eyes glanced at the herd at the other end of the compound, then looked back down into my face.

I was going to ride on her back?

"Oh," I said, looking at that glossy expanse of hide, higher and wider than my father's royal throne, almost as wide as my bed.

But what had I imagined? That we would walk together sedately through the palace gates, with the people waving us on our way, and proceed on foot to the ends of the earth?

Kalla's tail flicked again. I could feel her anxiety overlaid on my own. This would be her first time away from her herd, and it would be no easier for her than for me. But she was too stressed to understand that I—a princess, but all the same a puny human female—could not vault onto her back, higher than the top of my head. What could I say, that would not cause her shame in front of the herd?

What would the vizier do, that consummate old diplomat, in my position? His daily lessons had almost become second nature: I must let Kalla work out the problem for herself. I put up my right arm, tentatively, and touched her high on her ribs, barely brushing the glossy blue-black hairs. Her head turned and her eyes followed my movement and the extension of my arm. She blinked in what must have been a mixture of dismay and amusement.

"I'll kneel for you," she said, and settled gracefully onto the grass.

It was my turn for dismay. How could I sit on so wide an expanse of back? Kalla was three or four times the size of the asses and wild donkeys that men rode. The dress I wore was practical and simple, plain linen, well designed for dusty travel, with no golden fringes, no tinkling ornaments. Nonetheless, it was too tight for me to stretch my legs so far.

There was only one real possibility. I bent down to my right ankle and ripped the linen of my dress up to mid-thigh. I could pin it together when I needed to be respectable again. Then I lifted my bared right leg over Kalla's shining back—when I touched her hide, it was like silk from the fabled Orient, beyond the sunrise— and sat. My legs were wide stretched, and it would be painful in time, but for the first time in my life I was grateful for the tedious stretches and long poses of the lessons that I'd been forced to take, for the sacred dances day and night before the gods in their solemn festivals.

"You will not fall," Kalla said, but her voice sounded a little nervous to me. "Don't be afraid of that. The elders have arranged for an attachment spell to keep you safe. If you want, though, you can put your hands under where the wings connect to my shoulders. They tell me that you can hold firmly there without hurting me."

I felt thick muscle under my hands, sunwarmed and strong as stone. I grasped as tightly as I dared.

Kalla stood up onto all fours so carefully that I scarcely shifted, though I was seated so precariously there on her flat back. She turned then towards the herd, which had carefully been ignoring us. The winged beasts were better diplomats even than Father's vizier.

Kalla cried out to them in her own language, in her voice like a well-tempered bell. Her wide golden wings had already started beating.

"Farewell," I called, more softly, and waved. "Thank you." By the time I'd finished speaking, we were in the air above the palace, then flying south-east along the River.

• • •

It was as if my gilded silver bed with its duck down-stuffed mattress had taken wings and started to fly through the sky. I felt as safe sitting on Kalla's back as I would have on my own bed, and no more likely to fall off. Kalla's passage through the air was stately, but, even if she hadn't told me, it would have been clear that a magical force was operating to keep me safely positioned on her shiny-smooth skin. Luckily so: a tumble would have seen me dead, smashed and drowned in the great river which was our kingdom's life. Mentally, I thanked whichever of Kalla's herd it was who'd thought to use the spell.

The river Buranun—our land's lifeblood—was even lovelier from the air than from the earth. I gazed down on its turns and bends, the reedy marshes full of waterbirds, the farmlands irrigated with its water, and the great stone temples of the gods. Sometimes, when we were high or it was close, I even caught sight of our river's eastern twin, the Idigna. The vizier had taught me the names of the cities there, and their various strengths and weaknesses, in case Father chose one of their foreign kings as my husband. I'd never thought to see it from the air.

No one down below took the least notice of us. "I'm flying high enough that even the sharpest-sighted won't be able to see anything distinctly," Kalla said. "They won't understand how big I am; they'll think me an eagle, or something of the sort. And they won't see you at all, Geshtinanna. You're much too small, you tiny human. It would take two or three of you to make one of our newborn calves." She laughed deep in her massive chest; after a moment, I laughed too.

We flew for many days, or perhaps months, stopping in the evening only when Kalla sighted a small town, a few isolated farms, where she could stay concealed in the shelter of trees or rocks while I found a farmer's wife who would be happy to give me food and fill my water-skin for a small piece of gold, even though I was a woman travelling alone. When it grew dark, I slept curled against Kalla's warm back, comforted by her firm bulk. Her quiet snores made my sleep sweet.

On the first evening it could have been pure luck that I was met with nothing but kindness by a woman busy in her farmhouse. No threats, no violence, no greed at the sight of my gold. But I had learned too much of human nature, both in theory and in practice, to think it normal or natural, after three nights.

"I don't know," Kalla said, when I challenged her about the mystery. "It's not magic, or if it is I've never learnt it. The places I stop in just *look* right, *feel* right. They call to me."

"Snakes and dogs know when an earthquake is coming," I said. "Birds fly north from our marshes, every year, and back again, and winged butterflies build themselves from creeping caterpillars in their cocoons. The wise men call that unknown knowledge *instinct*. Perhaps you have an instinct for kindness."

"Perhaps," she said. "Kindness is good. It is worth seeking." She looked thoughtful, after that, until she slept.

The next night, as we lay together in the grass under some fig trees, and I apportioned her the larger share of the dates that I'd received from yet another pleasant woman, I asked the question which had worried me since my childhood, when I used to watch the blond slaves tending to the herd's needs: "How is it that your people are so large, and yet you eat so little?"

"Hmm," Kalla said, flicking the tips of her wings in amusement. "No one has dared ask us that before. But the answer is simple: we eat merely for pleasure, not out of physical need. We need no food as you humans do, or your animals. Would you like more of the dates?"

"Thank you, but no," I said. I was blushing with embarrassment. All my childhood, Kalla's herd had lazed in the compound at the palace, flicking away flies, munching slowly—but they were not mere cattle. Far from it. I said, "I should have known better. I was *taught* better. You are not mortal, as we are, but guardian djinn, more akin to the gods than to us."

"Yes, it's something like that," Kalla said, laughing the strange, deep laugh of her kind. "We absorb the energy from the sun, as plants do. But it's too complicated to explain. Push those delicious-smelling fresh dates closer to my mouth, human, and stop worrying about it." She grinned, then, and used a golden wingtip to brush my head softly.

I tried to treat Kalla more deferentially after that, more as one ought to treat an immortal guardian and less as a friend, but I kept failing. It was like water in the desert, after all my lonely years, to have someone to talk to.

One evening towards the end, as I dismounted, Kalla told me to get all the food I could carry, when I went to the farmhouse nearby.

"Can you see those mountains in the distance?" she asked. "Those little bumps on the horizon? They're the Mountains of Mashu, the boundary of your human realm, higher and wider than you can imagine. Some say they're impassable, that they stretch to the heavens. We will come to them tomorrow. There will be streams of pure water, but no farms—no human beings who eat the food that you do."

After that, we flew not over fertile river plains or even desert but over the rocks and boulders of the mountainside. In the evenings, Kalla refused any of my stores of fruit and cheese.

"I'm not sure how long this will take, trying to skirt around the side of these mountains," she said. "You need those good-smelling edible things, and I don't. No, don't argue, human. I'm older than you. And much bigger." Her face was serious; only the twitching of her tail told me that she was teasing.

After nine days of mountain flying—cliffs and ravines, springs and cataracts, stands of tall pines and regal cedars—the stocks in my food-pouch were almost gone. I tried not to worry. I had enough for tonight, just barely.

"Look," Kalla said, around noon. "The glitter, below us. It is the Garden of the Gods, I'm sure it is." She sounded relieved. Surely my guide and protector had not doubted that she could find it?

I looked down, and gasped.

I had grown up in a palace, surrounded by the riches of men and gods. I used to eat from silver plates, and drink from a golden cup set with gemstones. Mother glittered like the stars in the night sky when she was hung about with gold and jewels for state occasions, and Father's green alabaster throne set with carnelian and chrysoprase glinted in torchlight.

But this was a garden as big as our city, or larger, with each shrub, each tree, each lush vine scattered with bright jewels in place of fruit and flowers. It was just as Mother had told me, but larger, brighter, more real—and more *divine*. This was indeed the Garden of the Gods. How had I dared come here?

My awe and wonder at the jewelled garden only increased as we flew closer and I could see more and more gemstones encrusting the plants. And then I saw the sea. It was like our River in flood, but impossibly wide. It stretched to the far horizon and beyond. And then the truth hit me: the Mountains of Mashu, the Garden of the Gods, the wide blue sea—I was where Kalla's elders had sent me, the fabled ends of the earth. I must find Siduri, and ask her advice.

• • •

As it happened, I didn't need to find Siduri. She came to meet me while I was still scrambling down from Kalla's back.

"We must talk, girl," Siduri said to me, then looked at Kalla. "You—guardian being—what is your name?"

My massive mount said, "I am Kalla, Goddess."

Goddess? Of course, I thought. People called Siduri a wise woman, but how could she live here, brewing ale in a vat given to her by the gods, unless she too was one of them, a goddess in her own right?

Siduri nodded. "Kalla, you may now graze on the fruits of the Garden of the Gods."

Kalla bowed before Siduri. Her human-seeming face was almost impassive as that of the carved bull statues that guard my father's palace, but I could see the suppressed joy around those stony blue eyes. Kalla moved sedately towards the glowing jewels, her body a picture of restrained decorum.

"The jewels of the gods are a delicacy for Kalla's kind," Siduri told me. "They give them strength and wisdom."

I just stood there helpless before the goddess, my knees trembling, my mind almost blank. Siduri took me by the hand, led me to a bench in front of her tavern, and gave me a silver cup of ale, also pouring one for herself from a golden jug.

"But now," she said, "you must drink my ale. I have few mortal visitors, here at the ends of the earth, but my ale is excellent."

I sipped; it was the best I'd ever tasted, better even than the finest of wines in the palace.

"It is excellent indeed, Goddess," I said. "Thank you."

"So tell me, girl," Siduri said. "Why are you so sad?"

That much was simple. "Demons dragged my brother, beautiful Dumuzi, down to the Underworld."

"Ah, I heard about that. So you are the sister, valiant Geshtinanna, who tried to protect him."

Unshed tears made my throat hoarse. "I failed."

The goddess shook her head. "Whether you had failed or not, your brother would have died soon enough. He could perhaps have had ten more years, twenty, maybe even fifty, but death comes to all mortals. It is best if you accept it. Take joy in everyday pleasures: warm baths, clean clothes, good food and drink, making love with your husband, feeling your child's hand in your own."

Wise men and poets had said the same thing since the dawn of time. It didn't help.

I said, "That is excellent advice, Goddess, I have no doubt. But my city is falling to ruin. My mother has had no rest since her son was taken by the demons, and my father the king will not speak even to his closest advisers. Even the slaves and the sheep lament him. The sun burns the crops, and our fields are cracked, dry mud. To escape the sorrow of my brother's death, I would need to leave my city and my people, never to see them again, and still I would feel their grief and anger."

Siduri poured herself another cup of ale. "But, Geshtinanna, to leave her family is the lot of all women, whether peasant, noble or goddess. Every woman of marriageable age must leave her father's house and her mother's rooms and live instead in a house of strangers. The more exalted the family, the farther the woman must travel from her home."

I sipped cool ale from my cup before I replied. "That is all too true, Goddess. Indeed, if any of my suitors had paid my bride-price, he would have taken me far from my parents' palace. His mother would have become my mother, and his father my father. Perhaps, indeed, I would never have seen my own parents again, nor the place where I was born." Still, it did not help.

The goddess gestured around her. "So why are you here?"

The words came unbidden to my lips. "I must find Dumuzi."

I hadn't known, until that instant, what I was going to say. But it was true: the purpose of my quest was to find my brother—in the Underworld. Everything in my life pushed me towards that destiny.

The goddess sighed. "I was afraid of that. Your mortal race finds it so hard to accept death, though it is your lot."

Death is not the lot of the immortal gods, I thought. Why must it be *our* lot? Why must *we* accept it? But I did not speak.

Siduri drained her cup. I looked down and found that mine, too, was empty. The goddess said, "If that is what you want, you must go to the Dark Queen, Ereshkigal."

Ereshkigal, the Queen of the Underworld, the Queen of the Dead. Ishtar's sister.

For a moment, the world went hazy-white around me. If I had not been sitting on the bench, I might have fallen. But I remembered the vizier, and how he had trained me. I took a slow, deep breath, and lifted my head high.

"How do I find Ereshkigal?" I asked.

"Ah, that's an interesting question," the goddess said. "For mortals, there are many paths to the quiet realm of the Dark

Queen. I could slip a simple poison into your cup, or touch you with a single drop of the Waters of Death out there—" the goddess pointed to the sea, moving blue-green against the shoreline in front of us "—or merely wish you dead."

Gods! I took another deep breath.

Siduri touched my hand, gently and kindly, and said, "But you are fortunate, Geshtinanna. Kalla will take you to the Underworld."

My heart shuddered at the thought of exposing Kalla to that danger. "Can I ask that of her?"

"Perhaps you could not," the goddess replied, "though she is no mortal creature. But I will ask her, and she will not refuse me."

• • •

Soon I sat again on Kalla's broad back, my heart hammering, my fear-cold hands gripping the muscles below her wings. Siduri's kiss of farewell burned on my cheek.

This time I took no fruit, no water-skin. There was neither eating nor drinking in the Underworld.

Kalla said, "It would be best if you closed your eyes, Geshtinanna. Your kind is not designed for a journey such as this."

I squeezed my eyelids shut, and felt a sudden sensation of dropping through the void. My bowels were cold. There was darkness and confusion all around me: first whirling heat and pressure on my head and body, then a windy emptiness and a searing cold. I heard cries of terror, whimpers and moans. It could have lasted a moment or a year.

Then all was still and quiet, and I opened my eyes. I was in a great cavern, naked as a newborn baby, and stripped of my seven pieces of jewellery, gifts from my family and reminders of my past. Kalla stood beside me, shining blue-black in the light of the torches on the rough-cut walls.

In front of us stood the Queen of the Dead, Ereshkigal, incomparably lovely in her nakedness. A horned crown sat on her glistening hair. Strong dark wings hung behind her, from shoulders to knees. Her hands were almost like human hands, though her nails were talons, but her feet were the strong claws of a bird of prey. Those terrifying feet gripped the backs of twin lions, and two great owls, each as tall as a ten-year-old child, flanked her. She was as beautiful and as terrible as an army arrayed for battle.

"What do you want, mortal woman?" Ereshkigal asked. Her voice was that of a lion calling in the night, or of a huge owl hunting before moonrise. My breathing quickened at the sound, despite my fear.

I could not lie to her. "I have come to seek Dumuzi," I said.

The goddess bared her teeth, and the hairs bristled at the nape of my neck. She said, snarling, "Are you sent by my treacherous sister Ishtar? Are you one of her devotees?"

I trembled. "No, Goddess. I have no love for mighty Ishtar. I am Dumuzi's sister, Geshtinanna. My brother was Ishtar's husband, then her ransom to leave this place. The demons sent to free your mighty sister snatched my brother Dumuzi and brought him here, to your dark realm, in her stead."

The goddess settled her glorious wings against her back. "*Surely* my sister sent you. All men and women who walk on the earth serve the Goddess of Love and Battle."

I shook my head. "I do not do the will of Ishtar, no matter how great she is, and how much adored. If it were not for Ishtar and her *love* for my brother, he would still walk on the earth, living and breathing. Why would I do her bidding?"

"Then why *are* you here?" The goddess glowed with unearthly beauty. Her breasts were like ripe pomegranates, her eyes the colour of the night sky. I felt myself falling, helpless, into that deep, starry sky.

I took a breath. "Truly, Goddess, I am here for my own sake, and my mother's, and my father's, and my city's. My parents are mad with grief. Our city falls to ruin. The sun burns the crops, and the fields are dry. Even the slaves and the sheep lament him."

The goddess Ereshkigal asked, "Do you desire to come here, as his ransom, to take his place? Do you wish to live here in my kingdom?"

I gasped, and knew that this was what I had sought without understanding: to live forever in Ereshkigal's dark realm, in her fearful presence.

I bowed my head, ashamed. "My brother Dumuzi's beauty made him a god, or equal to one. He was beloved of a goddess. He was enough to ransom Ishtar, great goddess of the earth and sky, from your power. I am a mortal woman. Am I enough to free my brother, and take his place?"

Ereshkigal frowned. On her face, even a frown was glorious. "Perhaps not, my mortal Geshtinanna," she said. "But I will beseech the gods on high that they might allow the exchange, if that is truly what you wish."

She gazed into my eyes, into my soul. I fell into her darkness, and stars swirled around me.

"Yes," I said. "Yes. It is truly what I wish."

The goddess put out a sharp-taloned hand to my right breast— was she going to kill me now, slash me with those glittering claws? I held my breath, waiting for pain and death.

Instead, Ereshkigal pinched my nipple, tenderly. Fire ran through me, but it was the fire of pleasure, not of pain. Again, I gasped, and blushed.

The goddess smiled in delight. "You tell the truth, mortal. Truly, you *do* wish to dwell here with me."

"Yes," I said. I watched her hands, her eyes. I needed her to touch me again.

"You and I have something in common," the dark goddess said. "We are both sisters of siblings beloved by all."

"Yes," I said. *Touch me.*

"Beautiful Dumuzi, lovely Ishtar." She stroked my ear, my throat, with those clawed fingers. I shivered, but I was not cold.

"Yes." *Please, touch me.*

The goddess kissed my hair, my cheek, my lips. "To me, you are more beautiful than Dumuzi."

"To me," I said, catching my breath, "you are lovelier than Ishtar."

• • •

The gods on high decreed that I, a mortal woman, would not suffice to ransom Dumuzi entirely, but that I could take his place in the Underworld for half of every year; for that time, my brother would walk the earth.

It was enough. Our city rejoiced, the sheep jumped in the fields, the irrigated soil abounded with crops, and Mother and Father were filled to overflowing with happiness. I was pleased for their sake, but I could no longer live there, with them, after all that had happened.

For half of each cycle of the sun, now, I dwell in Ereshkigal's dark realm, sharing her fierce pleasures. No woman knows greater bliss. But when Dumuzi returns underground and the sun is hot in the sky, I am compelled to return to the world of the living. I travel the earth, then, with Kalla, best of companions. If you look carefully enough at the hawks and eagles that fly high in the sky, one day you might be startled to see her golden wings flashing in the sun. Look for me riding on her back.

❀

Afterword

I grew up staring hungrily at colour plates of lapis lazuli ornaments in my grandfather's old books about the excavation of lost Nineveh and Ur, the decipherment of cuneiform, and the astonishing rediscovery of the Sumerian language with its literature. Years later, when I finally saw the glorious winged bulls in the British Museum, I fell in love with them.

I know that it's a cliché of myth/fairytale retellings to start from the point of view of a minor character, but my choice of Dumuzi's less attractive sister as my main character wasn't at all mechanical. I'd spent my youth being described as the clever sister, not the pretty sister; when I was reading various versions and translations of the bizarre, contradictory myths that float around Tammuz/Dumuzi, I couldn't help worrying what life would have been like for a hypothetical (relatively plain) sister of a boy so terribly desirable. I was sure that I had invented the sister. I'd almost finished my story when I discovered that she had been a part of the Tammuz/Dumuzi myth for the last few thousand years.

The Oblivion Box

Faith Mudge

It is a white box in a black void. There were people once, she remembers, or believes she remembers; long enough alone and you might believe anything if only to slow the spreading gangrene of an unused mind. If the memory is real, there were hundreds of them, perhaps thousands, a long queue of the damned stretching behind and ahead of her to file down into the dark. When the grille slammed down behind each one it was like the chomping of vast steel teeth, and when it rose they were gone.

She, too, was swallowed. She woke up here.

Her name was Shaya. Stripped of her jangling jewellery and elaborate henna tattoos, she finds it difficult to recognise that woman in herself. The only colour left in her world is the cinnamon tan of her skin and the blue tracery of veins beneath. Everything else she sees is white or black. Muted white phosphorescence pulses from each side of the cube in which she is imprisoned; when she stands at the wall and squints against the light, all she can see beyond is unremitting darkness.

There are other cubes like her own. Shaya knows this the same way she knows there are stars and sunrises, intangible theory grown meaningless from too much contemplation. Sometimes she remembers faces from that day, that queue—a gaunt dead-eyed woman, a man heavily muffled in robes as though he thought he might get to keep them. She wonders whether they are still here, somewhere in the abyss. She wonders if they, too, are slowly going mad.

Food appears on a ridged circle in the middle of the floor. For a while she tried to judge time by that but she quickly lost track of how many times the food has come, and she has nothing with which to make a record—not even a knife to mark the tally on her own skin. Once Shaya coated her body in creams and studied it critically in the mirror with ideas for improvement. Given a knife now, she knows she would cut herself purely for something to do.

Sitting beside the circle, as she often is, she reaches quickly for the much-anticipated supplies. It is, as always, a small slab of coarse dark bread and two white nutrient bars, accompanied by a black enamel jug of tasteless dark liquid Shaya thinks is some type of water. Holding it up to take a gulp, she catches a blur of reflection: a pale oval of face swimming between shadow curtains of hair, punctuated by black blots for eyes. Her lips, her beautiful irresistible lips, which were once painted every shade between orange and vermillion, are too pale to be seen at all.

Her throat tightens. She drinks anyway. She will not receive more supplies until the emptied jug has been replaced and phased away, denying her the comfort of one small and useless object to break the emptiness of her cell.

With the food, though, she takes her time. She tears the dense grainy bread into small pieces and chews each to a fine mush before swallowing. The nutrient bars are hard and chewy with a sour tang. She does not need to invent tactics to make them last; by the time they are gone her teeth and jaws are aching.

On a full stomach it is easier to sleep, though she has never grown used to the inescapable light of the cube. Shading her eyes with hair, cushioning her head as best she can on her arm, she drifts into uneasy dreams.

• • •

The show was about to start.

The Royal East Pavilion was all old-world glamour: crimson glass walls swimming with shining fish, tasselled carpets patterned to look antique. Servitors in red robes glided between the private balconies in the treble-storeyed auditorium, bearing trays of sweet wine and decoratively shaped fruits to be picked over by disinterested patrons for whom this event was attended more as a display of wealth before their friends than for the formal entertainment. Teardrops of petrified oil dripped from the earlobes of beautiful women; tiger hybrids settled at their feet, growling softly as the servitors passed by.

Testosterone-enhanced men in gilded robes gathered in small groups at the balcony railings. They cast scornful glances through the curlicued wooden screens at the secondary seating below, teeming with an eager crowd. The Third Millennium Sultanate might be founded on co-opportunist philosophy, the new heart of modern democracy, but old capitalist feeling was bred into the bones of the urban elite.

Backstage with her zither strung across her back, Shaya tugged fretfully at her midriff-baring blouse until its fringe of bright bronze discs bounced and jangled a counter-rhythm to her many bangles. Rationally, she knew she was beautiful, but it was easier to take her nerves out on her looks than endure the wait peacefully. Running a fingertip over the cherry pink bow of her lips, she was suddenly certain she should have picked a different shade.

The gong sounded, a crystalline reverberation thrumming through her blood like electricity, and she swung her zither down into her arms, sashaying onstage as though she'd never possessed a doubt in her life.

The central podium was lit by a single golden spotlight. Shaya positioned herself on the stool provided and struck a pose there, fingers poised on strings, allowing her audience a moment to admire the picture. Then she struck the first chord, opened her mouth, and sang.

Later, Zali told her that was the moment he'd fallen in love with her.

"You must get a thousand proposals a night. God, your voice. You could make me believe anything. I hadn't cried since I was nine, until I heard you sing."

"Flatterer," she purred. "You'd never heard a balladeer before, that's all."

"You're not a balladeer, Shaya, you're a fucking hypnotist."

She bowed off-stage three hours later to thunderous applause. Laying the zither in its case, swaddled up in padding like a baby, she swapped her flamboyant costume for a light violet modesty robe and began the triumphant walk back to her apartment.

It was a sultry night. The street bazaar outside was fragrant with sizzling meat and aromatic spice, perfume, dust and sweat. Shaya stopped at an imaginatively constructed booth with stacked tyres forming a bench and a shuttercraft wing for an awning. She tossed over a couple of brass sequins to the stallholder, who caught them deftly and passed across a lamb skewer. Shaya bit into tender meat, her taste buds popping at the hot herb dressing, and strolled away through the crowd.

She liked this part of town. The street was a canyon of steel and glass, physical reminders of last millennium's disastrous alliance with the West Union, but the capitalist shells were not as abandoned as they seemed. The alleys between buildings were crisscrossed with treble-deep lines of washing, coils of jasmine trained around the concrete pylons of an underground carpark below. What had once been the domain of computer drones was now home to entrepreneurial families, many of whom held booths in the bazaar. This appropriation of property was not strictly lawful but the authorities turned a lenient eye, recognising the spirit of co-opportunism when they saw it at work.

Shaya didn't live here. Her apartment was a nice little pad in the residential zone of Aladeen three blocks away. In reality she'd never trade that up for what was essentially a modified squat, but her bohemian side sometimes indulged in a little wistful speculation. The bazaar looked at its most romantic at this time of night, lit by solar lanterns in a hundred colours strung overhead in the narrow laneways between booths. Music was playing nearby— tambourines, drums. *Dancing.*

Elbowing her way towards the sound, Shaya broke through a ring of watchers surrounding an improvised dancefloor where a bare-chested young man was doing handstands. He flipped back onto his feet with easy grace, snapping off a salute to the crowd, and bounded away, replaced by a trio of girls in matching headscarves performing synchronised pop-kicking.

Normally, Shaya was self-conscious about the way she danced. The Muslim Sisterhood school she had attended as a teenager had offered classes, but it had taken her rapidly growing limbs a long time to catch on and in the meantime two girls from her clique were putting everyone else to shame with their killer moves. They had gone on to join a dancesport company in the Ausasian Empire, but Shaya still felt stilted and slow when she danced in public.

Not tonight, though. She had wowed a pavilion of wealthy punters with just her zither and her voice—she could dance the world down if she wanted. The pop-kickers ended their routine to a flurry of applause and Shaya grabbed her chance, leaping into the emptied floor. A flute joined the drums and tambourines, a high sweet piping. Shaya swayed backwards until her spine arched, spun a tight pirouette, spun again—and nearly fell when a hand caught hers. A man had joined her in the circle.

She stiffened, astonished. Men and women didn't dance together, not in the Sultanate. He took full advantage of her confusion, spinning her neatly back into the crowd, and claimed the floor. Watching him, Shaya had to admit he deserved the spotlight. He seemed boneless, swinging his limbs at impossible angles, with moves that would have given Shaya's old friends a run for their money.

As he snap-footed past he flashed a bright white smile her way. Admiration re-ignited into indignation. She waited until he finally relinquished the floor and stalked over to intercept him.

"Hey, you. What was the idea? That was my turn."

He turned and grinned again. Dark-skinned and clean-shaven, he had a lean athletic body and chin-length black hair streaked with metallic gold at the temples. She could smell the incense of expensive cologne on him from a foot away.

"You're the balladeer," he said. "I was at your show. Maybe I just wanted an excuse to touch you."

Shaya felt her eyebrows brush her hairline. "*That's* your defence?"

She was charmed, though—she always fell easily to flattery. He swept her a flourishing bow and took her hand.

"Shall we start over?" he asked, and kissed her palm. "My name is Zali Scherade."

And that, she thought later, was the moment she had fallen in love with him.

• • •

The deluge comes.

Shaya is woken from her unsettled dreaming to a drenching spray of cold water jetting seemingly from every direction. There is no place inside the cube where she can move to escape; within seconds every surface is slick wet and her thin white shift is transparent, clinging to her body like a second, extremely ineffectual, skin. Knowing what to expect, she closes her eyes and endures.

The water stops. There is exactly a minute's pause before the heat comes.

Like a wind direct from the desert, warm air pumps through the cube, transforming it into a sauna. Shaya's hair and shift are still slightly damp when the heat shuts off and the temperature returns to its neutral standard. Throughout the entire business she has remained seated on the floor, not seeing the point in rising. Now she stands and looks upward.

The ceiling of the cube is exactly like every other side. For all Shaya knows it may not even be the ceiling but she calls it that to spare her sanity. She is sure there are sensors embedded into this cube to monitor her and that there is a warden somewhere out there in front of a screen, watching, so she tries to look strong. The resentment hot in her veins helps a little. She had been dreaming of home.

Anger feels good. It burns up her throat, stinging her apathetic brain into response. She must do something. There is nothing she can do. But she must do *something*. The two thoughts form an inescapable litany inside her head, triggering a surge of frustration and panic, until she suddenly flings back her head and screams.

The full power of her trained voice is unleashed in a raw siren of sound. It amazes her. She has not spoken aloud in so long she had almost forgotten she could speak or hear at all. As the aftershock of her scream fades from her ears, the silence falls again like a suffocating weight. Well, this she can change.

"My name is Shaya Scherade," she says. Her voice sounds raspy, her throat still sore from the screaming. "I am twenty nine years old. My father died from canine flu when I was three and I grew up with my uncle. He is the most honourable politician I have ever known. He fought to abolish the death penalty for thirty years. He's dead now too. I'm glad. It would have broken his heart to see me like this."

Her eyes blur with tears. Shaya rubs them away and keeps talking, pretending someone is listening, waiting for her to go on. She has never failed an audience yet. Even an imaginary one.

"He was awarded the Commendation of Service by the Sultaness herself before he died. I performed at the ceremony. I can play the zither, lute and mandolin. I know over two hundred traditional ballads by heart and wrote forty of my own. When I sing, grown men cry. I lived my life to the full. I was remarkable."

It does not sound convincing, even to her own ears. But it is true.

"I loved a man!" she shouts. "And he loved me. I know he did."

• • •

Zali was vain. Shaya knew that from the first time she met him.

He exercised religiously to maintain his gorgeous physique, adhering to a strict regimen of nutrient bars, protein capsules and power shakes, untempted by Shaya's diet of indulgences. She admired his dedication, but felt no need to emulate it—how he started the day without a strong Turkish coffee and a bowl of sweet, pitted dates, she didn't want to know. His apartment was a shrine to fitness and health and was possibly the blandest place she had ever been. She barely ever saw him there. Most nights, he came to her.

It was Zali who introduced her to genEx.

"It's no different from getting a skin rejuv or a hangover killer," he said persuasively. "It's great. You've already sampled the goods, I know you'll love it."

"What goods?"

He brushed a hand over his muscular chest in one of those extravagant gestures that were so *him* and Shaya laughed. They were in the sun swing on her balcony, watching the sun rise. The sky was streaked in vibrant pink, the tall palm trees lining the shady street below outlined with halos of gold. The winged silhouette of an ROC flew low across the city—one of the genetically engineered super-eagles used by wealthy risk-seekers for their joyflights. They scared the hell out of Shaya at close range, but from a distance filled her heart with an ache at their beauty. Dawn was the most peaceful hour of the day, she thought, the time when this overcrowded, overheated city of hers was at its loveliest.

"Just try it," Zali urged, breaking her reverie. Exasperated, she twisted to look at him. He was very attractive, it was true, but he would have to learn she didn't appreciate pressure.

"What improvements do you think I need?" she asked sweetly.

He shifted awkwardly, not stupid enough to take the bait. It won her nearly ten minutes of quiet before he found a comeback.

"Do you like this?" He held his arm against her nose and the faint fresh scent of citrus drifted into her lungs. "Is that cologne?" she asked. "It's a serious improvement."

He knew she didn't like his intense incense colognes but it would probably have triggered an argument anyway if he had not been so focused on persuasion. As it was, he laughed stiffly and drew his arm away.

"It's not cologne. The scent is a skin enhancement from genEx. Interested now?"

Shaya turned her face into his throat. The scent was there too, subtler than perfume, mingling pleasantly with the familiar smell of his skin. "Tell me more."

That was how two days later she found herself in the corporate sector of the city, in the pentagonal square outside the genEx building, with Zali a smug tour guide at her side. She had only been to this part of the city once before, joining a financial co-operative when she came of age at twenty. Her uncle had been with her, a big solid presence greeting every official they met by name in his deep slow voice.

It had still been unusual to see women in management positions then, despite the late Sultan's very specific equal opportunity decrees, but in the genEx lobby they were greeted by a stunning thirty-something in formal white business robes. Her hair was tucked demurely beneath a designer scarf, indicating her position as a second tier member of the Sisterhood. Shaya, in a thin azure modesty robe and glittering wedge-heeled sandals, was a third tier. She felt instantly overexposed. She had been lectured at school by women like this. *Men will try to objectify you,* she had been told. *They will ask you to wear sluttish clothes and demean yourself to please them. You must not allow that. Remember, you are a woman. You are precious as you are.*

Then again, she wasn't the one working for a cosmetic enhancements company.

The woman introduced herself as Yasmeen and ushered them into a modernist office furnished with 20th century antiques and white vinyl wall-liner. Shaya slid into an organically curved chair she'd swear was authentic plastic and tried not to stare. She was pretty successful for a musician, but this kind of luxury was way out of her league and spoke volumes for the popularity of genEx.

"You have to understand," Yasmeen said, sliding gracefully onto a lime green stool, "genEx is not really about looks. I know, I know—" she lifted one beautifully manicured hand to stall Shaya, whose eyebrows had soared upward. "That's how we're usually portrayed, but it's an unfair slant. What we do is enhance all that is wonderful about what you already are. We believe that everybody has the right to feel beautiful in their own skin."

Shaya thought about the delicate scent of Zali's sweat. She remembered friends who never put on weight or broke out, who swore by genEx and took shots of it in their coffee like sugar. She had always been comfortable with her own looks, safely ranked as the pretty one of the family by her younger cousins, but she didn't want to be left behind while everyone in her circle jumped aboard with improvements. What harm was there in an enhancement or two, anyway? A shot of antiblush and she would never be caught red faced again. A follicle augmentation and no more bad hair days, ever.

In the end she was uncharacteristically cautious, opting for a mild skin enhancement like Zali's. The procedure took less than ten minutes. She was then sat down by a smiling specialist who provided her with a pack of booster shots and instructed her to take one every six to eight days.

"Otherwise the augmentation stops activating," she explained. "If you're taking your boosters and you feel it's not working properly, though, come and see me. Some people do get reactions. Just sit quietly for a few more minutes, then you can go."

As it turned out, Shaya had to wait considerably longer than that, pacing around a stylishly spartan waiting room while Zali underwent some impulse augmentations of his own. She was beginning to suspect those muscles of his owed less to his health regime and more to some sneaky muscle stimulants.

He emerged almost hyper with energy, wanting to head straight out to a club. When Shaya quashed that one, he suggested some other forms of exercise involving the bed back at her apartment. She was still irritated at having to wait and kicked him petulantly in the ankle.

"Did you get a libido booster in there or something?" she snapped. "I want to go home. And no, not to get love drunk. I need to practice for tomorrow's show."

He jerked back, insulted. "You'd rather be with that string stick than me?"

"It's a *zither*!" Shaya shouted. "And right now, yes, yes I would!"

She didn't remember the rest of the fight, only that it was loud and bitter and very public. They ended up on the steps of the genEx building screaming abuse at each other. Zali grabbed her by the upper arms, gripping tight enough to hurt, and when she shrieked at him to let her go he shoved her away so hard she fell down the stairs into the square.

She landed awkwardly onto her elbow. The bone jarred numbingly; she made a sobbing noise of pain and shock and looked up in automatic accusation. Zali was white-faced. He started down the steps towards her, holding out his hands, saying her name, but she somehow scrambled to her feet, swearing at him, telling him to stay away *or else*. What exactly she would have done against him with one arm out of action, she didn't know, but Zali got the message. He fell back, watching her go without interfering.

Shaya caught a shuttercraft home. She was shaking the whole way. It was only when it dropped her off on a relay roof close to home and she was climbing down the steps into her street that she realised the sleeve of her modesty robe was ripped, stained with blood. But it didn't smell of blood. At some point during the flight, maybe even during the shouting match outside genEx, her enhancements had kicked in. Her torn skin smelled sweet, of sandalwood, and spice.

• • •

Shaya has always loved stories. That is why she became a balladeer in the first place. She remembers stalking a street storyteller when she was fourteen, ignoring his uneven teeth and the fifteen-year age gap, enchanted by the magic he made with his voice. He couldn't play an instrument; his accompaniment came from an eCord, plugged into a discreet speaker concealed by a fold of his robe. She thinks her uncle probably paid for balladry lessons just to end that particular crush. It worked. Shaya fell head over heels for the idealised hero of her favourite ballad instead.

It occurs to her like a bolt from the blue. She cannot remember the second verse of that ballad. She has forgotten.

Horror freezes her veins. She rifles rapidly through her mental catalogue of stories, wondering how many more are fading like ink-print left too long in the sun. A sob tears its way through her throat with an ugly ripping sound. Shaya rocks back and forth, her arms wrapped tightly around her knees, shuddering uncontrollably. She opens her mouth. She has to clear her throat three times before her voice emerges without cracking.

In a dead land beside a dead sea he was born
In the dying years of a century
The sky forever red, the ground forever black
But he was alive, alive as any man can be.

Halfway through the first verse she remembers how to begin the second. The melody flows from her throat, and she finds herself on the third verse, the fifth, the tenth. She has sung this ballad so many times but every time she seems to hear it anew—as though she, like the audience, has no idea what will happen next. How did Gashir end up in a robot-run junkyard, immune to the poisoned air of the radioactive wastes? Who is the beautiful girl imprisoned in the tunnels beneath the wrecking yard? Can he save her before she sickens and dies?

Shaya sings until her throat is dry and sore. By the fourteenth verse she has to stop, breaking off as Gashir falls into the fiery pit. Her panic has subsided, lulled by the familiar rhythm of a beloved story. She rests her forehead against her knees, chewing on her tongue to work up enough saliva to soothe her dry throat. When she looks up there is a jug of water in the circle at her feet.

She stares at it, nonplussed. This never happens. The water comes with meals, and unless she slept far longer than usual she is not due for more supplies yet. Is she really going mad, conjuring hallucinations from her wishes? But when she reaches out, the jug handle is smooth and firm to her hand, the liquid inside cool and wet. She tips it into her mouth, gulping gratefully.

"Finish the story."

Shaya drops the jug. It rolls away across the floor in a spreading pool, but she hardly notices; she is choking. Whether it is misdirected water lodged in her throat or her hammering heart, she can't tell. She has heard a voice. A voice. In this cube. Which is impossible.

"I said, finish the story. What happened? Did he fall?"

Shaya looks around wildly. The voice seems to come from everywhere, the way the light does; it is deep and husky, definitely male, completely unfamiliar. She is suddenly intensely aware of someone, somewhere, watching her. Listening to her.

Her throat contracts. "Who—who are you?"

"Just finish the fucking story!"

She has never failed an audience yet. Somehow, Shaya sings. She can barely hear herself through the pounding of her blood in her ears, which is a shame—she has always loved this part, when Gashir meets the cyborg queen in her time-locked citadel, the battle with her mechanised serpents. His return to Topaz, his love, only to find her dying from radiation poisoning.

She lay in his arms, the beautiful husk,
Of a beautiful heart, a beautiful love
Now just a dead woman beneath a dead sea
In a dead, dead land, in a dead century . . .

She falters again towards the end and once more a jug of water appears at her feet. This time she snatches it up without hesitating. Her brain has done some quiet calculations without her and now clues her in. Someone out there wants to hear her stories; someone who is not only prepared to communicate with her, but perhaps reward her. Is this, the first turning point in God knows how long, really the right time to fall apart? By the time she puts down the jug, Shaya has pulled herself together. She sings the final verses with a return of some of her old flamboyance. Her fingers quiver, the music of her zither playing on the inside of her skull. In the final verse she reveals the denouement no one ever sees coming, and lets the final notes ring out triumphantly.

They fall to silence. She waits, but there is no congratulation, no response at all.

The silence lengthens. Shaya drums her fingers nervously against the sides of the jug, then realises she is still holding it and quickly replaces it in the circle. It disappears. She is left with no reason to believe that anything out of the ordinary has occurred, only the ramblings of an unreliable memory.

She runs her wet tongue over her lips. She's not giving up so easily.

She chooses another ballad. An older one, full of bloodshed and tragedy and evil warlords, and begins to sing. Five verses in, she breaks off and waits.

The silence is very loud.

"Go on. Keep singing."

Shaya feels the corners of her mouth tug in what feels like the first smile in a hundred years. She has stories. She has an audience. This is solid ground.

She sings.

• • •

They got married. Third tier Sisters were allowed to date a man for one year before making the decision to marry or move on, and for some reason Shaya stayed. The wedding was very elaborate and arranged entirely by Zali's mother, who had more than enough enthusiasm to power the project alone—perhaps a good thing, since the actual couple spent the four months of their engagement engaged in either violent feuding or passionate sex. Zali's mood swings collided with Shaya's hot temper and resulted in explosions.

"It's the stress, my love, he is about to be married!" Zali's mother insisted. "You must try to understand him. You are very lucky to be marrying such a handsome boy."

Shaya found it hard to think straight. It was true, her cousins swooned over Zali every time he flexed his biceps and kept calling the two of them a 'glamour couple', the most hackneyed phrase in the entire language as far as Shaya was concerned. She was equally to blame in most of their fights, if she was completely honest with herself. She had slapped him across the face on more than one occasion—what was so much worse about the times he hit her? She loved him, didn't she? She wasn't trying hard enough.

The wedding was a blur of congratulations drowned in alcohol. By the end of the night she and Zali were in a minishutter, on their way to their new home in a leafy, family-friendly corner of town. They were both exhausted and more than a little drunk. Shaya suddenly desperately wanted to be walking through the teeming bazaar to her own little apartment to spend the night alone. Zali seemed to read her thoughts.

"Too late to get out now, beautiful," he slurred. "You're my wife now. Mine."

Shaya didn't know whether to burst into tears or kick him hard with her gem-studded slipper. Instead her body took over and she threw up, twice. It was mostly bile—she had barely eaten all day—but Zali recoiled from her in revulsion. He, she remembered, had received an augmentation a month or two ago to prevent involuntary vomiting. It was getting hard to keep track of his enhancements; he seemed to be in at genEx every few days, like a piece of faulty machinery that needed constant alteration. He kept trying to convince Shaya to come with him but after that first visit she had dug in her heels and refused. There were times she even thought about removing her only enhancement, but then she would arrive late at a show one day, coated in sweat, and would be complemented by the backstage staff on her perfume.

Compliments had, after all, always been her weakness.

Shaya had back-to-back matinees for a week shortly after the wedding. Zali and his mother had briefly joined forces during the wedding preparations, trying to make her cancel, but she had steadfastly refused; she had never cancelled a show and wasn't about to start now. Every evening when she got home Zali was there, taking up space, demanding her attention, complaining that she was never there for him. He would either ignore that she had had a show at all or question her minutely on every detail.

"Who was there? Did anyone talk to you afterwards? Who? What did he look like? What did he say to you?"

"What does it matter to *you*?" Shaya snapped. "It's not like you ever come!"

The next day she saw him in the audience, close to the stage. He was waiting when she came down, fully assured of his welcome. Shaya stopped uncertainly with her hand against the curtain, a foot or so away from him.

"You came," she said, flatly.

"I have to make sure you don't run away with another man," he said. He used to make jokes like that and she would laugh, knowing he didn't mean it, but there was something off in his smile that night. She didn't laugh.

"What's going on with you?" she demanded. "I don't know who you'll be from one day to the next. This isn't you, Zali. This isn't the man I love."

He jerked as though she had cut him. "You don't love me."

"That isn't what I said—"

"You don't love me!" he shouted. "I knew it! You're a liar, a cheating lying cow!"

"How can you *say* that?" Shaya shrieked. "It's you who's lying! It's you!"

He grabbed her shoulders, shaking her hard. They were screaming things at each other, terrible things, and then she was just screaming, teeth rattling inside her skull with each time Zali shook her. A passing servitor saw them. He called for help and two men came running, dragging Shaya's husband away from her, asking her what was happening, was she all right. His hands were gone, but she was still shaking.

• • •

Shaya sings.

She is still a prisoner. The daily humiliations are even harder to endure knowing that every time the deluge comes and plasters her shift against her skin, every time she performs her ablutions over the phasing circle, there's a man somewhere watching. She wonders what he's like, the owner of this disembodied voice. What he looks like. Not for the first time, she hopes fervently he is not a pervert.

But in another sense she is powerful. She has a head full of stories, a voice to sing down the angels, an eager listener—and she can play her audience like she played her zither. She takes longer breaks between verses, claiming tiredness, testing her unseen listener's patience. She tantalises him with snippets of stories and asks him to choose the next for her to sing. She is frequently surprised by his choices. The warden of a deep-sea prison apparently likes tragic romances.

Shaya sings until her voice throbs with sorrow. Her listener never applauds, but one night after finishing an epic thirty-verser the jug of water arrives with a plump red pomegranate. It is the first time she has tasted fresh fruit since she was imprisoned. She savours every mouthful and sucks her fingers until they're sore.

She begins to venture questions of her own.

"What's your name?" No answer. "Oh, please. Wouldn't you be curious?"

More silence. Then, finally, when she has given up hope of a reply:

"Xever. My name is Xever."

Gradually she eases little details from him, greased with many anecdotes of her own. He soon knows everything there is to know about her childhood, her career as a balladeer, the foods and colours she likes. She learns he is an only child. His parents, like her own, are dead. And the year is 3044. The breath goes out of her when he lets that detail drop. She has been imprisoned for two and a half years.

"Why are you doing that? Shaya. Shaya, what is it?"

He sounds uneasy. He should be. She is doubled over on the floor, racked so hard with heaving sobs that she thinks she might be sick. It takes her a long time to drag herself back together. As she leans her back against the wall and draws her knees up against her chest, she realises that was the first time Xever has used her name. The first time he has asked a question not directly related to the story she is telling. She wipes her sleeve across her sore eyes and looks up.

There is a handful of dates in the middle of the circle.

A choked laugh cracks from her throat. Is he trying to *comfort* her? If he is, it works. The sweet flavour of the dates overwrites the bitter salty taste of tears on her tongue. She licks her sticky fingers clean and looks up. She does not know from what angle Xever is looking at her, how he sees her at all, but as a rule she has decided to look up when she talks to him.

"Thank you," she says softly. "You're kind."

Xever says nothing. He is not a talkative man, Shaya has learned. She wishes she could see his face. It is so difficult to judge a man from his voice alone. But she returns his generosity with the comic ballad *The Zero Hounds*, one of her originals, and is rewarded when, during the chase scene in verse twelve, he laughs, a startled bark of sound. It is only the professionalism of nine years performing that keeps her singing while her mind is wiped white with shock. She wonders how long it has been since her taciturn prison warden last laughed.

These days, when the deluge comes, she does more than endure it. Xever has provided her with soap, an insipidly scented scrubbing tube for which she is ridiculously grateful, and already her hair is less lifeless, her skin brighter. When her supplies arrive they include small treats—fresh fruit, honey. Shaya forces her limp limbs into a few star jumps to get her blood moving before settling to eat. She makes sure to thank Xever after each meal. She is being entirely political, cultivating his good will. That does not make her thanks any the less sincere.

"That was wonderful," she tells him, when he thinks to include coffee. It is an explosion of caffeine; her brain feels kicked into gear, buzzing and alive. She jogs on the spot, hops up and down on alternate feet. Xever laughs again. A little peeved, Shaya taps into her old dance training and smooths out her motions, spinning slowly, sliding her feet across the floor, swaying her spine backwards into an arch with both arms stretched above her head. She is very rusty, but it comes gradually back to her. Her delight is edged with bitterness, remembering a different dance, that night at the bazaar. Zali.

"Why did you stop?" Xever is still watching. "That was beautiful."

Shaya looks up. "I didn't want him to die," she says. "My husband. I loved him. I told everyone that and no one believed me, but it's true all the same. I wanted to help him. No," she corrects herself, and it's her turn to laugh, a mirthless sound. "No, I wanted to *save* him."

There is a long, long silence. She has never brought this up before, though as a warden Xever must know why she is here. Perhaps now he thinks about it, he no longer wants to be involved with a murderess—a manipulative, dangerous woman who will enchant him and lie to him. Shaya's shoulders slump. She sits down quietly, cross-legged, on the floor beside the circle, feeling suddenly drained. Then Xever speaks.

"What happened?" he asks. His voice is hard, guarded, but he asks all the same.

She tells him.

• • •

"Insomnia. Mood swings. Paranoia. It's more common than you might think."

Shaya stared at the journalist on the other side of the table, her cooled coffee clutched tightly between her hands. Months venting to family and friends had divided everyone she knew into two camps: the 'Be A Loyal Wife's and the 'Leave The Bastard's. No one seemed to understand what she was really saying. Zali was no longer Zali. It was like she was living with a completely different man.

Then she had stumbled on a small column in an indie news feed, the only anti-augmentation piece she had ever read, and she had v-mitted her questions to the contact tag at the foot of the article. A couple of days later, she was in a coffee den in South Bezzir while Zali thought she was at a show. It was a reasonably safe cover; he had been banned from entering the pavilion where she staged most of her performances. She hated lying to him, but his obsessive behaviour gave her no choice.

"Three percent," she echoed. "Three percent of the population get this reaction?"

"So my research would indicate," the journalist said. He was an Ausasian expat with the distinctive accent that made his every statement sound like a question. "Not easy to be really specific, of course, because many people can't afford the augmentations or object to them on ethical grounds, but three percent is the rough figure."

"But why?" Shaya demanded, appalled. "Why weren't we told?"

The journalist patted her hand like she was a distraught toddler. "GenEx is in denial. They don't want to pay compensation so they say their enhancements aren't responsible for this strain of schizophrenia. Science is telling a different story. Sooner or later the government will have to step in, but in the meantime there is no mainstream recognition of the disorder."

"So what do I do? How do I help him?"

"That's a question better put to a medico. I'm afraid I can't offer you much advice. The first step your husband would need to take for any kind of recovery is the removal of his enhancements, but whether he will believe you is another matter. GenEx sufferers are often delusional and dangerous. I would advise you approach him carefully, if at all."

"I have to do something. He's my husband, I can't let him— *deteriorate* like this."

"It's up to you, of course." The journalist drained his coffee and cleared his throat. "Thank you for your time, Md Scherade, I appreciate you agreeing to this interview. Can I quote you by name in my next piece or would you prefer to remain anonymous?"

She remained at the table long after he'd gone, trying to think of a way to explain this to Zali. How could she make him believe her? The prospect made her stomach clench with fear, but she had to try.

It was late when she got home. She keyed open the door, steeling herself for indifference or inquisition, whichever she might find inside. She did not expect to be seized by the throat and slammed against the wall, a butcher's knife pressed against her jugular. Zali's face was contorted into a snarl. His eyes were red from crying.

"Whore," he hissed. Saliva flecked her face. "Betrayer."

"What are you doing?" Shaya wheezed. "Zali, let me go!"

"I saw you." He released her so suddenly she slid down the wall and crumpled on the floor at his feet, gasping for breath. "At a show, you said. Why did I ever believe you? I saw you with him. I saw him take your hand."

"No—no, Zali, you don't understand—" Shaya struggled to her feet. "Please listen to me. You're sick, Zali, but I'm going to help you—"

"*You want to kill me!*" He seized a handful of her hair, yanking her head back. The knife was a cold metal line across her exposed throat. "I know everything! You're turning everyone against me. You are a whore, a traitorous lying whore!"

He hurled her away from him as though it were she holding the knife, as if it were she threatening him. She collided with the couch, falling to the floor, scrabbled back to her feet as he advanced with the knife. She couldn't scream. She couldn't breathe.

"Zali," she rasped. "Zali, stop."

She backed away from him, through an open door; she realised too late it led onto the balcony. She was trapped. He was crying, she saw, tears streaking down his face.

"I loved you," he moaned. "I trusted you. How could you betray me?"

"I never betrayed you!" Shaya's voice was thin, breathless. He didn't seem to hear her. She was up against the balcony railing, and then he was there, grabbing at her, slashing at her, sobbing abuse at her. She grappled with him uselessly for the knife. He stabbed at her and her hands shoved with all their force.

Somehow they had got twisted around. He was the one against the railing. The old rusted metal gave way to his weight and he fell, screaming, into the street thirty feet below. Shaya heard his body smack against cement.

She didn't know how she got down there. She didn't remember using the stairs, although she supposed she must have done. All she remembered was falling to her knees beside Zali's beautiful, broken body, cradling what was left of her husband in her arms, screaming at the medicos who came to take him away. Someone gave her a sedative and called a cousin. She was led back to her apartment in the early hours of the morning and told to rest. Alone at last in a bed that smelled of sandalwood and citrus, she fell into a deep, drugged sleep.

She was woken to blinding mid-morning sun and a heavy pounding on her door. A pair of black-armoured demiGs were waiting outside. She had only ever seen them on guard duty at political functions before; she couldn't remember seeing them up close like this. They were huge, taller and broader than a human, and behind their dark visors burned eyes red as rubies. She and Zali had always argued over whether they were robots or cyborgs, pointless arguments that could never be settled.

Zali. Zali was dead.

"Shaya Scherade." Even the demiG's voice did not sound human; it was deep and booming like there was an amplifier built into his throat. "You must come with us."

As it turned out, someone had witnessed the fight. And so Shaya found herself on trial for her husband's murder.

From the start, everyone believed she was guilty. Even her cousins. They tried to excuse her, insisted Zali had been violent and deranged, but no one believed them either, held against his mother's tearful testimony. It took the jury—present in hologram to protect their identities—less than an hour to convict Shaya and sentence her. Fifteen days after Zali's death she was in a line of prisoners boarding the subcell penitentiary *Kraken*.

The *Kraken* was swallowed by the sea. Shaya was swallowed by the void.

• • •

"You didn't kill him."

Shaya can tell Xever doesn't believe her. There is open scepticism in his tone that reminds her of the aggressive prosecutors from her trial. She lets her forehead fall against her knees, her face hidden by a fall of dark hair, the only privacy she can claim.

"No," she says. "I killed him. But I didn't mean to."

Xever is silent for a long time. *"Like Gashir,"* he says eventually. *"And Topaz."*

Shaya looks up, startled. "What?"

"By trying to save her, he made her die faster."

Shaya's eyes sting with tears. She nods, not trusting herself to speak.

Xever says nothing more for a long time. She tries talking to him once or twice but receives no response, and she cannot tell whether that means he's no longer there or no longer wants to talk to her. She tries to sleep and can't. Eventually she gets up and circles her cube, rubbing at her arms. She turns around and there is someone there.

She screams.

It is a demiG. The carapaced black armour makes it resemble a vast black beetle, its red eyes emitting a hellish glow. It carries a scimitar longer than Shaya's arm. It steps off the phasing circle and advances towards her. She is still screaming.

"Shaya, it's all right. He won't hurt you. Go with him."

As though Xever's voice is a signal, the demiG sheaths its scimitar and holds out a vast gauntleted hand. Shaya is still trembling.

"Where will it take me? Xever, what's going on?"

"Go with him."

The demiG could rip her limbs from their sockets if it chose. Shaya gives in, accepting the proffered hand instead of waiting to be seized, and is drawn onto the circle. Blinding white light jets around her. She squeezes her eyes shut, throwing up her free arm to protect them against the glare, and when the light fades she is somewhere else entirely. It is a perfectly ordinary corridor, but the sheer size of it all is overwhelming. The wall to her right is punctuated with square portholes and through the nearest she can see the sea, the pale dawn sky. The *Kraken* is floating towards a cliff-edged coastline.

Shaya doesn't know why she has been brought here. A jailbreak? A retrial? She doesn't care. She has told the story that really matters and has been believed. This man she has never met knows more about her than anyone else in the world, knows tragedy when he hears it, and truth. And now Shaya is in a world outside her imagination, the world she almost stopped believing existed.

Light washes across her skin like liquid gold. Through the porthole the dawn sky is streaked in red and rose, dazzling her eyes with raw colour. The sun is rising. A black gauntlet lands on Shaya's shoulder, turning her from the porthole, but she twists her head back to catch a last glimpse and sees a winged silhouette launch from the cliffs.

She begins to laugh.

Afterword

For me, setting is always integral; once I know where I am, I know where I'm going. So I found the void first, and in it a woman in a box. Shaya's personality came within the first few sentences—flamboyant, extroverted, a bit vain—a performer. That was when I knew she was going to save her life with a story. That is, after all, what people do in the Arabian Nights. They tell stories, and stories help them to survive. For no one is this truer than Scheherazade herself, who married a madman and used her stories to remind him that other people were real, that they still mattered, that she mattered. Shaya didn't start out that way, but as I wrote she became like a futuristic Scheherazade. She talks herself back into reality after the dehumanisation of her long imprisonment, using words to escape a place that is inescapable, and she takes her gaoler with her.

About the Contributors

MARILAG ANGWAY is an author who has short stories appearing in publications by Bards and Sages Publishing, Deepwood Publishing, and Hadley Rille Books. She was born and raised in the Philippines for a time, but has since moved to the United States, where she currently resides in New Jersey (though she would like to note that she's a New Yorker at heart). She likes writing in ungodly hours of the morning, with cups of coffee and breakfast bars in constant supply.

• • •

CHERITH BALDRY was born in Lancaster, UK, and studied at the University of Manchester and St Anne's College, Oxford. After some years as a teacher, including a spell at the University of Sierra Leone, Freetown, she became a full-time writer. She has a special interest in Arthurian romance and medieval literature, and has published novels and short fiction for adults, young adults and children. She is currently part of the Erin Hunter team writing the Warriors and Seekers series. Cherith has two grown-up sons, and lives in Surrey in a household ruled by two cats. She enjoys music, especially early music, reading and travel.

• • •

• • •

ALAN BAXTER is a Ditmar Award-nominated author of dark fantasy, sci-fi and horror. He rides a motorcycle, loves his dog and teaches Kung Fu. He is the author of the dark fantasy novels, *RealmShift* and *MageSign*, and over 40 short stories which have appeared in journals and anthologies in Australia, the US, the UK and France, including the *Year's Best Australian Fantasy & Horror*. Read extracts from his novels, a novella and short stories at his website www.alanbaxteronline.com or find him on Twitter @AlanBaxter

• • •

JENNY BLACKFORD's historical novella *The Priestess and the Slave* was described by Alison Goodman as "a compelling blend of vivid storytelling and meticulous research". Her short stories have appeared in places as diverse as Random House's *30 Australian Ghost Stories for Children* and *Cosmos* magazine. Her first poem for decades was the only one selected for *The Best Australian Fantasy and Horror 2010*. Her current major project is writing the violent, sexy life of Bronze Age princess Medea.

• • •

JETSE DE VRIES—@shineanthology on Twitter—is a technical specialist for a propulsion company by day, and a science fiction reader, editor and writer by night. He's also an avid bicyclist, total solar eclipse chaser, beer/wine/single malt aficionado, metalhead and intelligent optimist. Sometimes, after fighting the good fight, he sleeps.

• • •

THORAIYA DYER is an award-winning Australian writer based in the lush, sweeping NSW Hunter Valley. Her short fiction has appeared in *Clarkesworld #75, Apex #35, Redstone SF* and *Nature*; it is forthcoming in *Cosmos #51*. Her collection, *Asymmetry*, is due in 2013 from Twelfth Planet Press (for a full list of published work, see http://www.thoraiyadyer.com/).

• • •

• • •

JOSHUA GAGE is an ornery curmudgeon from Cleveland. He is the author of *breaths* (VanZeno Press), the collaborative project *Intrinsic Night* (Sam's Dot Publishing), and *Zombies: Haiku in Four Acts* (Poet's Haven). He is a graduate of the Low Residency MFA Program in Creative Writing at Naropa University. He has a penchant for Pendleton shirts, rye whiskey and any poem strong enough to yank the breath out of his lungs. He stomps around Cleveland in a purple bathrobe where he hosts the monthly Deep Cleveland Poetry hour and enjoys the beer at Fat Heads.

• • •

RICHARD HARLAND migrated to Australia at age 22, played folk-rock music around Sydney, lectured for ten years at the Uni of Wollongong, then became a full-time author in 1997. He lives in Figtree, near Wollongong. His sixteen novels have spanned fantasy, SF, horror and, recently, steampunk. His latest novel, *Song of the Slums,* is steampunk/gaslight romance, and starts from a hypothetical: what if they'd invented rock 'n roll in the 19th century? Richard has collected 6 Aurealis Awards, the A. Bertram Chandler Award and the Tam-Tam Je Bouquine award (France). His author website is at www.richardharland.net.

• • •

FAITH MUDGE is a Queensland writer with a passion for fantasy, folk tales and mythology from all over the world—in fact, almost anything with a glimmer of the fantastical. She writes regular reviews and vignettes for her blog at beyondthedreamline. wordpress.com, enthusing about all things fairy tale on the way. Her head is a madly cluttered place that really needs new signposts and possibly a map; it is populated by a menagerie of stories, but the only other one currently released into the wild is "Oracle's Tower", which appears in FableCroft's *To Spin a Darker Stair.*

• • •

• • •

While writing is HAVVA MURAT's first love, her other passions include compulsive shopping for pets, purses, shoes, antiques and vintage trinkets, tearing apart interior design magazines to add to her voluminous scrapbooks, researching ancient history, mythology and the Victorian era, and creating stained glass pieces to fill her cottage which is about to sink into the earth. She is a member of the Romance Writers of Australia and you can follow her writing adventures on facebook or find her tweeting @MsHavvaMurat.

• • •

CHARLOTTE NASH took a long detour on the road to writing, completing degrees in engineering and medicine, and enjoying an eclectic technical career. She counts the best moments as building rockets, traversing the Pilbara mines, and learning medicine on an army base. These days she sails, motorbikes, ogles airplanes and writes fiction of many persuasions, often flavoured with technical, medical or nautical spice. Find her at charlottenash.net.

• • •

ANTHONY PANEGYRES is a Perth author whose latest stories have been published in *Andromeda, Dotdotdash Magazine, Overland Literary Journal* and *The Year's Best Australian Fantasy & Horror, 2011*. His story "Reading Coffee" was shortlisted for an Aurealis Award.

• • •

DAN RABARTS is a New Zealand writer of all things speculative— fantasy, horror, science fiction and the odd things in between. His fiction can be found in *Bloodstones, Beneath Ceaseless Skies, Andromeda Spaceways, Aurealis, Regeneration,* and at the *Tales from the Archives,* and *Wily Writers'* podcasts. He has twice been a finalist for New Zealand's SJV Awards, both for fiction and non-fiction. Find him lurking on the web at dan.rabarts.com, or in the dusty corners of the house tapping frantically at a keyboard.

• • •

• • •

ANGELA REGA's short stories have appeared or are forthcoming in publications including *The Year's Best Australian Fantasy and Horror, PS Publishing, Ticonderoga Publications, Fablecroft Press, CSFG, Cabinet Des Fees and Little Fox Press*. She is a lover of folklore, fairy tales and furry creatures and works as a Teacher Librarian in an inner-city high school. She is a graduate of the Clarion South workshop and is currently studying for her Masters Degree in Creative Writing. She drinks way too much coffee and can't imagine not writing.

• • •

JENNY SCHWARTZ is a contemporary romance author. She lives in Western Australia, loves Steampunk (what a way to misuse a history degree!) and delights in chatting with other readers and authors. Her website is http://authorjennyschwartz.com/ .

• • •

BARB SIPLES lives on the West Coast of North America and spends way too much time thinking about the inevitable planet-wide zombie apocalypse. The problem is not so much how to survive, but how to survive in style. You can read more of her stuff at barbsiples.com.

• • •

PIA VAN RAVESTEIN lives in Ellenbrook, Western Australia. She studied writing and scriptwriting at university, and has published short stories and won several poetry competitions. Recently, after several years of focusing almost exclusively on her artwork (including the cover of Juliet Marillier's *Prickle Moon)*, Pia has returned to hard science fiction, fantasy and Australian literature writing. She is hoping to find some kind of balance between the visual and written arts, which mostly involves chaotically bouncing between the two.

• • •

D C WHITE has been writing for several years. His work can be found in several anthologies including the *Scary Kisses, More Scary Kisses* and *The Killing Words*. Other fiction has appeared in *The Picture* magazine and on the internet. D C lives in Noarlunga, South Australia with his cat Toffee.

• • •

Acknowledgements

AVAILABLE FROM TICONDEROGA PUBLICATIONS

TICONDEROGA PUBLICATIONS LIMITED HARDCOVER EDITIONS

978-0-9586856-9-6	Love in Vain by Lewis Shiner
978-0-9803531-1-2	Belong ed Russell B. Farr
978-0-9803531-9-8	Basic Black by Terry Dowling
978-0-9806288-0-7	Make Believe by Terry Dowling
978-0-9806288-1-4	The Infernal by Kim Wilkins
978-0-9806288-5-2	Dead Sea Fruit by Kaaron Warren
978-0-9806288-7-6	The Girl With No Hands by Angela Slatter
978-0-9807813-0-4	Dead Red Heart ed Russell B. Farr
978-0-9807813-3-5	Heliotrope by Justina Robson
978-0-9807813-6-6	Matilda Told Such Dreadful Lies by Lucy Sussex
978-1-921857-00-3	Bluegrass Symphony by Lisa L. Hannett
978-1-921857-07-2	Bread and Circuses by Felicity Dowker
978-1-921857-16-4	The 400-Million-Year Itch by Steven Utley
978-1-921857-23-2	Wild Chrome by Greg Mellor
978-1-921857-27-0	Midnight and Moonshine by Lisa L. Hannett & Angela Slatter
978-1-921857-37-9	Prickle Moon by Juliet Marillier

TICONDEROGA PUBLICATIONS EBOOKS

978-0-9803531-5-0	Ghost Seas by Steven Utley
978-1-921857-93-5	The Girl With No Hands by Angela Slatter
978-1-921857-99-7	Dead Red Heart ed Russell B. Farr
978-1-921857-94-2	More Scary Kisses ed Liz Grzyb
978-0-9807813-5-9	Heliotrope by Justina Robson
978-1-921857-98-0	Year's Best Australian F&H eds Grzyb & Helene
978-1-921857-97-3	Bluegrass Symphony by Lisa L. Hannett

THE YEAR'S BEST AUSTRALIAN FANTASY & HORROR SERIES
EDITED BY LIZ GRZYB & TALIE HELENE

978-0-9807813-8-0	Year's Best Australian Fantasy & Horror 2010 (hc)
978-0-9807813-9-7	Year's Best Australian Fantasy & Horror 2010 (tpb)
978-0-921057-13-3	Year's Best Australian Fantasy & Horror 2011 (hc)
978-0-921057-14-0	Year's Best Australian Fantasy & Horror 2011 (tpb)

WWW.TICONDEROGAPUBLICATIONS.COM

thank you

The publisher would sincerely like to thank

Elizabeth Grzyb, Amanda Pillar, Marilag Angway, Charlotte Nash-Stewart, Joshua Gage, Angela Rega, Alan Baxter, Thoraiya Dyer, Barb Siples, Pia Van Ravestein, Havva Murat, Cherith Baldry, Anthony Panegyres, DC White, Richard Harland, Jetse de Vries, Dan Rabarts, Jenny Schwartz, Jenny Blackford, Faith Mudge, Lisa L. Hannett, Donna Maree Hanson, Robert Hood, Pete Kempshall, Penelope Love, Nicole Murphy, Angela Slatter, Karen Brooks, Jeremy G. Byrne, Felicity Dowker, Kim Wilkins, Marianne de Pierres, Jonathan Strahan, Peter McNamara, Ellen Datlow, Grant Stone, Sean Williams, Simon Brown, Garth Nix, David Cake, Simon Oxwell, Grant Watson, Sue Manning, Steven Utley, Lewis Shiner, Bill Congreve, Jack Dann, Janeen Webb, Lucy Sussex, Stephen Dedman, the Mt Lawley Mafia, the Nedlands Yakuza, Shane Jiraiya Cummings, Angela Challis, Kate Williams, Kathryn Linge, Andrew Williams, Al Chan, Alisa and Tehani, Mel & Phil, Hayley Lane, Georgina Walpole, Rushelle Lister, everyone we've missed . . .

. . . and you.

IN MEMORY OF
Eve Johnson (1945–2011)
Sara Douglass (1957–2011)
Steven Utley (1948–2013)

www.ingramcontent.com/pod-product-compliance
Lightning Source LLC
Chambersburg PA
CBHW031306280626
47169CB00017B/356